Page 152 *Pieces of flesh and bone and metal flew over their heads and all over the block. The force of the concussion drove both men back about twenty feet. Sam struggled to stand up, but fell over. Through his twisted vision he saw that the front of the Mad-Giles was no longer there. He became vaguely aware of a million pinpoints of pain in his eyes. He attempted to clear his vision as he searched for Charlie. He turned around on his hands and knees, finally locating the blurred, crumpled heap beside him. Loy's piercing scream made him turn his head again. His last recollection was the overpowering sensation of having done something incredibly stupid.*

Page 196 *Everything about Tsingy made him nervous. It was a completely foreign environment, like he was on a different planet, with no point of reference other than the sun, which was rapidly falling behind the giant spires. Lemurs taunted them constantly, throwing squishy, half-chewed pieces of fruit at the intruders. Giant hawks screeched overhead, volleys of bats flew out of holes in the limestone directly into their faces. As the shadows grew darker and more forbidding, he had to choke back the feeling that the towering minarets were closing in around him.*

A recent spate of O/Ds leads NYPD detective Lt. Charlie Bannerman to believe something of a sinister nature is going on. Ignoring orders to treat the deaths as simple drug over-doses, he enlists the aid of biology professor Gary Carswell. When Carswell's giant Cray computer suggests the presence of an exotic orchid native to the Island of Madagascar, he summons orchid specialist Dr. Sam Bloom to lend his expertise. The outcome is that Bannerman and Bloom will travel to the port of Toamasina to check out the *Lucinda V*, an old tramp steamer the DEA believes is involved in the movement of drugs.

After learning of the suspicious death of her husband in Madagascar's Tsingy National Park, Swiss physician Dr. Anna Grenier decides to conduct her own investigation. In Tana, Madagascar's capital, she runs into Sam and Charlie under dire circumstances, after which the three discover they have some-thing in common and decide to join forces.

The prestigious Zurich International Association of Naturalists (ZIAN) is run by Dietrich Brower, who answers to a board of directors comprised of eight former generals in the German Wehrmacht. Brower has just learned of disturbing events in Madagascar that prompt him to contact his associates at Interpol Paris to enlist the aid of agent René Simard.

Despite two blatant attempts on their lives, Sam and Charlie manage to uncover evidence that points to ZIAN's involvement in the movement of cocaine. But final proof can only be found by visiting ZIAN's HQ in Zurich, where snooping around the ZIAN premises late at night reveals something that shocks the hell out of the two Americans. Sam and Charlie must now return to the island and join CIA contractor Giles Lamont and several of his former military pals as they set out to penetrate the world's most forbidding piece of real estate. Here, a final terrifying twist of fate reveals the true evil that lurks deep in the heart of Tsingy's deadly limestone labyrinth.

PRAISE FOR SHADOW OF LIGHT

….Mr. Power is aptly named: he casts a potent spell from the first page and doesn't break it until well past the last one.

—MARK BUCHANAN, BESTSELLING AUTHOR

….Power is not only a master story teller, but a gifted craftsman who intuitively knows how to entertain and hold the reader's attention from beginning to end. What a great read from an imaginative, talented writer.

—SARAH NICHOLS, HOLLYWOOD SCREEN WRITER

….a terrific story, one I will read again just for the joy of it.

—GORDON PINSENT, AWARD-WINNING AUTHOR, ACTOR AND PLAYWRIGHT

….the work of an emerging master who is sure to be soon hailed by all readers…rich with insight, challenge and texture. A rewarding read, no matter your literary tastes.

—ROBERT MACDONALD, AUTHOR AND PUBLISHER

Shadow of Light has to be one of the most interesting fiction books I've read in awhile…a definite must-read! The events are quirky, humorous, entertaining and thought-provoking. The story kept me enthralled, with my fingers on the corner, waiting expectantly to turn the page to see what would happen next.

—CHRISSY LUTHER, AUTHOR AND RADIO HOST

Shadow of Light is one of the better books I have read…well laid out, excellently edited and very entertaining. You will fall in love with…the characters…

—RICK FESS, AUTHOR AND BOOK REVIEWER

The Case of the Golden Orchid

ISBN: 1478358041
ISBN-13: 9781478358046

Also by this author:
Shadow of Light Narrow Road Press (A division of Sheaf House Publishers)

See www.rodpower.com

The Case of the Golden Orchid is a work of fiction. Names, characters, places and incidents are products of the imagination or are used fictitiously. Any resemblance to actual events, locales, or persons, living or dead, is entirely coincidental.

Requests for information should be addressed to:
Editorial Director
MCW Publishers
4118 -15th Avenue
Vernon, British Columbia
V1T 8H1

Manufactured in the United States of America

RODNEY CHRISTIAN POWER

THE CASE OF
THE GOLDEN ORCHID

MCW Publishers

Vernon, British Columbia

PROLOGUE

A cold skift of snow followed the girl down the street, swirling around her naked legs, causing her to shiver and curse the night. The Mission was still four long blocks away and Jenny Beth moved quickly, clutching the twenty-dollar bill she had just been given by her stepfather in her small fist as if her life depended upon it. Her discomfort would soon be over, when she reached the end of her journey, the place where dreams were born.

The streets in this part of Queens were dangerous after dark, but such knowledge did little to discourage those who came to the Mission seeking solace from their trials and tribulations. The Reverend Bigtime Bantome made everyone feel welcome — young and old, black and white. He was their true friend, always there in times of need.

Around a corner and two blocks in the distance a sign mounted on top of a rundown old house proclaimed it to be the Mission of St. Anthony. Jenny Beth could not yet make out the sign, but knew it was there, waiting for her.

A soft voice from a darkened alcove startled her. "Hey there, little sister, what you all hurrin' and rushin' for?"

Two black men stepped out on the sidewalk, blocking her way. She had seen them before, never inside the Mission, but hanging around. "You stay clear, you hear? The Reverend Bigtime, he the daddy of my baby." The girl pulled aside the flap of her coat long enough for them to see she was several months pregnant. "You touch me, the reverend turn your heads into watermelon mush. Now get out of my way!"

The men mumbled something and shuffled aside. Jenny Beth smiled secretly to herself. It wasn't true about the baby; she didn't know who had given her that baby, but she knew she wanted it more than anything else. It was conceived close to her four-teenth birthday, around the time her stepfather told Jenny Beth he expected her to give him a little loving now that she was all growed-up. Maybe it was his baby.

The Mission was located in the upstairs floor of a three-story dwelling constructed for railway workers a hundred years ago. The girl climbed the wooden staircase and pounded her knuckles on a freshly painted door. A gruff voice asked who was there. She called out her name and the code word: *Stringy*. The door swung open, and the owner of the voice poked his head into the porch to glance around. Once inside, Jenny Beth watched the doorkeeper slide a steel bar back into place. Her heart raced as the first whiff of acrid smoke seeped into her nostrils. A dozen or so people were sprawled about the first of four rooms that made up the Mission, and stepping between so many stretched-out legs on his way to greet her was the Reverend Bigtime himself, the propri-etor of one of the most profitable crack houses in New York City.

"Hey, there's my sweet Jenny Beth. Now how you doin', honey chile?"

The girl smiled, not minding his big hands rubbing her breasts. "I'm doin' good, Reverend, real good. I brought you something."

The proprietor, a sad-faced heavyset man who once had a brief career in boxing, looked down at the crumpled twenty held in her hand. He took it, removing the crinkles as best he could, then put his arm around the girl. "You in luck tonight, sweet thing. Just got a new supply in, stuff so good it gonna send you so high, you ain't never gonna come down."

Jenny Beth nodded anxiously, aware of the powerful aroma of cocaine in the air. She was careful not to step on the people as she was led into the next room. The reverend selected an unused corner for the girl, near a rusty water-heated radiator that kept the place warm. He helped take off her tattered duffle coat and laid it on the bare wooden floor for the girl to sit on. With no furniture in any of the rooms, clients were forced to lay flat or sit up against a wall. Across from the girl sat a businessman, his dark suit and tie looking out of place, his eyes intently studying the ceiling. There was little talk, just occasional sighs, everyone except the reverend and his doorman either climbing, sitting up there in the promised land, or working their way down. Men with their women, other teenagers like Jenny, and an old man, his face a gray shadow in the smoke, sat with their butane torches flaring and burning, turning minuscule pieces of near-pure cocaine into heaven.

The reverend slid a glass pipe into her hand, and with the other hand Jenny took the small glass vial that contained the magic of her life. He laid the torch at her side, pinching her breasts one last time. "Sweet dreams, baby. Have a good one."

Like the majority of addicts in New York City, Jenny had been doing jumbos for over a year, having slipped away from heroin and its derivatives because they couldn't compete with the wild rush of crack. There were chemicals out there that were even better—China white, fentanyl in its various forms, ecstasy, weird designer drugs, new stuff hitting the street every week—but these were dangerous, and people died. She'd had friends who'd died horrible deaths. Jenny Beth didn't want to be one of them.

She was soon on her way up, racing past the colored lights, heart pounding, head swelling. She was beginning to float ... this was special, she knew it right away, good stuff, just like the reverend said. The sudden rush was wild and free, faster and better than ever before, everything fine now, even the baby was climbing with her. *I want to stay here,* she cried inwardly ... *if only I could stay ....*

The man in the dark suit noticed the girl's convulsive twist—one sharp toss and then stillness. He motioned to the reverend, who was patrolling the room checking to see who might be ready for their next hit. He followed the gaze of the businessman and knelt down on one knee to see if Jenny Beth was okay. The girl didn't respond to his hand on her shoulder. He moved closer, close enough so that no one else could see, and rested his finger on her neck. Nothing. He checked the other side—nothing.

The reverend stood up, saying, "Sure thing, honey chile, you want to sleep away the night here in the Mission, you're welcome to it. I call you in the morning, make sure you're not late for school." He nodded at the businessman, grinning a bit. "Little girl had a hard day, gonna stay and sleep awhile."

Downstairs in his private quarters, the Reverend Bigtime mulled over his predicament. He'd have to wait until the rooms thinned out, then get the body into the trunk of his Caddy and go past some old building they were wrecking so he could get a few chunks of concrete to weigh down the body. He had to be careful, because the fastest way to shut down a house was to allow stories of bad shit to hit the street. Then he had an even bigger problem on his hands: trying to figure out if that whole supply was bad, if any of it was bad, or if it was just the girl — problems with her pregnancy or something.

"Poor little Jenny Beth," he thought. A nice kid, quiet, respectful, let him feel her up whenever he wanted. She needed her dreams, she once told him. Why, he didn't know, but all junkies had their own private reasons; it wasn't his business to snoop. He just provided a service. "Poor little Jenny Beth," he whispered softly into the night. "Ain't gonna dream no more."

CHAPTER ONE

Lind Grenier was an adventurous man. Otherwise, he would not have agreed to spend two years of his life in an isolated forestry training center. But during the past fourteen months, the island of Madagascar with its strange and haunting beauty had somehow managed to lay claim to his soul. A dedicated photographer, he in turn had captured on film exquisite flowers and butterflies found nowhere else in the world.

Now he was its prisoner, in more ways than one.

He had returned to Tsingy in an attempt to solve the mystery of his recording machine, but this time had become hopelessly lost, despite having carefully marked his progress through the maze with pieces of red flagging. By the time he realized that the bright colors provided an irresistible attraction to a family of ring-tailed lemurs, it was too late. There was still enough light to see the animals spread out across the branches of one of the enormous tamarind trees found inside Bemaraha Tsingy National Reserve. Fortunately, he had brought along his ice pick, an old companion from his days of climbing mountains in his native Switzerland; otherwise, he would not have been able to even sit upon the razor-sharp limestone surface.

Located in the west central part of the island, Tsingy had once been a massive limestone plateau of some six hundred square miles. But over the course of millions of years natural erosion had cut deep into the plateau, turning it into so many thousands of jagged peaks. As he bent down to chip away a place to spend the night, Lind had to fight off a strong sensation that the wall of spires towering thirty meters above were slowly closing in around him. Pieces of rock flew in all directions as he scrambled to complete his task before darkness settled in. It would rain tonight, and perhaps another thunderstorm would add to his discomfort. At least down here, at the base of one of the pinnacles, he was safe from lightning. Constant storms on the westerly side of the island were responsible for a good number of deaths. Lind had reason to be cautious, as he had come across them himself, small bodies of the Malagasy, not all that far from the boundaries of the reserve.

Near the perimeter he had seen two natives and called out, but they ran from him. Probably hunters or honey gatherers who had mistaken him for the law. Lind stood up and listened carefully. Another huge flock of bats swarmed overhead. An owl called from nearby. He was certain he heard voices this time and experienced a sense of relief. They would know the way out.

Then it dawned on him that these men were speaking German, which puzzled him. French was common enough in and around the commercial centers of Madagascar, but never German. They had to be foreigners, like him.

"Hallo, guten tag?" he shouted.

No reply.

Lind called again, this time telling them his name, that he was lost and asking their assistance.

Still no answer.

After a few more attempts, he sensed no help was forthcoming from these foreign voices and bent over to finish off the last few ridges. In the morning he would travel east toward the sunrise and eventually find his way out. So he was not overly concerned as he laid out his jacket and pulled his poncho tight around him. At worst, he would spend a miserable night, a fitting punishment for being so stupid.

After settling in, he switched on the tape recorder, wondering again if it were possible to trace the source of the unusual feedback he had picked up during his last trip. He had been playing back a number of bird calls at his friend's home when Wilhem's dog, a mastiff, began to grow nervous. It didn't take Wilhem long to determine that it was something on Lind's recording machine that had caused his dog to react. A few days later, Wilhem told

Lind he was convinced the animal was reacting to an ultrahigh frequency feedback. At some point during his last trip to Tsingy, Lind had been close to a powerful radio transmitter. Impossible, Lind told him. Not only was Tsingy closed to the public, but the park was all but impossible to penetrate. There were no roads or trails, and even access by air was impossible. Thick rubber soles were required to traverse the weathered razorback ridges. No one in Tsingy would have a radio transmitter.

Nevertheless, Wilhem had fixed up a sensitivity indicator on the recorder that he claimed would solve the mystery. So Lind had returned, fascinated by Wilhem's absolute conviction that wherever he had recorded those particular calls, there also was a transmitter or something of an electronic nature. Lind had done his best to retrace the route he had taken on his previous expedition three weeks earlier, but soon found that once inside the limestone labyrinth, everything looked the same. He pushed the record button and slowly moved the unit in a circle, just as he had done all afternoon. The indicator light did not come on. The deep, slow roll of thunder in the distance confirmed his earlier suspicion.

With the first indication of a storm came the wind, tearing through the pinnacles and creating a peculiar chorus of sharp whistling noises. Lind reached out to shut off his recorder, but noticed that the indicator light had come on. He stared at it for a moment in surprise. Then it occurred to him: with so many overtones of sound being created by the wind, was it not reasonable to assume that some could be beyond the range of human hearing?

There was the answer, and a perfectly obvious one. So much for the electronic genius, upon whose solemn assurance he would now have to spend one damnable uncomfortable night. Radio transmitter indeed, he thought, grimacing as he settled into his limestone nook to await the rain.

Some two hundred meters northwest and twenty meters underground, three men were engaged in a heated debate. The language was German. "He is not one of the locals, Victor. Zap this man and you run the risk of an investigation."

The speaker was tall and gaunt and had seen little sun in the last few months. Overhead fluorescent lights made his face appear even more sallow. The other two were seated, each holding a glass of sherry. Behind a single desk in the room sat the older of the two, Victor. At eighty-three years of age, he was near bald and had been forced to wear thick lenses to compensate for his failing vision.

Victor tapped his desk impatiently and said, "An order is an order. Zurich has been told who he is, and a decision has been made. This leaves us with no choice in the matter. Therefore, I suggest you get on with it."

The third man had his chair tipped back against the wall to the left of Victor. His name was Erich. "Perhaps Karl is reluctant, Herr Doctor; after all, this one is not a miniature piece of shit like the others. He is a Swiss forester, a man capable of putting up a good fight."

Karl Schuster, a West German hired six months earlier to look after security, reacted by starting toward Erich. He felt the time had come to wipe that taunting sneer from his face.

Victor jumped up before Karl reached the man. "Erich is young, my friend, and youth and arrogance go hand in hand. Do not waste your energy. Besides, he is the only chemist we have. As for the intruder, take two of your men and seal off the southeast passage. Call in when you have him or if you encounter difficulties."

Lind rolled over as the first few sprinkles fell on his poncho. He was having unpleasant thoughts about Wilhem. It was completely dark now, with the thunderstorm drawing ever closer. He listened to the ringtails nearby; they too were restless. Lightning flashed across the sky, releasing its primary charges. He heard noises, probably tamarind pods falling to the ground. He thought of Anna and suddenly felt a deep longing for his mountain home and his beautiful wife.

The eerie, haunting call of the giant Indri, the largest of Madagascar's lemurs, echoed in and out the spires. The Malagasy believed these animals sometimes strangled humans in their sleep. They also claimed Tsingy to be a sinister place and that the spires were the devil's teeth, which chewed up intruders and then swallowed them. Lind knew these were just stories the typically superstitious natives made up. All primitive cultures had their evil omens and such. Even so, he began to feel an unaccountable sense of being afraid.

Karl had learned to traverse the reserve in the dark. The area surrounding the project had been aerial mapped the previous year by ZIAN, the Zurich International Association of Naturalists, with each spire assigned a number. The Swiss forester had scraped out a spot to spend the night near the base of 137. Karl would approach from the north, from behind 139. He eased back the safety on his MP44 assault rifle. A lightning flash created daylight for a split second, just long enough for him to see that his quarry was sitting up. This alarmed the German, and he suddenly wondered if the man was armed.

But the lightning had also exposed Karl. Seeing a man approach with a weapon held at the ready, Lind snatched up his ice pick and bolted around the limestone base.

"Herr Grenier, please do not run. You have nothing to fear and will only slip and fall on the razorbacks."

Lind stopped dead at the sound of his name spoken in German. Confused, he called out, "Who are you?"

"Please remain where you are, Herr Grenier. I will explain in a moment."

Lind was startled when two more armed men approached from behind. "Do what the nice man says, Herr Grenier, and you won't get hurt. And drop that nasty little toy."

He did as he was told and waited. Seconds later a powerful light beam scanned his face, forcing the Swiss to avert his eyes.

"You are to be congratulated, Herr Grenier. Only a handful of foreigners have dared to enter the maze, and none so deeply as you."

Lind did not care for the rough hands poking through his clothing. "To my misfortune, it appears."

The tall man who had called to Lind passed his light to another and spoke into a hand radio as the sky flashed its anger in a great sweeping arc. "All clear. We are returning to base." To the other two he said, "I want you to come back in the morning and make sure there's nothing lying around. And now, Herr Grenier, I will assist you to our humble little shelter where you will have a good bed and a decent night's sleep. So much better than trying to sleep on these damn limestone ridges."

After some ten minutes of stumbling along between the two men in the driving rain, Lind was astonished to see a brightly-lit doorway appear ahead of them. Once inside, the door closed automatically behind them as they began to descend a steep staircase cut into the rock. A powerful chemical odor strong enough to make him rub his eyes rose up to greet them.

They arrived at a landing, where a rough wooden floor had been laid down over the limestone. The excited swoosh of many small wings high above made Lind realize some of the pinnacles were hollow.

"Hell of a stink, isn't it?" said the tall man leading the way. "Takes some getting used to."

He paused to reach behind a door for a towel, then gave it to Lind with an unexpected smile. "I suppose I should have stopped long enough to let you put on your rain gear, but lightning makes me nervous."

The man behind Lind chuckled and said, "I can't imagine why."

Their destination was a large, office-like chamber with a couch, a desk, and a few chairs. An elderly man with pale features rose from behind the desk upon their entry. "Well done, Karl. Delighted to have you join us, Herr Grenier. So few visitors drop in these days, and you have no idea how lonely it can become down here. Please have a seat and tell us all about yourself. Erich, a sherry for our guest."

Lind shook his head, wondering if it was all a dream. Could he really be sitting in an office beneath the most forbidding piece of real estate on the face of the Earth? He leaned over the old man's desk. "A few questions are in order, it seems. For instance, who in hell's name are you people, and just what is it you are doing in Tsingy?"

Another man entered the room, carrying Lind's shoulder pack with his camera equipment and tape recorder. He laid the recorder on the desk. "Take a look at this sensitivity indicator. What do you suppose it is intended for?"

The old man's eyes narrowed as he ran his fingers over the crudely mounted dial. He gave the Swiss forester a cold look. "Perhaps Herr Grenier will be kind enough to tell us."

Lind remained silent, because in a darkened corner of the room he had spotted a sophisticated radio transmitter. He apologized to Wilhem in his mind, at the same time realizing that he had apparently uncovered some kind of criminal activity.

But what kind?

The younger man in the room was grinning away at the Swiss. "It seems our guest is not going to cooperate after all. A little sport would go a long way to alleviate the boredom of this enterprise. What do you say, Victor?"

The old man twisted his face into a deep scowl and told Erich to shut up. After a moment's hesitation, he pushed a button on his intercom. "How much time before this one passes over?"

"No more than fifteen minutes," another voice responded in German. "There's a follow-up due in around four."

Victor glanced up at the tall man who had brought in Lind. "Do we have a problem on our hands or not?"

Karl looked down at the tape recorder to study it for a moment. He turned it on, rewound it, and pressed play. Several birdcalls filled the room, lemurs chattering away, a faint roll of thunder. Immediately after the thunder, the indicator light came on for a few seconds, followed by the familiar sound of wind whistling through the spires. The security chief continued to stare at the recorder for a full minute before glancing at his watch and then at the radio transmitter.

He finally turned to the Swiss forester with a somber look.

Chapter Two

Lieutenant Charlie Bannerman sweated a lot. At five eight, he was two-twenty and growing. A constant diet of bagels, pizzas, and doughnuts had turned his body into a disaster, a fact his superiors frequently brought to his attention. Over the years he had developed the same tenacious attitude toward his food as he had toward his job: when he bit into something, he never let go. In the majority of homicide cases this trait was beneficial to the department. Occasionally, like right now, it was a pain in the ass; and Captain Harry Ulansky was fast running out of patience as he listened to Bannerman ramble on.

"Come on, Harry, we know there's lots of bad shit on the streets — too much. All I'm saying is we got enough similarities going to make a rational assumption that some of it is being put out there for a specific purpose. And that purpose is to kill."

Ulansky squeezed his eyes shut, but when he opened them, Bannerman was still there. "Charlie, Charlie, there is always bad shit on the street. This is not news. Bad shit kills. This is not news. You're asking me to believe the pushers are doing away with the source of their income, which is bullshit. Okay, we got twenty-three stiffs in a couple of weeks, with nineteen of them showing cause of death as aggravated heart failure. I'll admit the pattern is similar. So what?"

The veteran officer rolled his head around. "I didn't say it was the pushers. I'm not crazy enough to believe that. Look, just give me a few days. I'll get Rizzo and Little Sammy Carletti started on it. I'll feed the whole enchilada into the computer. I'll get the lab boys to —"

"Goddamnit, Bannerman, you're beginning to piss me off!" With that Ulansky stood up, which brought him a full five inches closer to the ceiling than his subordinate. "We have the best forensic people in the business and they're telling us any combination of this shit can kill. Yeast, baking soda, valium, a whole menagerie of amphetamines, freaking PCPs, a bunch of that synthetic crap like fentanyl, even heroin, all mixed in with pure cocaine! And you wonder why we got so much crow bait floating around. What I don't understand is why the number isn't ten times as high."

He sat down again, pissed off at himself for getting upset so easily, but Bannerman had that effect on people. "Let's not read into this sudden splurge of corpses some evil plot against New York City. The ones classified as homicide are ours. How many you got there—four? The ODs are accidental or suicide—out of our hands, finished. The narcs have the whole shemozzle on their plate, so let them play with it. It's their baby, okay?"

Bannerman rolled his head around some more. It was a particularly annoying mannerism of his, since it was impossible to tell whether he was agreeing or disagreeing. He had been standing the whole time in front of Ulansky's desk, holding the four files in his sweaty palms as if he were making an offering. "Look, Captain, I think the reason our guys can't find anything out of the ordinary is because it's beyond their capability. Things out there are moving too fast for them to keep up."

When the senior officer began to grit his teeth, Bannerman added quickly, "Look, forget Rizzo and Carletti. Just fix it so I can get my hands on the autopsy reports and samples of the recent stuff that's come in. Dolman told me about this computer whiz in the biology department over at Columbia. He says this guy created a program that can break down the components of any substance in the world. What do you say, Harry? That's not so much to ask."

Ulansky buried his head in his hands. Anyone but Bannerman, he could stare the man in the eye and discuss things rationally. He looked up to see the hangdog look, the face the guy wore when he was trying to wheedle something out of his superiors.

"When you came in here this morning I felt great, organized, in control of my life. You have succeeded in giving me heartburn, a headache, and a sense of insecurity. There is now some question of my ability to carry on as head of this department. What is this aversion you have to the word 'no'? Charlie, it is a simple word; it means you are to stop, that you must not go on, that this particular phase of your life has come to an end. And it means if you insist on pursuing this line of reasoning, I will personally rip out your balls and stuff them down your throat!"

"Gosh, Captain," said Bannerman, backing away. "You never told me there was Arabic blood in your family."

Ulansky's voice followed the detective as he made a quick exit. "You are dead! Do you hear me? Dead, dead, dead!"

"Having a disagreement, are we?" asked Nancy McIvor, whose desk was closest to Ulansky's office.

Charlie paused at her desk, the four homicide files now tucked under his arm. "It's not good for his health, you know, to get all worked up like that."

McIvor looked up, smirking. "It's only with you, Charlie. Somehow, you manage to bring out the best in people."

Bannerman made his way down a flight of stairs, wondering how he was going to get his hands on the exhibits. At the end of a long hallway, he pushed through the double doors leading into the police laboratory. He went to see Dolman first.

Dolman took in Charlie's crumpled suit, saying, "Lieutenant, I heard they're redoing *Jake and the Fatman* and you're gonna play the Fatman. That true?"

The officer's eyes flickered, but he said nothing. It was hard to tell with Charlie whether all the kibitzing got to him or not.

"What do you have on that professor at Columbia?"

"A name, Lieutenant, just a name. And a telephone number."

He took down the information, then stood by Dolman's desk for awhile, thinking. It was something he did on a regular basis anywhere in the building, so Dolman paid no attention.

Finally, Charlie asked, "Frank, how many crack exhibits we got on hand?"

"Hell of a pile at the moment—over a hundred."

"I need a dozen, the most recent we took in."

Dolman looked up from his telescope. "So, get the captain's John Henry on the bottom line, they're yours." Catching Bannerman's pained look, he added, "Ulansky won't go for it?"

"He prefers to believe that nineteen ODs with the exact same type of heart failure is a natural result of some new chemical shit they're adding in."

Dolman pushed his chair back, taking off his glasses to rub his eyes. "Which could be the bottom line, who's to say otherwise?"

Bannerman stared down at Dolman's bald spot for a bit before answering. "I got a bad feeling about this one, Frank. Something different is going on out there."

Dolman nodded. Charlie's gut feelings were legendary around the department. "Okay, Lieutenant, what do you want me to do?"

"Dr. Carswell?"

"Yes, speaking."

"This is Lieutenant Bannerman of the NYPD, Twenty-First Precinct, Homicide Division. Heard about your new program. I believe it might have some application in a case I'm working on."

"This comes as a bit of a surprise, Lieutenant. I hadn't realized word of BTI had leaked out. If you can give me some indication of the problem, perhaps I can tell you if I can be of help."

"This isn't something that should be discussed over the phone. What are the chances of coming over to see you right away?"

"I'll be free at two forty-five. You know your way around Columbia?"

"Yeah, you're in the Sherman Fairchild Center, aren't you? Park under the Computer Science building and take the stairs?"

"Or the service elevator. Check in with reception; the girl will direct you to my office."

"Gotcha. By the way, what does BTI mean?"

"Stands for 'biology to infinity'—just my way of telling God I'm hot on his tail."

It was mid-November and the first few wet snowfalls had already come and gone. The last leaves on the oak trees lining Fifth Avenue were beginning to die. Bannerman had spent most of his life thinking about death in one form or another. His old man had caught it in Iwo Jima — a hero, with two Silver Crosses sitting atop a whole mess of other decorations. Bannerman was not a hero. He didn't have a taste for violence and had yet to fire his weapon in a real-life situation. But he had friends in the force who bragged about how many people they'd blown away — killer cops. Bannerman knew these guys were necessary, because there would always be scum on the streets ready and willing to turn their corner, their block, or their district into a jungle.

He glanced at his watch and pulled in beside a street peddler to pick up a few bagels. Charlie never did marry. He had quit school in grade nine to help his mother support the family. On the docks he'd met Sofia and fell hopelessly in love. He bought her a ring, using every cent he had saved up. While strolling along the banks of the Hudson one evening, Sofia ripped off her engagement ring and threw it in the river. She had a fiery temper, something that only added to her appeal up till then. Charlie watched the tiny ripples disappear, then turned around and walked away. Sofia was the beginning and the end of serious women in his life. The following spring, at the age of nineteen, he joined the NYPD.

At the service entrance off Amsterdam, he flashed his badge at the black security guard leaning against a stone wall. He found a parking spot close to the staircase, locked the door and brushed the crumbs off his blue serge suit jacket. He made a fruitless effort to button it up while climbing the inside steps. The receptionist told him to keep on climbing; Carswell's office was seven doors from the head of the stairs on the fourth level.

Inside he found a bearded young man in a gray turtleneck sweater perched on a highchair before a green chalkboard with his runners hooked over the lower rungs, elbows on his knees, and head resting in his hands. He raised his eyes at Charlie's unannounced entry. "Lieutenant Bannerman, I presume?"

"Right. You're Carswell?"

"The very same," he answered, jumping off the chair with a sudden leap. He stretched and groaned for a bit before sliding into an armchair behind his desk. "It so happens that I like mysteries, Lieutenant. Do you have a little mystery for me to solve?"

Bannerman nodded, sensing the vast amount of energy in the guy. "Got one sure enough. But I doubt if it's going to be solved that easily, maybe not at all."

Carswell grinned, creating a hole in the wall of scruffy blond hair on his face. His blue eyes sparkled. "If it was easy it wouldn't interest me. Let's see what you have in the briefcase."

He placed the case on his knees and removed the exhibits Dolman had signed out from Property, then laid them on the desk. "This is street junk, crack. It's got all kinds of shit added to it, most of which is capable of killing if the dosage is high enough." The biologist fingered the little plastic bags while Charlie removed the autopsies and other paperwork. "These are the case files on nineteen drug-related deaths that occurred within the limits of the Twenty-First over a two-week period. During that same time frame, every other precinct that deals with our type of serious drug problem reported a similar increase in ODs. Most, but not all of these deaths were caused by severe paroxysmal tachycardia, meaning their heartbeat went crazy. Since various types of amphetamines have been around for years, paroxysmal tachycardia isn't news to us. But even with the most severe case of rapid heartbeat, the victim usually recovers. Now, all of a sudden we got a hundred junkies wiped out because their hearts went wacky."

"Has there been a comparative study done of the victims' blood and urine samples?"

Charlie rolled his head around. "Sure, the usual studies were carried out, and the lab found everything you can imagine, but nothing we hadn't seen before. The kicker is that in every single case crack was used, and for the most part the buys were made at the local crack houses. Naturally the bodies were removed from the premises and dumped on the street or in the river. Some were even weighed down."

"Which makes it homicide."

"Maybe. Maybe not. The houses have their reputations to protect. They get rid of the bodies as best they can. If the victim was known to frequent a certain place, the owner won't want his name linked to that death because his regulars might suspect he's selling them bad shit."

"So your victims could come from any part of the city?"

"They could."

Carswell swung his head around to study the figures on his chalkboard. "And you want me to try to determine which substance or combination is killing them."

"Something like that."

"You think it's being done deliberately?"

"I do."

"A sort of gang warfare, one faction trying to knock the other out of business?"

"That occurred to me, but I'm having real problems seeing the logic, because, well, nobody wins. By the way, these exhibits got nothing to do with the cases. They're examples of the current stuff coming off the street. If you could look over the autopsies and lab reports, then run an in-depth analysis on the samples, it might tell us something."

"Looking for some common thread."

"A common thread, yes—but one that kills."

Carswell took in Charlie's mournful look and the sad state of his attire. "You the investigating officer in all these cases?"

"Only four have been classified as homicide. They're mine. The files on the others are closed or about to be. I'm conducting this research on my own."

"I see," said Carswell, pulling the crack samples toward him.

Bannerman laid his stack of files on the desk. "You can have these until noon tomorrow." He watched Carswell open one package and then another. "Try not to mix up the contents, although I doubt if anyone would know the difference. What do you think, Doc, can your program handle it?"

Carswell didn't bother to look up. "You know what a gigaflop is?"

"Never heard of it."

"It's a term used to describe the performance of the big new mainframes about to hit the market. A gigaflop is the ability to conduct trillions of floating-point calculations every second. Downstairs we have a pair of interfaced Cray Y-MPs with a nine gig potential. In them is stored the known data on all the world's natural elements."

"Natural—"

"Just a moment, Lieutenant, I'm not finished. All that information is stored in memory. What do you know about AI?"

"Artificial intelligence, as applied to computers."

"Good. That is exactly what it means." Carswell popped up from his desk holding one of the exhibit bags in his hand. "No matter what is contained in this little bag, BTI will sniff it out. If it is a completely unknown substance, the program will conduct its own research and tell us what it is in generic terms. Even so, under these circumstances that may not be enough. You'll want to know where it comes from, and I can't guarantee we can provide you with that information."

Charlie used the edge of the desk to help himself up. "Over the years I've found that correct identification is the first requirement in these sorts of oddball cases. You tell me what we got, and I'll take it from there. Here's my card. I'll get back to you in the morning. And Doc, I don't have to tell you this is super-confidential."

Gary Carswell smiled, offering his hand. "You don't, but you did anyway."

Charlie Bannerman's Brooklyn apartment was not an exotic setting, yet it was much neater than its occupant. This was due to Charlie's three older sisters, who had given up recommending eligible women for his consideration and taken on the job themselves of keeping their brother's place in order. They also did his laundry and ironed his clothes, though Charlie still tended to live in the same outfit for days at a time. If he had a hobby at all, it was reading everything he laid his hands on, much of which he tended to store away somewhere inside his head for future reference. He never smoked, had only an occasional beer, and still went to church from time to time. His private life was a counterpoint to his public life, and Charlie was content, or at least thought he was.

That evening he killed two Budweisers while mulling over some loose ends in one of his current cases. He fell asleep with the light on and the case file in his hand. The telephone rang at 3:37. He glanced at his clock before answering it.

"Bannerman."

"Gary Carswell, Lieutenant. I have something to show you. Can you come over?"

"Right now?"

"If you can make it."

"Give me an hour."

A note pinned to one of the glass doors provided directions to the computer room downstairs. Carswell was all alone facing two oversize screens, each displaying a series of random numbers. He shoved a swivel chair across the floor for Bannerman.

"A little test for you, Lieutenant." He punched a few keys and the screens cleared. A few more keys, and both showed a pear-shaped ellipsoid. Inside was a configuration of numerous hexagons, much like a honeycomb. "What I've done so far is isolate the foreign elements from each of the samples you gave me. I must commend your people on doing an excellent job, because their reports list every trace element that Dan found."

"Dan?"

"This is Dan," he answered impatiently, throwing his arms in a sweeping arc to take in the computer apparatus. "Both monitors are showing us, in graphic form, the chromosome breakdown of a single cocaine cell. Can you spot any difference between them?"

Charlie squinted at the screens for a moment. "Uh-uh," he finally declared.

"I'm going to take the right display and overlay it on the left one." He did so and turned again to Bannerman. "Pull your chair in and take another look."

This time Charlie took a bit longer. "I can see only one figure."

Carswell took a magnifying glass from the desk and passed it to Charlie. He placed the tip of his pencil on the screen. "Tell me what you see here." Bannerman moved the glass back and forth until he focused exactly on the pencil point. All he could find was a slight bulge in one of the hexagon sides.

"A bulge, is that it?"

"You got it—just the tiniest bulge."

Bannerman rubbed his eyes. "Christ, how did you manage to find that?"

"I didn't, Dan did. I took a few grains from each the dozen samples you left me. Four samples showed an identical bulge in the same chromosome, and the odds against that being done artificially are in astronomic proportion."

"Shit," Charlie said. "So we're talking about a natural alteration, some environmental quirk in the development of the coca leaves."

Carswell stared at Bannerman for a moment, nodding finally. "You've drawn the obvious conclusion, but not the correct one. You mentioned the environment. After Dan pointed this out to me, I sent him on an environmental scan of the various pollutant factors spread throughout the atmosphere. We can be reasonably assured that two of these samples came from south central Bolivia, one from east central Peru, and the fourth from northern Bolivia, close to the Brazilian border."

Charlie scratched his head. "But didn't you just get through telling me—"

Gary Carswell broke out a wide grin. "Fascinating, isn't it? So we know it isn't something that happened in the development stage of the plant. And because of the variety of impurities and the amounts added, we also know these particular samples were cooked up in different locations—three, to be precise."

Feeling a touch of frustration, Bannerman said, "You tell me it has to be something natural, then you tell me it can't be natural. Where does that leave us?"

"Dan is presently conducting a geographical analysis of our mystery chromosome. Let's have a look at his progress."

Carswell went to work at the keyboard again, causing the screens to revert to rows of numbers. He studied them for a moment before keying in further instructions. "The BTI program allows Dan to put our scanning electron microscope to work. I've asked him to let us view the DNA configuration on the right screen."

This time the screen showed an array of colors, twisting and turning into the double helix that signified the basic genetic code of all life forms. "Now I'll ask him to show us those parts of the helix that have been affected by the altered chromosome."

Three small black circles appeared on the screen, moving along with the intertwining arms of the pretzel-like three-dimensional image. "The numbers on the left show the computer utilizing its AI capability. All we have to go on so far is a peculiar mutation that took place at the molecular level. Dan is using his own logic and knowledge to formulate a solution, or a series of solutions. While he's doing that, I'll ask him to note possible eccentricities in the DNA molecules and tell us whether such modification is capable of combining with pure cocaine or any of the foreign elements we found, in a form that could have a spasmodic effect on the heart."

About ten seconds after Carswell had keyed in that particular set of instructions, the colorful twin spirals of the helix gave way to lines of text made up primarily of chemical symbols and numbers. Then the screen began to scroll, allowing Carswell to read the output.

He stopped the scroll and highlighted two lines. "Define!" he said, touching a single key.

A long set of chemical symbols raced across the screen and froze there. Carswell studied them intently. "Don't jerk me around, Dan. Redefine!"

The screen cleared for a few seconds before another set of symbols appeared. To Bannerman they looked identical to the first set. "Problem?" he asked politely.

Carswell stood up and pulled the gray turtleneck over his head. "I'd say that Dan has overlapped my initial cellular search command with my second command to cross-reference the eccentric DNA molecules. He was apparently unable to find a direct correlation and used his own initiative to presuppose a solution. What he's given me is a formula for a nonexistent substance, which I can only surmise is a macro-amphetamine. The symbols jive, but the proportions are wild. This is rocket-booster stuff he's showing us, a drug capable of rupturing the heart muscle in seconds."

"But isn't that possible? That's not too far removed from the actual cause of death."

"No way, Lieutenant. Don't forget, only a single chromosome has been altered." He walked over to a small table and plugged in a kettle. "It doesn't matter whether we're talking natural or artificial modification; this scenario is just not possible." When he turned around to face Bannerman, once again he wore a pained look on his face.

"I just had a perfectly disgusting idea. Ugh! I hate to even think of it. You drink tea?"

"When I have to." Charlie stood up, stretched, and removed his jacket. "Are you getting anywhere?"

Carswell glanced at a wall clock. The time was 6:03. "When do you have to be at work?"

"I usually arrive around seven-thirty. Why?"

"Do you have access to the morgue?"

"Sheesh! You want a sample from one of the victims, right?"

Shaking his head as he unplugged the kettle, Carswell said, "You got it, Lieutenant. Specifically, the heart from one of your victims. Can you think of a better way to disprove Dan's conclusion?"

Charlie watched two tea bags sink into an ornate China teapot. "Have you ever considered, Doc, that you might have bugs in your program?"

Carswell set his mouth under the blond hair that covered it. "This program has an elaborate set of checks built into it. If a mistake has been made, Dan will let me know. He honestly thinks the answer he gave us is correct."

"Which you say is impossible."

For the first time, Bannerman thought he detected a tiny crack in the biologist's armor of self-assurance. Carswell poured the tea and passed the second cup to Charlie, then returned to his keyboard. "I'm going to ask for a status report on how the cell search is progressing."

While the left screen continued to run what appeared to Charlie to be random numbers, the right screen listed a set of headings down the left side: GROUP, ORDER, FAMILY, SUBFAMILY, TRIBE, SUBTRIBE, GENUS, SPECIES.

"Ah, so it is natural! This is the classification order of angiosperms, or flowering plants. Good boy, Dan. Now let's see how far you've taken it."

23

The computer immediately listed *Monocotyledonae* after group and *Liliiflorae* after order. There it stopped. When Carswell prompted it, the left-hand screen flashed insufficient data.

Carswell ran his fingers through his unruly hair. "Dammed unusual. It got us as far as a flowering plant of the *Liliiflorae* order and stopped dead."

"What do all these random numbers mean?"

"You're looking at the cell search being carried out in binary code. The monitor is showing you how Dan thinks. Lieutenant, this is going to take somewhat longer than I anticipated. What about the morgue—can you borrow a specimen or not?"

"They won't like it. Relatives get wind of something like that, they go bananas. How long will you need it?"

"At least twenty-four hours, maybe longer. From a male of good physical stature, if you can. I'll have to bully my way into the electron scanner, but I have seniority. Can you run it back here before you begin work?"

Bannerman smiled, a reasonably rare occurrence. "I began work in nineteen fifty-six."

By the time he reached the morgue it was seven forty-five. Several arguments later he was on his way back with a cold, unpleasant package. The receptionist informed him that Dr. Carswell had called in sick and wasn't expected in today. This threw Charlie into a tailspin for a moment, until he realized the obvious. The door to the computer room was locked, and he had to identify himself before Carswell let him in. Bannerman could tell from his grim look that something was wrong.

"I had to force the next two classifications. So far we have the plant fixed in the *Orchidaceae* family, in the subfamily *Epidendroideae*. We know it is an orchid."

Bannerman deposited his package on the computer desk, happy to be free of it. "An orchid?"

Carswell nodded, rubbing his eyes. "An orchid, though apparently one unknown to Dan, which by definition means it is an unlisted species. But something in the makeup of that chromosome is preventing the computer from using its logic to continue the identification process." He hoisted the package, feeling its weight. "I'm going to place this in the scanner and allow Dan to do a complete analysis on his own. The computer is off limits for the day. No one has access." He yawned. "That will piss off a lot of people." He glanced at the wall clock, adding, "My wife, especially."

"What about the exhibits?"

"Everything is in the computer. I don't need them anymore. Look, there's no reason for you to wait around, since I really have no idea how long this process is going to take. If I don't get back to you sometime today, how about dropping around early tomorrow morning?"

"Sure thing, Doc. Do I take it you're impressed with my little mystery?"

"Lieutenant, I called you early this morning because I was certain that I would have the answer by the time you arrived. Once the parameters were defined, Dan should have been able to spit it out in a matter of seconds. Instead, he's completely stumped. So yes, you definitely have my attention."

The call came just after four in the afternoon. "You better get over here, Lieutenant."

"On my way, Professor."

Carswell was biting his nails when he let Charlie in. He seemed on edge.

"What's up?" Bannerman asked.

"Come and have a look."

The right screen showed the faded image of a delicate golden flower attached to a twisted brown stem. Bannerman studied it for a minute. "Is that our mystery orchid?"

"It is."

Bannerman noticed the image was faded. "Anything you can do to make it sharper?"

Carswell gave the officer a hard look. "That is as far as Dan will go on his own. Watch what happens when I command him to enhance the image."

As the colors grew more vivid, in the background a pair of coal-black wings began to take shape and actually fluttered on the screen. Bannerman sat down and stared at the picture in awe. The divided wings appeared to be hovering behind and level with the top of the flower.

Both men watched for a few minutes before Carswell broke the silence. "It scared the living hell out of me when it first came on. For some unknown reason Dan seems unable to correlate the wings into the display—until I call for enhancement. And when I ask him why, all I get is the old incomplete data singsong. In some weird manner that I can't pin down on the program, there's enough info available to partly ID the orchid, yet not enough to even acknowledge these goddamn wings!"

Charlie glanced at the biologist, wondering why he seemed to be taking it so hard. "How do you interpret all this?"

"It's like Dan doesn't even know they're there. I suppose the wings could represent a moth or a bird feeding on the nectar. But the bottom line is what you see taking place in front of you is inconceivable." Carswell turned away from the screen. "We started out looking for a chemical and wound up with a chromosome. I hate to admit it, Lieutenant, but this is getting over my head. My field is really biotechnology, not botany. I put in a call to Sam Bloom, but he can't make it until Sunday evening."

"Sam Bloom?"

"Your orchid is almost certain to be an unlisted species from the island of Madagascar. Dr. Samuel Ignatius Bloom is one of the world's foremost botanists, and he *is* the leading expert on exotic orchids. I believe it is now imperative to get him involved without delay."

Bannerman picked up on the tone. "Something else you should be telling me?"

Gary Carswell ran his fingers over the keyboard, wiping clean both screens. "Dan didn't make a mistake this morning. His analysis of the super-amphetamine was correct. There's no longer any doubt that the majority of your victims died when this stuff, whatever it is, entered their bloodstream."

Charlie slumped in his chair, feeling no real sense of triumph. Instead, a great weariness seemed to take hold of him. Quietly he said, "It's being done deliberately."

"That's the only answer there is, Lieutenant."

"But it makes no sense. Would anyone really go through so much trouble just to knock off a bunch of junkies?" He rolled his head a little, puzzled. "Christ ... Madagascar. You sure about this?"

"The ratio is eighty-seven percent certainty, odds high enough to bet your pension."

CHAPTER THREE

"There is a Monsieur René Simard who wishes to speak to you, Dr. Grenier."

Anna looked up from her desk at Marie, her gray eyes widening. "René? My cousin René?"

Marie shrugged her shoulders. "I doubt if the security guard asked him *that* question. Do you wish to see him or not?"

After all her years in Geneva, Anna was still put off by the unnecessary abruptness of the French. She had been with the World Health Organization almost since the completion of her internship in Zurich. But unlike Zurich, where the real Swiss lived—she would never voice that opinion aloud—Geneva was French, and the majority of the staff at WHO headquarters were French.

She nodded at the sullen-faced girl. "I'll see him right away."

She rose from her seat, feeling a small tingling of excitement. Below her fourth-floor window the maples were at the peak of their crimson glory, but the sparkling surface of Lac Léman that usually greeted her during the summer was now shrouded over by the fall mists. The past came flooding back to her: René, on the banks of the Limmat River—he was fourteen, Anna fifteen, locked in passionate embrace; René, so handsome, so aggressive—even at that early age. That final year she had barely managed to escape with her virginity intact.

Smiling, she caught part of her reflection in the window and wondered what he would think of her now. People claimed she had a fine presence. Certainly she had inherited her mother's looks, a sort of Catherine Deneuve with cheekbones. By engaging in a relentless struggle to keep her weight in line, the final product was a moderately tall, well-built, attractive woman thirty-five years of age.

She had last seen René during the summer of sixty-seven. During that winter his family moved back to Paris, and he never again came to spend his summers with Anna and her brothers. They had met just once since then, at her father's funeral, and Anna had been too distraught to even remember him.

When the door opened and Marie stepped aside, Anna caught her breath. "René? My God, is it really you?"

René returned her smile and quietly closed the door. Anna shook free from her shock and ran the short distance between them, throwing her arms around his neck. She could feel the tears sting her eyes. They kissed with an intensity that left her breathless.

"Anna, Anna, my smart, sexy, older cousin," he said into her hair. "I never guessed you would become so beautiful, nor so successful. A physician yet." He held her at arm's length. "Let me look at you."

She instinctively reached up to wipe her eyes, then broke free and punched him hard on the shoulder. "We were friends, damn you!"

"Almost lovers," he added, rubbing his shoulder.

She took in his features, seeing how they had changed, but recognizing that same seductive glimmer in those same beautiful brown eyes. "Almost," she agreed, moving again into his arms. "All those years, René, couldn't you have at least written or called when you came home to visit your mother?"

"You were married. I met him at the funeral and felt insanely jealous, even if you were my cousin."

Anna broke free again. "That is hardly an excuse. I often told Lind about my handsome French cousin. You should have come to see us. Where have you been all this time?"

René pulled back, his smile dazzling. "Seeking my fortune out there in the big, bad world."

"Have you succeeded?"

He sighed. "Lady Luck and I did not get along so well. I did attempt university, but I am ashamed to tell you that it did not hold my attention for long. Eventually I became a simple government peon, just one of the masses, and made my home with the Bureau of Statistics, in Paris. Not very romantic."

Anna led him to a chair, then took her own behind the desk. She leaned across, reaching one hand toward him. "It is so wonderful to see you again, René. So tell me, what brings you here, after all these years?"

He took her hand in both of his. "I was just down the street, at the UN building. I have a few days to kill, and thought I would begin by taking you and Lind out to dinner. How is Lind, by the way?"

Anna smiled. Her husband was perhaps the healthiest man she knew. "Lind is wonderful, but he just happens to be in Madagascar at the moment. So he will have to gracefully decline your invitation."

René pursed his lips and was silent for a moment. Studying him, Anna concluded that his classic French looks would melt the heart—and the pants—of most any woman.

"Too bad. I was looking forward to finally getting to know him. However, my invitation stands. An evening at some quiet restaurant to renew old times. What do you say?"

Anna slowly withdrew her hand. *Damn you, Lind,* she said silently to herself. Her husband was just over halfway through a two-year contract with a Swiss-sponsored forestry training program on the island of Madagascar. During her frequent trips to the WHO headquarters in Brazzaville, she did manage to stop off for a few days now and then. But in the last few months she realized that she no longer missed her husband—a bad sign. After this project, they were to finally begin the family that Anna longed for so desperately. Lack of children was a major sore point in their twelve-year-old marriage, and it seemed like the longer they went without a child, the more distant they were becoming. She still loved Lind; at least she thought she did. She also knew that the flame from their early years had pretty well gone out, which made her very sad.

Now, gazing at her elegant and attractive cousin, Anna was very aware of the dangers of going out to dinner with him. Despite their differences and long periods of separation, she had always remained faithful to Lind, but …. "I would be delighted. So tell me, it's been twenty years. What have doing all this time? The last time I spoke to Aunt Giselle, you still had not married. And now?"

René rubbed a hand along the side of his face, feeling the dark shadow of whiskers. "I drove direct from Paris and arrived just a couple of hours ago. Would you be greatly offended if I went now to check into my hotel? There'll be time enough during dinner to cover the past."

Anna stood up, smiling radiantly. It was so good to see him again. "Of course not. And if Lind was home I would invite you to—"

René held up his hand, rising gracefully from his chair. "I understand perfectly. Write down your address for me, and I'll come by at, what, around eight?"

"Eight will be fine." Anna jotted down her address, then walked around the desk to link her arm into René's. She could feel the electricity between them, and it excited her.

She was surprised to find that René was staying at the Hotel de la Paix, a luxurious hotel on the lake. This is where he chose to take his cousin for dinner, a two and a half hour affair in the golden dining room with a bill of 240 francs at the end of the evening. Anna did not wish to inquire into the whys and wherefores of how an ordinary civil servant could afford such luxury, but the thought crossed her mind that he may have been trying to impress her. She was also surprised and a little disappointed when the meal was over that he did not invite her up to his room. Instead, they took advantage of the unusually warm mid-November evening to stroll along the lake and up Rue de Mont Blanc. They gazed into the shop windows at the great variety of timepieces for which Geneva was famous, joking and giggling like teenagers at the wild price tags on the Cartier bags and Lacoste shirts and other expensive items on display along the city's major thoroughfare.

They took a different route back, through the small red-light district that had popped up in recent years along Rue de Berne.

René asked a tough-looking blonde how much she would charge to spend the evening with both of them, but the woman knew he was joking and walked away mouthing a few classic French phrases. By now, Anna was beginning to come out from under the giddy effects of the champagne. A wind had started off the lake, and she snuggled close to René as they rounded the corner of his hotel. Directly ahead, the crest of the Jet d'Eau exploded into tonnes of spray as its pressure surrendered to the wind.

He paused near the front entry. "Home?"

Anna nodded reluctantly. It was all for the best, she knew, yet at the same time felt somehow cheated. She was convinced during dinner that he would at least try to seduce her.

They drove home in silence, a letdown for Anna, for which her conscience was giving her hell. Her flat was located in a quiet residential area on the left bank, across from Parc Bertrand. René parked the Citroen a few discreet doors back and turned off the motor. He immediately took Anna into his arms and kissed her hard. She responded hungrily. "Oh René," she said after breaking for air. "I thought you would never get around to it."

"I was unsure of how you would react."

"Don't you remember our pact that we would always remain kissing cousins? We said even though we could not have sex, we would always stay close. Do you remember that time?"

René chuckled. "Of course I remember. You were the older woman who instructed me in the technique, what I could do and what I couldn't do. I could touch you here," he said, running his fingers lightly over her blouse and caressing her nipple. "And here." His hand went under her skirt, touching the bare flesh of her thighs.

"God forgive me," she whispered fervently, pulling away. "Not here, not in the car. Come inside, quickly."

Once inside her flat, Anna locked the door and took René by the hand into her bedroom. *It's your fault, Lind. You and your goddamn orchids!* In their twelve years of marriage, Lind Grenier had spent close to five years in one African country or another. He had succumbed to the mystique of Madagascar because it had more varieties of orchids than any place in the world. Being an expert photographer, their whole flat was decorated with examples of his work.

Leaving off the lights, Anna tried to block out the unpleasant reality that she was bringing a stranger into their bedchamber. Well, not exactly a stranger, she thought as she began to undo the buttons on her blouse. René had his jacket and shirt off in a flash, then stopped her, wanting that pleasure for himself.

The sudden jangle of the bedside telephone startled both of them. "Leave it," René whispered urgently.

"It may be one of my people in Brazzaville," Anna said as she pulled away. "They sometimes call at night if there is an emergency."

René threw up his hands and left the room when Anna switched on her bedside lamp. She picked up the receiver. "Yes?"

"Anna, is that you?"

The man spoke German and sounded far away. She did not recognize the voice. "This is Dr. Grenier. Who is speaking, please?"

"It's Wilhem, Anna. Wilhem Strouss. I am calling from Analabe."

Analabe was a little town just north of the training center on the island. "Oh, Wilhem," she said, feeling confused and somehow disoriented. "Why are you calling so late at night? Where is Lind?"

"Anna, something terrible has happened—"

"Lind!" she cried. "Is it Lind?"

"I … I'm so sorry. I—"

She became aware of René standing in the doorway behind her. "Please, Wilhem, tell me how bad it is."

"He's dead, Anna, struck by lightning up near Tsingy. We found his body just before dark. It has taken us this long to reach Analabe. I'm so sorry."

She backed up to sit on her bed. Was all this really happening? The intensity of the last few hours had mixed up her emotions. Lind, dead? Never. He was indestructible. It was a ridiculous idea. "I don't believe you," she said in a weak voice.

René entered the room and sat beside her. "What is it?"

She turned toward him, taking in his tussled black hair, the sharp angles of his upper body. She at least had the presence of mind to place her hand over the receiver. "Lind is dead," she whispered in quiet desperation.

"Oh no, Anna. Dear Jesus, it can't be true."

Only then did she become aware of the enormous shame, of the great wrong she had almost committed. "You'll have to leave now, René. Please."

"Oh, my darling, how can I walk away?" He placed his hand on her shoulder. "Anna, listen to me — you need someone to be with you, and I am part of your family."

She had not the will to argue as she raised the receiver to hear Wilhem's anxious voice. "Yes, Willi, I'm okay. How did it happen?"

"We have been trying to figure it out. When he didn't come home on Sunday, I was concerned but decided to give him another day. When he didn't show on Monday, Gerhard and I went looking for him. I knew he had gone back to Tsingy to investigate a powerful radio signal he had picked up on his tape recorder a few weeks ago. We followed the tracks of the Land Rover and eventually found his body. He was over half a kilometer from his vehicle, in open terrain in the middle of a lightning storm. It's not like Lind to do such things. He was always very careful, Anna; he knew the dangers of lightning."

Anna broke free from René's grip and stood up. She was suddenly charged with an unaccountable anger. "Then what was he doing out in the goddamn open?" she shouted into the telephone.

"Please, Anna, we don't know the answer. Listen to me, I am taking care of matters here, but we need to discuss certain things. Now is not the best time. Call me at the station in the morning, whenever you feel up to it. He was my friend too, Anna. I can feel a small part of what you feel."

René had gone back into the living room. She ran her fingers through her hair, pulling at the strands. "God, Willi, I'm sorry for shouting at you. Give me a few hours, will you? Are you near the station?"

"It will take at least another hour. Do you have some pills to take? It will make things go easier for you."

She stared at the framed enlargement of a golden orchid over Lind's dresser. This had been one of his treasures, an unlisted species he discovered inside the Tsingy reserve. "I'll call you in the morning."

When René returned he was fully dressed. He pulled back the eiderdown and sat Anna on the corner of her bed. "Here, take this." He handed her two red cylindrical pills and a glass of water. She protested feebly but relented, the professional side of her nature whispering that deep shock would set in at any moment. He eased her listless body back and gently tucked her in. "I'll be outside, in the living room. There is no need to be concerned. Sleep well, my darling, sleep well."

With the door to her bedroom closed, Anna began to pray. She prayed not for Lind, but for his forgiveness.

The body of Francis Lindgren Grenier arrived at Geneva International on a Swissair flight two days later. He was to be buried the following morning. Although it wasn't necessary, Anna had come to meet the aircraft. It was a typical November day, with low clouds and the ever-present threat of rain. She had dressed in black, which ironically put her right in fashion, as blacks and browns were the current rage all across Europe. Since all the Swissair loading bays were full, his plane came to rest about two hundred meters out on the tarmac. She spotted Wilhem among the disembarking passengers, saw his blond hair get caught up in the light breeze, and noticed his anxious glance at the Mercedes hearse and the gray Citroen parked beside it.

René uncovered his ears as another noisy jet moved away from a nearby loading bay. "I wish you hadn't come," he said again.

Anna remained silent. His very presence made her feel uncomfortable. And yet he had been a godsend, taking charge of all the unpleasant arrangements and fending off the multitude of friends and relatives from both sides of the family. But the fact that she had come so close to betraying Lind was a tangible force that lay between them, and prevented her from drawing close. She wondered vaguely if they would ever be close again.

Lind's parents were inside the central lounge. Her mother was with them, plus a few aunts and uncles and Anna's older brother, Kurt. When she telephoned Wilhem back, he'd told her more about Lind's reason for taking that particular trip to Tsingy. The lightning strike had all the classic symptoms, but Lind's body was found about ten kilometers from the southeast corner of the reserve. This did not sit well with Willi. Because of his suspicions, Anna had requested that an autopsy be carried out, which drew heavy resistance from Lind's Catholic family. In the end she relented, agreeing that a superficial examination of the body would suffice. This was to take place at ten-thirty in the morgue at the Cantonal Hospital, under the supervision of Dr. Trembley, the city coroner. Dr. Trembley had agreed that Anna could be in attendance.

After the final busload of passengers had been transported to the airport complex and all cargo removed, the forklift operator gave a hand signal to the hearse driver. It wasn't considered good form to let the passengers know they had been traveling with a corpse. The black Mercedes drove slowly out onto the tarmac, followed by Anna and René in his Citroen. Transferring the aluminum casket from the bowels of the aircraft into the back of the hearse took about five minutes. The guilt Anna had been carrying around since that night was suddenly amplified by the sight of the coffin. She bit down hard on her lower lip, barely able to hold her emotions in check. René reached for her hand, but she would not allow him to touch her.

The drive back into the city, which entailed crossing the Rhône at the Pont de la Coulouvreniere, took eighteen minutes. Dr. Trembley was waiting. A tall, lanky man in his early sixties who wore glasses with half lenses, he had a small white goatee and a slight limp from an automobile accident four years earlier.

Seeing the victim's wife, he said, "My dear, I do wish you would allow us to conduct the examination on our own."

Anna shook her head, slightly resenting his patronizing arm around her shoulders. René took a chair near the door, folding his arms and setting his jaw. He thought the examination morbid and unnecessary and had done his best to talk her out of it. An assistant approached with a pale green gown for Anna and stood by to help fasten her mask.

Upon entering the autopsy room, a small alabaster chamber, she saw her husband's naked body lying on the gurney and steeled herself. Dr. Trembley nodded, pressed a button on the wall, then began his introduction. "Date: nineteenth of November, nineteen eighty-seven. Time: ten thirty-three. Subject: Francis Lindgren Grenier, a Swiss national. Age: forty-six. Weight: eighty-five point seven kilos. Height: one point eight six meters. Present in the examination room: Dr. Trembley, Dr. Lyon, and Dr. Grenier, wife of the deceased. The death certificate was signed by Dr. Maurice Terroux, a physician resident at the Befelatanana Hospital in the city of Antananarivo on the island of Madagascar. Time of death was approximated between two hundred hours and eight hundred hours on the fifteenth day of November, nineteen eighty-seven. The cause of death has been listed as massive arterial disruption brought on by a direct lightning strike. It is noted that this examination is of a superficial nature only and is being carried out at Dr. Grenier's request. Shall we begin?"

Dr. Lyon, a somber, horsey-faced man in his late forties, gave a quick nod. Anna was standing to the right of the gurney, across from Dr. Trembley. Her eyes were transfixed upon Lind's face. Except for his deathly gray pallor and the odor of decay that seeped through her mask, he appeared to be resting. "Dr. Grenier?"

"Oh yes, of course. Please proceed."

"Very well, we will begin at the cranium, where a ten centimeter diameter patch of hair in the center of the crown is missing. The flesh at this point is darkened and appears melted. The surrounding hair has been singed, as have the eyebrows and the eyelashes. The tips of both ears have a slight darkening ..."

Anna soon lost track of the droning voice. She moved a little closer, telling herself that she had seen many cadavers and this one was no different from the others. She tried to set aside the agony in her heart and the cries of her conscience to scan her husband's body in search of some clue that would explain why he had been caught out in the open during a lightning storm.

The west central part of the island was notorious for its killer lightning, which Lind had often mentioned. He had even come across a few victims himself. So why would he have been so stupid, she wondered. And this thing about a radio transmitter he was supposed to be investigating—what bearing did that have on his death? Willi had explained about the tape recorder and the apparent feedback. But the natives had found the Land Rover before the search party and completely stripped it, so his tape recorder was missing. The local police were searching nearby villages to see what they could recover.

The body was turned over, and Dr. Trembley continued while Anna slowly circled the bed. When the coroner had completed his observations, he asked if Dr. Lyon wished to state anything into the official record.

Lyon cleared his throat. "Dr. Grenier should perhaps be informed that I was invited here today because of my experience with similar cases during my sojourn in South Africa. I must say, this is the first example I have encountered where lightning has apparently entered the skull and exited both feet, yet left no outside path."

"Could you explain, please?" Anna asked.

"If the victim is wet, as is usually the case in a thunderstorm, the charge will run down the outside of the body, always leaving a distinctive path of burn marks. As you can see, aside from a certain amount of singed body hair, the only evidence of the strike is on the head, the feet, and the fingers. Which is the second inconsistency that should be noted. Unless the victim were to somehow have his fingertips touching the ground, they should not be showing burn marks. The conclusion in this case is that his fingers were grounded. Of course it is possible to strike such a pose, much like a runner at the starting line. Though it seems rather odd. A third inconsistency is the matting of hair around the wrists and ankles. If you look closely, you will notice that where the hair is matted, it is not singed. Was your husband in the habit of wearing cloth or leather bands on his wrists and ankles?"

Anna shook her head. "I have never seen him wear anything other than a watch. He did own a waterproof outfit with elastic around the wrists and ankles. I suppose he could have been wearing that."

Lyon nodded solemnly. "That could explain the matted hair. Do you know what he was wearing at the time of … when he was …"

"I'm sorry, I don't know. I will make inquiries."

"Also, if the subject were in the upright position at the time of the strike, as the entry point seems to suggest, one should see some indication of a fall. In this case there appears to be no exterior bruising or abrasions."

Dr. Trembley waited a moment and when he saw that Dr. Lyon had completed his observations, he looked at Anna. "Dr. Grenier?"

"I have nothing to add, except my most sincere thanks. Perhaps if you have a few moments, Dr. Lyon?"

Her cousin was on his feet when Anna came out, followed by Dr. Lyon. René appeared anxious. "How did it go?"

Anna turned as the hallway door opened, and Wilhem came in. She let out a sigh and went to meet him, knowing full well that she would no longer be able to keep it all together. Looking up at the Swiss forester, she said, "Willi, Willi," and the tears began to flow.

He swept her into his arms and held her tight. "Oh God, Anna, what can I say?"

They stood that way for a few minutes, while René questioned Dr. Lyon on the outcome of the examination. When Anna felt she had sufficiently recovered her poise, she introduced Wilhem to René and Dr. Lyon.

"What was Lind wearing when you found him?"

Willi was a big man, six centimeters taller than Lind, and towered over everyone else. As is often the case with big men, his voice was soft. He looked embarrassed as he answered Anna's question. "The Malagasy found him before we did. I'm afraid they didn't leave him with anything."

"Do you know what he was wearing when he left the center?"

"I didn't see him leave, but Lind nearly always wore some sort of checkered cotton shirt with a pair of khaki trousers. I should imagine that's what he had on. He usually carried a heavy wool jacket and a poncho for the rain. Why are you asking about his clothing?"

Dr. Lyon suggested they retire to a nearby office for privacy. A police officer had just entered the hallway with a distraught young woman who was sobbing convulsively. Once inside the office, Anna reviewed the observations made by Dr. Lyon.

In a sharper tone than necessary, René said. "Surely, no matter how many inconsistencies there are, the bottom line is the same: Lind was struck by lightning. Is this not so, Dr. Lyon?"

"Yes, yes, of course. I did not intend to imply otherwise. There are unusual aspects, I admit, but your husband most certainly died from at least one direct hit."

"Willi," said Anna with a slight tremor in her voice. "Can you guess why the … the … his body was hardly sunburned and untouched by animals?" She could not bring herself to use the correct term to describe Lind's condition.

It was obvious that Willi was exhausted. He sighed and leaned back against a wall. There was only one chair in the room and Anna was gripping the back of it. "I noticed that myself. Except for the missing clothing, it was as if he had lain down only minutes earlier. But the death certificate was supposed to be in with the body …?"

"Yes, it was," Anna confirmed. "But you said when we spoke on the telephone that you had found him a few hours earlier, on Monday evening. The certificate gives the time of death as early Sunday morning. Could his body have lain out there for two whole days and remained untouched? There are vultures in Madagascar—I've seen them. Why did they refuse to feed upon my husband's body?"

Anna's voice had cracked with her last question, and René walked over and took her by both shoulders. "What are you looking for? You just heard Dr. Lyon state that Lind had been struck by lightning." She struggled to get away, but he held on. "All else is beside the point. Your husband is dead, Anna, and there is nothing you can do to bring him back. It's time you faced up to it!"

Wilhem came off the wall, his anger flashing. He gripped one of the Frenchman's hands and squeezed. The color went out of

René's face. Wilhem drew him close. "You are never to do that again."

At that moment Anna watched a cloud draw over her cousin's face and saw something there she had not seen before. He quickly masked his pain and smiled a tired smile. "Please forgive me. I hadn't realized until this moment how much all this has affected me."

He withdrew, and Anna immediately felt sorry for him. "Willi can take me over to the church. Why don't you go and spend some time with your mother, then get some rest. Tomorrow I will need all the support you can give me."

He massaged his hand, nodding slowly. "I do have to return to Paris directly after the funeral. You're right, of course. I'll bring mother along to the service this evening." He kissed Anna on both cheeks, nodded formally to the men and left the room.

Wilhem turned the chair around for Anna to sit, then took his former spot against the wall. "Can't say I like your cousin a whole lot. What does he do for a living?"

"He is with the Bureau of Statistics in Paris. But believe me, René has been a blessing ever since your ...." She paused, aware of how close she had come to revealing her secret. "Since he heard of Lind's death."

Dr. Lyon glanced at the clock on the wall. "Was there something in particular you wished to ask me, Dr. Grenier?"

Anna looked out the window. A sprinkle of rain dripping from the edge of the balcony just above was caught up in a spiral of wind. She knew René was right. What did it matter now of the circumstances surrounding her husband's death? Lind had been struck by lightning. End of story.

She stood up. "No, and I have taken quite enough of your time." She held out her hand. "You must realize how very grateful I am."

Lyon's morose expression changed to a smile. "My dear lady, I was there, nothing more. I suppose now that you have accepted the will of Allah, as it were, the questions that have been raised should be buried forever. And yet ...."

"Yes, I know. But you see, it really doesn't matter, does it?"

"Perhaps not, but would you mind terribly if I asked Herr Strouss a question?"

"If you wish."

Looking up at the Swiss forester, he said, "I have been considering my comments in the examination room concerning the subject's posture when he was struck and the matter of the charge exiting his fingers. I suppose the same effect could be achieved if he were leaning forward against a large boulder. What was the terrain like?"

Willi rubbed his jaw. Anna noticed he had not shaved that morning. "It's a sort of desert east of the reserve, with scattered thorn trees and bunchgrass. The ground is flat and rocky, but with no rocks larger than thirty centimeters close to where we found the body."

Despite her previous resolve, she also had to ask Wilhem a question. "Have you figured out yet why he was found so far away from his Land Rover?"

The big Swiss moved close to Anna, touching her gently on the shoulder. "Lind may have been a forester by profession, but we both know that he was captivated by the natural world. I believe he spotted something — an animal or a bird, perhaps even a butterfly — and became so engrossed that he was quite unaware of the storm moving in."

"Yes," Anna nodded quickly, again choking back her emotions. "His true love was … nature."

She had chosen the most expensive cemetery in the city, near the Rue des Rois, the street of kings. Here many of Geneva's great men of the past, teachers and statesmen and philosophers alike, had been laid to rest. Lind was none of those, but even if they didn't see eye to eye on everything, she felt that her husband had lived as good a life as anyone there.

Death had become familiar to her by now and no longer made her afraid. Each of us has our time on stage, she mused while following the procession the short distance to his grave site, to give our performance, and without the benefit of rehearsals. We enter life cold and unknowing, and we leave it cold and perhaps a little wiser, but to what end? What had Lind's life been all about?

What is my life all about?

Anna was a Calvinist, as were so many of Geneva's citizens. She had a Calvinist's strong distrust of the simple answers provided by the Catholic Church. Despite that, she had found comfort in the words spoken by Monsignor Vanier in the great basilica of Notre Dame. He had a warm sense of compassion that Anna had not found in her own ministers. They tended to be cold and unyielding men, as Calvin himself had been.

When the procession came to an end, Anna held tight to her brother's arm as he led her to the front of the circle of mourners beginning to form around the open grave. At least half of the two hundred or so who had been at the church service had joined in the funeral procession in order to pay their last respects to her husband. The sky was threatening rain as they stood in silence while the coffin was being lowered onto a metal ramp. She had ordered a good coffin but nothing elaborate, because Lind had been a simple man and would not have wanted anything elaborate. His parents stood across from her, to one side of Monsignor Vanier and his two altar boys, and Anna felt their eyes upon her. They had wanted to bury Lind in an obscure Catholic cemetery, as if it meant anything to God where someone was buried. Anna had refused. She had relented on the autopsy, but when it came to Lind's final resting place, there was to be no compromise.

She continued to scan the crowd, looking for René. He had not shown up at his mother's apartment yesterday. When Anna telephoned his hotel in the morning, she was told that he had checked out early. His absence from the funeral led to mixed emotions; she desperately wanted him to be near her, but deep down knew that his presence would cause her to suffer even more. Perhaps René was aware of her feelings and had decided it was best for both of them if he didn't attend.

Monsignor Vanier cleared his throat and began the ceremony, but Anna did not hear his words because she was lost in her own world of sorrow and misgiving. After a few moments, Kurt placed a bundle of flowers in her hand — roses and carnations. Wrong, Anna cried inwardly, they should be orchids ... goddamn orchids! Orchids had lured him to Madagascar, and orchids had probably caused his death.

I'm sorry, my darling, I didn't mean it. But what am I going to do without you? What about our plans? What about the children? A boy and a girl, you said. Oh, Lind, how could you have let yourself be killed so … so needlessly? You knew about the lightning. Why did you have to be out there? Why? Why? Why?

By now, the people had gathered around her. Tears flowed freely from the Swiss of French descent. Those of German descent were a bit more reserved. Wilhem's eyes were dry but red. His wife, Meg, was an American, highly emotional at the best of times; Anna dreaded having to talk to her. She left the center of the crowd to seek out Aunt Giselle, René's mother.

Giselle was a pleasant, dumpy little woman whom Anna loved a great deal. "Have you heard from René?" she asked her aunt.

"Oh, Anna, you were always the strongest one. Would God that I could be like you." She dabbed her embroidered handkerchief at the corners of her eyes. "I'm certain he had to leave suddenly to return to Paris. It's part of his job, you know."

Anna must have looked puzzled, so Giselle added in a whispered voice, "Interpol; it's what he does, you know."

"But he told me that he worked at the Bureau of Statistics."

The woman nodded knowingly. "That is what he is supposed to say. René works undercover. It's very dangerous work, so he has to be careful."

"Oh," Anna replied. Suddenly it became clear, the intense cross-examination he had put her through the day after. She had thought at the time that he was simply trying to get her mind off Lind's death and her own indiscretion. Now that she knew he was a policeman, his questions made perfect sense.

She turned to Kurt. "Do you think we can leave now?" Her older brother was a veterinarian, a tall, gangly man with a heart of gold. Their youngest brother, Helge, was pursuing postgraduate studies at the University of Pittsburgh. His telegram arrived yesterday.

"Just a few more minutes, Annie. Shouldn't you go over and have a word with the Greniers?"

"Damn! Do I have to?" Lind's father was an angel, but his mother was something else.

"No, honey, you don't have to do it now. They'll be at the reception."

She made a face. "Wonderful, then let's get going." The thought of enduring all that sympathy at once was almost too much. This is where she would have loved to have René at her side. So far she had held up remarkably well, but once she took on a few drinks, what then?

The reception was held in the banquet room of the Rousseau, a private club of which Lind had been a member. It was a teary affair and went on until late afternoon. Kurt and his wife, Suzette, had agreed to drive Anna home. Her mother had insisted on spending a few days, but Anna would have no part of it under the circumstances. She needed to be alone.

Simply out of self-defense, to help get through the day, she had downed five cognacs. By the time Suzette helped her to the car, Anna was working hard to maintain her composure. When Kurt finally pulled his Renault up in front of her apartment, she stepped out, closed the door, and experienced a great sense of relief. She walked carefully up the front stairs, searched around for her key, let herself into the landing, then walked over to the lift where she punched the fourth-floor button. By now her mind was caught up in a myriad of thoughts. She was simultaneously feeling grateful it was behind her, wondering why René had left without saying good-bye, and picturing Lind as he lay upon the examination table. 'The Widow Grenier' was how some fool at the reception had introduced her. Which was now her official role in life, she supposed — a widow, like her mother.

When she directed her key into the lock, the door eased open. Anna caught her breath and felt her heart jump. Had someone broken into her flat? Was that someone still there? She ran down the hallway to the Salanders, but there was no answer to her knock. She huddled against the wall, alone and frightened. This was a fine introduction to widowhood, she thought. Within minutes her emotions reversed, and she felt outraged that some son of a bitch would invade her privacy. She marched back down the hall and pushed open the door. Holding her bag in front of her, Anna tried to recall the lines from an American movie she had just seen.

"I have a gun, you asshole! Come out now, or kiss it good-bye!"

Kiss what good-bye, she wondered, but thought she had said it correctly. She listened carefully, trying to pick up any little noises. What a time to have slurped down five cognacs. She stood completely still for a few minutes, then her eyes began to focus on the drawers that had been dumped on the carpet. Several pictures were missing from the walls. She took a few steps forward, fully expecting at any second for some big ape to leap out at her. She made it across the living room, paused, then angled her head to peer around the corner into her bedroom, where she found another mess, with articles of clothing strewn everywhere. She noticed that the large framed photo of Lind's golden orchid had been removed. She backed off, turning to tiptoe into the kitchen. Here the drawers were not dumped but merely pulled out.

The bathroom was last, but Anna was boiling mad and walked into it without hesitation. It was empty. She wondered if she should check the closets, but fully realized by now that she was alone. She threw her handbag down on the floor in disgust and balled her fists. "You bastards! Bastards, bastards, bastards!"

The telephone rang, and she jumped two feet. She pressed a hand to her heart, steadying it as best she could. It rang and rang, until she could stand it no longer.

"Yes?"

"Anna, is that you?"

She lowered the receiver. It was Meg, Willi's emotional wife. Except for a few words here and there, Anna had managed to avoid her all day. She just couldn't handle that now.

"Yes, Meg, it's me. I just arrived and my flat has been burglarized. I must call the police. I'll have to get back to you tomorrow."

"It's Willi. He had an accident." Her voice was soft, controlled. Even in her present state, Anna knew very well that Meg never spoke like this.

She took a deep breath, then asked, "How bad is it?"

First there was silence, but she knew the answer even before the words were spoken. "He's dead, Anna, he's dead. It was an accident, and he's dead. He's dead, Anna …" and on and on and on.

She slid down the wall. One of her legs was twisted under her, but she was not aware of it. Seconds later, she was not aware of anything.

The World Health Organization was comprised of five major operational branches, with the director general in overall command. Under him were five assistant director generals who oversee their respective branches. Dr. Anna Grenier worked in the third branch, which had four divisions. Hers was the Family Health Division, but because she also was in charge of the Status of Women, a newly-formed department, she answered directly to the assistant director general. Dr. Grenier's primary task was to see to the education of women in third-world countries, which necessitated a considerable amount of travel. While in Africa she usually worked out of the WHO HQ in Brazzaville, capital city of the Congo.

The assistant director provided her with an annual budget and allowed her complete autonomy. Anna came and went as she pleased. After each trip she prepared a report, and at the end of the year her reports were edited and published by WHO. The editing process was always a tug-of-war between Anna's determination to see the truth printed, and the ADG's insistence that WHO guidelines for non-interference in politics and local traditions be firmly adhered to. Her last excursion had been to the Sudan, where women were still considered chattel and she was unwelcome in those villages. She had since formulated a different approach — reaching out to the women through their husbands — and was now anxious to return.

But first she would stop off in Madagascar.

Five days had passed since Lind's funeral. After the police left her apartment that evening, Anna felt honor bound to go and comfort Willi's wife. As she made her way across town, something occurred to her. The next morning she placed a call to the coroner, Dr. Trembley, and asked where she could contact

Dr. Lyon. She was given three numbers in Bern and tried all three. The third was his home, where she caught up to his wife. Theresa Lyon was worried sick, because her husband had been due home the previous evening on the train from Geneva. He was supposed to have been in surgery that morning and had not even called the hospital.

Four people had gathered in that little office beside the morgue: René, Dr. Lyon, Wilhem, and herself. The first two had vanished. René's mother had only the phone number of his Paris apartment, which Anna tried repeatedly. Then she called the personnel department of the Bureau of Statistics and traced the five Simards who worked there. It soon became obvious that René was not one of them. Interpol came next, but even with Anna's claim that it was an emergency, they firmly denied he had ever worked for them. Wilhem was dead. A transport truck had run a red light just one block from his flat. He had been returning from taking home the baby-sitter following the funeral reception. The air brakes on the truck had failed — just another one of those insane coincidences that happen without rhyme or reason. As for Anna, her flat had been broken into, and among the missing items were stacks of ordinary photos and letters from Lind, plus several large framed photographs of flowers.

She decided to voice her suspicions to Inspector Lemieux, an old family friend with the city police in Zurich. Lemieux opened a file at once, but agreed with Anna that in view of everything else that has been taking place, she had every right to be suspicious of her husband's death on the island of Madagascar.

CHAPTER FOUR

Dirty little pieces of snow were messing up the windows in the police commissioner's reception room. By unspoken mutual agreement, Captain Ulansky and Lieutenant Bannerman had chosen to sit on opposite sides. Ulansky had an *Esquire* fixed in front of his face, but hadn't turned a page in five minutes. He just glared over the top at Bannerman. Charlie ignored the daggers and concentrated on the snow. He hated snow. There were those rare moments, on a still winter's night, when the stuff was falling and the clamor of the metropolis had faded to a murmur. At such times he felt as if he were looking at a whole new world. But usually he just hated it.

By going over his commander's head directly to the chief of detectives, Charlie had committed a no-no. The chief was impressed, and so was the PC, apparently. Ulansky was furious. He'd told Charlie in concise New York policeman's terms what he thought of all the high-tech bullshit Gary Carswell was feeding him: "You have the nerve to come in and tell me, after ignoring my direct orders to get your goddamn nose out of the OD files, that you think some mystery flower is responsible for most of these deaths? You expect me to buy that? This time you've gone too far ...." and so on. Which left Charlie with no choice.

But whether the PC had called him in for questioning or to ream his ass for going over the head of a superior officer, he didn't know. The police commissioner was an ex-military type who went by the book. What Charlie had done was not by the book. It gave him some consolation to see that Ulansky too was nervous.

When the CD came in, the receptionist rose from her seat and broke out her very best smile. She had good reason to do this, Charlie knew, because the commissioner was due to retire in about fifteen months, and Chief of Detectives Neil Greenaway was a shoo-in. In other words, this gal's next boss.

Greenaway nodded to the two detectives and went directly in. Another twenty minutes went by before the door opened again. "Gentlemen," said the CD, his face impassive. Charlie pulled in his gut as best he could and marched in behind Ulansky.

Bannerman had been inside the inner sanctum a number of times during his thirty-one years on the force. Just once had he caught hell, when he'd had to blow the whistle on a superior and chose to reveal his findings to the PC rather than Internal Affairs. But that was three commissioners ago.

The PC was staring out the window, shaking his head. "It's gonna stay this time, guaranteed." He turned and looked directly at Charlie. "You hear how much they got in DC last night?"

"Just over seven inches."

"Umm," Hennessey responded, rolling his lips around for a few seconds. "Seven freaking inches and it's only the twenty-third of November. This winter's gonna be a real bitch—mark my words. Sit down, you guys, take it easy. Nobody's here to catch shit; although Ulansky, a man with your experience should know better than to try and stop Bannerman once he's got his nose to the ground."

Ulansky deepened a few shades. "Sir, I—"

"Not looking for explanations, or excuses. When Lieutenant Bannerman says something's not kosher, even the cops in Jersey listen up. And you, his commanding officer, forcing him to go to the CD. I don't like it when the chain of command is broken. It reflects badly on me. And there better not be a reason for it to happen again."

The captain nodded, but remained silent. Charlie could hear his teeth grinding.

Hennessey took his seat, glancing over at Chief Greenaway, who had chosen to lean against a walnut table with a vase of red and white carnations stuck in the middle. Ulansky and Bannerman sat side by side across from the PC.

"My brother-in-law teaches at Columbia." He grinned at Bannerman's expression. "He knows this Carswell, claims he's brilliant. His new program is the result of six years of research. Did he tell you those Cray Y-MPs are tapped into every library computer in the country?"

"He didn't bother to mention that," Charlie replied.

Hennessey leaned back, resting his right hand on top of the single file folder on his desk. He stared at Ulansky. "What do you know about Interpol, Captain?"

Ulansky stared at the commissioner. "Interpol? I … ah … it's an organization used by different countries to coordinate search techniques, help track down international criminals."

The PC rolled his lips in and out, waiting to hear more. Finally, he said, "That's it?"

"Comes under the UN, I believe." Ulansky squirmed around a bit, then added, "They got an office down in DC."

"Know anything about their history?"

"Ah … not an awful lot."

"Ever meet or work with any of their people?"

The big man looked puzzled, wondering why the PC was grilling him on effing Interpol. "Not that I can remember."

"You, Charlie?"

"No, sir."

The PC leaned across his desk. "But I bet you know their history."

"Some," Bannerman agreed.

The commissioner pushed his chair back and walked over to the window. His size and height were about average, but he had a curiously small head, which he jerked to the right every few seconds. Possibly an old war wound giving him trouble, Charlie had thought the first time he noticed it. After a moment he turned around. "Tell us what you know about them."

Bannerman glanced at Ulansky, registering his own bewilderment. He reached deep into his memory banks. "I suppose it really began in 1914 when Prince Albert of Monaco convened the First International Congress of Criminal Police, although the organization itself didn't get off the ground until 1923, in Vienna, I believe, when the International Criminal Police Commission was formed. Because its original charter was a mess, the League of Nations refused to take it under its wing, so it ended up as a private organization, which it still is. Vienna was their first head-quarters, the Austrian chief of police their first leader. Up till 1935 it was more of an annual social gathering than anything else. But in 1935, when the Nazis took over, they—"

"Nazis?" The word escaped Ulansky's lips before he could stop it.

Bannerman cracked a tiny grin, warming to his subject. "The Nazis ran Interpol, directly that is, until 1972, when SS Untersturmführer Paul Dickopf retired. From 1938 to 1945 it was an organ of the Gestapo. Colonel Otto Steinhausel was the president from 1938 to 1940; Reinhard Heydrich, 1940 to 1942, and Ernst Kaltenbrunner, 1942 to 1945. Depending on which book you read, there are those who claim Interpol is still full of Nazis. It wasn't so long ago that the Jewish Congress accused them of looking after the security of Nazi war criminals."

He paused, squinting up at the commissioner. "This what you're looking for?"

The PC smiled. "How about some modern history—in particular, drugs."

Bannerman scratched his head. "That's where it gets cloudy, because Interpol does their own PR. According to them, they're pulling in traffickers every day."

"Which we know is bullshit," added the commissioner.

"Mostly bullshit, yet they do manage to pass on a piece of information here and there, to the French, or the Germans, or the FBI, which leads to a fair number of arrests. The refrain I keep hearing is they're in the business themselves and do what they can to pull the rug out from under the competition. It's a fact they had a thing going with the Mafia in the sixties and early seventies. Their guys were caught in the act. The agency claimed they had gone dirty, but you know how it goes. The French are running it, and we all know where they stand when there's a few francs to be made. The Feds withdrew financial support about fifteen years ago because the stink was getting too high. Nowadays most states refuse to have anything to do with them. They still maintain a branch in DC, but I don't know much about it. I can probably recall the specifics on a few heroin cases if you want me to go on."

Ulansky didn't like being upstaged by his subordinate. "Where did you pick up all this crap?"

Before Bannerman could reply, Hennessey snapped, "He reads, Captain. It's an activity you might want to look into."

Ulansky had been pissed off at Bannerman when they came in. Now he was boiling mad. The commissioner held up his hand, indicating peace. "You did well, Charlie. That's what I was looking for, a lead-in to their shady dealings on the drug scene. For the last five or six years they've been running an operation down in La Paz, 'watchers', they're called, agents who monitor the cocaine traffic. I've been told that some of those big ones the FBI pull off in Miami are a direct result of tips received from the Interpol office in Bolivia. Yeah, and from time to time a few of their guys get lead for breakfast, so it's not like they're not doing their job. The question is: What exactly is their job?"

Hennessey resumed his seat and pulled a second file out of his top desk drawer. He placed a pair of reading glasses on his nose and looked over the top at Bannerman. "When Chief Greenaway called Friday about this orchid thing in Madagascar, I had just finished reading a thirty-page FBI memo on recent Interpol activities in the United States, South America, Africa, and Europe. Now, I don't suppose it's a big secret that the FBI has been keeping tabs on these Frenchies. Just because they work with them doesn't mean they trust them. Too many of their guys over in Europe were caught in bed with the Italians, like you said, and there's little doubt that the Mafia still control the main heroin supply lines in Europe. Stateside, too. But this report highlights an interesting question: How much impact is the coke traffic having on the skag trade?"

Greenaway was a sharp dresser, and Charlie wondered if he was standing to keep the wrinkles out of his pants. "Heroin is down, way down," said the CD. "Coke, especially crack, is climbing daily. We're swamped with the shit. Pretty soon the shitface Colombians will own us like they own Miami."

The commissioner glanced up at Greenaway. "You liked it better when the Mafia controlled the marketplace?"

"The Mafia got some rules. For one, they don't kill cops — without good reason, that is. These other assholes got no rules; they're just insane animals who'd blow away a dozen cops just to smell the gunpowder."

Hennessey nodded, swinging his gaze back to Bannerman. "You agree?"

Charlie dug a little wax out of his right ear. "It's just business with the Mafia. They try to run it with a minimum of trouble. Most of the lower echelon Colombians are snow bunnies themselves. They don't believe in rules."

The commissioner grunted and lowered his head to read for a few minutes. "This report alleges that cocaine shipments destined for the European market may be showing up here in New York. By what means they're not certain, but the FBI figures the longer time to market is more than offset by the diminished risk factor, which fits. Any cocaine busts we've made in the past involve either stateside transportation or ships that work the coast. We don't expect cocaine to be shipped from Europe, so we don't look for it. Simple."

"But we're still picking off skag shipments," Ulansky reminded him.

"Few and far between these days," the CD commented. "Like I said, skag is losing out to the big C."

"The report goes on to say that about one year ago Interpol Bolivia went silent on the stuff going to Europe, which the FBI interprets to mean the La Paz operation has gone dirty — again. Right after that the DEA was turfed out, in July, as you probably heard, which leaves us with no ears in Bolivia at the moment."

Hennessey paused for a moment, giving his head a few jerks before going on. "I sent a copy of this to Narcotics, and would have filed it except for the chief's mention of Madagascar. Now maybe, just maybe, we're on to something here. The Feds obviously had a peek at the CIA's monitoring sheets, where they keep a record of the movements of just about every ship in the world. The only ship that matches the kind of profile they're looking for is an old tramp steamer called the *Lucinda V.* Panamanian registry. Half of its regular route is Buenos Aires to Venice, with ports of call at," he flipped over a page, "Toamasina, Djibouti, Alexandria, and Piraievs. That's somewhere in Greece."

He looked over the top of his glasses. "Toamasina, as everyone knows I'm sure, is the main port in Madagascar. So what have we got? A ship that *may* be carrying cocaine, which just happens to make its first stop out of Buenos Aires right where Carswell *thinks* there's some mystery flower that *could* be the source of some drug being used to kill off our junkies. No one else's junkies, it seems, just ours. How about it, gentlemen, am I reaching too far?"

"Anyone checked out the ship?" Bannerman asked.

"Venice Port Authority went through it in June. Found nothing."

"I wouldn't attach a whole lot of credibility to that," added the CD. "Plus, the ship could be a decoy. How can the Feds be so sure the stuff isn't being moved by air?"

The commissioner shrugged. "It's just a memo. They don't go into details. Let's hear Lieutenant Bannerman's opinion."

Charlie was way ahead of him. "It could provide the answer to one key question—how a deadly substance from Madagascar found its way into the recent shit we've been pulling in. If the cocaine is cut down right there on the island and then continues its journey to Europe and on to the States … well, it might also explain why there's so much of it around. Narcotics is looking in the right places, but for the wrong stuff. It's thin, real thin, Commissioner, but I like it."

The PC got up and went to the window. The snow had turned wet and heavy and all but obliterated the view from his fourteenth-floor office. With his back to them he asked, "Chief?"

"I'm with the lieutenant. Thin as fly shit, but possible."

"Captain?"

"No argument from me. But I'm having a big problem buying the Interpol connection. From South America to Africa to Europe and then to New York. An operation like that takes heavy planning. It's no midnight run on a DC-3. And the whole Interpol system can't be rotten, can it?"

"Charlie?" the PC prompted.

Bannerman rolled his head around a few times before replying. "I don't have enough to go on. Have you considered feeding all this back to the FBI?"

The commissioner turned around, his face tense. He didn't bother to answer Charlie's question. "I'm being leaned on and I don't like it. You saw Friday's *Times* — an eleven-year-old kid from a wealthy family, dead from an overdose. The vultures got their claws in it now. This morning the mayor ordered me to set up a special task force. Hell of a thing, isn't it? One white kid gets this kind of reaction from the press.

"Chief, I want you to take personal charge of this one. Grab who you want from Narcotics and Homicide. Set up your HQ in the Twenty-First. Captain Ulansky will be your Two IC. Pull every drug-related death over the last six months and look for some common ground. Find out how many were caused by heart failure. Get some history on this thing. See if you can run down the source, or sources. Check with Jersey and the big ones — Detroit, Miami, LA — see if they got a similar problem. Do whatever has to be done, but get me some meat I can throw to the vultures. I'm going to fire out a press release at two, but Bannerman's research and the Madagascar connection stay in this room. Any questions?"

"If I'm going to set up operations in the Twenty-First, I presume Charlie goes with the turf?"

The commissioner shook his head. "Lieutenant Bannerman is on special assignment, as of right now. If there are no more questions, I'll let you get on with it. I'll expect a verbal every morning at zero nine hundred, a written every three days."

Bannerman stood as the others left the room, uncertain whether he should be staying or going. He stayed. When the PC came back in, he told him to take a seat.

"You met Dr. Bloom yet?"

"He was due in last night. Haven't talked to Carswell this morning to see if he made it."

"Know anything about him?"

"Part-time professor, part-time research scientist. On loan to the Smithsonian from Stanford. World's leading expert on exotic orchids, according to Carswell."

The commissioner eased himself onto a corner of his desk. "I had him checked out. Interesting character. Clean, of course." He opened the folder on his desk, took out two pages and pushed them toward Charlie. "Here, take a few minutes and read this. Coffee black?"

"Yeah," Charlie muttered as the PC was going through the door. Clipped to the first page was a photograph of a young man in uniform. After committing it to memory, he started to scan the file. It soon became clear that Samuel Ignatius Bloom was not your average scientist. Grandfather arrived in 1894, Blumenauer by name, but changed it to Blum when the First World War broke out. His father changed it again when the next war came along. Bloom was born in Stillwater, Oklahoma, in 1942. Mother died in childbirth. Married to Virginia Dewhurst in 1963, just before heading off to Vietnam. Flew Intruders in Nam, shot down twice and taken prisoner by the Viet Cong. Took some heavy torture in the POW camps, but each time managed to escape and came back with a patrol to rescue some of his buddies. Never made it beyond lieutenant because he didn't take too well to orders. Charlie noted that the guy had been awarded four medals for valor, and after the war was cited for the Congressional Medal of Honor when the truth behind his unauthorized rescue missions was finally released. Wrote to the president and told him he would accept it only after all the POWs were home.

Upon his return, Bloom jumped into the academic life with a vengeance, earning four degrees, including doctorates in chemistry and biology, in seven years. His wife pulled out in 1970, and a divorce followed two years later. No children. Has a brother one year older who took over the family business in Tulsa. The second page contained a list of professional associations and a rundown on the father, Werner Bloom, whose name Charlie remembered as being heavy into the Oklahoma oil scene in the fifties. Died in 1985 and left an estate worth eleven million to his two sons.

After completing the second page, Charlie began to study the photo in earnest. The face seemed so familiar that he was annoyed he couldn't stick a name on it. The commissioner's secretary set down a cup and saucer on the nearest desk corner. In

Kelly green, with the Hennessey crest embossed in gold. Charlie was unable to slip his finger through the miniature handle.

The commissioner returned and seemed to read Charlie's mind. "Looks familiar, doesn't he?"

"Sure does, but I can't seem to—"

"Randolph Scott. You're looking at a young Randolph Scott. Damn near drove me up the wall until it clicked. Quite the boy, isn't he?"

Charlie nodded. "Mind if I ask why you ran a sheet on him?"

The PC watched Bannerman's attempt to wrap his hand around the delicate cup.

"Nancy," he said into his intercom, "for Christ's sake bring Lieutenant Bannerman a mug of coffee." Looking up, he said, "She must think you're here socializing. Bloom's been to Madagascar twice. Speaks French and German. I've been told the language down there is some kind of local thing, but French is common enough. You speak French?"

Charlie stuck a finger into the middle of his thick clump of curly black hair. "Not much call for it here in New York. Commissioner, are you heading where I think you're heading?"

"I made a few calls. The *Lucinda V* pulled out of Buenos Aires last week. It's due into Toamasina late Thursday evening. Charlie, I need to know what the hell is going on. We both know goddamn well the dealers aren't doing this—that'd be like using money for asswipe. I figure someone's fighting a war on my turf and using the junkies for cannon fodder. But before we can stop them, we gotta find out just who these shitheads are."

Charlie began to feel a bit uneasy. He'd been to Florida when he was twenty-five. Drove down, didn't like it. "Sending me isn't a good idea. Why don't you give it to the FBI?"

"Why do you keep asking me that? The FBI is full of candy-ass bureaucrats. They'll bring in the freaking CIA because it's out of country and we'll have two dozen Dick Tracys watching our every move. This is my city and my problem. Look, I'm not ordering you. But along with being the best detective this city's got, you just happen to be completely honest, so I know you're not going to piss away the expense money. Bloom is keen as—"

"You talked to him?"

The commissioner leaned back in his chair. The top joint of his right index finger was crooked into the handle of one of his little teacups. "He arrived at Carswell's shop at six. We chatted for about half an hour just before the CD arrived. He'll go. The way I got it figured is, you're the professional cop. You're gonna see things he'd never see. Bloom's the scientist, who's gonna spot stuff you'd never recognize. His line of work might be flowers, but his Nam background proves he's no wimp. And his cover is perfect. You willing to give it a shot?"

Bannerman let go a long sigh. He knew well enough that the PC might be asking, but in reality he was ordering. "Yeah, I guess so."

"Good. You got a passport?"

"Afraid not."

"Christ! Okay, go on over and meet Bloom, but on the way stop by a post office and pick up a form. Drop in to some Fotomat and get a picture taken. Fill out the form and send it and five photos back here via a precinct courier ASAP. Tell Bloom I'll need his. Nancy's got you booked to fly out of here tomorrow night and I need both passports to get your entry visas. You should get a malaria shot, Bloom too if he hasn't had one in the last year or so. Take your shield with you, but leave your weapon behind. I'll see what I can arrange with the embassy, assuming we have one down there. I'm pulling twenty-five grand out of a special fund — five in bills, the rest in travelers checks. One more thing — this little fishing expedition stays between us and Carswell and Bloom, for now anyway."

The commissioner frowned briefly as Charlie stood up. He had deleted a crucial part of Bloom's background and hoped to God he had made the right decision. He rose from his desk. "Bannerman and Bloom. Got a nice ring to it."

Charlie grunted. "Sounds like a couple of shysters to me."

Outside, the streets had turned to mush. Noon traffic was in a snarl. Pedestrians were getting splashed, and their curses filtered through his Chevy windows. He did the passport and snapshot bit, then flagged down a patrol car and sent them back down-town with a sealed envelope for the commissioner's personal attention. He cut right onto Central Park West, heading for West 116th, which would take him through the potholes of Harlem and onto Morningside Campus. The park was on his right. Charlie saw the wet snow dripping off the oaks and began to feel home-sick already. Madagascar — who would have believed it?

After passing under the archway, he took the left ramp and parked in a loading zone, then took the service elevator to the second floor. He asked for Dr. Carswell and was told he was downstairs in the computer center.

"Wondered when you would get here," Carswell said after he unlocked the door to let Charlie in.

The biologist appeared much more at ease than the last time Bannerman had seen him. "I just left the police commissioner. He's real impressed with what you've come up with. He's even decided to send me on a hunting expedition."

"Great! Spoke with him for a few minutes this morning. He said some nice words and then told me to keep my mouth shut." A tall man at the computer table was running one finger along a line of chemical symbols on the right-hand screen. "This is Dr. Sam Bloom. Sam, here's the guy who started it all."

Bloom muttered something harsh and cleared the screen. He wore his sandy-colored hair short, military style, which allowed a clear view of a thick scar that wound up into the back of his hairline. Charlie suddenly wondered why anyone who had inherited five big ones a few years ago would still be playing around with flowers. The man stood up and turned around to face the policeman. Bannerman took in the lean face, the square jaw, the steely blue eyes, and found the likeness to the movie actor disconcerting.

Bloom walked over and put out his hand. "Pleasure, Lieutenant. I hear you and me could be doing some investigating."

"Could be," Bannerman said as he felt his knuckles being crunched. "I suppose people are always saying you look like—"

"Yeah, Randolph Scott. It's a pain in the ass."

"You could have done worse—Bob Hope, for instance."

"Or Lon Chaney," Carswell added.

"Yeah, the Wolf Man himself." Bloom turned to face the C-shaped, bluish-gray computers. "Then I would come back during the next full moon and sink my fangs into computers that refuse to cooperate. You hear that, Dan?"

"Easy," said Carswell, grinning at Bannerman. "Dan is sensitive."

Bannerman pulled off his trench coat and hung in on the coat rack. "The commissioner needs your passport, Dr. Bloom."

"Sam's the name. Figured he would." He dug into a leather wallet strapped to his belt. "Don't much care to hand my personal effects over to strangers, but I suppose if we're going to be buddies ...."

Charlie looked up at the guy, six feet or six-one, struck by the fact that his soft drawl seemed a touch odd for a man with four science degrees. His overall appearance was more like one of those cowpunchers from Nebraska the patrols picked up on a Saturday night for being drunk and disorderly. Charlie stuffed the passport in a side pocket and lowered his bulk into a swivel chair. "Come up with any new insights into our little puzzle?"

"Not especially." Bloom sprawled his legs over a corner of the computer table. "More a matter of confirming what Gary has found. Truth is, I've never seen a species quite like this baby. Can't say it doesn't exist, but if it does exist, more likely than not it'll be in Madagascar. The island's sort of a biological Disneyland with about one thousand known species, most of which are native only to there. You see, Lieutenant, orchids are fascinating critters, and many are in a constant state of evolution. This one is probably a newly-evolved hybrid. It seems to belong to the *Vandoid* group and has several typical characteristics of the subtribe *Angraecinae* – cylindrical leaves, spurred lip, spiral shape, two pollinia, and a rostellum that is deeply notched. What I find truly mesmerizing is that the computer apparently has this knowledge, but is inhibited in some way from finalizing the classification. I suspect it may be the manner in which it was compounded with the cocaine molecules."

"And the wings?"

"Ah yes, the wings. Let's have another look at them, Gary."

Carswell slid into a chair and punched in a series of commands. The right screen blossomed with a striking golden orchid, complete with the same fluttering black wings. As before, Charlie stared at the screen in awe.

"*Angraecinae* are generally thought to be pollinated exclusively by moths, which may lead one to conclude that the computer has somehow managed, through its vast knowledge and its own intelligence, to assume that this particular species is pollinated solely by this particular moth. But that would be an extremely rare occurrence. Fidelity, the tendency of any one pollinator to return again and again to the same species, normally evolves through some kind of environmental constraint. Here, I'll show you something interesting."

Bloom walked back to the door and turned off the overhead lights. The effect was enhanced a hundredfold. "Moths' wings will vary a great deal in size but very little in configuration. With the lights out, these appear to be translucent. Look real hard and you can just make out three thin lines in each wing. Those wings belong to a bat, Lieutenant. The thumbs are missing and the bottom curvature is incorrect; but it is, after all, only a computer-generated image."

Carswell had obviously been made aware of Bloom's conclusion, as he showed no surprise. "A bat," Charlie repeated, wondering for the first time if he wasn't in way over his head on this one. "My knowledge of such matters would hardly register on the Richter scale, but it seems to me sort of illogical for a computer to suggest that a bat is feeding on this flower, unless it had reason to do so — like finding something in the analysis to leads it to make that conclusion."

Bloom flicked on the lights and strolled over to stand beside the screen. "I should imagine if enough clear and unambiguous data were available, Dan would be pleased to show us the creature's complete anatomy."

The flower man yawned and rubbed his eyes. "But you're right. A bat only compounds the mystery. To begin with, none of the orchids in this group have sufficient nectar to attract a bird or even a large insect like the comet moth. Truth is, the flower's relatively small reservoir forces it to rely upon other means, such as color, shape, or fragrance, to attract a pollinator. And bats have rarely been observed attempting to extract nectar from any orchid, let alone one from this group. What the screen is showing us is not known to exist free in nature. Again, I'm not saying it isn't possible, but if we were to discover such an orchid and then find it was being pollinated by bats, it would be the botanical discovery of the decade."

It was suddenly too much for Charlie. "There's a better than even chance this could drive me bats before we're done."

Both scientists laughed. Cary Carswell said, "You told me you had a mystery, Lieutenant, and you certainly do. I'd give my eyeteeth to be going down there with you guys. What an adventure it should be."

Sam Bloom unfolded a sheet of paper that showed a photographic image of the orchid without the wings. "I figure if we pass copies of this around, it shouldn't take more than a few days to track down our little golden child."

Charlie realized why the commissioner wanted a cop along. "If it turns out Madagascar is where the cocaine is being processed, advertising our presence would not be a smart move. A coke operation, especially a big one, is always bad news for snoopers."

"Good point," Sam said. "Figuring on carrying your piece?"

"Not possible. The commissioner said he would try to arrange something with the embassy. We do have an embassy down there?"

"You bet. It so happens the ambassador is a young fellow from my home state. I'm sure he'll do his best to help us out."

Bannerman glanced at his watch and stood up. "The boss says we're pulling out tomorrow night. I gotta go get a malaria shot. How about you?"

"Mine's good till May. I expect we'll be back by then."

Watching the dark wings continue to enact their mysterious fluttering motion, Charlie said, "Yeah, unless they bury us there."

Chapter Five

Herr Brower downed a small cognac, straightened his bowtie, then walked briskly out to center stage. A single glance told him the auditorium was less than one quarter filled. Little wonder, he thought as he adjusted the microphone. "Ladies and gentlemen, members and guests, I bid you welcome to another in our series of monthly lectures. I see many familiar faces out there, but in case there are newcomers among you, my name is Dietrich Brower, chairman of the board and a director of ZIAN. These lectures began as far back as 1954 and over the past several years have gained international recognition as a touchstone of the great naturalist movement. Our global membership is ever expanding and always alert for news of yet another threat to some poor species of flora or fauna teetering on the brink of extinction."

The director closed his eyes for a moment. An old man of eighty-five, Herr Brower was in his forty-second year with ZIAN. Lately he had been finding it difficult to project the proper degree of enthusiasm.

"As many of you know, the Zurich International Association of Naturalists continues to sponsor prominent biologists and zoologists to undertake studies in the field and report on the plight of endangered species. We are fortunate indeed this evening to have Roderick Hassel-Walker among us again. Dr. Hassel-Walker, as I am certain you already know, is recognized as the world's leading authority on exotic mushrooms. This time he brings us urgent news from the small African country of Rio Muni. It seems their Ministry of Lands and Development has ordered the filling in of a tiny swamp that contains an entire community of extremely rare locus mushrooms. Just one other community is known to exist."

He paused again, balancing in his mind the exact amount of mild outrage to inject into his opening commentary. It was important that the audience feel outraged, particularly since at the end of each lecture a collection was taken up and turned over to the visiting speaker as an honorarium.

"Here at ZIAN we take such matters seriously indeed. Truly, this is just one more sad reflection upon our primary role as caretakers of this poor ravaged planet. Therefore, I urge you to pay close attention to what Dr. Hassel-Walker has to say about this despicable undertaking by the government of Rio Muni. A slide presentation will follow the introduction, and after his summation, Dr. Hassel-Walker will be pleased to answer questions. As usual, a collection will be taken up at the end of the evening, after which coffee shall be served. There, I have said quite enough for now, so I ask you to join with me in welcoming our old friend, Dr. Hassel-Walker, back to Zurich."

Amid a smattering of applause, a tall, thin man of beet-red complexion walked onto the stage. Herr Brower raised the microphone, bowed once to the mushroom man, and left the stage. At the curtain, he hesitated for just an instant at the sight of his secretary. The look on his face told Herr Brower there was trouble.

The young man clicked his heels in respect. "My apologies, Herr Director. I have news from Geneva."

"Geneva? Very well, Hans, let us return to the privacy of my office, where you may tell me all about it."

The old man was trying out a new Teflon prosthesis and still had not mastered the stairs. Twice Hans reached out, but each time Herr Brower's look stopped him. Once in the long hallway, his limp was barely noticeable. The director's office was located near the front of the building on the fourth floor. The building itself was once a small opera house, having been purchased outright in late 1944 by Herr Brower on behalf of several members of the General Staff of the Third Reich. The funds had come from the systematic theft and sale of a number of choice art treasures seized by Reichsmarschall Göring during the rape of Europe.

The director settled into his big leather armchair and looked up at his secretary. "Is it the Grenier affair?"

"Yes, sir. René Simard called. He just found out that the woman departed for Brazzaville yesterday morning, but has booked a stopover in Madagascar. He thought you should know."

Herr Brower's heavy lids lowered in thought. After a moment's reflection, he removed his glasses and reached for the bottle of cognac he kept in his bottom drawer. "Perhaps to pick up her husband's effects, do you think?"

"Perhaps," Hans answered cautiously.

After pouring and taking a sip of cognac, Herr Brower leaned back and fixed his hooded stare upon his secretary. This made the young man nervous, the director knew, and so it should, as the director of ZIAN was even now one of the most powerful men in the whole of Europe. During his Gestapo days as a trusted field officer on the Reichmarschall's staff, he had been given a number of unpleasant duties to perform. Only a few of these unpleasant-ries had his name attached, but they were enough to inspire fear in those who knew the truth. And yet it was to Herr Brower, then Oberst Hermann Von Rudel, that the fourteen senior officers had come with their proposal, just one of many that had arisen out of the desperation of the last few months of the war. They had come to him not only because of his obvious logistical talents, but because they had recognized in him a special aptitude for survival.

His secretary was the grandson of one of the old generals, a weakling to be sure, but a man who obeyed unquestioningly. Herr Brower had discovered early in life whether in war or in commerce, absolute obedience was a primary essential in a subordinate.

"But you think not?"

The young man relaxed a little. He never sat while in the direc-tor's office, nor had the director ever invited him to sit. "Simard's report claims she is an intelligent woman. Perhaps the Strouss accident and the scouring of her flat may seem like too much to accept as mere coincidence. She may have even learned of the disappearance of the physician from Bern ...." Hans stopped there, wondering if he had said too much.

66

A hint of annoyance crossed Herr Brower's face. Based on Simard's telephone call after the coroner's examination of Grenier's body, each of these moves had been deemed necessary at the time. In retrospect, the director considered now that he may have acted somewhat hastily. Simard's original instructions were to stay close to the woman until she received news of her husband's death, whereupon he was to probe the extent of her knowledge. It was the best way to learn if Grenier had passed along his suspicions about the radio transmitter to his wife. The man from Interpol had also learned of the involvement of Wilhem Strouss in the Tsingy affair, which left the director little choice but to order his immediate termination.

The fact that Simard was Anna Grenier's cousin had been a fortunate coincidence. That, plus his immediate availability, were the reasons for selecting him over one of the more experienced consultants who made their home at St. Cloud. The vehicle accident in particular had been complicated and expensive to arrange, but a credit to the Frenchman for bringing it off on such short notice.

The director had often wondered in his later years if the truth about Interpol would ever become known. The Jews continued to make noises, but by now the world community viewed the Jews as the boy who cried wolf. Their continued accusations of seeing Nazis behind every rock had finally reached the saturation point; and there were few indeed, especially in Europe, who paid attention anymore, or even cared. Kurt Waldheim was a case in point.

Paris was a city of scandals, with at least one major one per week. Without such scandals to fill their newspapers, the French would probably not read at all. In the midst of these endless scandals the name of Interpol would emerge from time to time, but to the French such matters were not to be taken seriously. It was, after all, just entertainment.

As far as ZIAN was concerned, more than a few of Zurich's respected citizens knew of its Nazi origin, but could care less. All of ZIAN's eight surviving board members were millionaires many times over. Each had estates on the north shore of Lake Zurich, known locally as the Gold Coast. Each had villas in Spain, Greece, or wherever. Many of their sons, daughters, and grandchildren had married into old Swiss families. In the name of the mighty Swiss franc, all was forgiven. Herr Brower had found the complacent burghers of Zurich to be among the world's greatest whores.

"Is Simard still in Paris?"

"Yes, sir. He called from St. Cloud."

The old man refitted his glasses and swung his chair around to gaze out at the activity taking place along Bahnhofstrasse. The old opera building was in a choice location, on Fusslistrasse, just two doors west of the Bahnhof, considered by many to be Europe's premier shopping district. "The letters taken from her flat have confirmed to my satisfaction that her husband's suspicions were of a recent nature. And yet, these photographs tell us that he did manage to penetrate deep enough to photograph the golden orchid, something that concerns me a great deal."

He began to tap his fingers noisily on the desktop, which made Hans nervous. "Isn't it possible, Herr Director, that he may have come across such a specimen outside of the reserve?"

"This is a possibility of course, but unlikely. No, my young Hans, these photographs, together with the sensitivity dial mounted on his tape recorder, clearly indicate that Grenier had some knowledge prior to his final visit, which also raises the question of complicity. Were he and Strouss the only ones, or would they have shared their suspicions with the other foresters?"

"Grenier was a passionate photographer, Herr Director. The photograph of the golden orchid was just one among many. The other men would have no reason to single it out. As for the dial, Victor said he also recorded bird calls. Might it not have something to do with that?"

Brower swung the chair around again to face his secretary. "What you say has merit. Still, Grenier's widow now has every right to suspect Simard because of his unfortunate but necessary disappearance. Very well, Hans, here are my instructions: Alert Victor, and tell him exactly what has transpired. He will arrange to have one of our locals keep an eye on her. If she shows up in Tsingy, he is to arrange an accident, by the usual method if it is deemed expedient."

Herr Brower pulled himself up, grimacing as his new artificial leg cut a ridge into his stump. He would have to go in for yet another fitting. "I hope and pray this will not happen, of course, but it behooves us to be wary of this Grenier woman and her curiosity."

The words from an old proverb brought a smile to his shriveled features. "Curiosity killed the cat, didn't it?"

Bannerman jerked in his seat when the pilot of the 747 let down the landing gear. He turned to Bloom. "What the hell was that?"

Sam chuckled. Here was a man, a senior officer in the NYPD, who had never flown in an aircraft until they pulled out of Kennedy the night before. A seasoned traveler, Bloom knew there was no way their luggage would make it through two quick changes of airlines. So by now, after scrambling with their bags through two major airports, a kind of fledgling friendship had developed.

"It's the landing gear, Lieutenant. The big plane has to let down its little wheels so we don't become an inkblot on the tarmac. You asked me the same question when we landed in Cairo."

"Yeah, but it sounds different this time—heavier, sort of."

"Same sound, bigger plane." They had taken a United DC10 to Amsterdam, scrambling around the airport in the wee hours of the morning and barely making it aboard their KLM flight to Cairo, where they hooked up to an Air Madagascar Boeing 747. He watched Bannerman's knuckles turn white again. "You a churchgoer, Charlie?"

"Sometimes," the policeman answered nervously. The plane was dropping fast now. In the distance off to his right, the sun hovered directly over a lone, high mountain. It was exactly half an hour since they had passed over the port city of Mahajanga. After leaving Cairo, Sam had insisted Charlie take the window seat, and when they left mainland Africa behind them, he began to speak seriously about Madagascar.

"How much do you know about the island?"

"Zip."

"Then, my friend, a brief geographical, ethnological overview is in order. We are now crossing over the world's fourth largest island, close to a thousand miles from north to south. The people are descendants of the Malayans who first arrived around eight hundred years ago, and of the Africans who found their way here some three hundred years later. Prior to that, Madagascar was populated by a primitive race called the Vazimba, who have since gone the way of the dodo bird. Naturally, the two races intermarried, and during the next few centuries a whole raft of little kingdoms was formed, each one struggling for control over the other. The Merina eventually came out on top and had everything in good order by the time the French took over in eighteen ninety-six.

"The country has five distinct climatic zones. The capital is located on the Hauts-Plateaux, the high plateau, a region of moderate rain, mid-temperatures, and open rolling terrain. To the west is a large, dry area of grasslands. Years ago much of it used to be forest, but the natives burned it off so often to produce feed for their huge cattle herds, that it will never grow again. To the east we head down to the coast, the only large strip of tropical rain forest left on the island. That's where Toamasina is located, and it's hotter than hell and just like a bloody sauna. Way down south is a strange little area unlike anywhere else in the world. Giant cacti, huge tamarind trees, and several species of baobab trees hang out together in a sort of spiny desert environment. Most of the lemurs are found down there, along with bats with four-foot wingspans, and of course hundreds of the rarer species of *Orchidaceae*. If we find ours, I'm certain it will be down there. The last zone is smaller again, right up in the northwest tip, called the Sambirano. Except for seasonal cyclones, it's probably the nicest part to live in."

Charlie was impressed and said so.

But Bloom had something to add. "Unfortunately, Madagascar has a serious problem. A terminal illness, like a cancer, has taken hold of it. The place is in such a sad state, I could cry just thinking about it. Hell, it wasn't that long ago much of the island was a tropical paradise. Look below, and tell me what you see."

70

Their aircraft had just left behind the Betsiboka River delta and was making its way over a scarred, rust-colored landscape. Here and there in the rugged terrain, a few small clumps of trees survived as remaining witnesses to the lush growth that had once thrived in the area.

It was not at all what Bannerman had expected. "Looks like a war zone down there. What happened?"

Sam shook his head slowly from side to side. "The story is long and sad and boring, and you don't want to hear it, believe me. In many ways it is the typical African story, with the colonial powers turning the country back to the locals, only to have the locals proceed to screw it up royally. Granted, such stories are old news in this part of the world. But this poor little island didn't have a lot going for it in the first place. Once its socialist government got underway in 1961 — would you believe the ruling party is called the Advance Guard for the Malagasy Revolution — in typical socialist fashion the natives out in the country were left to fend for themselves. All the poor devils were trying to do was survive, but in their effort to survive they've damn near wiped out the entire virgin forest. Now they're left with hundreds of square miles of near-desert conditions and about twenty million zebu cattle, which make sure the forest will never grow again. And they usually don't even kill the stupid creatures except for weddings or funerals."

Bannerman wondered about the trace of anger in his companion's voice. "Some kind of religious thing?"

"It always is, isn't it? That little quirk probably originated two hundred years ago with some medicine man drunk on corn brew saying the more cattle that are killed when a man dies, the better his standing in the afterworld. Stupid, stupid, stupid, like so much of Africa, just plain stupid."

They began skimming over flat green fields with terra-cotta houses and barns scattered sporadically about, then the sinuous shoreline of a big lake, and then clunk ... bounce ... clunk .... Dr. Samuel Bloom and his assistant, Dr. Charles Bannerman, botanists from the world-renowned Smithsonian, had arrived at Ivato International Airport.

Charlie let go of the armrests and flexed his fingers. He wiped his sweaty palms on the sides of his pants and tightened his tie.

71

Through the window he spotted what appeared to be clumps of residential areas with low gray hills in the distance. "So this is it, Antananarivo, the capital of Madagascar. Yeah, I can tell right away it's not Brooklyn."

"Call it Tana, just Tana. Only foreigners use the whole spelling." Bloom glanced at his watch: 1703 hours. Once they checked into the hotel, there would be time for a quick look around the city before sunset. In the morning they were to take a local flight down to the coast, to Toamasina, where the *Lucinda V* was due to arrive late in the evening.

Commissioner Hennessey had obviously been successful in plucking a few political strings, as they were warmly greeted by a member of the embassy staff who escorted them through customs with hardly any delay. The air was hot and dry, and the sun still high.

"The ambassador said to tell you he is entirely at your disposal, Dr. Bloom," said the young American. He wore a white short-sleeved shirt with a flowery tie and looked like one of those young Mormon kids who patrolled upscale neighborhoods looking for fresh funds to help run the big Salt Lake City machine.

The car was a Ford, one of few American cars to be seen weaving in and out of the mishmash of motorbikes and miniature European automobiles. A team of horses pulling a covered carriage full of dark little faces made its way along the side of a muddy street that abruptly gave way to rows of tattered three-story buildings. The city core appeared to be somewhat of a hilly island, with shops and residential quarters crowded together into steep terraces rising one above the other. Pedestrians gained access by the use of stone staircases cut into the hillside.

Curtis Johnson used both hands on the wheel and never took his eyes off the road. "I've been briefed, of course."

"Of course," Sam said as he turned around in the front seat to give Charlie a wink.

"Guns are a problem. The Kung Fu were getting in shipments from South Africa. Last year the police cracked down and outlawed private ownership of weapons. So now there's a stiff penalty if one is found in your possession. Which doesn't apply to embassy personnel, of course."

Sam turned around again to tell Charlie that the Kung Fu was an outlawed anti-government party.

"Violent buggers," the driver went on. "Nineteen eighty-five they had a big shootout just four blocks from the embassy. The military even used tanks. The outcome was kind of messy."

They began to climb a steep incline where a church spire at the top of the hill poked up above the city's red and white gabled roofline. Although dark-skinned, the people appeared more Oriental than African, with the placid, resigned faces of peasants everywhere. Aside from assorted straw hats worn by the men and boys, the brightly colored clothing was the sort to be seen in Harlem during the summer months. Many were barefooted. A number of foreigners dressed in business suits, probably Europeans, towered over the diminutive locals.

The new Tana Weston was of stark North African design, the color of sand and heavily columnated on the lower two of its three floors. Outside balconies on each floor extended around the inner sections of its U shape, which enclosed a large courtyard of packed red clay. Considering the eight-hour time loss and the fact that they had been on the move for over twenty hours, Charlie had no wish to do anything other than grab a quick meal and hit the sack.

As they climbed the courtyard steps behind Johnson and the porter, a woman of intriguing beauty came out of the lobby and stood for a moment on the landing. Bloom paused in mid-stride and stared, drinking in the quality that radiated from her like a fine perfume. She took no notice of the three men and appeared deep in thought as she adjusted a pair of sunglasses. Once she began descending the steps, all three turned together to continue with their appraisal.

"There goes one nice lady, hombres," Sam said, taking in the crisp white blouse and China-blue skirt as she walked across the courtyard. "You know who she is?"

Johnson shook his head. "But it won't take me long to find out."

After collecting their passports, Johnson went on ahead to take care of registration. Once the woman disappeared from view, Sam followed him in. But Charlie had noticed a movement at one end of the near-deserted courtyard. His detective's instinct told him to stay put. From behind the columns a dark face peered out again, then a man stepped into view. He walked rapidly toward the entrance to the courtyard, staying behind the columns. He was a nondescript little man, probably a local, but he moved with an intent that Charlie had observed many times over the years.

Bloom came back out and stood beside his new partner. "Well, Lieutenant, what have you found out so far?"

"I've found out the lady has a tail."

"Whaaat?"

"Look at that little sucker just scurrying around the corner. Hundred to one he's a tail."

"I'll be dammed. We're at the hotel less than two minutes and you got something already. What should we do?"

"Nothing," Bannerman told him. "The guy could just be a watcher hired by a jealous husband. She is an attractive woman."

"Or he could be someone out to commit rape, or even murder."

Charlie smiled wearily, rubbing both hands over his face. "Not our concern, Professor. This here's a foreign country and we got our own problems to look after."

"Shouldn't we at least report it to the police?"

"It's not smart to draw attention to ourselves. I'd advise against going near the police for any reason."

"Damn it, Bannerman, it's not right. I'm going to chase her down and tell her she's being followed. At least that way I can live with myself if anything happens to her."

Johnson came back out at that moment. "Something wrong?"

Bloom explained what was taking place and asked, "You able to find out who she is?"

"Her name is Anna Grenier, a physician. Swiss. She's with the World Health Organization. Say, why don't we jump back in the car and offer her a ride to wherever she's going? It might just be a pickpocket, but the Kung Fu killed a priest and a school-teacher just three weeks ago right here in the capital. I believe we have an obligation to tell Dr. Grenier we think she's being followed."

"What the hell," said Bannerman, fully aware that both men were using the tail as an excuse to meet the woman. "If you two are determined to make fools of yourselves, I might as well come along and watch you do it."

Less than two blocks downhill from the hotel, the China-blue skirt showed up like a flag. But the tail blended so well with the sidewalk traffic that it took Charlie a minute or two to spot him.

"On the right, just passing that shop with the turtle sign, in a red checkered shirt."

Johnson slowed the Ford to a crawl. He turned around and grinned at Charlie. "Want to have a word with him, Lieutenant?"

"Forget it," said Bannerman. "He'll just deny—"

"Pull up ahead of the woman and let me out," Sam said abruptly.

Their car eased by the tail and then by the woman, who walked quickly and with purpose. Johnson pulled in just past a small alley on their right while Bloom shucked his tie and jacket and threw them over the seat. "Don't bother waiting for me, amigos. I see a need for a deed. Catch you back at the hotel."

Once Bloom was on his way, Charlie opened the back door and went to lean against the trunk. He was curious to see how Randolph Scott would make out with the good-looking Swiss physician.

A couple of blocks uphill, Sam stepped directly in front of her and spoke in French. "Pardon, madame, there is a man following you. If you have no objections, I will ask him to stop at once. It is very impolite to follow people, especially a beautiful lady."

To Sam's surprise, the woman took him seriously. She removed her glasses and started to turn around. "No, don't. Let's just talk for a moment and then say good-bye. You continue on down the hill and I'll go back and have a few words with this fellow."

Anna looked up, puzzled as much by the man as by his actions. "What makes you believe that I am being followed?"

He noticed her wedding ring and felt a jolt of disappointment. "We saw you leave the hotel a few minutes ago. Soon as you cleared the courtyard, this character came out from behind one of the columns and took off after you."

"Do you make it a practice to concern yourself with the affairs of others?"

"No, ma'am, I usually keep pretty much to myself. But I thought you should be warned."

She continued to stare into his eyes, listening to the words being quietly spoken, yet sensing that something was wrong with her would-be rescuer. She glanced down at his hands and saw that they were shaking. "Are you feeling all right?"

Sam had been keeping an eye on the red shirt. He could see the guy was getting restless. He leaned over and kissed Anna on both cheeks. "A pleasure, Dr. Grenier. So nice to see you again. Please carry on as before, as if nothing has happened."

Sam set out to cross the street, working his way around the Vespas and motorbikes that were charging down the hill. On the other side, he ducked into a wicker shop and waited a few minutes before looking out the window. Red shirt took one last glance in his direction and began to move out. Sam felt his breath coming in great gulps and choked back on it as best he could. He knew it was starting up again. After all those years.

He also knew he should stop, now, while there was still time.

Two minutes later he was back across the street. He easily picked up the blue skirt further down the steep sidewalk, but the tail had vanished. Sam put on some speed and had almost closed on the guy before he saw him again. But the tail was intent on business and didn't bother to glance back.

Looking ahead, Sam noticed a sheltered alley coming up fast. It was the right place if he could make it in time. He was practically running when he reached the man. One jerk on his arm had him off the sidewalk and into the alley.

The Malagasy was miniature and in shock for a few seconds. Sam continued to pull him deeper into the alley. Then the guy gave a vicious kick, catching Bloom behind the right knee. His legs buckling, Sam knew he had been struck a professional blow. But he managed to hang on and bring his prisoner down with him. Then the tail exploded in a flurry of fists and knees that forced the American to let him go. The guy was off in a flash, but stopped dead when he saw Johnson and Bannerman blocking the exit.

Without hesitation he reversed direction, leaving the ground in a classic flying kick aimed at his assailant's head. Bloom was ready this time and stepped back at the last instant to grip the Malagasy by his ankle, using the man's own momentum to swing him around and slam him into a brick wall.

"Jesus Christ!" Bannerman shouted as he came running up. "You probably killed the poor bastard."

But Bloom was now beyond reason as he turned on the lifeless heap at his feet and kicked the guy in the ribcage, feeling the bones give way. He reached down with one hand and pulled him upright as Charlie struggled to fix a hammerlock on his companion, but Bloom continued to beat on the guy in any way that he could.

"Lieutenant Bloom!" Bannerman shouted into his ear. "You are to cease and desist. That's an order. Right now, Lieutenant, or you'll never see the inside of an A-6 again. Do you hear me?"

Bannerman hung on as the big man slowly came out of it. By now Sam was shaking so violently that he caused both of them to vibrate. "Let the guy go. Let him go, goddamnit!"

Once Bloom released his hold, Johnson caught the Malagasy and lowered him to the ground. He felt around for a heartbeat, then looked up. "There's no pulse!"

Charlie turned Bloom around to lean him back against the building. Too late he realized that he had laid him up against the splotch of blood made by the tail's face when it connected with the brick wall. Then he bent over and thrust two fingers between the guy's rib cage. Nothing.

Straightening up, Bannerman noticed several brown faces at the end of the alley peering in. He could imagine what they were thinking, seeing three white guys beating on one of their own.

"Let's move it, fellows," Johnson said. "Right now, if you please."

Charlie said, "What about—"

"Forget him, out to the car we go. Dr. Bloom, are you okay now?"

Bloom was still shaking and squinting hard, trying to focus his eyes. "I ... my eyes are—"

"Just hold onto me," said Bannerman. The huddle of a dozen or so silent little men with impassive faces gave way for the trio. Charlie led Sam another twenty paces to the car, but then had to wait for Johnson to bring the keys. Looking back, he saw Johnson saying something to the watchers. When the young man finished, he ran down the hill and unlocked the door for Charlie.

Soon as they were underway, Bannerman asked Johnson what he had told them. His words tumbled out rapidly as he kept glancing in his rearview mirror. "The Malagasy live in constant fear of the ghosts of their ancestors. I told them Dr. Bloom was the reincarnation of that man's grandfather who had come back from the dead to punish him for murdering a tourist. It was all I could think of. I said if any one of them were to tell a living soul what had happened, the grandfather would return and do the same to them."

"Sheesh, they'd swallow that?"

"Oh yeah," Sam said in a quivering voice. "Johnson touched on the one part of their nature that has remained absolutely inviolate—fear of their ancestors. You can bet your life's blood that none of those particular few will tell. You couldn't beat it out of them."

Johnson pulled an old towel out from under his seat and passed it back to Bloom. "You better get that blood off your hands, then put your tie and jacket on before we get back to the hotel."

"Where did the woman get to?" Bannerman asked, aware of how their driver had suddenly taken over the show. Young Johnson was not quite as innocent as he appeared.

"Must have ducked into one of those tourist shops near the market," Johnson replied. "Dr. Bloom, please stay out of her sight if you can; and if she questions either of you, on no account are you to tell her what happened. She may not believe it was an accident—which it was, wasn't it?"

"Of course it was," Bannerman said. "The guy came at him. Sam reacted. The brick wall just happened to be in the wrong place."

Sam pulled his tie up, then looked at his hands. They were still shaking. "Look, fellows, please believe me, I had no intention of hurting that little guy. I just wanted to talk to him. I … it just … got away from me."

Charlie was uncertain of how much he should say with Johnson listening in. He decided to save the questions for later. "These things happen. Let's hope nothing comes out of it."

Back in the hotel courtyard, the Ford stopped behind an open-backed truck being used as a taxi. A group of noisy British tourists were unloading their bags.

Johnson turned around, his nice Mormon boy look now gone. "You'll have a better chance of avoiding the woman if you eat away from the hotel. There are two cafés just outside the north gateway; the Arabic one is the best by far. I'll come by at zero nine hundred and take you back out to the airport. The ambassador will have to be told, of course. We'll keep our fingers crossed, but in case there are any complications, here's my card. Good evening, gentlemen."

Charlie collected both keys, and they walked up the stairs in silence. He opened Bloom's door first and followed him in.

Sam turned around and stared at the NYPD cop as best he could. His eyes still were not focusing properly, and he cringed at the thought of facing up to the next stage in the process. "I suppose an explanation is in order."

Bannerman rubbed a hand over his face and lowered himself into a sofa chair. "I read your sheet. It's the past, isn't it?"

Bloom looked puzzled. "My sheet?"

"You didn't think the commissioner would send us on an assignment like this without knowing something about you."

"No, I suppose not." Sam sat on the corner of his bed and looked down at the traces of blood on his hands. "Yeah, the past. Twenty years, and sometimes it's like it's still going on, you know, like I'm still trying to escape. Back home I could control it, but down here it gets complicated because—"

"Because they remind you of your Cong torturers."

Bloom nodded, his face twisted into a painful grimace. "But I've never gone off the handle like that before. In the Philippines and even the last time I was down here, it ate into me a bit, but I was able to stay above it. Jesus, it grabbed me so hard back there I would've killed that little fellow no matter what. Soon as I felt that kick, I reacted out of pure instinct. God, Charlie, it's like … like trying to stay alive, you gotta survive, and you gotta kill this guy before he kills you. It's one god-awful nightmare that goes on and on. It never ends, Charlie. Twenty years later I'm still trying to get away. Jesus ...."

Bannerman stood up, a bit embarrassed when he saw the tears. He didn't remember ever seeing Randolph Scott cry. "What about your eyes, is that a medical problem?"

"It's psychosomatic, so the experts say. They should be okay in the morning. Look, I'm going to have to pass up dinner. Just give me a call before you go for breakfast."

"Sure, Doc. Sorry this came up so sudden. Try and put it out of your mind. I'll see you in the morning."

Bannerman closed the door and paused for a moment. The implications of what they had just done were just now hitting him. Leaving the scene of the crime, or even an accident, went hard against all his years of training. Still ... Johnson was the embassy, the man in control, probably concerned that the guy's death could turn into something international. What troubled Charlie most was his partner's sudden burst of instability. If he had known about Bloom's problem he would have turned down the job, no matter how hard the commissioner leaned on him. He wondered how the PC had missed the psycho bit.

If he missed it.

Being stuck on an island with a goddamn psychopath, a man who could come unglued at any time just by the sight of one of the locals, was not his idea of how to run an investigation. As he dug out his room key, Charlie had the unpleasant sensation that the little guy's freak death was just the beginning.

CHAPTER SIX

Anna came away from her meeting with the police inspector disappointed and a little angry. Her questions about Lind's death clearly puzzled him. "Madame Grenier, already this year we have had over one hundred reported deaths by lightning. It may be our worst year on record. For sure, there is a high increase in the west, near the Tsingy reserve. Poof — that particular area is often riddled with killer storms. It is to be expected. Since the weather office confirmed there was indeed a storm on the night in question, what is it you expect the police to do?"

Inspector Gannett was French, from Marseille, with a large moustache that seemed to compensate for his lack of hair elsewhere. He was a fatherly figure whose eyes twinkled as he spoke. "Even if you suspect certain inconsistencies, surely these suspicions must be set aside in the face of such irrefutable evidence: Monsieur Grenier was most certainly struck by lightning, and that, madame, can only be arranged by God."

It was soon apparent that her cries for help had fallen upon deaf ears. Gannett laughed outright at the idea of a radio transmitter inside the park. "In Tsingy? Someone has been filling your ears with impossible tales. Did you not know that only the birds have access to Tsingy? It is an impenetrable maze of limestone needles joined at the base. *Mon Dieu,* who would wish to even visit such a place?"

"Naturalists, biologists, photographers, even tourists who collect butterflies. Perhaps the local natives hunt there. I don't know who. I just know that my husband's body was supposed to have lain in the open for two days, and yet it was untouched by wild animals. Even you, Inspector, must agree that this is illogical."

The kindly policeman reached across and took Anna's hand. "Madame Grenier, naturally I am distressed when such a fine lady cannot accept the death of her loved one. But you are reaching for shadows. Someone should have told you that the ozone which lingers inside the victim will keep the animals at bay for one to two days. Ozone makes all animals nervous, even those in the insect world. Alas, madame, your quest is for naught. But you are still young and beautiful. I implore you to put all this behind you and begin again."

Knowledge of the ozone badly upset her resolve. Her immediate reaction was anger at herself, because as a physician working in Africa she should have been aware of it. Standing outside on the police station steps, she reviewed all the events that had taken place since poor Wilhem's terrible call. Anna possessed a logical mind, and certain incidents refused to fall into place. Then she recalled that the last noteworthy event was this stranger telling her she was being followed.

The sun had almost set as she descended the steps, wondering now what had happened to him. He was a handsome man, she recalled, tall with broad shoulders. And there was a certain disconcerting familiarity, as if she may have met him a long time ago. Then there was his accent. In Geneva one hears French spoken in every possible manner, yet his accent too eluded her.

The hotel was several blocks away, up a steep incline. Anna would gladly have taken a taxi, except taxis were usually group affairs, with the driver collecting as many passengers as possible into his vehicle, usually an open-back truck, before setting off to deliver them. Aware of the dangers of walking the streets of Madagascar's capital after dark, she set off at a brisk pace.

Two blocks from the police station, she came upon an ambulance and three police cars outside a narrow alley. Drawing close to the gathering crowd, she saw two men exit the alley carrying a stretcher between them. The man on the stretcher seemed to have no face at all, just a mass of bloody pulp. She shuddered and moved slowly around the crowd. This terrible Kung Fu thing seemed to be growing all the time. Lind had told her their members were joined in a blood bond, a covenant of violence and death. This poor devil had obviously undergone a brutal beating. Then someone threw a sheet over him, and Anna realized she had been staring at a corpse.

This knowledge caused her to hurry even more, cursing the fitted skirt because it hampered her stride. She would have gladly welcomed the company of the big man who told her she was being followed, stranger or not. She recalled what he had said, about seeing her leave the hotel, and wondered if he was staying there.

There were many blacks on the street, descendants of those men who had not married into that vast family of islanders known as Malagasy. They hung around open doorways in small groups, cutting short their conversations at her approach. The hissing noise they made was both rude and vulgar, yet accurately embodied one of the many pulses of Africa: a restless sensuality that translated into nothing more than a raw desire to copulate. She was intensely aware that every man on the street wanted her, and would not hesitate to take her if the opportunity presented itself.

The lights in the hotel courtyard were fully lit when Anna finally made it up the hill. Almost out of breath, she thanked God for having seen her through another anxious moment and stopped to compose herself beside a small fountain near the courtyard entrance.

The place had come alive since her earlier departure, the center of activity a small band playing their exuberant Afro-jazz style of music. Three black women swiveled their hips seductively while crooning the harmony background to a young male singer's lead. Hotel guests were scattered along the full length of the veranda, dining or lounging about.

The desk clerk smiled at Anna. "*Bonsoir*, Dr. Grenier, did you enjoy your walk?"

"If only you had not built your hotel on top of a hill," she replied, feeling her leg muscles beginning to tighten up.

"Ah yes," he answered as he placed the room key into her hand. "But the view of Lake Anosy is magnificent, is it not?"

"It is. Yes, I admit it is." She was about to turn away when she remembered the stranger. "Earlier on a man spoke to me who may be staying here. He is tall, above one eight, I should think, with sandy brown hair cut very short and a somewhat squarish jaw."

"Yes, that would be Dr. Bloom." The clerk's eyes twinkled, and Anna could almost read his thoughts. "He arrived early this evening, and I placed him in room two fourteen, just three doors away from yours. He is a nice man, Madame. And he happens to be in at the moment."

Anna nodded, lowering her head as she could feel the blood rush to her cheeks. A nice man, she thought while climbing the staircase. That was the impression she herself had formed.

She paused in front of 214, her curiosity making demands that she would have to satisfy sooner or later. But not now, she thought. She was hot and sweaty and longed for a bath. A sound stopped her—a long, drawn-out moan, an agonizing sound, like someone in deep pain would emit. She placed her ear against the door and listened. Yes, it was definitely coming from this room. Anna put up her hand, hesitating for just a second, then knocked.

The sound ceased immediately. A man's voice called out in English, "Who is it?"

"Anna Grenier. May I speak to you for a moment?"

The door opened to a room in darkness. He filled the doorway, the man who had come to rescue her, and looked down at his visitor. Her original impression that something was wrong with this man was immediately reinforced.

"I do apologize for intruding," she said in English, "but I wanted to ask if you—"

Her words broke off when she saw that his eyes appeared to be twisted up into his head. "Your eyes—my God!"

Bloom tried to smile through the pain, but didn't quite make it. Pain had been his constant companion ever since his POW days, and according to the experts it would remain that way. But the real killer stuff came infrequently, thank God, usually after something kicked his memory into reverse.

"I would invite you in, but I'm not in such good shape at the moment. Perhaps I could call you in the morning."

Anna pushed her way into the room and turned on the lights. "Are you a medical doctor?" she asked quickly.

Sam leaned against the doorframe, forced to shut his eyes against the light. "No," he told her.

"Well, I am. And I wish to examine your eyes," she added firmly. She took his hand and sat him under a lamp, which she switched on. Anna closed the door, and when she turned around again, her eyes fell upon a dark red stain in the center of the bed.

"Good Lord!" she whispered, the image of the little man on the stretcher hitting her full force. "You're hurt," she said as she looked over the clothes he was wearing. "Where? Where were you struck? Was it a bullet?"

The pain inside Sam's head was threatening to explode. Without waiting for his reply, the woman dropped to one knee and began to pull up his shirt and undo the buttons. "Lady, my head is coming off. Please believe me, there is nothing any doctor can do. And it isn't my blood you're looking at. Could you leave now?"

He began to get up, but the woman was firm. "Absolutely not," she answered, clasping his wrists to pull him down again.

Once she had the shirt off, she examined his chest and stomach, then pushed him gently forward to look at his back. There was a patch of dried blood, but she was able to remove it by using the tail of his shirt. After a few moments of close examination, she was convinced that he was speaking the truth. Then the scars took her attention. So many scars.

All of a sudden it hit her. "You are an American! The war—the Vietnam War. Is that where this happened to you?"

But her patient was silent, his eyes closed, the veins in his temple bulging like they were threatening to burst. She switched off the lamp, and then, with only a brief hesitation, reached over to the wall to turn off the overhead lights. "Lean back now, I am going to relax you and ease the pain." She spoke softly, her gentle tone caressing him. "The best healers in the world come from Switzerland, did you know that?" Her hands slowly closed to either side of his head. "It's psychosomatic, isn't it? Something they did so that you would never forget. No matter, in a few minutes you will forget, because I am going to draw away the pain." The throbbing was unlike anything she had encountered before, and for a second considered calling for the hotel physician, but then closed her own eyes and began to concentrate.

She moved in close, her breasts touching the back of his head. "What you must do now is clear your mind. It is not so difficult. I want you to place yourself inside a dark tunnel, where you will feel safe and secure. You are warm, content, loved. But inside your head is a pain that refuses to go away. This pain, this terrible pain, if only you could be rid of it, everything would be so wonderful. At the end of the tunnel there is a small glowing light, a golden light, unlike anything you have ever seen. You are curious, and you watch as it continues to grow. Before long the whole tunnel is caught up in its glow, and you are pleasantly surprised when the light begins to wash over you like a gentle breeze. Layers of warm light brush against your skin, each caress reaching deeper than the last, penetrating your mind, taking control .... It is a loving thing, you realize, that has entered your consciousness ...."

She continued to massage gently, using the power that all humans have to draw pain from one another. It took an enormous degree of concentration, and despite the air-conditioned room, she was aware of beads of perspiration building up on her forehead. She had stopped talking and lost all track of time when she was startled by his hands gripping hers.

A sudden fear took hold of her. Anna had acted out of instinct to help someone in need. But she was in a dark room with a stranger — a stranger who may have been responsible for one death already.

"How does it feel now?" she asked lightly as she pulled her hands away.

"You must be an angel. The pain fell away in layers, just like you were describing it. What an extraordinary gift you have — little wonder you became a physician."

"May I turn the lights back on?"

"Yes, please do." Sam stood up and turned around to face his benefactor. "Could you allow me a few moments to clean up and put something on? I feel sort of uncomfortable without a shirt."

Then he caught the drained look on her face. She smiled at him. "This kind of therapy is quite exhausting. I suppose that is why so few people are competent at it."

"Please, use my bathroom to freshen up."

Anna arched her back and ran her fingers through her hair. "Yes, thank you, I'll go and rinse my face."

Bloom watched her walk across the room and could not believe his good fortune. His headache had not completely left him, but was now well within the tolerance level. He still had not unpacked and was pulling things from his suitcase when the beautiful lady reappeared.

"You'll have to excuse me," he said. "Hadn't quite got around to this yet."

She took the chair where he had been seated earlier and watched him lay out his things. The scars along his back were long and thick. It seemed to her they had been put there for the sole purpose of inflicting pain. "Did you ever catch up with the man you thought was following me?"

Sam turned around. "No, he gave me the slip. You know, it might have been a mistake on my part. I couldn't be absolutely certain he was following you; it just appeared that way."

"I see," Anna said ponderously. "But you did get a good look at him?"

He busied himself again with his unpacking. "Not really, these little fellows all tend to look alike to me."

"I don't suppose he could have been wearing a red checkered shirt?"

Sam was undoing the buttons on one of his own shirts when her question stopped him cold. "I really can't remember. No, I don't think so. Why do you ask?"

"Because on my way back to the hotel, I saw the body of a little man in a red checkered shirt being carried out of an alley. The alley was about one block past where you stopped me. His face was badly bloodied. And I cannot help wondering about the blood on your hands and shirt."

He hung over the bed, motionless for a moment. What in hell's name could he possibly tell her? She would never believe it was an accident, since she already knew he had gone to seek the guy out. Sam turned to face his benefactor. "Can you think of any reason why you would be followed?"

She shrugged, an odd little movement that seemed wrong for her. "Well, the truth is … terrible things have been happening in my life of late, so it would not surprise me greatly to learn that I was being followed."

At that point, a stack of papers Sam had placed on the edge of the bed fell to the floor, among them a color printout of the mystery orchid. He bent down to pick them up, but the splash of color had caught Anna's eye.

"Was that a picture of a flower you picked up? Could I see it, please?"

Sam observed the intense look and wondered what was going through her mind. He removed a copy and stared at it for a moment. He could see no harm in letting her see it.

She took it from his hand and twisted her head slightly to one side. "Where did you get this?" she whispered.

"Why do you ask?"

She looked up at him, her face now covered with suspicion. "For one thing, this is an unlisted species."

Her answer almost floored Sam. "How in hell's name do you know that?"

"No! I want to know where this came from. This is a computer printout, isn't it?"

"Yes, it is. It came out of a damned computer, where else?"

"What is your doctorate in?" she asked abruptly.

"Chemistry, biology. But my field is botany."

"Of course, now I remember. Dr. Samuel Bloom. No wonder you seemed so familiar." She smiled at him and added, "Considering your rather distinctive name, I should have picked that up right away. Your picture is on the back flap of *Exotic Orchidaceae, A Guide For Orchid Lovers*. My husband used to swear by it."

Sam cleared a spot on the bed and sat down. Despite his growing excitement, he'd caught her use of the past tense. "Doesn't he use it anymore?"

"No," she answered slowly. "He was killed two weeks ago, right here on the island. Over near the Tsingy reserve."

"Killed? What happened?"

"Lightning. But since his death certain questions have been raised that I would like answers for."

"Is this why you're here in Tana?"

"Yes. I suppose you already know that the golden orchid comes from Tsingy."

"How do you know? How can you be so sure?"

"My husband was a forester by profession, but his passion was photographing flowers, especially orchids. He was especially proud of this one, as it came from inside a nature reserve that is supposed to be impenetrable." Anna studied the man for a moment and decided to go on. "Our home in Geneva was covered with examples of his work. On the day of his funeral, my flat was burgled. Among the missing items was a blowup of an orchid almost exactly like this one, although the stem is different. Will you tell me how it came into your possession?"

Sam stood up. "Dr. Grenier, you and I have a great deal to discuss. There are certain things you should be told, and you obviously have information that could be helpful to us."

"Us?"

"My assistant, Dr. Bannerman, is in the next room. This really is the most extraordinary coincidence, and all because Charlie thought you were being followed. Look, have you eaten yet? I didn't feel like it earlier, but why don't we —"

"You killed him, didn't you? The man who was following me. I insist that you tell me what is going on. Was he out to … to do me in?"

Her anxiety touched something deep inside him, and Sam had to hold himself back from reaching for her. "I have no idea. The truth is that it was an accident."

"That cannot be true. I saw his face. The man had been badly beaten."

"Because his face connected with a brick wall. But it was still an accident. I swear to you that it was an accident."

He had remained standing by the bed, holding his partly unbuttoned white shirt. To Anna it seemed that Dr. Samuel Bloom was a man incapable of lying. Everything about his demeanor confirmed this impression. And yet, she knew this to be a characteristic of the very best liars. "On the street you called me by name. How did you know my name?"

"After you left the hotel, we inquired at the desk."

"Why?"

Bloom smiled. "Surely that's obvious."

Anna lowered her head. If only she didn't blush so damned easily.

"Let me get cleaned up and I'll give Charlie a shout. This orchid thing is more important than you realize. You won't leave, will you?"

"There are so many mysteries floating around this room that you couldn't drag me out of here. By all means, Dr. Bloom, do go ahead and wash away the evidence. I'll wait."

Charlie had already eaten, of course. He was studying a map of the port city of Toamasina when Sam knocked at his door. He answered clad in his blue and white polka dot boxer shorts. Bloom was a completely different man from when Charlie had left him — all cleaned up, eyes bright and alert, even sporting a wide grin. Then Bannerman spotted the Swiss woman behind him and sensed a certain familiarity between the two.

Bloom stepped inside the room and whispered enough of what he had learned from the woman to entice Charlie into joining them. "You recall that place Johnson mentioned, the Arab café?"

"Just outside the north entrance. Okay, give me a few minutes to get dressed."

At the top of the stairs, some sixth sense warned Bloom that it might not be wise for Anna to be seen with him. During their long hours onboard the plane, Bannerman had filled Sam in on the FBI memo concerning the possibility of unknown quantities of cocaine being shipped from Buenos Aires to Madagascar. The NYPD, for whatever reason, seemed to believe there was a strong possibility that the drug then underwent some kind of chemical alteration right here on the island, which turned it into the deadly amphetamine presently taking a devastating toll on New York's addicts. He admitted to Bloom that the purpose behind such an elaborate scheme was shrouded in mystery. Nevertheless, if there really was a cocaine operation underway on the island and he and Charlie were caught up in it, this could spell even more danger for Anna.

He touched her arm before they reached the bottom of the staircase. "I'd just as soon the people in the hotel don't see us together, so I'll go on ahead. I'll wait for you just beyond that small gate at the right-hand side of the courtyard. Just dawdle a bit, take in the entertainment and slowly work your way along the veranda. Okay?"

For a moment Anna thought he was joking, but his eyes were deadly serious. "If you wish," she replied, then watched him go on ahead. By the time she reached the bottom of the stairs, Sam had already exited the lobby.

The band was on a break as Bloom passed behind the wooden stage that had been set up facing the dining area on the veranda. Wailing sirens in the distance played their own sad song, and he wondered how long it would take before the local authorities caught up to him. Johnson's threat of ghostly revenge had only covered the immediate onlookers. But there had been others on the street, people who would remember three foreigners in a late model American car. Sooner or later the police were bound to learn the truth.

The café was full when Sam and Anna walked in. The music was loud and the crowd boisterous, made up mostly of British and European tourists, although the few Slavic faces they spotted were probably Russians. The density of tobacco smoke was appalling. They were given a choice of waiting or taking the last available table near the kitchen entrance, a restricted little nook that would force them to sit close together. They decided to take it and asked for an extra chair for Bannerman. Twenty minutes later Charlie strolled in.

Sam spotted his new colleague and waved him over. As Bannerman made his way between the tables, a hefty belly dancer threw a veil over his head and held on for a moment while wiggling her hips seductively against him. When Charlie reached the table, he was twisting his head around as if he couldn't decide whether he had enjoyed the experience or not.

Bloom introduced Dr. Grenier, who was smiling up at him. She and Sam had lapsed back into French again, so she greeted Charlie in French. Bannerman nodded politely. "Nice to meet you, too."

"Dr. Bannerman doesn't speak French."

"But I find that strange," said Anna, switching to English. "You look more French than most Frenchmen I know."

"You're absolutely right," Sam said. "I never noticed it until this moment—those solid jowls, those marvelous ears, and of course that magnificent structure fixed to the middle of his face. Not quite in the de Gaulle class, but …."

"Is he always so disrespectful, Dr. Bannerman?"

Charlie shrugged. "Don't even hear him."

"Dr. Bannerman's doctorate is in applied physics. He is a renowned computer expert who has volunteered his valuable time to help this poor botanist keep his research in order."

The cop marveled at his companion's straight face.

"I am so impressed," said Anna while drumming the fingers of both hands on the table as if she were using a keyboard. "You can do such fantastic things with computers these days—like run off full-color prints of unknown flowers."

At that point a waiter interrupted the conversation. Charlie waved away his menu. "Perhaps a little dessert later."

After a prolonged dialogue with Sam and Anna, the young waiter, who seemed more Indian than Arabic, went into the kitchen wearing a resigned look. Then Bloom got down to business. He related everything that had come out of his conversation with Anna, through which she sat in modest silence. From time to time, Charlie would interrupt with a pointed question. When he was finished, Sam added that he thought Dr. Grenier had a right to be told what they were about.

"Before you begin telling me what you are about," Anna said, "would it not be in order for the three of us doctors to stop calling each other 'doctor'? I never realized Americans were so formal. My name is Anna, you are Sam, and you are Charlie. Now, will one of you please tell me what is going on?"

With that, Anna leaned back and folded her arms. Sam felt her moving her feet and realized she had just kicked off her shoes. He looked at the detective. "It's up to you, Charlie."

Bannerman sighed. On this whole island of ten million people, a single person is placed off limits. So who does his partner take to dinner? "Let me put it like this, Anna: There appears to be every possibility that you have certain knowledge, or access to certain knowledge, that others consider a threat. That little fellow in the checkered shirt was a tail. Far as we know, there are a whole bunch of reasons why he could have been following you. So let's try the most obvious — that he or his employers have something to gain by monitoring your every move. Since you came here to investigate your husband's death, which you have reason to believe happened under suspicious circumstances, the tail probably had the job of finding out if you were likely to uncover something that could prove dangerous — to them, that is."

The cop was squeezed against one end of their small table with waiters whizzing by his head every few seconds on their way in and out of the kitchen. The other two were seated tight against the wall. Before going on, Charlie couldn't help but think what a striking woman Anna Grenier was. Her beautiful but intense gray eyes had pinned him down, waiting for what he would say next.

"I will give you some good advice, Anna: Get up from this table right now and walk away. Deny ever knowing us, and go home, or wherever it is you are going. I think you're already in trouble, probably something to do with your husband's death, and being seen in our company could make it even more dangerous for you."

Bloom shook his head. "I don't buy that, Charlie. She's given us valuable information, and now you want to walk out on her."

Bannerman wondered why simple English always seemed so hard to grasp. "I didn't say anything like that. What I said was —"

"If the decision is mine to make, then I will make it."

Both men stared at Anna Grenier, waiting for her to make up her mind. But Charlie had read her correctly. Here was a woman of resolve who would not give in easily. She finally broke into a smile. "It looks as if you are stuck with me, for the moment at least. I promise not to cause any complications or get in your way. How long will you be staying in Tana?"

"We're off in the morning, I'm afraid," Sam told her. "Heading down to the coast. How about you?"

"Tomorrow I will fly over to Morondava and spend a few days with Klaus and Marina Scheuchzer. Klaus is the manager of the forestry station where my husband worked. I intend to speak to the physician who signed my husband's death certificate, then to the police to see if they recovered any of Lind's personal belongings that were missing when the body was found. After that … I don't know. Perhaps I'll visit those villages closest to Tsingy. I am curious about the relationship between the number and severity of these storms and about the number of victims in that particular area. Then there is this problem about a radio transmitter supposedly operating inside the reserve. I will certainly have to check into this."

"Oh," said Bannerman, his brain going on full alert. "Where did you hear about the radio?"

"Another forester who worked with my husband, Wilhem, told me this is why Lind was in the reserve in the first place — to try and locate the source of this powerful transmitter he had picked up on his tape recorder a few weeks earlier."

"The man you said was killed on the day of your husband's funeral."

Anna nodded. "An accident — supposedly."

One of the waiters swooped down on their table with a large plate of various seafood in one hand and several tiny bowls of delicious-smelling sauces in the other. Their exotic odors were downright sensual to Bannerman.

Sam was becoming impatient with the detective's reluctance to part with information. "Come on, Charlie, loosen up. If you don't tell her why we're here, I will."

"Am I permitted?" asked the policeman, his mournful look aggressively fixed on the hors d'oeuvres.

"Do help yourself, Charlie," said Anna sweetly. "But only on condition that you tell me everything."

He already had his fork poised by the time her second sentence hit home. "Have it your way, lady. I just hope one day I don't get asked to ID your corpse."

Bannerman's eyes had a certain fire in them when he was eating. Now his eyes positively glowed. "These are wonderful. Please, try some."

Sam shook his head, glancing at Anna. "Nice of you to ask."

They watched in silence while Charlie devoured half the plate. Even while munching away on his second meal of the evening,

Bannerman's investigative logic was hard at work. It seemed an incredible stroke of luck to have pinned down the location of the mystery orchid so quickly. And he had always been suspicious of incredible strokes of luck. After a few minutes he stopped, wiped his mouth and fingers, leaned back and looked across the table at Anna.

"You want to know the whole story? Well, there isn't one, just a few facts and lots of speculation. Until you identified the orchid, we couldn't even be sure we were in the right country."

"You are a policeman, aren't you?"

Charlie smiled. "Guess I don't come across as much of a physicist, huh?"

"It isn't that. Perhaps it's more the way you construct your reasoning. Interpol?"

"No, ma'am. Try the New York City police department. Lieutenant Charlie Bannerman, Twenty-First Precinct, Homicide. What made you say Interpol?"

Anna didn't answer immediately, because the whole thing — having dinner with a world-renowned biologist and a homicide policeman from America — suddenly struck her as highly implausible. "Oh, it's nothing, really. I have a cousin who is supposed to work for Interpol. But he …. Never mind, please go on."

Charlie caught the hesitation but went on to outline their reasons for coming to the island, telling most of what they had learned to date, but not all. He stored away the bit about the cousin for future reference. By the time he finished, Anna had several questions ready, which she fired at him nonstop.

Sam was content to eat his meal in silence, enjoying the pleasure of watching two keen minds at work. Every now and then he would turn his head to observe Anna's habit of pushing her mouth forward just as she was about to speak, like she was getting ready to bite into the words. Occasionally she would become aware of his attention and turn toward him with a quizzical look on her face. Her near shoulder-length hair was tawny, the color of a coconut. Sometimes a few strands would fall forward as she dipped her head to eat, and then she would give a quick little toss to put them back in place. He sensed that she was an unusual woman, not only because of her extraordinary looks, but because she was both intelligent and sensitive and cared deeply for her fellow human beings. Bloom had experienced that caring first-hand. He had no doubt that she could have had a lucrative practice somewhere in her native Switzerland, but instead she had chosen to work with the poor of Africa.

Dinner was over, the second bottle of Bordeaux finished off, and their little Arabic café now three-quarters empty. It was seven minutes past midnight. Bannerman insisted on paying the bill, which he did in US dollars; in return he received a handful of Malagasy francs for change. They entered the street in time to see an open truck full of soldiers lumber by, their cherry-red berets at odds with their jungle camouflage outfits.

Anna noticed the tense look on Sam's face. "They patrol the central city core every night after dark," she said as she took his arm. "I understand it has been going on for years."

Sam nodded. He had not considered what would happen if uniformed soldiers came to take him in for questioning. The sudden thought of having to face up to another interrogation caused him to break out in a sweat.

She sensed Bloom's anxiety and tightened her grip. "These soldiers are here to protect the tourists. Lind told me they are well-disciplined and do not behave badly, as they do in many other African countries. You are a tourist, are you not?"

He was amazed at her perception and touched by her concern. Charlie was staring at him as well, and Bloom didn't need to be told what was going through his mind.

Bannerman shook his head a couple of times, setting aside his personal predicament, and took up the rear as they set out for the hotel. He wondered about these two drawing so close in so little time.

The Tana Weston had been constructed upon the ruins of an old fortress and commanded a view that was unmatched anywhere in the city. They turned to look down over the flickering lights that enclosed the moonlit circle of Lake Anosy while a smiling little man unlocked the courtyard gate to let them in. The air had cooled considerably in the last few hours, which Charlie thought was odd until he remembered that they were close to the five-thousand-foot level. Inside the courtyard, band members were packing away their instruments. The number of guests on the veranda had dwindled to a few small groups. Tana, apparently, was a city that retired early.

Charlie collected his key and said good-night in the lobby. His brain felt a bit spongy and he longed for bed, even an unfamiliar bed in a strange land. They parted with an agreement that he and Bloom would conduct their investigation in Toamasina, which he expected would take a few days, then fly over to Morondava and meet with Anna. Bloom didn't want her to go wandering around the countryside by herself, and Charlie agreed wholeheartedly.

Sam and Anna climbed the stairs silently, side by side, each harboring their own thoughts. Bloom's room was nearest the head of the stairs, and there they stopped.

"Will you be spending Christmas in Africa?" he asked. Christmas was just one month away.

"Yes, I suppose in some little village in the Sudan, where they have never heard of it. And you?"

"Haven't given it a lot of thought just yet. I'm presently on loan to the Smithsonian from the university where I teach, Stanford. If it can be arranged, I wouldn't mind staying on here awhile. After all, Madagascar is every botanist's dream."

She looked down, noticing the red mud on her shoes. "What about your family?"

"I have no family — oh, I shouldn't discount poor old George, my brother."

She kept looking down, wondering why her pulse was racing. "No mother or father, no wife and children?"

"None," he answered quietly. Sam desperately wanted to invite her into his room but hesitated, fearing it might cheapen the relationship that seemed to be developing between them.

"Look, we're off at nine. Can you ... will you have breakfast with us?"

Anna smiled, raising her eyes to meet his. "Of course I will. Who knows, I may owe you my life." Her smile fell away when she recalled the terrible state she had earlier found him in. "Can I ask you one question, a personal question? But I want you to promise not to answer if it makes you feel uncomfortable."

"Go ahead."

"You never answered me about the Vietnam War. Is that where all those scars came from?"

He looked away, wondering if she really knew how personal her question was. Finally, he nodded. "They aren't so bad. It's the ones you can't see that play hell."

She knew exactly what he meant. He was leaning against the door with the thumb of his right hand hooked into his belt. Anna gently closed her fingers on his wrist. "Will you tell me what they did to your eyes?"

Bloom tensed. The woman had just crossed into forbidden territory. "That's two questions," he said sharply.

"I am asking because I may be able to help."

"Lady, it's been twenty years. A whole raft of experts has gone to work on me since then. I was a pilot, and when the Cong shot me down a second time, they made damn sure I would never fly again."

Anna increased the pressure of her grip. "I don't understand what they could have done to cause your eyes to react only under adversity."

But all her questions did was place a wall between them, the same wall that had caused his separation and eventual divorce seventeen long, lonely years ago. He pulled his arm away and turned to place the key in the lock.

"Please, I didn't realize how sensitized you were. I am truly sorry."

Bloom stood in the doorway of his darkened room, just like she first found him. "So am I, Dr. Grenier. So am I."

CHAPTER SEVEN

Curtis Johnson's official title was Naval Attaché to the US Ambassador to the Republic of Madagascar, though he had yet to board a naval vessel of any kind. When he informed his boss about Dr. Bloom accidently knocking off one of the locals, Ambassador Wright's solution was to draw up two special identity cards stating that both men were bona fide members of his staff and recipient of all rights and privileges that go with it, including diplomatic immunity. The cards were dated the day of their arrival. Johnson explained on the way to Ivato Airport that the embassy was supposed to submit the names, ranks, position, and so on of all foreign diplomatic personnel to the Madagascar government prior to their acceptance. However, in reality this rule was seldom followed to the letter.

Their diplomatic cards, which now formed part of their passports, also permitted them to board domestic flights without having to pass through the usual security checks. This was important because Johnson had arrived with two boxes of cartridges and a pair of Colt .45 semi-automatics he had borrowed from Marine Corps personnel stationed at the embassy. These were large weapons, which they decided to place in their carry-on bags for the time being. Charlie checked the action on his and loaded the magazine before putting it away.

"What happens if you uncover evidence of cocaine on board the *Lucinda V?*" Johnson wanted to know.

"Nothing, for now," Bannerman replied. "But in case we do run into difficulties, what kind of relationship do you have with the local police?"

"The civil authorities are mostly French, easy to deal with. But the military controls the police. This means that anything of significance is usually handled by the big boys, who are all Malagasy and a touch unpredictable. Madagascar doesn't have a serious drug problem, so they have practically no experience in that field."

Johnson had chosen a different route to the airport, and their present hillside road allowed them to view a swath of white parasols covering the streets below where crowds of people were milling about. "The Zoma," Sam explained to Charlie. "Tana's eternal marketplace. Whatever you need, they have, or will find it while you wait."

It was a fine clear day. The air was scented with spices from the Zoma, and the scenic view across the winding outline of Lake Anosy first class postcard material. The temperature was in the low eighties. Bannerman pulled out his map of Toamasina. "What about the port authorities — any suggestions?"

Their driver didn't respond until he had successfully needled the Ford between a pair of plodding two-horse carriages. "I'm telling you this in confidence, so keep it to yourselves. For the last eighteen months the Soviets have been upgrading the port to take larger ships. We have a small ... operation in Toamasina that monitors their progress. The man in charge is French, a local who's worked for us for several years. Name is Giles Lamont, runs a small bar near the docks. Show him your IDs and ask his advice. The bar is called the Mad-Giles, hyphenated."

"I hope that isn't an accurate description of Mr. Lamont?"

Johnson smiled oddly at Charlie's question. "I expect you will find both Monsieur Lamont and his bar a little out of the ordinary."

The single strip of tarmac outside the port city of Toamasina had just been resurfaced, so the odor of fresh asphalt was overpowering as their aircraft taxied a short distance to the modest airport terminal.

"It's a goddamn sweatbox!" Bannerman declared as soon as he hit the tarmac.

"Welcome to the coast. Don't worry, it only gets worse. Let's pray to God our hotel has air-conditioning."

Bloom signed for the car while Charlie went to the money exchange. He noticed right off that the people milling about the airport were somewhat larger in stature and darker, more African-looking. The car turned out to be a 1978 Citroen, without air, that had recently been occupied by a herd of goats, or so it seemed. Sam drove while Bannerman navigated. Protruding smokestacks indicated the presence of some kind of industry, but there appeared to be little wealth in evidence. Many buildings were old and worn, their once brightly-colored façades peeling away, their balconies rusted, their doors twisted permanently open.

"What a godforsaken place," Charlie ventured. With two-horse taxies more common than automobiles, the streets were sprinkled with piles of fresh horse manure, which in turn were covered by thick clusters of flies. An old Chinese shopkeeper smiled at them as Bloom steered around a particularly large mound. As they neared the ocean, the harsh stink of burning garbage rushed up to meet them. "Yeah," Charlie whispered to himself. "This place even got Harlem beat."

The harbor came into view, a shimmering blue mirror under the boiling midday sun. Several ships were docked, while a dozen more waited their turn to unload or to take on cargo. Bloom pointed out four gray vessels anchored on the south side of the harbor, just inside a long breakwater.

"Russians. Two frigates and a missile carrier. Smaller one looks electronic, maybe one of those new data collectors they deployed a few years back."

It was the first time Bannerman had seen a Soviet warship in the flesh. "I thought this was a French island."

"Not anymore. They turned it back to the locals in sixty-one."

"Who want to turn it over to the Russians, I suppose."

"Hell, who knows? This is Africa; anything is possible. Next year it could be our navy out there."

The Mangola Hotel was jammed in beside all the other buildings along a street that had once been paved, but was now inundated with serious potholes. The building's façade appeared as if it had at one time been painted white and later covered over with a single coat of blue paint. The result was an unpleasant chalky blue.

Bannerman peered through a glass storefront window into the lobby while Sam extracted their bags from the back seat. Sniffing one, he commented, "We'll never get rid of this goddamn stink."

The hotel was full up, French, Russians, Cubans, Koreans, a few traveling locals from out of town. Just one room had been reserved for them, which neither man appreciated at first, until they considered the security angle and decided to go with it.

"Popular place," said Bloom after they had settled in.

"Yeah. How about let's grab a bite and take a drive down to see this Lamont character."

"You're the boss, Lieutenant. You get to call the shots."

The Mad-Giles was one of several run-down bars located along both sides of the main access leading to the dock area just down the street. A lone security guard could be seen lounging in the shade of a tin gatehouse reading a newspaper. The bar itself had such a disgusting exterior that it offended the sensibilities of both men. Three mangy mongrels sprawled across the doorway had left their trademark: heaps of fresh turds scattered all over the place. Pieces of bare clapboard stuck out everywhere. The single-story building appeared to be standing more by the grace of God than by its state of repair. Only the bright green sign mounted on top seemed in good condition, with four buxom gals painted one into each corner.

Bannerman gave his head a shake. "Lower and lower we descend."

"I never saw anything in Nam to outdo this. What kind of a person would spend his life working in this rathole?"

"That's what we're here to find out. Buy you a beer?"

Bloom grimaced. "I don't know … the old stomach might not be able to handle it."

"Probably something to do with all this quality fertilizer."

The dogs didn't bat an eye as the two mid-afternoon customers stepped over them. The inside was dark and gloomy, and the stink of last night's puke and spilled beer quickly supplanted the heady aroma of dog feces. Aside from a hefty stained-glass lamp hanging over the bar, the dim light came from several hurricane lanterns mounted on the walls. Four Peter Lorre wicker fans in the ceiling kept the air moving. A dark kid of indeterminate race was working a mop around the two dozen heavy wooden tables left standing. He had piled nearly all the chairs and some of the tables at the back in order to get more working room. Aside from the boy and an attractive black woman leaning over the bar reading a French pocket novel, the place was empty.

"Good timing, I'd say," Sam muttered.

The woman picked up the English words. "Oh la, American. Is ya?"

"Is ya," Charlie agreed. "Old friends of Mr. Lamont. Is he around at the moment?"

She smiled and thrust out her breasts, showing both the space between her middle top teeth and her amazing cleavage to good advantage. "Yankee doodle dandy!" she exclaimed happily.

"*Très bon,*" Sam said. He asked essentially the same question in French.

She cocked her head to one side and blew out over her bottom lip several times before firing off a question to the kid. The boy barely looked up as he gave a sharp "*Non!*"

The barmaid smiled again, saying in French, "My husband is sleeping. His brat will not wake him, and I will certainly not wake him. If you stay for two, maybe three drinks, he will come and you will see him."

Bloom pulled out a picture of Ben Franklin and waved it in front of her. She snatched the hundred and placed it under her nose. "Oh la! For this he will surely rise."

Bannerman had once seen a TV program of a grizzly emerging from its den in springtime. So it was with Giles Lamont as he emerged from the back of his hovel, scratching and farting as he made his way across the floor with the hundred clutched in his left hand. He was a short, barrel-chested man with a gut that even outdid Bannerman's. He came to a stop in front of Bloom and cast his bloodshot eyes up as his right hand hit the bar to receive the drink already poured by his wife.

"I look at you and I say CIA. I look at this bill and I say CIA. But I look at him," he said, indicating Bannerman with a flick of his eyes, "and I say not CIA."

Charlie was intrigued. "You're Lamont, I take it?"

Some of the drink he had thrown into his mouth missed and found its way into the ragged black and white hair surrounding it. His hand hit the bar again and his glass was instantly refilled. Charlie noticed his wife was pouring from a bottle of ouzo.

He was more careful with the second drink and worked it around his mouth for a few seconds before swallowing. "Ahhh ... okay!" This was followed by another great burst of flatulence, which brought a small grin to his face as he pulled up a shapeless gray shirt and began aimlessly moving his fingers among the coarse black hair. "Okay, okay. Business. Order up and come into my office."

His wife had not understood the words, but she understood his motion. "Please?"

"Nothing for me," Charlie said quickly.

Sam pointed to the bottle of ouzo she was holding. "A little of that would be fine."

Compared to the public section, Lamont's living quarters were definitely upscale. With a good cleaning, a fresh coat of paint, and one of those machines used to get rid of odors, the place might even be livable. A pair of what looked to be human skulls boxed in clear plastic sat atop an old Heintzman piano. They were small and bleached pure white.

Lamont caught Bannerman's look and strolled over to the piano. "A perfectly matched set. Twins," he added proudly.

Sam entered the room and went over to join them. "South America?"

"No, no, certainly not. The Mekong River delta, nineteen fifty-three. We surrounded this miserable little village and killed off the whole goddamn works. We set her afire and out run these kids. I nailed them both and walk up and see they are twins. So I say to the commandant, 'These make good souvenirs — okay if I keep them?' 'Sure,' he says. And here they are. Nice, eh?"

Bloom found it difficult to mask his disgust. "You were with the French forces?"

Lamont grinned, showing off a mouthful of gold fillings. "Paratroopers. Our motto was 'kill or be killed.' Original, eh? We shoot first, second, and third. We don't ask questions at all!"

This gave way to a hearty laugh. "You guys went in with daisies in your teeth. No wonder they throw you out."

Bannerman had found a reasonably clean wicker chair to sit in. He pulled out his passport with the embassy ID attached and held it up for Lamont to inspect. "You recognize this?"

"Sure, CIA. So I am wrong. What is it you want Lamont to do this time?"

Charlie started to tell the Frenchman they were not CIA, but then figured it didn't matter a damn what he thought. "You ever heard of the *Lucinda V*, a freighter that stops in here a few times a year?"

Lamont sat down on the piano stool. "She's an old one. Sometimes the crew comes in. Sure, I know her."

"We heard rumors she might be carrying a little extra cargo out of Buenos Aires. You ever hear anything like that?"

"Extra cargo — meaning guns or drugs, maybe." He considered this for a moment. "She's an old scow, been working the east coast for thirty years. Greek captain and crew, Liberian — no, Panamanian registry. Poof — I think she carries just the usual cargos."

Bannerman was breaking new ground with this kind of unorthodox investigation. He had considered earlier what steps to take. "We have reason to believe cocaine is being shipped to Europe via Madagascar, but we don't know how. We'll need to find out everything we can about the type of cargo the *Lucinda V* normally brings to the island, plus details on whatever she takes on here in Toamasina."

Giles Lamont remained still for a full minute, then began using both hands to smooth over his mass of unkempt hair, all the while staring down at the floor. "If you mean lists — cargo lists — the ship's manifest tells you these things and more. It names all the ports, what is being left behind, and what they pick up at each stop. But I think you want to look at this cargo, eh? To see what is inside the boxes. This is not so easy. But it's crazy to think drugs come here."

"Why?" Bloom asked after sampling his shot of ouzo.

"Why? Because this poor island is full of socialists who have no money for drugs, very little even to drink—" He stopped abruptly, knitting his bushy eyebrows into a deep furrow. "Did you not just say these drugs go to Europe? Ya! So, what is the difference about cargo going off, cargo going on here in Toama? Please, you explain."

Bannerman eased his back off the chair, as his gun was digging into his kidneys. "It's a bit complicated, but we believe the stuff is unloaded somewhere on the island, run through some kind of special treatment, then loaded back aboard ship. It might be the same ship, or it could be a different one."

"Maybe not even Toamasina, eh?"

"Maybe not," Charlie told him. "But the *Lucinda V* is our prime suspect at the moment."

Lamont glanced up at the clock. "She's in dock now?"

"Due in this evening, apparently. Can you help us?"

"Of course! I am big friend to CIA. How many days in port?"

"Afraid we don't know."

"Okay, okay. I find out some things. Where do you guys stay?"

"At the Mangola."

"Okay, give me five hundred dollars for *baksheesh*. I talk to some sailors, maybe—only maybe. Please, the afternoon shift comes soon, so better you take off now. I come to your hotel tomorrow, at three." He grinned as he took the bills from Charlie. "See, for CIA I miss afternoon siesta for two days."

With the holidays coming up, Bahnhofstrasse was dressed in its finest. Lights and decorations sparkled in store windows as the merchants and early morning shoppers greeted each other with cheery smiles. Herr Brower's regular route to the old opera house, which is how he always referred to ZIAN headquarters, took him across the Quai bridge and on to the Bahnhof. From the rear seat of his Mercedes limousine he was able to glance left and right to see what changes were taking place along the famous street. As he had every Christmas since first settling in Zurich, he eagerly anticipated having his family gather around him once again. This year a fifth great-grandchild had been added to the list. It was such a wonderful time.

The limousine turned left onto Fussli and pulled over to the curb. His chauffeur opened the door, and Herr Brower stepped out into the fresh snow that had fallen overnight. The air was frosty and sweet. He made his way carefully up the steps while returning hearty greetings from nearby merchants busily sweeping their sections of the sidewalk. Ah, Zurich, he thought, how good you have been to me. For some time now, he had been considering some special way to express his thanks. But Zurich already had so much.

His secretary greeted him at the top of the staircase with a not-so-happy look on his face. "Fresh snow, Hans, good skiing on the weekend. What could possibly make you look so serious on such a beautiful day?"

"Good morning, Herr Director. Another transcript from the island arrived overnight. Wassel has just now delivered it."

Herr Brower handed his hat and scarf to the young man and turned to allow him to slip off his topcoat. "Bad news, is it, Hans?"

"I don't believe you will consider it good, sir."

"My dear boy, one must learn to accept the bad with the good and then make adjustments. Such is life."

"Yes, Herr Brower," his secretary answered patiently.

Including the men who worked in the taxidermy studio deep down in the bowels of the old opera house, the Zurich International Association of Naturalists kept twenty-eight employees on permanent staff. It had become a time-honored tradition for the administrative staff on the fourth floor to stand in the hallway outside their office doors to bid the director good morning. Herr Brower always had a smile and a kind word for all. However, only Hans and the six controllers who manned the powerful satellite transmitter in an old house up behind University Hospital had complete access to the inner world of ZIAN.

The controllers at Moussonstrasse had several duties to perform, their main task being to keep track of each phase of ZIAN's multifaceted operations, from the initial harvesting of the opium in central Turkey to its transformation into heroin. Its final destination was usually a warehouse in one of five major US cities. The number of individual projects varied seasonally, never exceeding an upper limit of fifteen. Competition from the vast Indonesia-producing areas was always present, which in recent years had become a vital secondary function of the controllers: To monitor and coordinate the flow of information from ZIAN's own field staff and then to pass the data directly to Interpol's Paris headquarters. Interpol verified and re-coordinated this information with its other sources and then notified the appropriate national police agency.

The controllers also monitored the Tsingy operation, where the most daring experiment ever undertaken by ZIAN was nearing completion.

Along with his other talents, Herr Brower possessed a remarkable sense of vision. He had observed the astonishing growth of the cocaine trade and had foreseen the imminent downfall of the lucrative heroin business long before any of his wartime colleagues. It had taken sixteen years of complicated maneuvering for ZIAN, working hand in hand with the old guard who still maintained control over Interpol, to seize the lion's share of the heroin market from the Italian Mafia, and Dietrich Brower was determined not to allow a handful of South American gangsters to step in and destroy his hard work.

Despite warnings to the contrary, the first decision of the board of directors had been to communicate with the Colombians. This turned out to be a disastrous mistake, as they quickly found it impossible to deal with men who had so much money that they stored it away in mountain caves. General Enrich Swetmeyer, the youngest of ZIAN's directors, plus six others, including two Interpol agents, had been murdered in a single evening—at a dinner put on in their honor! The Colombians had effectively communicated to the upstart Swiss that they were to keep their noses out of the cocaine trade.

Long-established morning protocol began with a visit by Vera Foch, head of International Affairs, who arrived with a tray of coffee and fresh pastries from the bakery across the road. A stout woman of sixty-three who had dedicated her life to the preservation of species, Frau Foch possessed an ardor that occasionally bordered on militarism. She also had several grandchildren, and much of each visit often covered their recent activities. Herr Brower did not mind this at all and frequently indulged in stories of his own. Of course, he never mentioned such incidents as the time the Gestapo rounded up a dozen young schoolgirls in Dresden and had them boiled alive in the main square. Such memories inflicted pain now, but he was able to draw comfort from knowing that he had been acting under orders; and in wartime examples did have to be made, even among one's own people.

Frau Foch knew there was more going on inside ZIAN than what was outlined in the stated objectives, the primary one being the investigation and documentation of worldwide reports of threatened or endangered species. The second was the collection, mounting, and distribution of the more common species of birds and animals to museums and centers for natural history throughout the world. This secondary activity, while on the surface appearing to be in conflict with the main goal, created a constant infusion of capital and was accepted as ZIAN's principal source of funding. But Vera Foch had long ago learned that the association tended to have more money on hand than could be expected from such transactions. The director claimed this additional funding came from certain wealthy foundations that preferred to remain anonymous. Since ZIAN was the preeminent organization of its kind, she did not find this explanation unreasonable. However, from time to time she had seen strange, hard-faced men enter the director's office. As well, occasional rumors of illicit activities flitted about Zurich like hummingbirds, but she took such rumors as a personal affront and reacted accordingly.

She also knew Herr Brower well enough by now to sense when he was preoccupied, and in such instances tended to cut her visits short. After she left, Hans came back in and shut the door. He removed the transcript from his coat pocket and passed it to his boss.

The old man pulled his chair in, changed his glasses, and began to read: "'Local assigned to follow AG beaten to death. Two US citizens seen in the area, but their complicity not ascertained. ID: Charles Bannerman, Ht. 1.75; Wt. 100; est age 58; thick black to gray hair. Samuel Bloom, Ht. 1.85; Wt. 85; est age 41; short brown hair. Hotel registration shows both as botanists from Smithsonian Institute. AG met with Tana police yesterday, expected to leave today for Swiss Forestry Station. US citizens due to depart this morning for Mangola Hotel in Toama. Await your instructions. Victor.'"

Herr Brower looked up. "Beaten to death, Hans. Does that sound like the work of two American scientists? What nonsense. Bloom happens to be a world-renowned botanist and is one of our own members. He spoke here in ... eighty-three? No, eighty-two. It is perfectly natural for him to be in Madagascar. And if he has an assistant, does this not also appear to be in order? Only their arrival at Toamasina on the very day the *Lucinda V* is due to dock is suspect. Give me your opinion, Hans."

The younger man had been standing behind the director watching a new snowfall gather intensity. "I should think you will need to know considerably more, sir. There appears to be too heavy a degree of speculation to act definitively. Perhaps Paris could make a few discreet inquiries ...?"

"That is exactly where I shall begin. Get Henri on the telephone and I will outline our position. And have Wassel contact Captain Demetrios to warn him of the Americans, just in case."

Hans clicked his heels. "Immediately, Herr Director."

Four minutes later the director of the Zurich International Association of Naturalists was speaking to the head of European Affairs at Interpol, St. Cloud. After the usual banalities, Herr Brower got down to business. "Henri, there is a possibility that we may have a situation developing on the island. Do you have someone available if a need should arise?"

"There is always someone available to you, Dietrich, my good friend."

On sudden impulse the old man asked, "Where is René Simard at the moment?"

"He and Arond went down to Palermo to see if they can help keep a few of the witnesses alive until the Cosa Nostra trial is over — difficult, with such a huge price on their heads."

"Ah yes, our poor competitors." Henri was referring to the large number of Sicilians who had recently been charged with everything from drug running to murder. "How is the trial proceeding?"

"Excellent. The officials know they have to be tough this time, and they will. The whole thing is expected to finally end next week. I should think having some four hundred mafiosi put out of business is bound to strengthen our market position."

"Indeed, and you have also provided an excellent alibi for young Simard to have left his cousin so abruptly. Would you be kind enough to have him call me as soon as possible? Plus, Henri, I have two names for you. I want you to contact your people in Washington and have them find out what reasons were given on their visa applications to visit the island."

The director read off the names and other information from the transcript. "Have them find out whatever they can. One man we already know, but perhaps not well enough. Time is critical, Henri. I must have this information quickly, within hours if possible."

"And so you shall, old friend, and so you shall."

Henri Lapierre radioed his formal request to Washington via regular channels with an urgent code prefix. The task was assigned to Dan Glover, a US citizen and Interpol veteran of twelve years. Glover had to wait until 8:00 a.m. Washington time before getting on the telephone. His first call told him that the visas had not come through the embassy, but through the consulate in New York. A woman at the Smithsonian told him that Dr. Bloom had taken a sudden leave of absence. She didn't know why. No, there was no Dr. Bannerman working there. No, she had never heard of a Dr. Bannerman practicing in the same field as Dr. Bloom.

Like Vera Foch at ZIAN, Dan Glover was aware that not all was kosher at Interpol. Stories floated around the capital and books had been written condemning Interpol for 'selective' handling of drug runners. From time to time, it even turned out that such stories were not without substance. Yet he was convinced the work they did in Washington was honest and without bias. What he didn't know, of course, was the true identity of the source behind many of the requests that came from Interpol Paris.

During the next half hour, Glover learned that just one of eleven Charles Bannermans listed in the New York City telephone directory was out of town at the moment, and that particular one happened to be a policeman. The NYPD precinct list, a computerized printout updated once a month, told him Charles Bannerman was a lieutenant in homicide at the Twenty-First Precinct. The terse voice answering at the Twenty-First told him Lieutenant Bannerman was on special assignment and no one knew where the hell he was.

This information was received at Interpol Paris and relayed back to the director by Henri Lapierre. It was just after lunch in Zurich when Herr Brower called Hans back into his office.

"Bannerman is a policeman, a homicide detective with the City of New York. What do you make of that, Hans?"

After taking time to mull it over, Hans replied, "It does not look promising, Herr Director. It almost leads one to believe something has happened in New York that tipped off the police."

"And yet, we know that the altering of a single chromosome cannot be detected by any known means. Even if this were possible, how could such knowledge lead them to Madagascar?"

"I agree, sir, but unless this detective is an amateur botanist or they are old acquaintances or even related in some way, then the unfortunate conclusion is that the police must know something."

"That, my dear boy, would indeed be unfortunate." Herr Brower kept an old briar pipe on his desk, a memento from bygone days. Occasionally he liked to stick it between his shiny capped teeth to suck on it and imagine there was real tobacco in the bowl. He did this now, while considering his secretary's observations.

Hans remained at a modest form of attention exactly one meter in front of the director's desk, attending to his unofficial role of chief sounding board. He knew the next question that would be asked of him and was preparing the answer in his mind.

"So, Hans, we are faced with a dilemma. It seems we must now give serious consideration to these two Americans who have appeared in Toamasina at such an inopportune moment. The question which raises its ugly but necessary head is, what do we intend to do about it, if anything?"

His secretary was ready. "As I see it, sir, these first small shipments were in the form of an experiment, the successful culmination of which has just recently come to pass. It has allowed us to see what would happen to the cocaine trade under killing pressure, so to speak. And our sales have climbed by seven hundred percent in the last ten days. But all of those shipments together were barely enough to maintain the supply for a few weeks in one major center. When the *Lucinda V* leaves port this time, it will have on board enough chemically-altered substance to last for years, and the operation on Madagascar will be permanently shut down. Is this not true, Herr Director?"

The old man nodded, listening attentively to the carefully chosen words.

"Then the plan *must* go ahead at all costs. If these Americans are a threat, and it appears almost certain that they are, my advice is to play it safe. What better place to play it safe than in such an isolated part of the world? The blame could not possibly fall upon ZIAN's shoulders."

Herr Brower removed his pipe and looked up at his secretary with a new sense of respect. Perhaps there was hope for the lad after all. "And the woman?"

"Her intentions remain unclear. The main question concerns the man following her. Why was he killed? Were the Americans protecting her? I doubt if that was the case. Nor do I find it unusual for her to wish to visit her husband's colleagues."

"And if we were to learn that she is connected with the Americans in some way?"

Hans looked over at the thick snowflakes melting against the windowpane. "I should think, sir, that such a connection would seal her fate."

The director nodded. "Then I believe the time has come for Monsieur Simard to resurrect himself and take care of these problematic loose ends."

CHAPTER EIGHT

Morondava was a small port located on the central westerly coast of Madagascar, eighty kilometers due west of the Swiss forestry station, a training center where young Malagasy were taught how to care for and harvest their forest without destroying it. The station was positioned about one hundred and twenty kilometers south of the Tsingy National Reserve of Bemaraha.

Marina Scheuchzer, wife of the station manager, met Anna Grenier at the Morondava airport and drove her to the station. During the bumpy drive, Anna mentioned nothing of her recent troubles; but that evening, seated around the big table in the main house among her late husband's closest friends, Anna told her story.

The telling took considerable time, during which several bottles of good Swiss claret were consumed. Other than an occasional gasp as her tale unfolded, not once was she interrupted. When she finished, the silence hung dark and heavy over the table. Marina's sympathetic countenance was fixed upon her, and this angered Anna.

"I do not believe for one moment that Wilhem's death was an accident," she added in a sharper tone. "A clever murder, more likely. Both my cousin and Dr. Lyon have since vanished. You may believe such coincidences are possible. I do not!"

"But surely, Anna," Klaus asked gently, "in the case of Lind, when a person is clearly struck down by lightning, where can we go from there?"

Perhaps she had taken on a little too much wine, because then her temper really flared. "I am not satisfied; I am damn well not satisfied! And before leaving this island, I want some answers."

Klaus did not respond, and the other five foresters, all in their mid to late twenties, were clearly embarrassed. Even Marina was somewhat taken aback. "You have told us some disturbing things, Anna," she said. "But this is the outback of Madagascar. There is nothing evil here, unless you count the state of famine that has befallen the poor natives. I know there are stories about Tsingy, tales the natives make up, but this is Africa, after all. Tsingy certainly has no radio transmitter. Heavens, there is nothing at all in Tsingy besides the wild creatures that live there."

Anna took another good swig of claret and put her glass down slowly. "Then I will have to find this out for myself."

"Dr. Grenier, there are no proper roads leading into the reserve," said one of the young foresters. "Willi and Gerhard even had to use a winch to reach the perimeter."

"So, perhaps I will hire a helicopter."

"But what will you look for?" asked Klaus. "I have flown over these limestone spires a few times. It is a complete maze; everything looks the same."

"And we found Lind at least ten kilometers east of the reserve," added Gerhard, the one who was with Wilhem when Lind's body was recovered. "I know Willi said Lind had gone into the reserve to look for a radio signal, but the truth is that he was found a good distance away. I don't see how you can associate his death with Tsingy."

"Nevertheless, that is what I believe and will continue to believe until I am faced with irrefutable evidence to the contrary."

After a moment's awkward silence, another of the lads cleared his throat. He was the youngest of the foresters and had said little throughout dinner. "If Lind and Willi really were murdered, as you seem to believe, then I would pray to God that I can lay my hands on those responsible."

Anna smiled at him. Like Lind and Willi, all the foresters were huge men. She had earlier noticed the size of his hands. His quietly spoken words made her feel better immediately. "Thank you, Danny. I just know that something is very, very wrong. For all these things to just … happen is preposterous. All of you were Lind's friends, and I hope I can count on that friendship if a need should arise."

Marina stood up and walked down to the other end of the table where Anna was seated. She leaned over and gave her a big hug. "Such a silly thing to say, Anna. Of course you can count on us."

Gerhard was the last to leave. Anna walked with him toward his cottage, breathing the sweet perfume from a pair of jacaranda trees just beyond the compound. The moon had cast an unearthly lustrous glow over the courtyard, broken here and there by dark shadows extending from the tops of a clump of tamarind trees behind the manager's house. Muted calls from a troop of nearby ringtails prompted Caesar to issue a low growl.

"It is odd, you know. During daylight hours the lemurs are his playmates. Even the little ones jump up on his back for rides. But once darkness falls, he somehow knows that the security of the camp becomes his responsibility. Not a single item has been stolen since Willi brought him down."

The mastiff's great head rubbed against Anna's elbow. She ran her fingers through the stiff golden hair on his neck. "I suppose in the midst of all of you, he doesn't even know Willi is gone for good."

"No, I suppose not. To tell you the truth, I don't believe it really came home to any of us until tonight. Somehow it was too much to accept that Willi was killed just hours after they buried Lind. God has not played fair with us, Dr. Grenier."

"Please, you must call me Anna." They had reached the outside steps of Gerhard's cottage, which fell within the shadow of a fine old baobab tree. "What exactly did Willi say when you two were out searching for Lind?"

The young man thought about this for a few moments. "You know about the radio signal, and how he came to suspect it?"

Anna said she did, but wanted to hear how Willi explained it to him.

"He said Lind's tape recorder had picked up several high-speed bursts somewhere in the low megahertz range. Just like spies would use, he said. He found it amusing, as if this poor island had anything worthwhile to spy upon."

Hearing Gerhard describe the actual type of transmission gave Anna a sudden twinge of excitement. "Do you believe Willi knew electronics well enough to be certain of his analysis?"

Gerhard nodded. "I believe so. Willi looked after the camp radios. There was nothing he couldn't fix."

Anna went on to question Gerhard about certain other aspects Willi had related to him, and then about the actual position of Lind's body, the weather, and everything else she could think of. They were quietly discussing all this when Anna heard the telephone in the main house.

Gerhard stopped talking when Klaus came out on the porch. "It's for you, Anna," he called out.

Her heart leaped at the sudden surprise. Only her mother and the two Americans knew her present location. "Who is it?" she asked as she approached the bottom of the veranda steps.

Klaus shrugged. "A man."

It must be Sam Bloom, she thought. How nice. "Hello? This is Anna Grenier."

"Anna, thank God I've found you at last."

The reception was terrible, but there was no mistaking the voice. "Is it really you?" she asked, searching around for a chair.

"Yes, Anna. I'm so sorry for having to run out on you like that, but there was absolutely no choice, I assure you."

"Where are you?"

"I'm still in Palermo. I found out just an hour ago that you called the office looking for me. They are supposed to pass along all such inquires immediately, but I have been out of touch since I left you."

Anna ran the fingers of her left hand through her hair, an old childhood habit that returned whenever she was under stress. "René, whatever are you doing in Sicily, and which damned office are you talking about?"

"You know the one, Anna. I'm sorry about the Bureau of Statistics story, but that is my standing cover."

"Then you are with Interpol?"

"Yes, for eleven years. You must have heard of the big Cosa Nostra trial here in Palermo. St. Cloud was asked by the Italian police to send in two of the original undercover men who helped set up the bust. There was strong evidence that the top mafiosi had put out a one-billion-lira contract to murder the five key witnesses in the case. Two of us went back into the hills to uncover the identities of the hit team. They did get one of the witnesses, but we managed to keep the others alive until they were able to give their evidence. They shot another one since then, and I suppose sooner or later the poor devils will all be killed. I had no way of knowing you were trying to reach me until I contacted the office. Then I called Geneva and heard your message."

"But the message said I was going to Brazzaville. How were you able to locate me?"

"Anna, Anna, I am a policeman. It was a matter of making enough telephone calls. But what are you doing in Madagascar?"

She suddenly found it all very confusing. "Then you haven't heard about Wilhem and Dr. Lyon?"

"I have heard nothing at all. What about them?"

"God, René, don't you even know that Willi is dead? And Dr. Lyon vanished on the day of the funeral, just like you did. Damn you, René, I thought you were dead, too. What else was I to believe?"

"I can't believe what you are telling me, Anna, it's—"

"And my flat was burgled the night of the funeral, and a man was following me here in the capital."

"What happened?"

"Two Americans happened along, thank God, and took care of that problem."

"You mean two strangers just came along and told the man to stop following you?"

"Yes, René, something like that."

"What in God's name is going on? Do you know?"

"I bloody well do not. Don't you see? That is why I had to come down here. And now I am more convinced than ever that something terrible is happening and that Lind and Willi were killed because of it."

118

"Anna, listen to me. You are not to leave that camp. I will telephone La Sûreté and have them contact the island police. They will send over some men to watch you. I'm taking the first plane out and will be there as quickly as possible. I have excellent contacts in police agencies all over the world, and I promise we will get to the bottom of this. You will be my number one assignment from now on. Now, get some sleep, but let me speak to Herr Scheuchzer for a moment."

Anna said good-bye and passed the receiver to Klaus. "It's my cousin, the one who was missing."

The station manager spoke to René for a few minutes, mostly answering questions. Marina had been standing across the kitchen by the stove. She turned now, smiling. "It's good news, I can tell."

Anna nodded happily. Her load was growing lighter by the second. In Geneva she had detected something hard in her cousin, giving her cause to wonder. But working undercover among dangerous criminals would do that to any man. Now he was coming here to look after her.

"Thank God he's okay," she said after Klaus hung up. "He works for Interpol, an undercover agent. No wonder he had to leave so abruptly. He is coming down tomorrow or the day after. Can you put him up, Marina?"

"Of course we can."

"Oh, I'd almost forgotten. The Americans I mentioned at dinner are also flying over in a couple of days, or at least they said they were. Is there room for them?"

Klaus stroked his heavy red beard. "They have not even signed up our new foresters yet, so we still have two vacant cottages. Ah, your cousin speaks good Deutsche, but with a strong accent."

"Because my aunt married a Frenchman, a disgrace back in those days, so I am told. But René is a sweetheart, and I just know he is going to sort out this mess."

119

Bloom and Bannerman went for a late dinner. After their meeting with Giles Lamont, Sam had suggested that they get on with their cover and promptly drove twenty miles out into the rainforest to search for orchids. He told Charlie he needed a crash course and set about giving him one. But the combination of stifling heat and oppressive humidity was too much for the NYPD detective and damn near killed him. He needed a few hours to recover.

But even while he was out there sweating profusely and battling insects, Charlie hadn't missed the change that came over Sam Bloom when he entered his element. Bannerman would have sworn the man got more pleasure from examining these exotic flowers than most men got from sex. Bloom refused to pick any, claiming there was no point if he didn't have the equipment to preserve them properly. He settled instead for a dozen photos whenever they came upon a species he considered rare.

Bloom explained to the policeman the various ways orchids pollinate, how aggressive they are, the little tricks they use to attract their pollinators, and the selective processes they go through while attempting to cross-pollinate. Charlie was surprised to learn that many orchids carried no nectar, depending instead upon mimicry or deceit. Part of this fascinating system was the exquisite scents they provided to attract bees and other insects, including a wide range of multi-colored butterflies, which to the detective were far more interesting than flowers. For a mind like Bannerman's, listening to Sam Bloom's informal overview was a real pleasure. After all, the man was considered the world's leading authority on exotic orchids, and Charlie realized the rare privilege he was being given.

The bistro was located on top of the hotel, with the back half covered over by a Polynesian-style thatched roof and the front half open to the sky. A sprinkling of lights in the harbor disclosed the relative positions of the many cargo vessels and Soviet warships at anchor. Fainter lights in the distance signified other vessels moving up and down the coastline. One set of lights, according to Giles Lamont, might even be the *Lucinda V* on her way into port. Walking through the beaded curtain entry, they saw the place was jammed to the rafters. The music, mellow and bluesy, came from a five-piece ensemble backing up a female vocalist. Bannerman, accustomed to hearing the best, knew this was good stuff. A pair of Koreans seated at a table near the door smiled their wide smiles at the Americans, who were searching for a break in the line of bodies at the bar.

"Look around at the faces," Sam said after they ordered. "Tell me what comes to mind."

Charlie reached over some guy's shoulder to take his beer, then turned to study the clientele. Not being a world traveler like Bloom, he had only his fifty-one years in New York City to call upon. He could tell right off that the patrons came from many nations, but it took him a minute or so to catch Bloom's drift.

"Commies!" he proclaimed.

Bloom nodded. "Slavic features over there, Russians for sure. Cubans at that table, a bunch of East Europeans right in front of us, could be Czechs or Poles. Koreans to your left, northerly type I expect. A whole corner of Chinese, probably not followers of Chiang Kai-shek. Christ, you'd expect old Lenin himself to walk in and begin preaching."

Minutes later, one of the Koreans came over and bowed slightly. "You are American comrades to work on dam?"

Sam glanced at Charlie before shaking his head. "Nope, not us. We're the flower brigade."

"Ah? You are military personnel?"

Bloom smiled. One must learn to watch one's words. "No, no, just a little joke. We happen to be a pair of wandering botanists from the Smithsonian. You ever hear of the Smithsonian?"

"Oh yes, this is a velly good place. You are scientists, yes?"

"Sort of, but nothing to do with the military. What are you boys doing over in this part of the world?"

The man removed two business cards from his wallet and handed one to each American. "Goon Ha-rung, marine engineer, representing Democratic People's Republic of Korea. We are to assist in improvement of dockyard facilities."

Sam introduced himself and Charlie, leaving out the doctor bit. "That's nice, Mr. Ha-rung," the cop said.

"Please, you call me Goon."

Bannerman seemed to consider this for a moment. "Fine by me," he said at last. "You can call me Charlie."

"Please, you have no table. We would be honored to have distinguished scientists to sit at our table — as guests of Democratic People's Republic of Korea, of course."

"Sure, why not?" Sam said. "I'm all in favor of improving international relations."

Bannerman hesitated for a few seconds, concerned about the similarity between the stocky Koreans and Bloom's Vietcong prison guards. After yesterday's performance, it was all too easy to envision his new colleague having a sudden desire to throttle the representative of some Communist country.

The second Korean stood up as they approached. Goon introduced Dun Najin to the Americans. The Orientals took the settee with their backs to the wall, leaving Sam and Charlie the other one on the outside. Dun turned out to be a civil engineer, with both men part of a team that specialized in designing both military and commercial dockyards. They had just completed three months in Diego Suarez, recently renamed Antsiranana, located on the northerly tip of the island.

"Such a beautiful place, but too many Russians," said Dun emphatically.

His comment raised Bannerman's eyebrows. "You don't say?"

"Is true," said Goon. "Maybe two thousand or more." He grinned and succulently added the word, "Assholes."

Such a fitting word, Sam thought. Hearing it gave him a nice warm feeling. "Just to make sure my geography is correct, you are from North Korea?"

"Yes, is true," Goon replied, narrowing his slity eyes even more. "But nowhere is written we must love Soviet peoples. Americans now having big romance with Gorbachev. Soon everyone in America love Soviet peoples. I spit on Soviet peoples!"

His remark started off the first of several stories about the difficulties they had encountered with Russian engineers, first in Angola and later in Diego Suarez.

It was long past midnight when Bannerman noticed a big black guy at the bar. The man turned his head away soon as Charlie's eyes lit on him.

Bannerman stood up, saying he had to go to the can. The man hulked over the bar as Charlie walked behind him. Instinct whispered to him that this character spelled trouble. This was quickly confirmed when he spotted another man leaning up against the wall near the staircase. The guy looked away when Bannerman rounded the corner.

Gotcha, you bastard, Charlie said to himself. How many more were around, he wondered as he relieved himself of his fifth beer. The local stuff, which everyone called THB, meaning Three Horses Beer, tasted a lot better than he had expected to find down in this godforsaken part of the world.

He came back, sat down, and reached under the table to grip Bloom's arm. "You know Sam, I had a long day and not much sleep last night. I think it's time we turned in."

Bloom looked at Bannerman's half-full glass of beer, then at his own. He glanced at Bannerman's face, wondering what was up. "You sure?"

"Yeah, I'm sure."

The good-byes were profuse, with promises to meet again and so on. But then, to Sam's surprise, Bannerman didn't head off to their hotel room.

Charlie wanted to be somewhere out in the open, where he could identify and cope with a potential threat. He broke the news soon as they hit the street, then voiced his concern about Bloom's state of alertness and his ability to stay cool.

"Come on, Lieutenant, I'm in great shape. You give the orders, I obey."

The silly grin on his partner's face didn't do much for Bannerman's confidence. "Your gun loaded?"

"You bet your ass."

Just ahead of them a foursome of Brits was staggering down the street, arms locked around each other, hollering out the lyrics to an old sea shanty. An oxcart being pulled by two big zebu oxen creaked and clunked its way over the broken asphalt.

"No rough stuff this time, Sam. Let's see if we can learn who's behind it—providing it really is us they're after."

They paused at the first street intersection on the pretext of considering a proposal put to them by a couple of tiny Chinese girls. "Son of a bitch!" Charlie said when he glanced back. "I guess we're it. Here they come!"

Bannerman glanced both ways and chose the darker street to the right. "It would be real nice if we could pull this off without guns."

Bloom was listening to the British sailors, now behind them: *"The cabin boy, the cabin boy, that dirty little nipper, stuffed his ass with broken glass and circumcised the skipper."*

"So what's the plan, Charlie? You going to say, 'Excuse me, but I think you nasty black boys are following us. Now please explain why, or we'll take away your bubble gum.'"

"Away, away, with fife and drums, O here we come, all full of rum, looking for women to peddle their bums, in the North Atlantic Squadron."

"Love that song," Bloom said, easing his .45 around to the front. "I'm still waiting to hear the plan."

"My guess is those boys were hired to do more than spin a tail. Let's wait a bit, see what happens."

They began walking downhill on the darker side of a narrow, foul-smelling street caked in horseshit, with garbage strewn in all directions. The cloudy half-moon cast more light than the grimy yellow street lamps. A few doors ahead of them the heavy pounding on at least two big drums sounded to Bloom like something from Haiti, the kind of frantic rhythm that enticed zombies to come out and play. Gave him a creepy feeling.

A lone sailor put in a sudden appearance and sauntered toward them holding in one hand what seemed like his penis, except it looked abnormally large. Slowing down as the guy drew near, Bloom asked, "You own all that?"

"Sure thing, hotshot. Wanna have a closer look?"

"No thanks," he replied as they moved past. But Sam's curiosity made him turn around. "What's the purpose, sailor?"

"Just out trolling for homos. One comes along, me mates pop out of that doorway there and beats his friggin' skull in. Bloody slow tonight, I'll tell you. Only got three so far."

"I see ... well, good fishing."

"Nice little town we got here," said Bannerman, wishing he was back in the Bronx. He took another quick peek over his shoulder. "They're closing. Let's act it up, make them think we took on a bit too much booze."

Sam immediately wrapped himself around a lamppost and opened up with verse five or whatever from the very first song he had learned at Naval Academy: *"The Eskimo women, they are the shits. They have no cracks, they have no tits. They jack you off with their frozen mitts, in the North Atlantic Squadron."* Watching the big blacks put on some speed, he wondered if his singing made them nervous. The next thing he saw made his hair stand on end.

"Charlie, they got machine guns. *Hit the deck!"*

Sam dropped to the street, using the bronze base of the streetlamp for cover; Bannerman threw his bulk into a doorway. The sputter of lead scattered pieces of garbage all around them. *Silencers!* The black men were now less than fifty feet away and walking forward with both weapons extended from the waist, watching for movement.

Bloom figured they were up against a pair of professionals and felt his breath coming in gulps. A quick glance at the doorway told him it was impossible for Bannerman to fire without exposing himself. It was up to Bloom. He pushed the safety off, jerked the breech back and let it slide forward.

As if echoing his thoughts, Charlie called out softly, "Nail the pricks, Sam. Now!"

They were about thirty feet away when his hand snaked out from behind the post. He fired four times. The blasts made his ears ring. He waited a few seconds before easing his head around the other side of the lamppost. One man had keeled over on his side while the other was on his knees, holding his chest with a look of surprise on his face.

Bannerman came out with his pistol held at arm's length, not taking any chances. He stuck the gun into the face of the one on his knees and kicked his machine pistol out of reach. Sam reached down and gingerly extracted the second weapon. The guy was still twitching but wouldn't be around for long.

"Better start asking. I don't reckon we got a whole lot of time before the local gendarmes drop by, see what all the fuss is about."

Bannerman realized the fisherman and his mates were watching from half a block away. He dropped to one knee. "Listen, friend, we need to know who hired you. Tell us that, and we'll call an ambulance. Otherwise you bleed to death."

The guy seemed like he wanted to cooperate, but had trouble getting the words out. When he finally did speak, it was in a foreign language.

"Marvelous!" Charlie exclaimed. "You ask him."

Bloom noticed blood seeping out between the guy's fingers. He knelt down beside Charlie and spoke to the dying man in French, but he didn't seem to understand.

Bannerman cursed. They were losing him. "Ask him again."

But then the heavyset black man tipped to one side as his eyes closed for the last time. A single word escaped his lips, which sounded like *sheen*.

Sam placed his finger on the guy's neck, shook his head and stood up. The sound of sirens suddenly broke through the night, and not that far away.

Charlie hauled himself up. "Sheen – I wonder if it means something in Malagasy."

A flashing blue light appeared at the end of the street. Sam glanced down at the bodies, then at Bannerman. "You figure on hanging around and trying to explain what happened?"

Bannerman grimaced. It went against all his principles to run. But with the Tana killing hanging over their heads and now this, they'd be deported for sure, diplomatic passports or not. And the secret of the golden orchid might never be known.

Charlie's indecision prompted Sam to grab him by the arm. "Come on, Lieutenant. We hang around here, the shit is going to hit the fan. Let's move it!"

Bannerman nodded. The sailors worried him, but a glance up the street told him they had vanished. In the upper floors of the old buildings, more lights were coming on. The cop car was closing fast, so they took off down an alley and covered two more blocks before slowing to a walk.

"I guess the word is out," Sam ventured.

Bannerman was still breathing hard. "We've touched a nerve, no doubt about that. Christ! Machine pistols — with silencers yet!

We are two very fortunate lads. That was pretty fine shooting by the way, considering you couldn't really take a good look. How do you feel?"

Sam had to think about that for a minute. He had killed three men in two days and got to smell the flowers in between. "The old pulse is still racing like crazy, but I'm okay. I think I am. You figure there's more where those two came from?"

Bannerman puffed a few more times before answering. "You can bet the whole bundle on that."

CHAPTER NINE

At eighteen degrees south latitude in the middle of summer, it didn't take long for things to heat up. By 10:00 a.m. the temperature had risen to ninety-three and the humidity wasn't far behind. Nevertheless, Bloom was determined to return to the forest and search for more orchids. Charlie declined as gracefully as he could. Allowing Madagascar's voracious insect community a second opportunity to feast upon his tender city flesh was not going to happen.

Bloom went anyway, and Bannerman was more than happy to return to bed. There were things he could be looking into, but both men had agreed to wait for Lamont to report before deciding on a course of action. Sam returned just after two, took a shower, then went upstairs with Bannerman to grab a bite of lunch.

"Hell of a pattern you got going," Charlie said after they ordered up some beer and a couple of shrimp sandwiches.

"Meaning?"

"You break a guy's neck, then go off to smell the flowers. Shoot two more, then hightail it back for another sniff. Some people would consider that a mite peculiar."

Sam stared at the NYPD cop for a moment before replying. Bannerman varied his droll Peter Ustinov expression so rarely that it was difficult to tell if he was being serious. "Tell you what, Charlie, from now on you can take over in that department. I'll just stick to my advisory capacity."

A small boy strolled out from the lounge area with a bundle of newspapers under his arm. Bloom took one and gave the kid a five-hundred-franc note. "Maybe there's something on last night," he said as he began to scan the local French paper.

Their table with its big white parasol was near the edge of the hotel roof. Charlie shaded his eyes against the reflections and turned to look across the patchwork of tiled rooftops that lay between their hotel and the dockyard area. The ocean itself had already begun to shimmer in the heat, creating a light haze over the harbor. He noticed one of the Soviet frigates had moved out during the night. Stacks and masts of several freighters poked up above the trees and housetops. Presumably, the *Lucinda V* was now down among them somewhere. Taking in the geography of the whole bay area, he saw that a narrow peninsula of land swept gracefully away from the south end of the city, curving north and then hooking slightly west to form a fine natural harbor. At the end of the peninsula, a breakwater extended northward for another half mile or so. It appeared as though there were enough docking berths for about twenty ships. Dozens of long, low metal sheds, some old and rundown, some gleaming new, paralleled the docks. In the center, a huge white granary rising to ten or twelve stories dominated the whole yard. The rumbling of a diesel shunting back and forth blended with the squeal of swiveling cranes going about their business of loading and unloading containers.

A waiter showed up with their beer and two glasses. Bannerman poured his and waited for the suds to disappear. "Mind if I ask you a personal question?"

Sam looked up. "Go ahead."

"Your sheet said you and your brother were left an estate worth eleven million. Why work at all?"

Bloom laid the newspaper on the table and took a sip of cold beer from his bottle. "You believe money is that important?"

"Not if you got a whole lot."

"Yeah, I guess you're right." He paused for a moment, staring pensively across the harbor. "Money is one thing I never had to worry about. My old man could've even pulled me off the draft if I had agreed. He got George off. My big brother watched the war on TV. Told me when I came back that the whole thing was a 'silly macho game'—his exact words. Anyway, when the old man died, I let George take control of all the money. Money means a lot to him. He tells me I'm worth about thirteen million now."

"The rich slob act holds no appeal?"

"Not to me. Never did. Someday I intend to give most of it away, which will probably give George a heart attack. That will be my way of paying him back for all his stupid 'Nam jokes."

Bannerman broke out one of his rare smiles. "Gotta great charity in mind when you get ready to start spreading it around."

Sam grinned. "Like the Charles Bannerman Foundation, I suppose?"

"Sounds good to me — shit! Here comes Lamont. He's early."

The burly Frenchman and his wife were just crossing the street leading toward the hotel entrance. Sam glanced down over the railing and noticed they were all dressed up. "Just look at them, would you. You'd never think they crawled out of that stink pit. I suppose we should go down to the room. He might not appreciate being seen with us."

"Yeah," Charlie replied. "Especially after last night."

"There's no way Lamont could know we were involved," Bloom said. He placed a five-thousand-franc note on the table and took his beer. "Dammed if I'm leaving this behind. You go on down. I'm going to rustle up our sandwiches and grab a few more THBs for our guests."

Sam walked down the stairs about five minutes behind Bannerman. By then the Frenchman and his wife were already in the room. Lamont had combed his hair and trimmed his beard. He wore a fine pale blue linen shirt with Greek-style dark blue trim. His wife was decked out in a ruffled golden blouse cut so deep her ample breasts seemed ready to pop out at any moment. A white miniskirt over pale yellow silk stockings showed off her shapely legs. She was a tall woman, of African descent, but unlike any other he had seen. Sam guessed her homeland to be Libya or Ethiopia.

"Where do you think she comes from?" asked Lamont, grinning.

Bloom found it disconcerting that the Frenchman was able to read his mind. He told him somewhere in North Africa.

"More like East Africa. She is Somali. I will tell you a secret known just to a few: The most beautiful women in the world come from Somalia. And beauty, my friends, is but one of their charms. They are passionate. *Mon Dieu!* So passionate you would not believe. And loyal. This one would lay down her life for me — without question! They work hard and are obedient. So I ask you — what more is there to ask of a woman?"

Lamont's wife smiled and preened, as if she knew her husband was extolling her charms. Closer appraisal told Sam she was indeed beautiful, possessing a haughty profile that would make most men pause and stare. "What's her name?"

"Ah, her real name cannot be pronounced. She is now Loyola, the name I gave to her because once she shielded me when the bullets were flying." Lamont was seated on a chair beside his wife. Reaching over, he pulled up the left side of her blouse and placed his fingertip on a small round scar. "This bullet was meant for me. It nearly killed her. Does your wife have such courage?"

"I'm not married. Neither is Charlie."

Lamont's tiny dark eyes lit up. "Loy has four sisters. The youngest is yet unmarried. Perhaps you are interested?"

"Not me," Bloom replied. "I already have my eye on one." A sweet vision of Anna Grenier swept across his mind. "How about you, Charlie?"

Bannerman shrugged. The Frenchman's words had a certain logic and appeal that he found surprising. It had been his experience that after the first year or so, most men considered their wives a burden and would gladly be rid of them. It was apparent that this gorgeous Somali woman was anything but a burden.

"Why should any young woman wish to take up with a fat old bastard like me?"

"The hell you say!" said Lamont indignantly. "Is it Tyrone Power who sits in this chair? Errol Flynn maybe? *Merde!* Americans think the whole world revolves around youth and beauty. But Somali woman, she looks for courage and wisdom. And sensitivity. A fine poet will sweep her off her feet. Their values are different, thank the good Lord. Appearance has little meaning to Somali woman."

Lamont must have caught something in Bannerman's expression that made him stop and study the policeman. "You never married?" he asked abruptly.

Charlie shook his head.

The Frenchman's face lit up again. The afternoon sun reflecting off the windowsill danced a tune on his golden teeth. "By God, you will be!"

Then he lapsed into a foreign tongue Sam was unable to follow. The Americans were astonished when Loy flew off her chair, flung her long arms around Charlie's neck and began hugging him without reserve. Bannerman's face was a few shades deeper when the woman finally let go. He looked to his companion for help, but Sam seemed a little dazed himself.

Lamont stood up and crossed the room. Bloom had brought down a case of Three Horses with the sandwiches. The Frenchman pulled out a bottle and popped the cap with his thumb, no mean feat. "So, maybe I have CIA brother-in-law. This I drink to."

Charlie stood there in shock, with the beautiful black woman pressing him into her near-naked bosom, and watched Lamont down the whole bottle without pause. He gave a long belch, then walked over and slapped Bannerman on the shoulder. "You will never regret this decision, *mon ami,* never! Somali woman is finest in the whole world. Shaleen is nineteen years old, even more pretty that Loy, and built like the Golden Buddha of Siam. She will peel twenty years off your life—I guarantee it!"

Sam fell into the mood of things and came over to take Bannerman's hand. "Congratulations, old buddy. This all happened so fast I almost missed it. But I think you're onto something that has a lot of potential."

"Christ—" was all Charlie managed to get out before Loy smothered him again.

"We're talking the will of Allah here, Charlie. This is gift city, man, so you better think twice before turning it down. Maybe someone up there has decided it's time for a change."

"Enough," Lamont said in French. His wife unwrapped herself and returned to her chair. "These things we can discuss later."

He pulled out another four beers, popping the caps as he had before, then passed the bottles around. "Now, business. The

Lucinda V, she is due in early last night. Instead, she arrives at four this morning. She is often late these last few years, according to my friend, Pierre Leclerc, the harbormaster. An old scow, with an old engine that keeps breaking down. One day, he said, it will happen in a storm, and that will be the end of them. So this morning in walks three of the crew, and we get talking."

Lamont's eyes narrowed and his features began to cloud over. "Sailors will talk, they like to talk — by God, this I know. But these guys say nothing about their ship or their cargo — not one goddamn word! They look back and forth at each other like they are guilty of something, you know. So I let it be known that someone wishes to have some information about their ship, then they get up and leave — without finishing their drinks! Lamont will tell you now that someone has put the fear of God into them."

"Which means, of course," said Bannerman, still recovering from his sudden betrothal, "that they're covering something up. Good! Now all we have to do is find out what it is. Did the harbormaster say anything else?"

"So, we are old friends. I put to him the question of drugs on board this one."

"And?" Sam asked, forcing his mind onto the subject at hand. Loy had just uncrossed her legs, allowing him to see all the way to China.

"He says it is doubtful. Their cargo is the same for years — automobiles and commercial products from France and Italy, machinery parts from Spain and Brazil, petroleum and steel from Argentina, some fruits and vegetables. Nothing out of the ordinary."

"And outgoing?" asked Bannerman.

Lamont removed a folded sheet of paper from his shirt. "So, I have a list. You read it yourself."

Bloom took the papers and walked to the other side of the room, where he took one quick peek at Loy before starting to read. The document was in French. "This is a copy of the ship's manifest. How were you able you get your hands on it?"

"Yesterday I tell you this information is for the public to know. I ask Leclerc, and he gives it to me."

Sam nodded. "Okay, let's see what we got ... coffee, raw sugar, vanilla, cloves, black pepper, melons, bananas, and a list of miscellaneous items. Umm ... three companies in Cairo are to receive twenty-seven containers of well-drilling equipment. An antique carving goes to a Meru Katalle in Piraievs. A shipment of one hundred and seventy-three cases of animals—it's got 'dried' in brackets—is bound for an outfit in Zurich, spelled Z-I-A-N."

Charlie glanced at the Frenchman. "You know who they are?"

Lamont was about to respond when Bloom cut him off. "That stands for the Zurich International Association of Naturalists. Yours truly happens to be a member. They're heavy into the conservation business, but their main source of income comes from selling certain stuffed birds and animals, even butterflies, or any species at all that's abundant. They get permits to set up little operations in Africa, Malaysia, or South America, which usually last from one to two years. I get their yearly report, but I rarely read it. Not too surprising to find them down here. The last items on the list are ten sets of zebu horns for Anton Wigalie in Djibouti. A water tank, used, for a Said Faffar in Alexandria, and that's the lot."

"You find out their loading schedule?" Charlie asked.

"Sure I did. The unloading is finished tomorrow around noon, and the loading begins right away. All cargo for the *Lucinda V* is stored in warehouse D, in the central yard. She is one of the new ones, just a twenty-minute walk from the Mad-Giles. If you want to look, you look tonight. Tomorrow night is already loaded, maybe."

"Maybe?"

"*Qui,* maybe. Leclerc says ZIAN shipments come from across island, near Beza Mahafaly Reserve. Some comes by railroad, some by truck. All railroad boxes have arrived, but one truckload is late. Tomorrow it will arrive, maybe."

"Why do you keep saying maybe?" Bannerman asked.

Lamont smiled. "You have not traveled our roads too much, I think. When it rains, sometimes the road, she is gone for days. So one learns to say maybe."

"Yes, I see. And you figure it's no deal getting one of the crew to talk?"

"I tell them money is waiting for the one who helps my friend. Who knows if someone will talk? But I think not."

Sam had been leaning against the wall opposite to where Lamont and his wife were sitting. The woman had continued to spread her legs a little more every few minutes, which finally forced Bloom to take a seat on the corner of his bed to hide the growing lump in his trousers. "Is there a guard on the warehouse?"

"The central section is patrolled by seven gendarmes. If you want to get in, I arrange it."

"Well, Charlie, what do you say?"

Bannerman's mind had been wandering. He pulled it back in. "Do we need to bust locks or anything?"

"For another five hundred dollars you walk through the gate and into the warehouse. And stay all night if you want to."

"Okay," he said, peeling off five bills from the roll he took out of his pocket. "I suppose you're keeping the other five in case one of the crew shows up?"

The Frenchman stood up, grinning. "This is so, my soon-to-be CIA brother-in-law. It is better you learn to trust Lamont, you know. Maybe by tomorrow night I have some good news."

"Oh?" Charlie inquired cautiously. He had a feeling the conversation had come full circle.

Lamont's wife was four to five inches taller than her husband. She twisted her arm into his, smiling away at Bannerman. "You see those tits, *mon ami?* I tell you the rest is even better. Shaleen is young and tender, a virgin of course. Oh, you are a man to be envied!"

Charlie rolled his head around. It was a bit much for a quiet bachelor of his late years. "When are you going to get back to us?"

"No telephones. Someone will come at midnight." He squinted at Bloom for a few seconds. "You I have seen before somewhere, this is for sure. Maybe North Africa, yes?"

"Maybe," Sam agreed, not wishing to get into the Randolph Scott thing. "If you're going to send over someone we don't know, perhaps we better settle on a password."

"Good! I agree. Mekong—where you and me, we shed a little blood. Okay?"

"It'll do. Look, Charlie's sort of in shock at the moment, but I'd like to say that we sure as hell appreciate you helping us out. I doubt that we'd get too far on our own."

"Ah, CIA and me, we are old friends." The Frenchman placed a hand on Bloom's arm. "I like you two. These other guys are young and cold and mean bastards, you know? Now they got smart and got some real men. So, Lamont has everything under control. Maybe tonight I see you, who knows?"

Sam watched the woman's swaying hips as the oddly matched couple made their way down the corridor. He closed the door, shaking his head in disbelief. Charlie was standing perfectly rigid in the middle of the room. "Man, you should see the look on your face."

"What a comedian! And that woman — she damn near smothered me in those big black boobs."

Sam pulled out another THB. It was a long time till midnight. "You think he was joking? No way, Charlie my boy. You're it, the next family relative. Here, have another drink. I think you could use it."

Bannerman eased back toward the nearest chair and dropped into it. "What do you think he meant about tomorrow night?"

"Who knows? Somalia is just up the road. Maybe he'll have her flown down here." He caught Bannerman's look and nearly choked on his beer. "Hey, it's not so bad. I can be your best man and we can invite Anna Grenier. Good opportunity for me to get to know her a little better."

"This is bullshit! The guy is putting on a real good act, I'll grant you. But why should he think I want to get married at all, let alone to his sister-in-law? I might be a faggot, or a white supremacist, or even a card-carrying member of the Klan for all he knows."

"I'll tell you why. Because Giles Lamont is a very perceptive man. He sees through people. And he likes what he sees in you. In his own crude way, he has probably paid you the finest compliment you're ever likely to receive. Don't throw this thing away without some careful thought, my friend. You could be throwing away a future most men can only dream of."

Bloom walked over to Charlie and touched their bottles together. "Here's to you, Lieutenant Charles Bannerman, and to your beautiful fiancée, Shaleen whatever-her-name-is. And just to complicate your life some more, I'm going to lay a little dowry on the line. If she turns out to be all Lamont said she is, and you *do* decide to marry her, I *will* make that contribution to the Charles Bannerman Foundation—one million bucks! So you don't have to worry about your goddamn pension and that kind of nonsense. You can forget about working and go live wherever you want to live. How does that grab you, old buddy?"

Charlie was acutely aware that his life was in the process of being turned upside down—a million dollars, and a woman like Loy to keep him company for the rest of his days. Loyalty, the Frenchman said. Somehow, that single word went deeper than any other. He looked up at Samuel Ignatius Bloom, war hero, scientist, cowboy, and friend, and wondered why Fate had decided to throw him a curve ball this late in life.

"Why would you want to give me a million dollars?" he protested.

"I told you this morning I'm going to give it away. Who in hell's name needs thirteen million dollars to live on? Your name just made top of the list. Congratulations. There's just one little catch."

"That being …?"

"We both have to survive Madagascar."

The physician who signed Lind's death certificate lived in Tana, but ran a small clinic in Analabe. He came on Sunday of each week and usually stayed until Tuesday. Dr. Maurice Terroux was in his mid-sixties, long and rangy, the product of a French father and a Malagasy mother. He seemed just as astonished as the police inspector in Tana that this beautiful young widow should be questioning her husband's death.

"My dear, dear Dr. Grenier, this is Madagascar, a country which must surely have the greatest number of lightning fatalities in the world."

"I am aware of this. But you see, when the body was shipped home, an examination was carried out. There was a physician in attendance who had practiced for many years in South Africa. He referred to certain inconsistencies."

"Regarding the death certificate? Surely not."

Tiptoeing around the man's professional integrity, Anna chose her words carefully. "There is no argument that my husband's death was caused by anything other than a direct lightning strike. Dr. Lyon merely pointed out the absence of an outside path of burn marks along the body. And he was unable to reach any conclusion concerning exit burns on the fingertips. He also wondered why a near vertical strike would leave no evidence of a fall to the ground. I've read that lightning can hurl a victim several meters."

She watched the good doctor's brow continue to deepen with each sentence. He turned away from her intensity and remained silent for several moments. Finally, Dr. Terroux rose from his chair and began to pace back and forth in front of his office window. Outside, a magnificent array of scarlet bougainvilleas was in full bloom.

"For thirty-six years I have traveled back and forth to Analabe. This is where my mother was born, and where she came to practice as the very first physician to settle in the west. My father was a merchant who did not spend a great deal of time at home. The summer I turned thirteen, lightning killed three boys from one family, and when the last charred remains were brought in, their father committed suicide. One week later my youngest brother was struck down and died. Ah yes, many terrible memories linger still inside this old skull of mine. As storms approached, we would think, us children, that one or more of us would surely die. We thought lightning was a word interchangeable with death. When the missionaries first appeared, they told the old people that God had cursed their lack of faith, so within weeks our whole village turned to Christianity. But fierce storms continued to rage along the coast, just as they do today, and the Christian God was soon forgotten …."

"But …?" Anna prompted, sensing that this gracious gentleman was trying to tell her something else.

"The fact of the matter is, you are the first person to make such inquires. And yes, more than once I have pondered the very same questions you have just asked. But you see, my child, there are no easy answers."

"Were the marks on the other victims similar?"

Terroux stopped pacing and returned Anna's unwavering look. He nodded, slowly. "In several, yes."

Anna felt her jaw muscles tighten. "And would those several have been struck dead in the same general proximity — somewhere near the boundaries of the Tsingy reserve?"

"That is also the case. And, for sure, all died from a direct strike to the crown, just like your husband."

"Since the head is usually highest, would it not be reasonable to expect lightning to reach for the nearest part of its target?"

The doctor sighed. "Yes and no. Lightning does not necessarily move straight up and down. Victims have been struck on the shoulder, or on the elbow. It is not as predictable as you may think."

Anna felt her pulse begin to bubble. At last she was on to something. "Has there been a noticeable increase in the number of victims of late?"

"Yes."

"From what date?"

"Oh, perhaps from two years ago. An elderly British couple, amateur naturalists I suppose you could call them, were among the first. They would come down from Kenya every few months to nose around Tsingy. It was forbidden of course, but no one minded their being there. I remember looking at their burns and wondering how both could have been struck in identical fashion. As you say, their hands were another puzzle, as if the victims had been poised on the ground like a runner preparing for a race."

"Yes, that is exactly how Dr. Lyon put it." Something occurred to her. "Has there ever been an autopsy conducted on any of the victims?"

Terroux shook his head. "It seemed rather pointless, don't you think?"

Anna frowned. She knew damn well she had made a serious error in judgment by allowing Lind's parents to talk her out of the autopsy. "How many others do you think there may have been?"

"Ah, well, I am no longer the only physician available to sign death certificates, but I did make inquiries last month, just prior to your husband's death. The number seemed high. Over the past two years the bodies of eighteen victims have been found inside a single area of some twenty-five square kilometers."

"This is the area where Lind's body was located?"

"It is. Yes, indeed it is."

Anna realized that in her excitement she had been nervously fingering silky strands of her hair. She pulled her left hand away and forced herself to remain calm. Terroux resumed his chair and stared at her for a moment. "But madame, no matter what the circumstances—"

"—they were all struck and killed by lightning!" Anna barked. "Yes, I know. This is where the story ends each time. An act of God, and so on. Well, it is not going to end there this time."

"But what can you hope to accomplish by pursuing the matter? If you were to request an investigation, the police would consider you crazy. Do you not think that it has not occurred to me to do so?"

Anna stood up. "My cousin will arrive soon. He is a professional police officer with Interpol. I have two other friends at Toamasina, Americans. One is a New York detective. These men have all agreed to help me. Before I leave this island, Dr. Terroux, I *will* have answers."

Chapter Ten

It was Lamont's surly kid who arrived just before midnight. His job was to take them through the main gate, he said.

"What about the guard?" Bloom asked in French.

"He is supposed to take a piss behind the gatehouse. So what?"

Sam took in the scraggly black hair and insolent look, wondering what could have turned the boy so cynical at such a young age. "Who takes over from you?"

"How am I supposed to know?" he snapped.

"Well, Charlie, I guess we're onstage again. Ready?"

"You sure the kid knows what he's supposed to do?"

"He knows, all right," Sam said as he locked their hotel room door. "But he doesn't much like it."

They could have walked the ten blocks or so, but Bannerman preferred to have their smelly Citroen nearby in case they needed to make a hasty departure. Bloom parked the car near one corner of the Mad-Giles and followed the boy down the street toward the gatehouse. The night was hot and sticky, and the many grubby bars along the street were in full swing. Every time a door opened, snatches of music and laughter broke free into the darkness. From a nearby swamp, a lively bullfrog chorus provided a resonating background, while large bats swooped and dived at insects drawn to the yellow streetlights.

The guard watched the three approach until they were about fifty paces away and then vanished behind his little tin house. Once inside the gate, Lamont's son turned on his heel and went on back up the street without a word.

The pungent sea air was now invaded by the reeking stink of diesel, bilges, and oiled machinery. "What happens next?" Charlie asked.

"No clue. But I don't much like hanging around out here in full view. Let's mosey over to the back of that shed."

Somewhere nearby a heavy motor started up. The two intruders had just reached the shed's protective shadow when the machine, a big yellow forklift, came out from behind a warehouse and moved toward them.

"I don't like the looks of this," Sam said, vividly recalling the previous night's events.

Two glaring yellow lights, like the eyes of a dragon, pinned them to the shed. They were about to hightail it when a voice called out in English, "Messieurs, your chariot has arrived."

"Lamont!" Bannerman exclaimed.

"Son of a bitch! I thought we were in deep shit for a moment there."

The Frenchman came alongside them and lowered the lift to the ground. On it was a four-foot-high wooden container box. He grinned down at them, calling above the noise of the motor, "I do a few odd jobs for these guys now and then, so the guards, they are used to seeing me around. You got lights? Good. Into the box you go. Then pull over the lid and make sure it don't bounce off. How about guns?"

"Why, you expecting trouble?" Charlie asked.

"No, but Lamont, he is the good Boy Scout, you know. Lots of shitty things happen since these Ruskies set up shop. Toama is not so safe anymore."

"Certainly agree with you there," Bloom said as he helped Bannerman climb up and into the box. Once inside, he refitted the top and held onto it with one hand as the forklift got underway. There was just enough room for them to sit snugly side by side.

"If we end up doing a lot of this, Lieutenant, you should consider losing some weight. A little deodorant wouldn't go astray, either."

"You don't exactly smell like a rosebud yourself."

"The hell!" Bloom retorted. "I showered twice today. That stink is either you or this goddamn box."

"Thanks for the benefit of the doubt. What do you suppose was packed in here before us?"

"Probably horse manure. Seems to be a regular commodity around this town."

Their box pitched and swayed as the forklift picked up speed. They heard Lamont call out a greeting to someone. "Just think, Charlie, if it was Shaleen in here instead of me. Mind you, it might be difficult to assume the position."

Bannerman grunted. The forklift came to an abrupt halt, with the container rocking dangerously forward. They could feel Lamont climbing down from the cab. Next came the screech and grind of a heavy metal door being raised. Lamont climbed up again and moved the machine ahead for another couple of minutes.

He stopped again and lowered the lift down to floor level. He reached down and tapped the top of the box. "Hey, CIA, this is it."

Bloom eased the cover aside and hauled himself up and out. Then he reached back to take hold of his overweight colleague. In attempting to straddle the edge, Charlie fell forward into Bloom's arms while the heavy box tipped to one side, missing Lamont's toes by inches.

"Hey, be careful with your future brother-in-law." He chuckled away to himself as he helped Sam lift the box back on the forklift. "Come on, I show you where the *Lucinda V* cargo is stored. That is her you can see just outside. They unload for the whole night."

Lamont had driven the forklift around the corner of a section of containers piled thirty feet high. Through the open doorway, they were now able to make out several thick patches of rust erupting from the *Lucinda V's* stern. "She is no beauty queen, that one," Lamont commented.

A ring of upper windows in the warehouse allowed the ship's lights to play off the sheet metal ceiling and cast muted shadows around a vast array of boxes and containers.

"I hope all this isn't going aboard ours," Bannerman wondered aloud. It would take forever to check out so much cargo.

They followed Lamont down a long aisle until he stopped and extended his arms in a right angle. "Okay, this corner is for the *Lucinda V*. But everything has not come yet."

"What's missing—that truckload belonging to ZIAN?" Charlie asked.

The Frenchman nodded. "Maybe they come tonight, so you find a place at the back somewhere and stay out of sight. I will come to get you no later than six. See, against that wall, there are some crowbars and hammers and nails."

He laughed and placed his hand on Charlie's shoulder. "We got big rats down here who think they own the place. When you hear lots of noises, it's just those guys. And the loading bay door is the only way out of the building. So, I wish you good hunting, CIA."

After the Frenchman had driven the forklift out of the building and pulled down the steel door, the two Americans switched on their flashlights and walked over to grab a crowbar.

"Split her down the middle?" Sam asked.

"Yeah, I'll start at the far end. Forget about the boxes of fruit. That should leave us with about one-third of this group to pull apart. Be careful with the stuffed birds and whatnot, and try to fit the lids back on properly."

Bloom nodded. "So tell me, Lieutenant, just what is it I'm supposed to be looking for?"

Bannerman scratched his head in silence. "Not all that sure myself. We're still a long way from knowing exactly what the hell is going on. If they're shipping the stuff out now, it must have been brought in previously, either in this ship or by some other means."

The NYPD detective had just started to read the writing on the sides of the crates when he muttered under his breath, "Son of a bitch!"

"What is it?"

Bannerman turned to look over at Bloom. "Last night—what was the last word that guy got out before he croaked?"

"Sheen. That's what it sounded like—sheen."

Charlie shook his head. "Uh-uh. He was saying 'ZIAN.' That's what he was trying to spit out. ZIAN hired him to kill us."

"Don't be ridiculous. ZIAN has been around for more years than I can remember. Every biologist, naturalist, botanist, or ecologist who has made it to the top of his profession belongs to ZIAN. It's the finest organization of its kind in the world. I gave a lecture at their Zurich headquarters in '82. The director, old Dietrich Brower, has dedicated his life to the preservation of our environment."

"Sounds like a great cover to me."

"No way, Lieutenant. You're way off base on this one."

Bannerman wasn't even listening. "We open every case with ZIAN stamped on it. Leave the others."

Charlie walked down to the end of the pile of containers and glanced back to see Bloom still standing there. "Let's move it. Morning's gonna be here before we know it."

Bloom began twirling the crowbar around. "I don't believe this. All this trouble to get in, only to piss away our time once we're here."

Bannerman's voice was cold when he said, "I can't order you to do anything, friend. Sit on your ass and watch me, if it makes you feel any better."

Reluctantly, Sam moved in among the cases with his light, locating a ZIAN crate right off. He studied the stamp for a moment and was all set to jam his crowbar under the lid when the hum of a nearby motor stopped him. Next came voices and the harsh squeal of the metal door being raised.

"Talk about timing," Bloom whispered when Charlie reached him.

They walked along the east wall toward the back of the warehouse. Charlie turned into a narrow aisle between the last two rows of containers and climbed upon a pile of straw mats, scaring away a few large rodents as he did so.

Once Bloom had joined him, Bannerman said, "This might be a good time for you to tell me everything you know about ZIAN."

Sam groaned as he played with the batteries in his flashlight. "I can't believe you're serious about this. Getting a fixation is one thing, but you should at least have something tangible to back up your position."

"You said it started up years ago. Before or after the war?"

"I don't know, somewhere around that time."

Exhaust fumes from the truck drifted back to them. "You know who started it up?"

"A group of Swiss businessmen, I believe."

"You sure they were Swiss?"

"Come on, Lieutenant, spit it out. Just what is it you're trying to say?"

"Why don't you play around with the letters, see what you come up with."

Moving headlights reflecting off the walls provided enough light for Sam to make out his companion's face. As usual, he couldn't read it. He ran through the combinations in his mind: IANZ, ANIZ, NIAZ …

His startled gasp told Bannerman he had made the connection. "So what's the verdict, Professor?"

"It's … it's too preposterous for words. All these years and I never once heard it put that way. But … no, it's impossible!"

"Oh, and why is that, Professor? Because you're a member?"

"Well, I'm not a goddamn member of the Nationalsozialistische Deutsche Arbeiterpartei," Bloom snapped, "if that's what you're getting at."

"Touchy tonight, aren't we."

Sam didn't speak for a few minutes, as the ramifications were downright staggering. "When did you put it together?"

"I caught the Nazi bit right away, but didn't make a connection to the last word that black guy spit out until I saw it spelled out in big letters."

Bloom sighed. "It has to be a coincidence, and yet …."

"Right. So perhaps now you wouldn't mind telling me what you know about them."

Bloom struggled to recall everything he knew about the Zurich International Association of Naturalists, which wasn't much, and he could think of nothing at all that might lend credibility to Bannerman's theory.

Once the truck motor was switched off, Charlie strained his ears to pick up some of the chatter echoing back to them. "You know what language they're using?"

Bloom listened for a minute. "German."

"You speak German, right?"

"I can get by. You want me to sneak back up there and have a listen?"

"It might be dangerous."

"Only if your assessment is correct, Charlie my boy. And I still think you're way out in left field."

Bannerman eased himself down off the mats, pulled out his Colt semi-automatic and loaded a round. He let the hammer fall forward under control and checked the safety. "I'd better follow along behind, hang back a ways in case there's trouble."

The overhead lights suddenly came on, which stopped Bloom for a few seconds. He took the last few paces as quietly as he could, then knelt down at the edge of a row of containers. Poking his head out, he saw four men watching a forklift remove the newly-arrived crates from the back of a three-ton Mercedes truck and lower them into eight-foot-high containers. The ZIAN insignia was emblazoned on the side of the truck.

An elderly man seemed to be in charge. "Keep watch for the box containing the weapons!" he called out.

A big man still aboard the truck said impatiently, "Stop worrying, Victor, I know where they are."

The men from ZIAN continued unloading the merchandise and making sure it was packed securely in the shipping containers. Several minutes went by before the big man called out, "Got it!"

Their activities were halted while he pried the top off one of the crates. Bloom watched him remove two automatic rifles and pass them down to Victor. The last few crates were then unloaded and packed into their containers; but just before the process was completed the workers were interrupted by a lone man walking in through the open loading-bay door.

Victor greeted the new arrival in French. "Ah, Demetrios, my old comrade-in-arms. How goes the battle?"

"Hey, Victor, you ancient warthog, I see you're still alive."

Bloom eased his head out a little more to try to put faces to the names. He knew Demetrios was captain of the *Lucinda V*. He and Victor both looked to be in their early eighties.

After embracing the Greek, Victor placed an arm around his shoulder. "I intend to outlive you, you seagoing rhinoceros. Did you leave that decrepit old tub just to come down and see if Victor still knows how to run the show?"

"Not at all. Herr Brower just called in on the radio and wants to have a word with you."

The old man seemed genuinely surprised and glanced down at his watch. "At this time of night? It must be important."

Victor used a handkerchief to wipe his face while calling out instructions to Karl, still up on the truck. Then he took Demetrios by the arm and walked back toward the doorway. Their conversation began to fade as Bloom strained his ears to pick up what he could.

"Did he tell ... all about?"

"A shooting ... night ... Americans ... young ... Interpol ... take care ... vodka ..."

The voices melted into the night. Bloom became aware of beads of sweat dripping from his brow. Nothing had been specifically stated that would indicate this enterprise was anything other than what it appeared to be. But throw in the guns and piece together the dialogue, and the moving finger pointed toward Zurich. He walked back to where Bannerman was patiently waiting.

After Sam related his findings and suspicions, the detective said, "It's finally surfaced."

"Meaning?"

"The Interpol connection. The commissioner was right all along." After a few minutes of silence, he added, "I don't have a good feeling about this; the picture seems to be changing. Maybe we shouldn't be nosing around those crates."

Having already developed a healthy respect for Bannerman's instinct, Bloom said, "They're almost finished. I'll go back up and keep my ears open."

Sam took up his position again, listening carefully. Tiny scuffling noises behind him took his attention, and he hoped they were being made by the local rats scurrying about. After the last crate was packed away and the container sealed, Karl handed the weapons to the last two men, then walked over to the wall and pulled the light switch.

Before leaving he said, "I doubt if they will try to break in here tonight, but we can't assume they won't. So keep your ears open. And don't forget, Herr Brower wants them alive, if possible."

One of the men gave a harsh laugh. "Come on, Karl, nothing is going to happen. So how about changing your mind and sending in a couple of those young Chinese whores?"

The tall man was on his way out. He turned and pointed his finger at the speaker. "No women, Gratin. That's an order."

Karl walked through the doorway and once outside, lowered the metal door into place. Sam watched for a few more minutes to see if the guards were going to split up, but they seemed content to sit together on one of the smaller containers and discuss the female situation in Toama. Their conversation led Sam to believe these two hadn't been around women in a long time.

"We have a problem, Lieutenant," he said upon returning. "A big one, I would say. They left two guards behind, which sure as shit rules out any search, but what happens when Lamont returns?"

Charlie thought about it for a minute. "Have you considered what might happen?"

"Hopefully, they'll assume he's just another worker and stay out of sight."

"Maybe. And?"

Bloom strained to read his companion's face. "And once Lamont sees we're not around, he'll probably call out to us."

"Possibly. You just heard the captain mention Americans. Who do you suppose this Karl was talking about when he said Herr Brower wanted them alive?"

"Us, I suppose."

"Don't suppose, Professor. Last night they just wanted to put us away. Tonight they would like to talk to us first us, then put us away. Nice man, your Dietrich Brower. I take it his dedication to the preservation of the environment doesn't include the human species."

"So what happens if they grab Lamont? What do we do?"

"Nothing."

Bloom could feel his frustration getting all mixed up with his growing sense of unease. "Let's just suppose they beat on him. Maybe they'll threaten to kill him. We're just going to watch?"

The NYPD detective gripped Bloom's arm, suddenly concerned that the guy might be getting ready to come unglued again. "Listen to me, we know the cargo is hot, and that's what we came here for. Those crates are going to be under armed guard until they're loaded aboard ship, which leaves us out of the picture. It gets checked out at some other port, maybe even at its final destination, Venice. If they find out we were nosing around, they'll scuttle the shipment or bury it somewhere. Don't you see? No matter what happens, we can't show our noses. Which means Lamont is on his own."

As it turned out, soon as he rounded the corner with his forklift just before six, the wily Frenchman noticed right off that the rest of the ZIAN cargo had arrived. Even though he had no reason to suspect the Zurich operation, he knew from the few little snippets of information gleaned since the ship's arrival that something was going on with the *Lucinda V.* When the Americans didn't show, he took out a piece of paper, looked around, let out a few choice oaths, and waited another two minutes, just in case. Then he backed out of the aisle and drove his noisy machine to the end of the long warehouse.

They were waiting for him. As soon as the lift touched the floor, Bloom had the top off the box and began to push Charlie over and in. He glanced up at Lamont. "There's two characters with automatic rifles standing guard over that new shipment."

The Frenchman grinned down at them. "So what? Don't worry, Lamont takes care of his friends."

It seemed like hours before Sam heard the metal door screech back into place, though it had taken just a few minutes. He let out a deep sigh of relief and turned to Bannerman. "All that worry over nothing."

Charlie felt the tension drain out of him; it had been a long six hours. "Yeah, this Frenchman, he's been around the block a few times."

"Yes, sir, he'd make a real fine brother-in-law. Maybe you could help him clean up his operation, make it the top bar in Toama and entertain all those Russian sailors."

When the forklift stopped again, Lamont tapped on the lid. "Hey, CIA, we are behind the gatehouse. When you get out, go around front by the fence. My kid is waiting for you just outside. Okay? Loy cooked up a few flapjacks if you feel hungry. I come by in a little bit. Wait until I make sure no one is around before you get out."

"Flapjacks," Bannerman muttered. "Got a nice ring to it."

After Lamont gave the all clear, they scrambled out of the box and walked through the gate, heads down, trying to look as if they had just come off the night shift. A few trucks passed by while they waited for Lamont's son to exit a small treed area bordering the chain-link fence.

The great blood-red orb was just now clearing the rim of the Indian Ocean, turning the rolling waves beyond the breakwater into pure gold. They had heard rain drum upon the corrugated steel roof overnight, a short but heavy downpour that had cleared the air and made it sweet to breathe again. The bullfrog chorus had quieted down to just a tremor in the soft morning breeze off the harbor.

"You got a name, son?" Sam asked.

"Everybody has a name," the boy replied as he fell in beside the Americans.

"You want to tell me yours?"

"Why should I?"

"Okay, how old are you?"

The boy looked up at Bloom. "Sixteen."

"How long have you lived in Toama?"

He shrugged. "Maybe ten years, I don't know."

"And you don't like it a whole lot?"

Again he looked up. "Do you?"

"Haven't seen enough of it yet to tell. Tell me, son, what is the thing you want most in this world?"

"A Ferrari," he replied without hesitation.

"I see. Does your father have a car?"

"An old Peugeot that breaks down every week. I am ashamed to drive it when my friends are around."

"Do you have a driver's license?"

"Of course!"

Bloom had been fingering the Citroen keys in his pocket. "We're going to stop in and have a bite to eat. Our car isn't a Ferrari, but if you want, you can run it around the block a few times, as long as you have it back here in half an hour. That okay with you, Charlie?"

"Yeah, sure."

The boy could hardly believe his good fortune. He took the keys and stared at them for a few seconds. When he looked up, all traces of his earlier insolence had vanished. "Oh, thank you, monsieur, I will be very careful."

He broke into a run but stopped and turned back to the Americans with a shy smile. "And my name is Robert."

Bannerman watched his heels kick up dust. "Bet that was the fastest change in attitude you ever saw."

Sam chuckled as the boy unlocked the door, then carefully pulled it shut. Once inside he lowered the window and waved enthusiastically at his benefactors. They were about fifty paces away when Robert turned over the key in the ignition.

It was almost as if Bloom knew what was going to happen, because a curse escaped his lips at the same instant the car vanished inside a giant ball of fire.

Pieces of flesh and bone and metal flew over their heads and all over the block. The force of the concussion drove both men back about twenty feet. Sam struggled to stand up, but fell over. Through his twisted vision he saw that the front of the Mad-Giles was no longer there. He became vaguely aware of a million pinpoints of pain in his eyes. He attempted to clear his vision as he searched for Charlie. He turned around on his hands and knees, finally locating the blurred, crumpled heap beside him. Loy's piercing scream made him turn his head again. His last recollection was the overpowering sensation of having done something incredibly stupid.

Chapter Eleven

News of another bungled attempt to get rid of the two pesky Americans reached Herr Brower at two in the afternoon on Saturday, the twenty-eighth day of November. First came word that his oldest grandson, Medall, would not be coming for the traditional Christmas family gathering. Why? Because his wife just started divorce proceedings and he did not feel in the festive spirit. Ten minutes later Hans showed up at the door. Herr Brower led the way into his study. He poured two sherries and told his secretary to be seated—a first! The report was brief. Despite his instructions that the Americans were to be taken alive and interrogated if at all possible, Simard had gone ahead and wired a bomb to their car. Both men had been caught in the blast, but were a good distance away from the car when the device exploded. Bannerman was apparently unharmed, while Bloom was taken to the hospital with minor injuries. The net result was the death of some local urchin.

"These two are beginning to seem indestructible. How was the device set?"

"It was wired to the ignition. It seems this teenage boy asked if he could drive their car. They gave him the keys, and that was the end of him."

The old man removed his glasses and stared at the multicolored Brower coat of arms hanging over the doorway to his study. It had a solid and distinguished look about it. Occasionally he wished that he could lay rightful claim to the name. "I detest having the local police brought in at this final stage of our operation. Hopefully, Simard's being with Interpol will deflect any awkward questions, should they arise. What time did the explosion occur?"

"Approximately six-thirty a.m. Madagascar time. The car was parked close to some derelict drinking establishment beside the dockyard that was more or less destroyed by the blast."

"Beside the dockyard …. I wonder what these two were doing at such a place so early in the morning."

"I admit it seems odd, Herr Director. There is something else you may find of interest. During their investigation, the police learned that both men were carrying diplomatic passports."

Herr Brower swung his gaze back to the young man. "For Madagascar?"

"Yes, sir."

"A diplomatic passport spells diplomatic immunity. I do not care for the implications. It seems this thing has suddenly taken on an entirely new perspective. Is it possible, do you think, that the United States government has somehow learned of our little venture on the island?"

Hans did not reply immediately, but instead took a sip of his sherry. "I suppose a leak is always possible, sir. Still, I have difficulty accepting this. Other than Karl, staff members assigned to this enterprise are long-serving, trusted employees who receive generous compensation. So I must ask what reward or benefit might ensue to turn one of them into a traitor. No, I am inclined to believe, Herr Director, that the diplomatic cards were issued for another purpose, perhaps nothing more serious than allowing them to have free run of the island."

Herr Brower grunted. "Your reasoning is open-ended, my boy. Until we find out why these two men have shown up like this, we must assume the worst, the very worst."

The previous evening he had spoken directly with Victor and Simard to personally warn them of a possible attempt by the Americans to break into the special ZIAN cargo for evidence of the altered cocaine. After all, if the Americans were in fact the enemy, why else would they be in Toamasina? "Why else, indeed?"

"I beg your pardon, Herr Director?"

"Nothing, Hans, just thinking out loud." It continued to torment him, the fact that they were unable to tie the Americans to the drug shipment. It disturbed him that Bannerman was a homicide detective. If there was an investigation of the *Lucinda V* underway, he would have expected it to be conducted by the US Drug Enforcement Agency, the CIA, or at the very least by a narcotics police officer. But Interpol had been assured by the American authorities that no drug investigation was underway anywhere in Africa at the moment. So just what were these two doing in Madagascar with diplomatic passports?

"Very well, the ship has now left port, but has the cargo been tampered with? That is the first question that must be addressed. Radio Captain Demetrios and have him check the seal on every crate in the entire shipment, the regular as well as our special crates, and get back to me by morning. If the merchandise is untouched and with Dr. Bloom in the hospital, there appears to be no need to further concern ourselves with the Americans. In the meantime, Simard has agreed to fly over to the west side of the island and take care of the Grenier woman. At least that problem will be eliminated."

The Frenchman's recent telephone conversation with Anna Grenier not only confirmed her determination to seek an answer to her husband's death, but also exposed her involvement with the Americans. But Simard was her cousin and would have become her lover, except for being interrupted by an untimely telephone call. So he should be able to carry out his task with a minimum of difficulty. Her death would be a costly affair, as the Frenchman had initially balked at the idea of murdering his own cousin. But the director quickly recognized this as a bargaining ploy, and Simard had agreed to do the job for much less than he might otherwise have received if his reluctance had been sincere.

Charlie knew that Dr. Fiantarre had at first refused to come to Toama. On the telephone Curtis Johnson told Bannerman that it had taken considerable persuasion on the part of Ambassador William Wright to convince the resident eye surgeon at Befelatanana Hospital in Tana to leave his summer retreat in the north end of the island and fly down to Toama to examine Sam

Bloom. The ambassador had even sent his personal aircraft to pick the man up. Fiantarre had arrived just after three that afternoon, a tall, haughty man of mixed French and Malagasy blood, and had yet to speak a single word to Bannerman. It was now eight-thirty in the evening, fourteen hours since the bomb went off, and Charlie hadn't seen the physician since his arrival. He was worried.

Since there did not seem to be a single soul at the hospital who spoke English, Bannerman felt pretty much at a loss. During the afternoon one of the policemen standing guard had tried to get him, through the use of sign language, to go back to his hotel and get some rest. But he still had no idea what was happening with Sam and wasn't about to leave until he found out.

Both men had been knocked over by the force of the explosion, and Bloom was unconscious when Charlie reached over to touch him. Though Bannerman had been unable to find a single mark on his new friend, Sam was still out cold when the ambulance showed up twenty minutes later. He didn't come to until they were wheeling him through the emergency entrance, and the sight of his eyes rolled up into his head had given Charlie a start. He'd grabbed Bloom's hand and told him he would remain close by and keep watch on things.

In the afternoon Charlie had given his statement to the investigating officer, the biggest pack of lies he had ever told in his life. But what choice did he have?

Bannerman was dozing when he heard the doors to the trauma room swing open again. They had a peculiar squeal that he had earlier tuned into his subconscious, allowing him to sleep through the regular hospital noise. Fiantarre looked weary when he came over and sat down beside the American. He started speaking in French, so Charlie held up his hand.

"I don't speak nothing but English. You got someone around here who speaks English?"

The physician rose and walked over to the nursing station. Five minutes later the elevator door opened to allow a Malagasy nurse of diminutive stature to step off. Fiantarre had a few words with the woman before she came over and introduced herself.

She had large dark eyes and a captivating smile. "I am Marbella Haughton. You are Dr. Bannerman?"

"Yeah," he told her, grateful to hear words he could finally understand.

She introduced Fiantarre and began to translate his rapid explanation of Bloom's condition. "After the medical team was certain that the patient had not been struck by flying debris from the blast, they went on to conduct a detailed examination of his eyes." She waited for a few more sentences. "This was followed by Dr. Fiantarre and his colleagues examining a number of X-rays. Since there did not appear to be even a mild concussion, the prognosis is that Dr. Bloom's status may be entirely psychosomatic, something that has been brought on by the extreme stress of the explosion." She paused again, listening to the doctor. "Dr. Fiantarre discussed his findings with the patient, who confirmed that this kind of reaction has happened before. The only treatment that can be recommended in this case is for the patient to rest quietly in a darkened room, perhaps for several days. There is every reason to expect that over time his eyes will return to normal."

Marvelous! Bannerman had just gone from having an unstable partner to having no partner at all. "Yeah, well, I guess that's about it. Tell Dr. Fiantarre I'm real grateful to him for coming all the way down here. Ah, I take it Sam can be moved?"

The nurse asked the question, to which Bannerman received a cautionary yes, provided his eyes remain covered. A few minutes after they left, Bloom was wheeled out. His eyes were bandaged. Charlie walked along beside the gurney and laid a hand on his shoulder. "Sorry about all this, Sam. How do you feel?"

The corners of his mouth rose slightly. In a weak voice, he said, "I was relieved to hear you came out of it all right. Make a piss-poor partner, don't I?"

"That's a dumb thing to say. The goddamn bomb wasn't your fault. You in pain?"

"They shot me up with something pretty powerful. You spoken to Lamont yet?"

Bannerman rolled his head around. Facing the Frenchman after the death of his son was not number one on his list of fun things to do. "I hung around here all day. But don't worry, I'll take care of it."

They were back in Sam's room by now, a private room with a good view of the harbor. Charlie watched the two gendarmes take up their positions outside the door. He waited until the nurse and two male orderlies had left before taking a seat by the bed. "I'd say it's time you considered pulling out of here, Professor. Bombs, submachine guns — hell, a rocket or a grenade fired from one of those rooftops, and it's all over."

Bloom eased himself up against the back of the bed. He placed the tips of his fingers against the bandages over his eyes. "Your bedside manner is the shits, Lieutenant. Most hospital visitors I had in the past brought flowers or candy. You show up with an armload of paranoia."

Bannerman felt a bit stupid. Maybe he was getting carried away. "Yeah, you're right."

"Fiantarre told me about Ambassador Wright putting the arm on him. I guess us Oklahoma boys have to stick together."

Charlie stood up and yawned. "I'm going back to the hotel and call the commissioner. I'll shower and eat, maybe grab a nap, then I'll be back. Okay?"

"Sure, but don't pay a lot of attention to whatever Fiantarre told you. Couple of days, I'll be as good as new. Listen, can you call Anna Grenier and tell her what happened? Tell her our plans haven't changed — "

"Haven't changed, hell! The only place you're going is stateside. You're all done with the frontline stuff, Professor."

Bloom was still protesting when Charlie went through the door. Outside he told the two Malagasy cops, "That guy in there is my friend, you understand? Anything happens to him, you two don't want to be around when I get back."

They nodded, smiling happily while Bannerman waited for the elevator. Silly buggers didn't even know they'd just been threatened.

Commissioner Hennessey listened carefully while Bannerman rattled off his update. "So what's your honest opinion, Charlie? Is he out for the count, or is he likely to want to carry on?"

"The guy is tough, no doubt about it, but I'd say he's had enough."

"That's not what I asked. Does he want to go on or not?"

"Well, as a matter of fact, he's still pretty keen, told me his eyes will be cleared up in a couple of days. A recurring problem, apparently. I'm kind of surprised it didn't show up on his sheet."

Hennessey wasn't biting. "Okay, Lieutenant, you've answered my question. Bloom stays. When did the ship pull out?"

"Early this evening." Charlie had watched it steam out of the harbor himself.

"With the next stop Djibouti, due in on the fifth. This gives you exactly one week to get something on this Swiss organization. I'd say we're already running a heavy risk that our special cargo will disappear faster than a whore's drawers. Too bad you couldn't take a peek inside one of those crates." The PC paused for a few seconds. "Charlie, I take it you believe this ZIAN organization is the key?"

"Beginning to look that way."

"Okay, then your next logical move is Zurich. Bloom speaks German, so as soon as he can travel, you're on your way. Meanwhile, I'll run a profile on ZIAN and send it over. I'll see if I can't set up a contact with the local commandant to make it easier for you."

Bannerman figured the PC was making a mistake sending them to Zurich so soon, but didn't say so. "How about the ship? Anyone do a rundown on the owner yet?"

"Belongs to a consortium of Swiss businessmen from Zurich. All well-known names in the community, old respected families and all that."

"Any chance Dietrich Brower is one of them?"

"No, which doesn't mean he isn't. They got ways to cover up ownership in Europe we haven't even heard of over here. I'll forward the list once I know where you're staying."

"What about the Grenier woman?" he asked, wondering vaguely if his telephone could be bugged.

"Interesting coincidence, isn't it, her knowing about that orchid? What do you think we should do?"

"She claims it came from some nature reserve on the west coast. She also told us her cousin is with Interpol, which could give us a foot in the door we can use later on. Look, Bloom can be moved; it's only his eyes that are the problem. So why don't we spend a couple days over there before Zurich?"

"I don't know, Charlie, one week is cutting it real thin as it is. If we can convince the authorities in Djibouti that the cargo is hot, they'll search the ship. But in order to do that, we need to show them something, and so far we got nothing. Wasting two valuable days traipsing around in a wilderness reserve might not be a smart move."

Bannerman remained silent, letting the PC figure it out on his own.

"Well ... hell ... maybe you're right. If this flower is for real, it's better we find out now. But Charlie, machine pistols with silencers, plastic RDX bombs — this is desperate stuff, which tells me they won't let up until they get you, or you get them. My advice is to take the next flight out before that island becomes a death trap for you guys. Assholes might use a tank the next time."

"They might. But the way I got it figured is they'll probably check out the cargo, make sure we haven't been sniffing around. Then it's just possible they might back off a bit, especially after that bomb screwup. The local cops are really stirred up, swarming all over the city like ants. Once they found out we were carrying diplomatic passports, the shit really hit the fan. They put two guards outside Sam's room and two more at the hospital entrance. They probably figure we're spies checking out the new dock works, and that it was the Russians who wired the bomb."

"Good Christ, Lieutenant, I don't want you to turn this into an international incident. As it is, my ass is hanging out so far I might never see it again. How's the Frenchman taking his son's death?"

Charlie suddenly realized that his new life had gone down the tube with Robert's death — no more luscious Somali woman, no more million dollars. "Haven't talked to him yet, but he's gotta be real pissed off at us. This'll probably blow his CIA cover as well."

"Too bad. Look, if he wants to believe you're CIA, leave it like that. But tell him the US government is willing to help out. Find out if he had insurance on his building, what his general status is. We'll fix something up for him, okay?"

"Sure, I'll run it by him, if he'll talk to me. What's happening with the special task force?"

"So far, a complete waste of time and money! They picked up another new twist—coca leaves soaked in kerosene, a real killer—bazooka's the street name they pinned on it. And the ODs are back to normal, like the supply of killer stuff has suddenly run out. So now crack is king again, with heroin on its way to the bottom rung. It's goddamn scary how fast the word gets around. Oh yeah, and last night a couple of crack houses up on East One Thirty-Second were torched."

Bannerman nodded to himself; this was a natural course of events. He was just about to hang up when something tweaked his memory.

"The local harbormaster told Lamont the *Lucinda V*'s got an old engine that keeps breaking down. So from time to time they're late getting into port. You got any friends in the CIA?"

"No, I'm happy to say. But there's a few guys down in Langley who owe me. What have you got?"

"Probably nothing, but if the stuff is being shipped over from the west side of the island, how did it get there in the first place? It might have arrived by truck or train, but I figure crossing the island twice increases the risk disproportionately."

"What are you getting at, Lieutenant?"

"I remember you mentioning that the CIA can monitor ship movement by satellite. What do you think the chances are of finding out if the *Lucinda V* made a little detour up the west coast, maybe to unload a special cargo? This way the coke is treated right away, then they ferry it overland to Toama while the ship makes its way around the island. It don't make a whole lot of sense to me for the stuff to sit idle two or three months until the ship returns. If they're using the same ship, that is."

"You've been giving this matter some thought, good. Call me when you get to Zurich, maybe I'll have something."

After the commissioner hung up, Charlie figured he'd better find out where the Frenchman had moved, then go and apologize for the death of his son. The notion depressed him. Dog weary, he pushed himself up off the bed. At the hospital he had washed off most of the dust from the explosion, but he didn't feel too clean at the moment and began peeling off his clothes to take a shower.

In the shower he began to formulate a plan. The ambassador's plane was still at the airport. Charlie wondered if he could talk him into allowing the pilot to ferry him and Bloom over to the other side of the island before returning to Tana. From a security angle, it would have public transportation beat all to hell.

He reached the ambassador through the number Johnson had given him. After inquiring about Sam's health, the man agreed that it would be wise to get him away from Toama. He said he would talk to the pilot personally, and made Bannerman promise to keep in touch with him or Johnson and to let him know if they needed anything else.

That left Anna Grenier. Although it was late, she wasn't surprised to hear from the Americans. After all, they had promised to come over as soon as their business in Toama was finished. She told him about her visit with Dr. Terroux, but Charlie seemed only mildly interested. He asked if Morondova was the nearest airport.

Anna told him that it was.

"How long a ride is it to the forestry station?"

"More than two hours, I should think."

"What kind of condition are the roads in?"

She laughed. "This is the real country over here. I would describe them as barely drivable in places. A four-wheel drive is the standard vehicle, I'm afraid."

Bannerman figured all that bouncing around wouldn't help Bloom's condition any. "Is there somewhere closer a small plane can land?"

At that point Anna sensed something was wrong. "Has anything happened to Sam?"

"Yeah, he was standing too near a bomb when it went off. He's all right, except his eyes are buggered up again, like the night

162

he had the run-in with the guy who was following you, except maybe a lot worse, I don't know. The ambassador is allowing us to use his plane tomorrow, which is due to take off around nine-thirty."

"There is a gravel strip near Analabe used by small aircraft. I'm certain it will be suitable, unless there is heavy rain. Can you tell me what happened?"

"They rigged a bomb to the ignition of our rental car. Sam gave a local kid the keys to take it for a drive. We were still on the street when the thing went off. Neither of us got a scratch; but Sam, well, something happened inside his head, I guess."

"Oh, Charlie, is the boy dead?"

"It was one big mother of a bomb. Pieces of that kid will never be found."

"That is so ... awful. And Sam's eyes, are they taped?"

"Yeah, the doctor said he's gotta stay in the dark for awhile."

"I am not so certain that is the correct approach in Sam's case; however, we shall see. Charlie, whoever these people are, they must be growing desperate. Thank God I now have an official police escort."

"How did you arrange that?"

"My cousin did, the one I told you about. He called last evening."

"The guy with Interpol?"

"Yes, and he is arriving in Morondava tomorrow, around ten in the morning. When do you think your aircraft will get here?"

"The ambassador figured if we got away on time, we'd make Morondava about twelve thirty. If we can put down on that strip you mentioned, maybe a bit earlier."

"When you are about one hour from landing, tell the pilot to radio through on the forestry band and have Marina contact the clinic. They will send an ambulance. I'll try to make it back in time to be there to meet you. If I'm not, tell the driver to take you to the Swiss forestry station."

This is one organized lady, Bannerman thought. "I don't think he really needs an ambulance, but what the hell. Okay, that's the way we'll play it. And I'm looking forward to meeting your cousin."

"Oh, you will like René; everyone does. And I'm certain he will be a big help in finding out just who all these terrible people are."

I just bet he will. He took down the call sign and frequency. "Ah, there is one big favor I'd like to ask, but you're going to have to trust me. Figure you can do that?"

"Yes," she answered hesitantly, "I think I can. What is it?"

"Interpol. There's a better than even chance they're mixed up in this. It's probably got nothing to do with your cousin, but why don't you play it safe until we can check him out?"

She was silent for a moment, and when she responded, her tone was cold. "What is it you wish me to do, Lieutenant?"

"I would advise against wandering off with him somewhere alone. And secondly, I'd like you to keep everything we told you to yourself, probably just for a day or so. It won't take me long to figure out whose side he's on."

"Everyone is assumed guilty until proven innocent, is that how it works?"

He was aware of the edge in her voice. "Look, lady, I'm just trying to do my job as best I know how. And part of that job now is keeping you alive. Besides, if you don't do as I say, you could be endangering our lives as well."

That modified her tone somewhat. "It will be difficult for me not to say anything. After all, René's sole purpose for coming down here is to help me out. I must tell him something."

"Okay, just stick to the investigation of your husband's death. Don't say a word about what happened in Tana. Got it?"

"Yes, Charlie, I got it." She didn't dare tell him that she had already mentioned the incident to her cousin. "Then I will see you tomorrow. And tell Sam ... tell him I will take good care of him."

It was one-ten in the morning when Bannerman finally checked the windows to make certain they were locked and hauled his bed across the room to place it tight against the door. He was exhausted and knew he wouldn't hear a thing until his alarm went off.

To his surprise, he found he was unable to pop off as easily as he thought. The first formative pieces of the puzzle were starting to come together and he couldn't help mulling them over. NAZI, alias ZIAN, a group of ex-Nazis who had gotten together at the end of the war to set up a legitimate front to handle funds accumulated during the war. Who had since managed to get involved in the business of marketing cocaine — which is where the logic began to break down. If they were in the coke trade, the most lucrative enterprise the world has ever known, why were they apparently producing the deadliest concoction ever to hit the streets? Why set up such an elaborate scheme, just to kill off their own clientele? Even if they were trying to ease out the competition — mainly Colombians and Jamaicans — they weren't going to do it by selling killer crack. Or could it be, even after all this time, they were still working on Hitler's master plan to rid the world of its derelicts and misfits?

Bannerman told the cab driver to wait. He had only a few minutes to spare, just a few minutes to tell Giles Lamont he was sorry his son's body had been scattered over the neighborhood. Charlie had been through this before, but it never got easier. The house was a surprisingly neat two-story bungalow in a pleasant residential area just southwest of the city proper. A wrinkled old woman who had to be pushing eighty answered the door just as the rain began. She eyed Bannerman coldly for several seconds before calling to someone inside the house. Lamont's wife showed up. When she saw who it was, she smiled, then broke into tears and threw her arms around Charlie.

Lamont appeared behind her and gripped him by the elbow. "Come in, *mon ami,* come in."

As Loy led Charlie inside, her husband plodded out to the taxi, took some bills out of his pocket, and sent the guy on his way before Bannerman realized what was happening.

"Hey! I gotta be back at the hospital in half an hour."

The Frenchman wanted to know why.

"Because we're pulling out this morning and I gotta get Sam to the airport."

"So, he is already recovered?"

"Hell no. His eyes are still in rough shape."

"Where will you go?"

"Across the island to a place called Tsingy, just for two days. It's near a Swiss forestry camp where there's a doctor we know who can look after Sam. Then we're off to Zurich."

Charlie followed Lamont into the kitchen, where he caught sight of a flash of red disappearing around a doorway. There was another child, a dark little girl of three or four years old, seated at the table. She promptly jumped up and backed out of the room.

"Sit," ordered Lamont. "I will drive you. Maybe we are late a few minutes, so what? Loy is whipping up a batch of French toast, my favorite. Here is a cup of good Indian tea while we wait."

He studied Bannerman for a few minutes before continuing. "So, you have come to extend your condolences, maybe."

"I could hardly leave town before coming by to tell you how sorry—"

"Enough! We have all accepted the fact that Robert, my poor, unhappy Robert, is no longer with us. *C'est la vie.* For you to live, he had to die. Loy is a Muslim; to her it is only the will of Allah. So who really knows, *mon ami?* Maybe it is, maybe it is."

Charlie heard the sizzle of bread behind him. "There's something else. I spoke to my boss last night. He wants to make good on the damage that's been done."

Lamont raised one bushy eyebrow.

"Except for your son—nobody can make that up to you. I'm talking about your home and business."

"So, the CIA has developed a conscience. This is a new policy of appeasing the natives?"

The hell with it, Bannerman thought. "Look, I figure it's time I told you we're not CIA. Bloom is a scientist, a world-renowned botanist. Me, I'm just an ordinary cop, New York Police Department, a lieutenant with Homicide."

Lamont frowned, and seemed to give it considerable thought before commenting. "But you are here to do a job for your government. Is this not so?"

"Yeah, drugs, just like I said. What about the settlement? Why don't you give me a figure? Was your place covered by insurance?"

"Does it matter?"

"No, I guess not."

"Okay, one hundred thousand dollars I would consider fair. Would you consider that fair?"

Loy placed a large platter containing six pieces of fried home-made bread in front of him and left the room. "Sure, why not. I'll recommend it. When is the funeral, tomorrow?"

Lamont shrugged. "There are a few problems. Maybe Tuesday. Eat up; Loy stepped out for just a minute, but she will make more." The Frenchman sipped his tea as Bannerman dug in. "You and me are alike, I think. We like to feed our bodies too much. Ah, when I was in the Mekong, I was one hundred thirty-five pounds, can you believe? A skinny runt running around with a great goddamn machine gun blowing away all these stupid gooks who never understood why the hell we were there."

Loy returned, gave Charlie a pleasant smile, and continued with her task. It was at that moment that Bannerman got the feeling that all was not what it seemed. He had caught the slightest eye movement directed by Lamont at his wife as she came back in.

The Frenchman continued to ramble on about his days in Vietnam and later in North Africa. Charlie heard voices in the next room, the old woman and the two children, he supposed. Another quick exchange of eye movements put Bannerman on full alert. Words like 'revenge' were beginning to find their way into his thinking process. A guy who displayed human skulls on top of his piano might not be all that predictable. The taxi had been dismissed immediately, and Lamont seemed to be taking his son's death with unnatural equanimity.

Bannerman wolfed down the last pieces of toast as fast as he could. "Slept a bit late this morning, so this is really great. Ah, *merci beaucoup*, Madame Lamont. But now I gotta get back and get Sam packed up."

Lamont rose from his chair. "Come into the parlor and sit for a few minutes, then I will drive you."

Which left his visitor with no choice but to follow behind him. Charlie took the opportunity to move his semi-automatic around to the front, where he could reach it in a hurry. "Listen, Giles, I'm real sorry about your boy, and so is Sam. I really appreciate the great breakfast, but now I'd better head back. If you're not able to drive me, why don't you call a taxi?"

Lamont took a seat on one end of a big orange sofa and smiled up at Charlie. "Why are you nervous, my friend?"

"The plane is due to leave at nine-thirty. My watch reads eight-twenty. That doesn't leave me with a whole lot of time."

He reluctantly took the matching love seat and wondered what kind of a game was being played. He didn't have long to wait. The perfume gave him the first indication—some kind of exotic foreign scent that penetrated the kitchen odors and made its way into the room where the men were sitting. First came Loy, who walked directly over to Bannerman. When she began to speak, Charlie stood up.

So did Lamont. "Loy asked me to translate for her. What she says is that she is happy you came over this morning. She feels awkward because of Robert's death, and because she knows that we must all be in mourning." He waited until she said another few sentences. "She asked if you and me, we put aside our sorrow for a few minutes while she introduces to you someone very special."

Charlie could feel the same kind of knot building in his gut that he got when he thought a killer might be drawing a bead on him. When she entered the room, he was almost bowled over by the sheer beauty of her. It made him gasp, turning his throat so dry that he could hardly speak.

Loy said a few more things, and Lamont waited for her to finish. "She says this is her favorite sister, Shaleen Hazall El-Ramar Ahwaz, the youngest of a family of ten. Their father was a warrior in the north, where Loy and Shaleen were born. Then he becomes a government official and the family moves to Mogadishu. These two are really stepsisters, because her old man married again after Loy's mother died. He married a good-looking Italian woman, which is where that trace of red in her hair comes from. So, what did I tell you, is she not beautiful?"

Bannerman felt hot and flustered and tried to clear his throat. "I'm real pleased to meet you, Miss Ahwaz."

The girl smiled for the first time. "It is a great honor for me to meet you, Mr. Bannerman."

Jesus! She even speaks English.

"English is compulsory in many of the schools up in the old British territories," said Lamont in a matter-of-fact voice. "She also speaks Italian, French, Arabic, and Somali, naturally."

"Unreal," Bannerman managed to stammer out. So this is why Lamont was stalling, to allow his sister-in-law time to get all dolled up. The outfit she wore was right out of *The Arabian Nights*, a wispy swath of azure blue material wrapped around her shoulders and breasts, with another piece of deep indigo wrapped around her hips. She was also sporting a lot of gold: bracelets, necklaces, earrings, and he knew they weren't fake.

Her skin was lighter than Loy's, that special kind of coppery bronze sun worshipers would kill for. He attributed this to her Italian mother. Her features were so perfectly formed as to appear almost unnatural. Where Loy's hair was long and full, hers was cut and curled in around her neck, framing an oval face. He wondered how a woman so young could achieve such aristocratic bearing. She might have been a princess, or even a goddess.

Charlie was more than a little shaken up by the whole thing. He tore his eyes away from the woman's hypnotic stare and turned to Lamont. "Could we step outside for a minute?"

The Frenchman glanced out the window. "The rain .... Let us go into the sunroom."

"Ah, excuse us," Bannerman said to the women as he followed Lamont back through the kitchen. The elderly woman and child he had seen earlier took off again when they saw him.

Once they were inside the profusion of bright flowers and greenery, he let loose. "I'm going to level with you, Giles. I live in New York City, where we got beautiful women coming out of our ears. It's no big deal to see a beautiful woman, okay? But, Jesus Christ, I can't say that I ever, in my entire life, saw a woman like that. She's like a storybook princess or something."

Lamont grinned. "Good! You like her."

Bannerman rolled his head around. "Of course I like her. But we're talking the real world here. First, there is no way a young woman like that should end up with the likes of me. Look at me—I'm a slob, for Christ's sake. How could I ever hope to make such a woman happy? Woman—hell! She's still a teenager.

It wouldn't work, Lamont. Even if I married her and took her back to New York, every asshole I know, and that's a whole lot, would be trying to get into her pants. And besides that, the city is a mean, dangerous place. I couldn't be watching out for her all the time. Look, God knows I appreciate the offer, and I'll take it to my grave as the nicest thing anyone's ever done for me, but it won't work."

Lamont turned away to watch the rain beating against the glassed-in room. "Have you travelled much?"

"This is my first trip outside of the country."

"I see. So tell me, what do you know about Africa?"

"Not a whole lot, *National Geographic* stuff mainly."

"Not too much about tribal customs and beliefs?"

"Not much."

"Your whole life has been lived in America?"

"Yeah, like I said, New York City."

His host turned back again and moved in close to Bannerman, nose to nose. "Then maybe you forgive my saying so, but you don't know shit! There are many lands, and you know only one. So you use American standards now to judge this girl. You are wrong to do this, by God, and Lamont will show you. Shaleen!"

The woman came out quickly, followed by her sister, an inquisitive look on both their faces. Lamont held out his hand to Bannerman. "Give me your gun!"

Charlie frowned. The idea did not appeal to him. But before he could say anything, the Frenchman pulled up his shirt, extracted the Colt, then gave it to Shaleen. "Charlie thinks you might have problems, you know, looking after yourself in the big city. What is this?"

She palmed the weapon, studying it for a moment. "It appears to be a standard US military issue .45 caliber Colt semi-automatic."

She extracted the magazine, examined it, then laid it on a small counter used for flower pots. She pulled the action back, checked the chamber, then released the front sear and in just seconds had the whole thing apart. "The serial number tells me it was manufactured in nineteen fifty, maybe for the Korean War."

Placing it to her nose, she said, "I think it was fired not long ago." She glanced through the barrel, shaking her head. "Very dirty."

"It's not mine," Charlie protested. "I just borrowed it."

Watching her long, tapered fingers assemble the weapon with such familiarity made him wonder if she stripped and assembled guns for a living. "Where did you learn to do that?"

"In defensive classes." Smiling down at him from her near six-foot height, Shaleen jammed the clip back in place and returned the weapon, grip first. "Like English, it is mandatory now in most schools in the north. I attained perfect marks in weaponry, karate, and stealth."

"Stealth?"

"Yes, how to get close to your enemy and kill him before he knows you are there. It was very exciting."

Bannerman soon realized that he was lost in the sheer force of her presence. He looked down at her golden slippers and then back up into those enormous dark eyes again and shook his head. The pair of overhead wicker fans that kept the air moving had little effect on the temperature, and he was suddenly conscious of beads of perspiration breaking out. He wished Bloom was around for support.

Lamont placed a hand on his shoulder. "You see, *mon ami*, there is much more to Somali woman than beauty. Loy and me, we are married seven years, and even now sometimes there are new surprises. So, what do you say?"

Charlie was having big trouble with the logic. A young woman, who could have her pick of available men anywhere, coming down here on a moment's notice to meet, and probably marry, some guy, a perfect stranger yet, who's got thirty-two years on her. But, like Sam said, this is the kind of stuff dreams are made of.

"Ah, you know, in my country, Miss Ahwaz, it's sort of the custom for a man to court a woman, to take her places and get to know her, to ...."

It came to his attention at that moment that he could see right through the top part of the blue outfit she had draped around her, which caused him to freeze up. It had been so long since he'd made love to a woman that he kind of figured he had gotten over the physical desire bit completely. Not so, he realized now.

"I gotta go," he said quickly. "The plane is waiting. Look, I'm going across the island for a few days, but I'll be in touch, okay?"

Shaleen put out her hand, smiling warmly. "Okay. I will say a prayer for you."

They were on the road a few minutes when the implications of that one hit him. "Isn't she a Muslim?"

"Shaleen was raised as a Roman Catholic. You see, that is one of the problems."

Now the truth comes out. "Why none of the locals will marry her, you mean?"

"Yes."

"So what are the other problems?"

"There is only one other problem, but maybe it is a big one. Tell me, do you like little children?"

Bannerman dared take his eyes off the road for a second time. Lamont was a wild driver, weaving his little Peugeot in and out of the traffic with no regard for pedestrians jumping out of his way. "I got a few nieces and nephews. Didn't care for them too much when they were little, but now they're okay, I guess." He recalled the little girl back at the house. "Are you saying Shaleen's got a kid already?"

"Quite the contrary, *mon ami,* quite the contrary."

"I see," said Charlie quietly. He digested this in silence for several moments until Lamont glanced at him anxiously.

"Bad news, eh?"

"I don't know, Giles, I honestly don't know. I never figured on getting married, so I never gave much thought to kids. What is it, a medical problem?"

"A birth defect — tilted tubes or something they can't fix, you know."

"Too bad. Women tend to take that sort of thing seriously."

Lamont stopped the car across from the hospital entrance. "Think carefully on this, *mon ami.* She would be good for you, this I know for sure. Will you return to Toama before Zurich?"

Bannerman frowned. His life was growing more complicated by the hour. He opened the car door. "I doubt if we'll have time. But you'll hear from me. And God knows how sorry we are about your boy. Was Robert your only son?"

The Frenchman held out his hand, smiling. "Only the good Lord knows how many little ones Lamont has sired." Then his face grew serious. "Maybe someone has told you this Tsingy is an evil place. The Malagasy call those big limestone spires the devil's teeth, because some of them go in and never come out. The natives believe Satan eats them. You watch he don't eat you, eh?"

CHAPTER TWELVE

René caught Anna up in his arms and twirled her about. "Ah, chéri, you have no idea how difficult it was for me to walk away from you in Geneva. They came for me just as I was ready to leave for church. I called your home, but naturally you had already left. By nightfall I was in the hills and cut off from all communications."

She kissed him, a soft, lingering, loving kiss. "It's okay, René, I understand."

"I would think of you every night, what you must be going through, what you must think of me for deserting you at such a time."

They were momentarily caught up in a crush of people entering the airport terminal through the double glass doors. "I thought you were dead," she told him. "Willi was dead. Dr. Lyon had vanished. What else was I to think?"

René removed his sunglasses. "Poor Lyon. His body was found on Friday in a thick clump of trees just a few meters off the track, thirty kilometers out of Bern. His neck was broken. It appears that he either fell from the train or was pushed. In any case the police are treating it as homicide and really going at it. An Inspector Lemieux was placed in charge of the investigation, which seems odd, since he belongs to the Zurich city police. Do you know him?"

They withdrew to the perimeter of the knot of passengers pushing toward the luggage rack. She glanced up at her cousin. "Don't you remember that really tall man with the big moustache who came on Sundays to play chess with my father? Sometimes

THE CASE OF THE GOLDEN ORCHID

he would give me a few coins, which I often shared with you, as I recall."

"But of course. No wonder the name seemed familiar."

"I went to see him a week before leaving and told him everything. I'm glad he is looking after it. Poor Dr. Lyon, I just know his death is somehow related to Lind's and Willi's."

"But you said Willi died in a motor accident."

"It was intended to look that way."

"But you don't believe it was. What about the police, what do they believe?"

"They found the whole thing very suspicious. In time they will learn the truth, I'm certain of that."

The man from Interpol picked up his bag, but was promptly relieved of it by Anna's police escort, a diminutive Malagasy named Moussavi. They followed the man to the Land Rover and watched him place the bag in the front seat. René fixed his dark glasses and paused to take in the sundrenched forested hills behind the city. Then he swung his gaze around to the contrasting Prussian blue of the Mozambique Channel in the distance.

"I must say, Morondava seems like a perfectly delightful little spot. So peaceful."

Anna smiled, accepting his hand to help her climb into the back of the Land Rover. Once they were underway, he asked, "No more incidents, I trust?"

"Nothing, I am pleased to report." She leaned in close, whispering, "Moussavi is even reluctant to allow me to go to the bathroom on my own."

René took her hand again. "My darling, that is exactly what he is supposed to do. I told his commandant that all hell would break loose if anything were to happen to my favorite cousin."

She smiled, squeezing his hand. "Thank you for that, and thank you for coming. You have no idea how much it means to have you here."

"After deserting you the way I did, it seemed the least I could do. Will I be staying with Herr Scheuchzer and his wife?"

"No, Marina's decided to put you in one of the spare cottages," Anna replied. She added nonchalantly, "I'm sure you will find it much more private."

René allowed the tips of his fingers to trace a line along the seam of her jeans. "I'll do my best to persuade you to come and visit."

The heavy overnight downpour had turned the dirt roads into a sea of mud in places, requiring all the skill their driver possessed to keep the vehicle moving forward on the steep grades. Twice they had to stop to allow small herds of zebu cattle to cross the road. When they finally reached the flattened mesa, Anna glanced at her watch.

"Oh, damn. We're going to be late. Moussavi, do you think you could drive faster? I'd like to make the Analabe airstrip before two, if possible."

The little policeman nodded, grinning, then switched on the flashing blue lights mounted on top of his windshield.

"Late for what?" René inquired.

Anna took a good grip on the roll bar with her left hand as the Land Rover picked up speed. "Do you remember my mentioning those two Americans I met in Tana? They are coming over for a visit, but one of them was injured just yesterday. A bomb exploded quite close to them, and I gather they are fortunate to have escaped more serious injury. Since the drive up the escarpment is so bumpy, they are using a small aircraft to fly into an emergency strip just south of Analabe."

René tightened his grip on her hand. "I heard something on the news. Over in Toamasina, wasn't it? Some kind of terrorist activity, I suppose."

"Yes," she agreed. "It usually is when bombs are involved."

"How well do you know these men? Didn't you meet them for the first time in Tana?"

"You're hurting my hand, René."

"Oh, sorry. This road ...."

"Yes, like I told you on the telephone, they came along and, well, made that man stop following me."

"I see. But why are they coming to an isolated little place like Analabe?"

"For the same reason they were in Toamasina, I suppose: to study orchids. Both are professional botanists from the Smithsonian Institute in Washington."

René seemed impressed. "Really? And where do they intend to stay?"

"Dr. Bloom, the injured man, will stay in the main house, where I can keep watch. His friend will take one of the other spare cottages."

Her cousin nodded solemnly and remained quiet for the remainder of the trip, while Anna mulled over Charlie Bannerman's warning about Interpol.

The first blast hit with the impact of an artillery shell exploding overhead. Bannerman threw aside the covers and pushed open his cottage door. A second blast almost knocked him off his feet. With it came a flash of light as brilliant as the surface of the sun. René Simard called out from next door, "Have you ever seen the likes of this?"

"Jesus!" Charlie exclaimed. "The goddamn thing just sneaks up without a sound, then lets you have it with both barrels."

René carried a pair of jeans in his hand. He was halfway between the cottages when a third ear-piercing blast at point-blank range drove its shaft of supercharged electricity into one of the tamarinds beside the compound gate. It split the huge trunk down the middle and scattered pieces of wood all over the compound. Simard's sharp curse drew Bannerman's attention. The Frenchman was flat on his ass, having stumbled over a flower box while watching the display. He cursed some more as he struggled to pull on his jeans.

Branches and chunks of bark continued to rain down upon them as Simard leaped up the three steps to Charlie's veranda. "*Merde!* I can see now why they call it killer lightning."

The ringtails, whose instinct warned them of the danger lurking in high places, had all scampered down from the treetops to sit beside various buildings within the compound. Each family was curled into a tight ball of fur to watch the awesome display.

A few drops of rain touched Bannerman's bare feet as he stood with Simard at the edge of the narrow veranda. He was aware of his heart pounding. "Goddamn scary, isn't it?"

Simard nodded. "This is the nearest thing to the wrath of God I've seen in my lifetime."

Bannerman agreed. "I once read these things zap down to earth at around two hundred miles per second and build up to about a million volts. A single flash is capable of spitting out forty or more strikes. Make a great weapon."

The storm was just one of many that swept down from the northwest coastal region during the hot summer months. In less than five minutes the rain had peaked to an intensity that obliterated the lights in the main house across the compound. Klaus and two of his foresters had run out to inspect the damage, but were forced to retreat as rising winds caused the heavy downpour to spiral violently across the open space. When it began to bite into the bare flesh of the awed spectators, both men decided they'd had enough.

Once inside, the reality of the storm diminished sharply, and Charlie could not help comparing his own slovenly physique to Simard's, who weighed in at one fifty, if that, in his designer jeans and dark, smooth skin. He was a man who worked out and stayed in shape. Bannerman, with his candy-striped boxer shorts and pasty rolls of fat, could only stare in envy.

There was some Australian lager, Foster's, in the half-size refrigerator. Charlie twisted the caps off a couple and handed one to Simard.

The Frenchman grinned. "So here we are, two cops on an island off the coast of Africa, scared shitless over what is probably no more than an average storm for this part of the world. I believe this calls for a toast, Doctor — or Lieutenant. Which do you prefer, by the way?"

Bannerman shrugged. The truth had come out over dinner, as Anna Grenier had already told Klaus Scheuchzer that both men were policemen and had not thought to warn the Swiss to keep his mouth shut. "Charlie'll do just fine. As for a toast, why not to Interpol? I've heard a lot about it over the years, not all good either, but you're the first real agent I ever met."

René seemed to consider this for a moment, then nodded before raising his glass. "To the agency, then." He took a few gulps as Bannerman watched him closely.

"Tell the truth, I didn't even know you guys worked covert. But that Palermo bust, hell of an operation." Once the foresters learned there was a real live Interpol agent in their midst, they prompted Simard to relate some of his undercover experiences. He ended with the huge Cosa Nostra trial, very prominent in the news at the moment.

"If there was more of that going on in your part of the world, it would take a lot of pressure off our guys working the streets," Charlie added.

Simard eased back a little into the sofa chair. He looked out from under his long lashes at the New York cop and said softly, "But I think heroin is not such a big problem these days, eh?"

"True enough," Charlie agreed. "Cocaine pretty well got it sewed up in my neck of the woods. Crack, mostly."

"Terrible stuff. In Europe the volume has been rising steadily over the last few years. I was told the Colombians have set up an exchange operation — two kilos of heroin for every kilo of cocaine delivered. The reason being, presumably, that the going price of cocaine in Europe is twice what it is in your country. Our narcotics division now has a full-time staff, ten men, who do nothing other than monitor the movement of cocaine."

"They just keep an eye on it?"

"Not exactly. As perhaps you know, Interpol has no authority to make arrests. Our functions are primarily coordination, infiltration, supplying information — stuff like that. When we learn something of importance — a name, a date, a place — we pass it on to the appropriate authorities."

He paused for a quick sip, never taking his eyes off Bannerman's. "Sometimes, in order to come up with certain crucial pieces of information that could result in important arrests, it is necessary to work undercover. A job, I might add, which is often dangerous and usually thankless. Only the most spectacular results will bring a note of thanks from the host country."

Bannerman nodded in sympathy as he listened to the sky rumbling in the near distance. Simard's voice had taken on a bitter edge. "I know what you mean. It's much the same in my line of work. The everyday stuff goes unnoticed."

Simard waved his hand in an angry gesture. "At least you are not at the mercy of many governments. At least you have the power to act. Sometimes we are forced to beg, simply to get permission to monitor the movements of known criminals."

Here was another cop who had not received sufficient recognition for carrying out the job he was paid to do. Get in line, buddy. "You know, I always wondered where Interpol's financing comes from these days. Didn't the US government cut off support years ago?"

The Frenchman smiled. This obese creature would be astonished to learn that his death would result in a contribution of fifteen thousand Swiss francs to the Interpol coffers, twenty percent of the seventy-five-thousand-franc price tag on his head. "That is more in the administration end. I try not to concern myself with such mundane matters."

"As long as your check shows up each month," Charlie added with a knowing nod. "But what about these stories I hear about some of your people getting caught in the act, you know, actively marketing drugs?"

Simard shrugged. "Oh, these are true stories; there is no doubt about it. We have some rotten apples, who has not? Does each member of your New York police department have lily white hands? I think not."

Charlie had no argument with that. "'Let he who is without sin cast the first stone'."

"Exactly." René stood up and glanced at his watch. "So there, twenty minutes and it is all over. Just one more tiny but ferocious storm working its way down the coast of Madagascar. Thank you for the refreshments." He held the bottle out to glance at the label. "Australian. Not bad. I hope we are both able to get back to sleep. Good night, Lieutenant."

After the guy closed the door, Bannerman switched off the lights. He had just learned something about René Simard, but what it was exactly, he couldn't quite grasp.

The helicopter arrived at seven-ten, an old Bell G-2A that had been painted over a number of times. It was now blue and gold, the colors of the Virgin. From the veranda Bloom watched the machine land through his still-blurred vision. In Pensacola he had taken a short course on helicopters, and it was the G-2A he had trained on. The pilot who stepped out was a very tall Malagasy with little meat on his bones, but with a lot of teeth and an instant smile.

Gerhard, the young forester who had been with Willi when Lind Grenier's body was found, emerged from his cottage with a canvas bag containing their sandwiches, four thermoses, several cans of spray paint, and his camera. Since the Bell was a three-seater, he and Anna were to go first; the pilot, Rinday, would then return to pick up Charlie and René.

Anna came out of the kitchen and stood beside Bloom. "I feel rather guilty about leaving you behind, but I do want to take advantage of René's visit to see what we can find out. And having your friend along will be very helpful, I'm sure."

She saw that he had removed the bandages. "Your eyes have improved greatly, even since last evening. At this rate you will certainly be able to join us tomorrow. Still no headaches?"

Sam looked down at Anna's slightly fuzzy face and smiled. "Still no headaches." This is precisely what made this attack so different from all the others. While the explosion had severely affected his vision, the usual killer headache that accompanied each relapse over the last twenty years had yet to show up.

Bannerman strolled out to the middle of the courtyard to inspect the helicopter. He poked a finger at the bubble, testing it. It seemed like such a flimsy contraption to get airborne, and his stomach was already rolling at the thought of going up in it. The six Swiss foresters crowded around as soon as the rotors wound down, giving Charlie the impression that he was standing in the middle of the Pittsburgh Steelers. They knew the pilot and seemed fond of him.

As Charlie backed away, he saw Anna leave Bloom's side and walk over to stand beside Simard. Last evening Charlie had felt it necessary to caution his friend about telling her too much. When Sam asked why, Bannerman had reluctantly told him that in his opinion, the relationship between the two seemed a little too intimate for his liking, which upset Bloom more than Charlie would have thought.

Once they were airborne, Anna's curiosity burned to see this piece of unearthly terrain that Lind had raved about. She recalled his telling her that the Malagasy believed it to be an evil place, where spirits of the long-dead Vazimba returned in the midst of each storm to lay claim to the souls of those who had taken away their land. Lind had found their tales amusing.

On the way to Tsingy they crossed over the westerly corner of a swath of country known as the thorny desert, where every living plant was covered with thorns. Here lived the Antandroy, 'the people of the thorns', a tall, dark race of African descent, with their large herds of humpbacked zebu cattle. They waved with great enthusiasm at the helicopter. Within ten minutes they had entered a bowl-shaped desert-like valley that supported nothing other than occasional patches of low spiny scrub. There they picked up the single track that wound its way along the reddish-brown hills and craters that made up the westerly edge of the central plateau. From time to time the track would vanish completely; but their pilot, Rinday, knew the route along the escarpment and always managed to find it again.

When the aircraft was still ten kilometers distant, Anna could see the morning sun glistening off the spires. Tsingy, Lind had written in one of his letters, was the Malagasy word for spikes. As they drew closer, the weathered limestone pinnacles appeared like endless rows of giant shark's teeth. Numerous green dots on the horizon showed where clumps of trees had found sufficient soil to take root and grow even higher than the pillars surrounding them.

Rinday had not been keen about flying into Tsingy, and decided to warn his passengers once again. "In the whole reserve there is one place to set down, and I am not so certain I can find it. Even if we were to survive a crash, maybe we do not find our way out."

Anna was seated between the two men. She was aware of Gerhard tensing up. She did not wish to endanger her life or anyone else's, yet felt a near-desperate longing to view the tortured landscape that had not only awed her husband; but, she was certain, had also lured him to his death. The chopper had slowed to a mere crawl now as the giant pinnacles loomed up below them.

"What do you think, Gerhard? Would you prefer to wait for us out here?"

Gerhard was in his mid-twenties, an age when adventure was high on the priority list. He had been bending over to point his camera directly ahead through the bubble. He straightened up and turned to Anna, grinning. "If you are willing to risk it, Dr. Grenier, then I am too."

"Good. Well, Rinday, onward. Let's see the whole damn thing."

Anna was surprised when the pilot crossed himself, but she knew he was right: Their chances of surviving a crash were minimal, and their chances of finding their way out of the labyrinth were even less. They picked up speed and moved into the six hundred square miles that made up the reserve. A huge brown and white hawk fluttered out of its nest in alarm. Close up, the pinnacles seemed old and cracked and weather-beaten, some joined together, some solitary; yet to Anna they appeared stately and proud, harboring a certain primitive harmony in their ghostlike pallor. Perhaps they knew they were unique on the Earth's surface. There was only one Tsingy.

Suddenly, several columns of bats erupted out of a great bushy tree, forcing Rinday to veer sharply to the right while applying power for a steep ascent. He shook his head and muttered something that Anna didn't catch. She knew from her own experience in mainland Africa that a helicopter's blades could be thrown off balance by striking even the smallest object. For a moment she thought of turning back; it seemed pointless to risk three lives just to satisfy her curiosity. But she remained silent, because she felt it was more than mere curiosity that had called her here. Somewhere below, in this hellish maze of bleached limestone, her husband had met his death. She was convinced of that.

"Look," cried Gerhard. He pointed to a troop of red-fronted lemurs scurrying down a razor-edged spire. In seconds they had vanished into various shafts and crevasses at the base of the tsingy. A minute later they saw a tall, black indri rise from the crown of a tamarind tree to its full height to seek out the harsh sound that had invaded its solitude.

Rinday flew at fifty kilometers per hour about two hundred feet above the tops of the spires. Anna was struck by the great number of bats, large and small, which spiraled out of their roosts at their approach, and wondered what they would feed upon in such sparse undergrowth. Gray parrots and fat green sunbirds shied away from the aircraft, little kestrel-like falcons danced in front of it, miniature owls stared at it, swarms of butterflies fluttered in fear beneath it.

They were twenty minutes into the reserve, flying in a northwesterly direction, when Gerhard spotted a bright flash from a peak several hundred meters off to the left of the aircraft. He touched Anna's arm and pointed it out, so she asked Rinday to head in that direction.

When they arrived in the vicinity, however, there was nothing to be seen but more pinnacles. They circled the area once and moved on. As they were coming out of the turn, Anna saw a face staring up at them.

"Rinday—stop! I saw a man down there."

The pilot pulled up the chopper's nose and did a stationary turn. Anna removed her dark glasses and searched the area surrounding the base of the pillar. "He was right there, standing against that tree trunk. He glanced up the instant we passed over him. He seemed to be wearing glasses."

"He had a white face?" asked the pilot.

"Yes, very white."

"An old man, perhaps?"

She turned to the pilot. "You saw him?"

Rinday smiled. "If Madame Doctor will excuse the opinion of this poor pilot, I think she was staring into the face of a sifaka, our tall lemur. The old ones have so much white fur surrounding their face that in the distance they can look like little old men. There are many in Tsingy."

Anna felt a little miffed, as she resented being told that she was unable to distinguish between a man and an animal. "Just circle the area slowly. There is someone down there, and if we don't see him again, it is only because he has moved away."

But there was neither man nor animal to be seen. She studied the ground in detail, this time noticing the wide variety of flowers, among them, she was reasonably certain, the golden orchid.

Gerhard turned to Anna wearing a puzzled expression. "But how would a man be able to penetrate this far into the maze, Dr. Grenier, and then find his way out again?"

"Lind told me that the natives regularly enter the reserve to gather honey. Dr. Terroux mentioned an old British couple from Kenya who often came here. So there has to be a trail of some sort, probably more than one. There must be. Rinday, do you think you could find this spot again?"

"Oh no, Madame Doctor. Look around and you will see that everything looks the same. Even a magnetic compass does not work properly in Tsingy. There must be an underground ore body that throws it off. Only by the sun and the stars is it possible to tell direction. But location? Never."

"What about maps? Surely this country must have some decent mapping by now."

Rinday nodded. "Yes, everywhere but in the west. Here we still navigate by the one in two hundred thousand stuff the French did in the early eighties—small scale and poor quality. Tsingy was not done at all."

He had turned the helicopter back on a northeast bearing, directly into the sun. Anna replaced her dark glasses and glanced at her watch, thinking of René and Charlie waiting back at the station. She knew it was important to have the two policemen on site. "Very well, Rinday, return to the plateau. Gerhard, see if you can direct us to the spot where you found Lind's body."

The young man nodded; he was not unhappy about leaving the reserve. "We will have to go back to the southeast corner of the reserve and drop down close to the ground. Like I told you last evening, Dr. Grenier, it will only be my best guess. Everything out there looks the same too."

Bannerman always had a tendency toward motion sickness, probably the very reason he managed to avoid airplanes up till now. He climbed aboard the blue and gold helicopter with considerable apprehension. Simard was amused, as the American's nervousness was apparent to everyone. But after the initial shock of seeing the world go by beneath his feet wore off, Charlie settled down and enjoyed the forty-minute flight.

Rinday took his passengers over the corner of the reserve to give them some idea of the terrain. Simard shook his head. "I doubt if hell itself is more forbidding than this."

Bannerman couldn't have agreed more. Medieval mapmakers would surely have drawn a line around Tsingy and added their customary notation: *Beyond this place there be dragons!*

Anna and the young Swiss forester were waiting beside a four-foot-high rock cairn in the middle of nowhere, or so it seemed to Charlie. The landscape was completely devoid of character. There was nothing: no trees, no flowers, just tortured red earth strewn with rocks and sprouting a few wizened clumps of bunchgrass. To the west was Tsingy, its serrated ridges barely visible ten to twelve kilometers distant. To the north and east, a series of tabletop mountains sprouted out of the horizon, looking just as bare as the land they were standing on.

Anna rushed over to them before the engine was turned off. "Did the pilot tell you Gerhard spotted a flash deep into the reserve? When we went over to investigate, I looked down and saw a man staring up at us."

Bannerman wondered why the pilot had not bothered to mention such an important find. René seemed shocked. "What happened?"

"Oh, nothing. He vanished, of course. But I saw him, so I know someone is in there. Rinday tried to tell me it was a white lemur I was looking at, but it was a man. I am certain of it."

Bannerman shaded his eyes. He was the only one who had not thought to wear dark glasses. "You see any roads or trails, or figure out how he got in?"

Anna shook her head. "We spent barely half an hour looking. I believe the only way we are going to determine the access points is to fly the perimeter again and again until we locate one of them."

Gerhard said, "If the natives go there for honey, would it not be easier to ask around? For a few francs and a promise not to inform the authorities, I'm sure someone will cooperate."

"Good idea," René commented.

"Then why wait?" Anna said with enthusiasm. "Gerhard, why don't you and Rinday do that while we look around here. The name of the village where they found Lind's things is Manera, almost due east of here. Start there. If they know nothing, try the next two. I don't know their names; perhaps Rinday does. Do you have money?"

Gerhard grinned. He found Anna's excitement infectious. "Enough, I guess."

"Can you speak their language, Rinday?" Anna wanted to know.

The pilot shrugged, a movement that seemed to carry all the way down his slender frame. "Someone will always speak Malagasy. We can go. If you wish, we can go."

When the chopper departed and the dreadful noise abated, Bannerman asked Anna what she had learned in the hour and a half she and Gerhard had been wandering around. She gave a disappointing shrug and swung her hand around in a sweeping arc. "Look at this place; it is all the same. Gerhard said the spot where they found the body could be up to a kilometer away in either direction. We built this mound of rocks for a reference point and covered five hundred meters to the south and to the east. Since there are three of us, I will take the northwest quarter and Charlie, you take the northeast. René will cover the southwest. You are both policemen, so I need not tell you what to look for."

Bannerman found himself smiling. There was no doubt who was in charge of this little expedition. A woman who handed out orders like that might be someone Sam was better off without. "I guess we're looking for anything," he ventured.

Simard nodded. "Anything out of the ordinary, which should not be difficult to find; provided, of course, that there is something to find."

A shadow made them look up. A lone vulture was circling almost directly overhead. If only it could talk, Anna thought.

"Gerhard told me that is how they spotted Lind's vehicle — by the vultures circling." She brushed a few strands of hair from her face and said quietly, "I believe Lind was killed inside the reserve and his body was taken out here and dumped. Granted, he was killed by lightning, but how? And if his death was accidental, why would anyone want to move the body?"

"To draw attention away from the reserve," Charlie replied. "If something is going on, the last thing they'd want is a search party scrambling around."

"Which still doesn't alter the fact that he was killed by lightning," René said. "Let's say that whoever is in there, if anyone, moved it out. Moving a dead body is not such a serious crime, Anna. So I'm still not completely clear on what it is you hope to accomplish."

"If Willi had not been killed, if Dr. Lyon had not been murdered, if my flat had not been burgled, if I had not been followed in Tana, and if I had not seen a man in the middle of those damn razorbacks, then maybe I might not have anything to get suspicious about."

"She's got a point," Bannerman said. "In fact, she's got a whole bunch."

Twin red spots had appeared on Anna's cheeks. "Look around you! What in bloody hell do you think Lind would be doing out here in the first place, especially in the middle of a lightning storm?"

Simard placed a hand on his cousin's arm. "Okay, okay. I'm not disagreeing with your conclusions. I'm just trying to get some sense of direction in this whole matter. Let's say that I — that we — agree he died inside the reserve. Let's say that there is a super-secret government operation going on — chemical research or some such thing. Maybe it isn't even this government, maybe a foreign government — France, for instance. And Lind happened to wander into this secret installation. He watches, probably climbs up a tree for a better look, and a bolt of lightning strikes him. The next morning they discover the body and make a decision to dump it somewhere outside the reserve." He glanced at Charlie. "Does that make sense to you?"

Bannerman figured the time had come to lay a few cards on the table. "More or less. The super-secret government concept might be a bit thin. Why not a processing center for some big international drug cartel? Maybe they bring in cocaine from Bolivia, process it into crack, then ship it out again. No one would ever suspect Madagascar, and even if they did, Tsingy would be the last place they'd look."

René seemed a little startled at first, but quickly composed himself. He shook his head. "That idea has even less merit than mine. A drug cartel in Madagascar? Interpol has never heard so much as a whisper about cocaine being shipped to this island. No, it makes no sense at all."

Charlie had gotten what he was after and decided to back off. "I thought we were talking hypothetically. Hell, it could be a slave market or an atomic storage depot. It could be anything. But the question Dr. Grenier has to ask herself is whether she really wants to find out."

Anna had caught René's reaction, and it disturbed her. "The answer is yes, yes, yes! I must find out the truth behind my husband's death. And believe me, I will."

Charlie didn't doubt for a minute that she would. He had learned long ago that nothing short of death could keep really determined people from doing what they set out to do. He headed off into his sector as Anna turned north into hers. Simard hung back for a few minutes before slowly walking south.

René began to purposely kick up dust with every swing of his right foot. His cousin was definitely growing tiresome, and it was now clear to him that she and that fat American cop were working together. And it was also obvious that Bannerman knew, or at least had a damn good idea, about what was taking place inside Tsingy.

Figuring out how to get rid of all three and make their deaths appear accidental was becoming more difficult with each passing day. He needed help. Somehow, he had to get in touch with the ZIAN personnel inside the reserve. He knew their frequency and could contact them, if only he had a few moments alone in the helicopter. It was also his duty to warn Victor of a possible penetration, if and when they managed to locate the entrance.

René had no idea where they parked their vehicles, but assumed that it was probably in one of those caverns Karl had mentioned. It surprised him that the four men had returned from Toamasina so quickly. He supposed they were all anxious to return home, but before they could do that, there was the matter of destroying all evidence of the great experiment, whatever it had been. He knew cocaine was involved, but no one had bothered to provide him with details of what exactly Herr Brower's men were doing in Tsingy.

His foot slipped down a hole, an animal den of some sort. Simard cursed. He had come close to breaking his ankle. He desperately needed a plan, he thought, kicking up more red dirt. A tube-shaped glassy-looking rock caught his eye. He picked it up and studied it as he walked along. Then it occurred to him that he was holding a fulgurite — a glob of glass that formed when lightning struck the ground. This was certain proof that lightning had touched down in the immediate vicinity.

He thought of taking care of these two now. It would be simple to do it right here, but he would have no alibi.

He became aware of a shadow on his right. For some reason the vulture had decided to follow him. In frustration René tried to project Anna's next course of action. He assumed Gerhard would be able to convince one of the natives to show them the way into the reserve. They would then be entering a world controlled by ZIAN. And then what? What would they find in Tsingy? That was the question worrying René. He knew the operation was being carried out below ground, but perhaps not all of it. If only he had known while he was down on the coast that he would wind up in Tsingy, he would have asked more questions. As it was, there was little he could do to stop Anna and the others from entering. Perhaps Victor, if warned beforehand, could arrange a welcoming party. Perhaps there was a big crevasse into which the whole gang could disappear. Somehow, he had to contact Victor — and soon.

A crevasse .... This gave him an idea. He turned toward his cousin. She was about a hundred paces away, with her back to him. The American was also facing north. René retraced his tracks to find the hole he had stepped in. He bent down and pulled in enough sand and earth to cover most of it. Then he placed the fulgurite about three feet from his side of the hole and stood back.

He called to Anna. "Come over here and look at this!"

She spun around and began to walk quickly toward him. As she drew close, he pointed to the rock. "Is this what I think it is?"

She saw the shiny surface reflecting the sun's rays and anxiously increased her pace for the last few steps. Her hard fall knocked the wind out of her.

René rushed to her side. "What is it?"

The pain was evident on Anna's face as he reached down to remove her foot from the hole. René undid the laces on her soft leather boot as she groaned in agony. "My bloody ankle …." She twisted the leg toward her and felt the bone. "God, that hurts. Damn! Damn! Damn!"

Bannerman arrived, puffing heavily. "What happened?"

Simard looked up. "She stepped into some kind of animal hole. I called her over to look at this fulgurite—at least I think that's what it is."

Charlie saw that Anna was biting her lip. He noticed the swelling had already started. "Figure it's broken?"

"I don't think so, just a bad sprain."

He picked up the odd-shaped rock and turned it over in his hand. "Saw one like this in a science center once. The temperature of the bolt fries the sand and forms one of these things." He glanced around the area. "I guess it proves lightning's paid a visit or two to this place. Not exactly what you wanted to hear, I guess."

Anna took René's arm to help herself up. "The whole country may be full of fulgurites," she said defiantly. "It changes nothing."

Simard allowed the ghost of a smile to cross his face. *Oh but it does, dear cousin; it means that you stay at home tomorrow while I take care of your new American friends.* He had already worked out a plan whereby the three of them would explore the reserve alone, providing they were able to penetrate it.

They waited a full hour for the helicopter to return. But it didn't return; instead, it flew right over them as Gerhard waved. By the time they realized it wasn't circling to land, it was too late to signal them in.

"What the hell is going on?" the Frenchman asked.

"Bet they found someone who's agreed to show them the entrance to the reserve," Bannerman told him. He glanced down at Anna, catching the effort she made to hide her disappointment. They had used most of their water to keep the kerchief on her ankle damp in an attempt to control the swelling.

"I hope they come back this way before bringing the man home," she said with a thin smile. Charlie had since come across four more fulgurites, confirming just how prevalent lightning strikes were in the region. But he had yet to find evidence to indicate that the place had been visited by another human being—ever.

Another forty minutes went by before they saw the helicopter again. As soon as it touched down, René marched over and proceeded to blast Gerhard for being away for so long. The young man seemed completely devastated by Simard's tongue-lashing and stood by in awkward silence as they helped Anna into the machine. But then Gerhard decided he had better break the news before Dr. Grenier took off.

"The native, Jinnar, showed us the entrance, which I labeled with a square meter patch of fluorescent orange." He held up a can of spray paint. "You can see it from two kilometers with the naked eye. When we walked a short distance into the reserve to see how the trail was marked, I found this small piece of red flagging in some lemur droppings. This is the same kind we use to mark the trees; it is shipped to us from home."

Anna's pain left her for a moment. "Which means—"

René finished the sentence for her: "—that Lind somehow knew about that particular route into the reserve. But whether it was his first trip or his last, we will never know. Anna, do you think you could wait another twenty minutes so Rinday can fly us over to the entrance? We still have a good three hours of daylight left. This will allow sufficient time for Gerhard and I to have a look around while Rinday brings you and Charlie back to base."

Bannerman was about to protest, but something stopped him. He was aware of Anna's gaze, of her seeking Charlie's sanction. He shrugged, shouting at her, "It's okay by me, if you're willing to hang on."

192

"Yes, of course I am," she shouted back, climbing down again with her cousin's assistance. "But do you think it is dangerous, René?"

He looked thoughtfully over at the ridges in the distance. "You feel certain that you saw a man, but I am inclined to believe Rinday that it was just one of those old white lemurs. In my opinion there is no danger." He smiled at her, a dazzling smile of movie star proportions. "In any case I am not defenseless, should the need arise."

On their way back to the forestry compound, Anna and Charlie decided not to discuss the current situation as far as René was concerned with the pilot listening in on the headphones. But she did tell Bannerman about spotting the golden orchid.

"That's a step in the right direction. Problem is, Sam and me only got tomorrow to look around. Next day we're off to Zurich."

"Why Zurich?" she asked, puzzled.

Bannerman cursed silently. Letting the next stage in their investigation slip was dumb. "Just a quick stopover to pick up a few things."

"Ah, Zurich at Christmas — lucky you. I will give you my mother's telephone number and I insist that you and Sam go there for dinner. Will you?"

"Sure, if we have time." Charlie thought about Shaleen again, and wondered if a woman's opinion on the issue might help him make up his mind. "You know, when we were over in Toama, a strange thing happened to me ...."

By the time Charlie completed his story, they were just coming into Analabe. Rinday had assumed that Anna wanted to go to Dr. Terroux's clinic, but Anna said no, it was just a simple sprain. It seemed the whole population had come out to wave at them as they headed due south, toward the high plateau where the forestry station was located.

She had found Charlie's tale an extraordinary one, if the woman was as beautiful as he claimed. She hardly knew what to say at first, since he was obviously asking for her advice. "I know little about Somalia, but I can confirm that when it comes to love and marriage, most African cultures have different values than we do in the West. But nineteen, and so beautiful .... Then again, a woman living in a predominantly Muslim society and not able to bear children—yes, I can see where she would be considered a liability. Unless they come from a well-to-do family, most women who find themselves in her position end up as prostitutes or as the mistress of some rich man—the same thing. So yes, I suppose it is possible that the offer is exactly what it appears. How do you feel about this girl? Are you considering marrying her?"

Bannerman tried to force an answer, but every time he went to say no, a vision of Shaleen with one million bucks floating over her head stopped him cold. And when he tried to say yes, a vision of his three sisters giving this poor African girl the third degree presented itself. They were sure to think that he had turned into a dirty old man. And his fellow cops—it would be years before they stopped ribbing him.

At last he said, "Sheesh—it's a tough one. Seems like I'm having this wild fantasy and sooner or later I'm gonna wake up, and that'll be the end of it."

"What does Sam say about it?"

"Well, he kind of figures I've been presented with an opportunity most guys can only dream about. Said he'd be my best man, even volunteered you as the, ah, bridesmaid or something."

"Did he?" she asked pensively. "Did he really?"

Bloom heard the rotor blades chopping the air and looked at his watch. He sensed something was wrong. After tucking his drawings under a pillow, he ran out into the courtyard. Marina, the only other person who had remained at the station, was already there.

He watched Bannerman get out and then offer his hand to help Anna down. "What did you do?" Bloom shouted above the noise of the machine.

"Stepped into a hole," she replied with a weak smile.

"Is it broken?" Marina asked.

"Thank God, no. Just a nasty sprain."

Bannerman shrugged his shoulders to Sam's questioning glance and went off to his cottage. Inside he took two beers from his little refrigerator and walked back across the compound. Marina had taken Anna inside to get some ice for her ankle. Charlie glanced at Sam's eyes. "Looking better all the time, Professor. How's your vision?"

"Ninety percent. Ready for action, Lieutenant. So what's the story?"

Charlie handed his companion a beer and slumped back in one of the veranda chairs. He took a good swig from his own bottle before covering the day's activities.

Having digested all this in silence, Bloom finally smiled. "ZIAN, Simard, Interpol: a home run every time at bat. I'm beginning to see why Hennessey insisted you take this case. Are you ever wrong?"

"All the time. The only difference between a smart cop and a dumb one is the smart one catches his mistakes before it's too late. But everyone screws up. Everyone."

"For Christ's sake, Bannerman, stop being so bloody modest."

The policeman set down his Foster's and ran a hand through his mess of curly hair. "If you think we're making any real headway on this thing, forget it. All we know for sure is someone is trying to kill us. And you don't need to be a genius to know they're not done yet."

CHAPTER THIRTEEN

Simard glanced ahead at the thick rubber-soled boots worn by the forester and then down at his expensive Capstan runners, which were being cut to pieces. As it was, he had to look carefully each time he placed a foot upon the cursed razorbacks. Which is exactly what they were: blades of limestone honed so thin in places that it was like trying to make your way across a mishmash of guillotines. The oaf had warned him, of course, but René had been anxious to get into Tsingy before the others. He hoped that somehow he would get lucky and make contact with Victor. If he didn't do so soon, they would be forced to turn back. Since he had yet to see a place suitable to lie down, René did not relish the idea of spending the night.

They were now about one and a half hours into the maze. Gerhard had used his can of orange DayGlo spray to mark their passage, but even this knowledge did little to offset Simard's growing sense of unease. Everything about Tsingy made him nervous. It was a completely foreign environment, like he was on a different planet, with no point of reference other than the sun, which was rapidly falling behind the giant spires. Lemurs taunted them constantly, throwing squishy, half-chewed pieces of fruit at the intruders. Giant hawks screeched overhead, volleys of bats flew out of holes in the limestone directly into their faces. As the shadows grew darker and more forbidding, he had to choke back the feeling that the towering minarets were closing in around him. After millions of years of erosion, the limestone sentinels had grown to look so identical in shape and proportion that several times he could have sworn they had already passed the same point. A dozen times he had to reach out to prevent himself from falling over, and now both hands were sliced in several places. The young forester, still smarting from his tongue-lashing, kept up a brisk pace and did nothing to make things easier for the Frenchman.

René was far from certain that they were even following a trail, since there was nothing at all to indicate that the Swiss was following a marked route through the maze. Finally Gerhard stopped and bent down to study something on the floor of the tsingy. Simard approached carefully and looked down over his shoulder. All he saw was more limestone.

"What is it?"

The big forester straightened up, his features drawn. "Lind was here. He spent the night here."

The Frenchman studied the limestone again, this time noticing a series of narrow grooves chipped into the base of one of the pinnacles. Then he spotted loose fragments lying around the perimeter. The grooves took the shape of a nook, large enough for a man to curl up in.

René nodded and stood up. "What makes you think Lind did this?"

"His ice pick. Lind always carried it. These marks were made with an ice pick."

"I see," said Simard after a moment of thought. "Anna's theory grows stronger all the time. You are to be congratulated, Gerhard. I would not have recognized those grooves for what they are." He glanced at his watch. "We'll push on for another quarter hour. Then we must turn back."

After ten minutes of delicately weaving their way through more razorbacks, the Swiss stopped again. This time he was looking up. Simard closed on him and followed his gaze. They were standing in a narrow gap about four feet across. Gerhard had spotted a two-inch diameter hole that seemed to have been drilled into the rock. The hole was about eight feet up and surrounded by a dark patch. He reached up to insert a finger into the hole and then placed his finger beneath his nose.

He tasted it. "Yuck! It's something vile—burnt, like carbon."

But Simard had already spotted an identical hole on the other side of the gap. Then his eyes were drawn unconsciously to the dark patches at his feet. He sensed that there was something sinister about these three points of darkness.

He pointed them out to the Swiss. The young man nodded and backed away a few meters to study the whole gap. Simard bent down to run his fingers along the darkened limestone. It smelled like carbon. Then he noticed that the surface of the rock was grooved, but not by an ice pick. By something infinitely more powerful. Looking up, he saw the forester standing with his arms outstretched in the form of the crucified Christ.

It gave Simard a start, as the sun was directly behind his head, creating a halo effect. "What are you doing?"

Gerhard remained silent, moving his arms slightly as if attempting to fit them into a certain position. It wasn't until he stood on his tiptoes that the man from Interpol understood the full implication of the terrible secret they had uncovered. He knew then that Anna's theory was correct.

The exit burns on Grenier's hands and feet, which had puzzled Dr. Lyon, were no longer a mystery.

"Well," he snapped at the forester. "What the hell are you doing?"

When the words came, they were spoken so softly that René could barely hear them. "This is where he died—where he was killed."

"Explain yourself!" Simard shouted in frustration. He knew too well if news of this discovery leaked out, the repercussions would be severe, perhaps even disastrous.

"Don't you see? They wedged a bar into these holes and tied him to it. Some kind of device capable of holding a rod long enough to reach above the spires. When the lightning came, he was … murdered. Do you hear me? Dr. Grenier was right. Lind was murdered!"

The young man's eyes began to well up. "Willi said it wasn't right, that Lind would never be caught so far from his rig in a storm. But why? What monstrous thing did he uncover in this godforsaken pile of limestone that killed him?"

Karl had heard enough to know that he would soon have the blood of yet another Swiss forester on his hands. It was something that he found particularly distasteful. Memories of the last execution were still vivid in his mind: A powerful man reduced to begging for his life, then his whispered prayers as his hands were strapped to the bar. Nor did he die easily. Three separate strikes burned through his body before he finally ceased struggling.

Sophisticated directional antennae hidden in the tops of several of the hollow spires allowed them to accurately trace the movements of anyone who entered the reserve within a two-kilometer radius of the operations center. They had been anxiously monitoring the progress of the two men as soon as they heard the helicopter approach for the second time. The first time Victor had climbed the steps himself to see who was in the machine, and had felt reasonably certain it was the Swiss woman from the photograph Simard had shown them just two nights previously.

Three men stepped out together, their automatic carbines held at waist height. René reached for his weapon, but stayed his hand when he recognized the German chief of security he'd met in Toama.

The Frenchman grinned, letting out an audible sigh of relief. "Your timing is impeccable. I trust you overheard the conclusions this lout has drawn."

Karl nodded. He himself was a tall, powerfully-built man. But the forester was even taller and broader. "An intelligent lout, it seems. Your conclusions were dead accurate, young man. Dead accurate."

Another guard stuck his rifle in Gerhard's ribs. "The emphasis is on *dead*, chum."

Gerhard stared into the Frenchman's face in disbelief. René smiled back. "I cannot claim responsibility for Lind. Your buddy Wilhem is another matter. He came like a sheep to the slaughter. And now you. If we continue at this rate, soon Herr Scheuchzer will have no one left but his Dutch cow."

His taunting laughter was too much for Gerhard, who rushed Simard with a ferocious roar. But Karl had anticipated the move and drove his rifle butt into the side of his head. Gerhard crumpled into a heap.

"That was not a wise move," Karl said patiently. "Now we will have to carry him."

René removed his dark glasses and rubbed his eyes. "He knows, so it is out of the question to let him go. But when I return without him, there's going to be hell to pay. That New York cop, Bannerman, knows something is going on here. He even suspects I am involved. If this one disappears, they are sure to launch a search party that will easily find this place, since he left a string of paint slashes on the rocks that anyone could follow. A search party is bound to notice these holes and will probably draw the same conclusion. It's getting muddled, and I don't like it."

"That's too bad, I'd say. You brought him in here. There are no storms in the immediate forecast, so what do you propose?"

René took a drink of water from his canteen and ran his eyes over the jagged spires. "Supposing we became separated, he going one way, me another. Supposing he climbed up one of these things, perhaps to try and get his bearings, and then fell."

The big German shook his head. "I have a much better solution. No need to worry, no blame will be attached to you."

The call disturbed a pleasant reverie of the previous holiday season, when all the children had gathered at his feet. A man of his late years had little to care about besides his family. To Herr Brower a happy family was worth more than all the gold in the world. He thought about not taking the call, as it was probably that fool from Mali again, still trying to scrape up funds to buy a small preserve to gather the country's surviving giant anteaters. In his day-to-day dealings with environmentalists and other would-be do-gooders, the director ran into a great deal of rabid paranoia, usually from the Brits. They were the worst. Then came the Yanks, waving their flags and their money.

The phone rang again. The old man glanced at his wall clock, a gift from the Royal London Museum. It was ten minutes to four, the hour when he set aside the demands of office and returned to the arms of his family. They had already begun to arrive for the holidays. He had decided not to take the call, but then his secretary came in.

"Yes, Hans, what is it?"

"Superintendent Milland is on the line, Herr Director. He says it is important."

Milland was an old friend, a member of his exclusive men's club and Zurich's senior police official. Brower nodded, and his secretary withdrew.

"Horst, my old friend, a pleasant surprise indeed. Are you keeping well?"

"Well enough for a man who is ten kilos overweight. And yourself, Herr Brower, still putting in a full day at the office?"

"If the truth be known, from time to time I leave a little early. But I want your solemn promise that you will not tell on me."

The policeman laughed. "You have it, by God. And what of Frau Brower and all those lovely little ones?"

The usually civilities took up another five minutes. It was a sort of ritual the Swiss had, these endless inquiries after the health of every family member. When Milland got down to business, his tone changed. "Listen to me, Dietrich, this call is off the record. If anyone learns I contacted you on this matter, my neck is in a noose. Agreed?"

"Naturally. You have known me long enough to know I am a man to be trusted."

"By God, I do. Which is exactly why I made the decision to call you. I just received a confidential inquiry from the police commissioner of the city of New York. The wording is subtle enough, but there is little doubt that they suspect ZIAN of having dealings with the criminal element—in particular, aiding in the movement of cocaine. At first I was shocked, but then I found it quite humorous."

The director was startled. He instinctively reached for his heart pills and held the plastic vial in his hand for comfort. "I suppose I would react in the same way if I had been in your position. It is curious, though. We have no permanent staff in the United States, so what would lead them to suspect ZIAN of running drugs, of all things?"

"Nothing about that. He asks that a full *and* confidential inquiry be launched immediately into all business dealings of your organization, and into the personal holdings of each director."

"Umm, I wonder … I wonder," said Herr Brower, pausing for effect. "As you know, over the years we have had our share of

RODNEY CHRISTIAN POWER

threats, and not all from individuals. Rio Muni is quite angry at us right now. So is Japan, for our role in publicizing their ongoing slaughter of the dolphins. Do you think it might be possible that someone has found a new way to get to us by placing ZIAN under a cloud of suspicion?"

"The very thought has been running through my mind, Dietrich. In the end this is the very conclusion I came to."

"How do you propose to treat this insane accusation?"

"The commissioner will receive a terse reply, I assure you. I will tell him that his request is denied and will not be entertained under any circumstances, short of their providing positive proof that ZIAN is involved. That should put an end to everything. Mind you, I am not certain what to do about this Bannerman chap."

"How's that?" the director asked, his voice breaking slightly.

"I hope you are not coming down with the flu this close to Christmas. They are sending over a homicide detective, a Lieutenant Bannerman, and asked that we cooperate with him in any way we can."

"I see," said Herr Brower. He removed the cap from the little container and reached across for the jug of water.

"But again, if this man has no proof of ZIAN's involvement, then we will not be cooperating in anything. Just leave it with me, old friend. This kind of thing leaves a bad odor around. I will make certain that nothing comes of it."

"Thank you, Horst. I sometimes wonder why life is so complicated, but I suppose those things are sent to try us."

"You have no idea of the senseless accusations that are filed with me, and often by those in high office. It is an unfortunate fact that the revenge mentality is often at the root of such matters. The only other item on the telex was a request that Interpol not be informed under any circumstances. Now that I do find strange. No matter, the chips will fall where they will. I'll see you Thursday night?"

"I will be there for a short while. A nice game of chess, perhaps?"

"Excellent. I shall look forward to it."

Hans came in after the director hung up. He walked across the room to remove Herr Brower's coat from the rack.

202

"Leave it!" his boss said in a sharp voice. "And shut the door. I am not going anywhere. Neither are you."

While taping Anna's ankle, Marina told her about Sam's asking for paper and a pencil. "'A pencil with a good eraser', he said. When I went in later to make up the bed, he turned the paper over so I was unable to see what he was up to. What do you suppose it is?"

Anna said nothing, since she had no more idea than her hostess. She stood, testing the pain level; finding it tolerable, she hobbled out to the veranda to join the Americans.

Bannerman rose and pulled out a seat for her while she and Sam inquired after each other's injuries, which quickly turned into laughter.

Twenty minutes earlier the Swiss foresters had returned from the highlands, some thirty kilometers to the south. Upon learning of Dr. Grenier's injuries, each man had come over to make a personal inquiry after her health. Then they all trooped off to their cottages to shower for dinner.

The crackle of the radio transmitter in the kitchen caught Bannerman's attention. It was now dusk, and they had yet to hear from the helicopter. Marina was worried, especially since Rinday knew the forestry station frequency and should have called in if they were going to be late. After Klaus came home, he tried to raise the pilot, but without success. However, the station manager himself was unperturbed, telling his wife that helicopters often fly close to the ground and their signal could not be expected to carry far.

Charlie did not feel nearly as confident as Klaus appeared. He had been apprehensive about leaving the young forester behind in the hands of a man he considered a killer. With their little machine capable of carrying just two passengers, he'd had no choice in the matter.

The policeman was deeply immersed in this train of thought when a sound crept into his thinking process. It began as a low moan, but quickly turned into a terrifying cry of agony.

"Jesus Christ!" Sam exclaimed as he jumped up. "That's Marina!"

"Something came in on the radio," Anna said, rising from her chair as Sam and Charlie raced into the kitchen.

Marina was in shock, her deathly pallor indicating that she was about to faint. Bloom quickly placed his arm around her as Klaus came running in clad only in a towel. He snatched the microphone from his wife and barked a question into it.

Bannerman took hold of Anna's arm to help her reach Marina. As he was unable to understand what was going on, he asked her.

With a shocked expression on her face, she turned to the policeman. "It's Gerhard," she said quietly.

Anna wrapped her arms around the Dutch woman, muffling her anguished sobs. "What about Gerhard?" Charlie persisted.

"Dead," Bloom said, his mouth a tight line.

Bannerman felt helpless and frustrated. He was the only one who did not understand what Rinday was broadcasting. He backed away from the little knot of people and paused by the kitchen door, where he was almost bowled over by two of the lads, as Klaus called his foresters. They arrived in bare feet and without shirts, with the camp mastiff at their heels.

Once they were told, both men immediately broke into tears. Charlie withdrew to the veranda where the other two young foresters came flying by. Bloom soon came out to join him, taking a seat across the table from Bannerman. Charlie could see he was having a tough time maintaining his composure. "So what the hell happened?"

Sam looked away, up at the top of the jacaranda tree and then across the compound, where the logging equipment was parked. He finally angled his head back toward Bannerman. "An accident. He fell into a crevasse in the limestone. He was leading the way, and René was unable to reach him in time. Simard walked back out to the perimeter and got Rinday and a rope. Then he climbed down the rope and tied it around Gerhard's body. He was able to climb back up by using the rope, and then both of them pulled the poor kid up. He was dead when Simard reached him. It took them this long to carry his body out to—"

He stopped, noticing the dark expression on Bannerman's face, and leaned across the table. "It was an accident, pure and simple."

"An accident, sure, and I'm the effing blue fairy! That young man was murdered, and you want to know who's responsible? This stupid asshole seated right here, that's who! I knew dammed well that Frenchman was rotten to the core. It seeps through his skin, like frigging garlic."

Bloom knew his companion well enough by now to know that he would not make such an accusation lightly. "You think he might have uncovered something inside Tsingy? Something so important it warranted another murder?"

"Looks like," Charlie answered, suddenly weary. He placed his head in both hands. "This one's getting away from me, Sam, I can feel it. It's running all around this thick skull of mine, but I can't find the key."

The radio was still blaring away in the kitchen. Bloom leaned back in his chair. "I don't see how we're going to dispute it. Rinday said it was an accident. Gerhard fell into a hole — he just said it again — and was killed by the fall. Case closed."

"Yeah, that's the shitty part."

The radio finally stopped. Anna came out a few minutes later. She sat beside Bloom but said nothing.

"Are they bringing the body here?" Bannerman asked. "Because I want to have a look."

Anna bit down on her lip. "You suspect René. But why? He has nothing to gain and everything to lose."

"Unless the poor bugger saw something he shouldn't have," the policeman commented.

Klaus poked his head around the door. "Anna, they're taking the body to the clinic. Terroux has agreed to conduct an autopsy. Danny and I are driving into town. Are you up to coming along?"

"Of course. I'll be right there. Do you mind if Lieutenant Bannerman joins us?"

"Charlie is welcome to join us," he said, but his voice was cold.

Bannerman realized this was kind of a family matter and that he was the intruder. "I've seen my share of accident victims — and murder victims. Maybe I can be of some help."

Klaus began to say something, but Anna cut him off. "I'm certain there is no question of murder. But in view of recent events, I would like to be assured that this is indeed the case."

She gulped down a couple of strong painkillers before joining the others for the bumpy ride into Analabe. Gerhard's death had been her doing, and she could feel the hard stares of his companions as she made her way down the veranda steps. Not one of them offered to help her, but Anna understood. She had brought death into their midst, and they resented it. She was also very aware that she had worn out her welcome.

The man from Interpol sat silently between Herr Scheuchzer and another forester, Danny, in the clinic's tiny waiting room. He had the distinct feeling that he was being held prisoner, at least until the results of the autopsy were known. The police had arrived earlier, three slender little men wearing solemn expressions and short pants. The senior officer cocked an eyebrow when he was told that an autopsy was in progress, but made no comment. The results would be sent to him, would they not? Klaus Scheuchzer said they would. After taking René's statement, they went off to interview the helicopter pilot, who was spending the night as Dr. Terroux's guest. Simard's clothing was torn in places, and he was confident that the bandages wrapped around both hands and various cuts and bruises along his arms and legs added to his credibility. Climbing down into that hellhole had been a real challenge, perhaps the most physically demanding feat he had ever undertaken. But it had paid off, and Karl's solution was working even better than René had anticipated.

There was no question of the autopsy revealing the truth, as a chunk of limestone had been driven into the forester's head to cover the blow from Karl's rifle butt. Then the body was carefully dropped in the same way that a person would be expected to fall. It was foolproof, and it gave him some degree of satisfaction to know this. Unfortunately, the incident did nothing to resolve the reason he had been sent to Madagascar in the first place.

The Americans puzzled René. Bloom was a well-known botanist who was now, apparently, a close friend of his cousin. He had been astonished at the degree of intimacy that seemed to exist between the two. Bannerman was a policeman, but he too was a botanist. Why those two appeared to be mixed up in something usually handled by Interpol was quite beyond him.

Rarely did René concern himself with the whys and wherefores of any task, since the bottom line was usually his completing a successful assignment. And he had many to his credit. Back in his early twenties, a dark and troubled spirit had laid claim to René's soul. Peace came to him only after giving in to the terrible yearnings inside him. He had finally given up the struggle and begun reaping the rich harvest waiting for those without scruples or conscience.

The slovenly American detective would be the first to go. He knew, or at least suspected, too much. His cold look told René that he also suspected the truth about Gerhard. But Bannerman carried a large semi-automatic pistol and would be vigilant.

Anna came out shaking her head. She removed her mask and dropped heavily into a chair. "We found nothing to indicate that death was anything other than accidental. There were several marks on the body, all indicative of a fall along a jagged limestone surface. And he was alive before he fell."

Klaus was standing. "Then there is no doubt it was the fall that killed him?"

"None whatsoever. And Charlie and Dr. Terroux concur." She looked over at René. "I'm truly sorry about all this, but in view of everything that has gone on since Lind's death, I just felt I had to be certain."

René took in a deep breath. "There is no need to apologize, Anna. Herr Scheuchzer did the right thing. If only I had been closer to him. But he moved so fast, it was difficult for me even to keep him in sight."

Klaus nodded. "Gerry was like that—in superb condition and accustomed to traversing rough terrain. I'm not surprised you were unable to keep up with him."

And that was that. On the way back, René bemoaned the fact that he hadn't been of much help to anyone since his arrival. "You just arrived yesterday," his cousin told him. "I didn't expect a miracle, you know."

Bannerman took it all in silently. He could see that the Frenchman still had the woman wrapped around his finger, despite her suspicions. As far as Gerhard's death was concerned, Charlie knew there was more than one way he could have ended up in that crevasse. He wondered why they'd found no indication of the man having grasped at the undergrowth that was supposed to have covered up the hole. There had been flecks of paint on both hands, but nothing else. Bannerman felt there had to be a reason — and a dammed serious one — for Simard to run the risk of exposure.

At Bloom's suggestion he had commandeered the manager's office that afternoon to make a call to Johnson at the embassy. He asked for a rundown on Simard's movements since he hit the island. If it could be shown that the Frenchman was in Toama while they were there, Charlie figured this would make him number one on the suspect list for the bomb fiasco. But how Bannerman, even with his diplomatic card and police ID, would go about having an Interpol agent arrested, was beyond him. Who would believe him?

There was another option, the Final Option, something he had criticized throughout his whole career. It was a known fact, even an accepted one by many senior officers, that from time to time during the course of events, a situation would arise that warranted drastic action. As repugnant as it seemed, he realized for the first time in his thirty years as a cop, that he might just be faced with such a decision.

Klaus Scheuchzer was a religious man, a Presbyterian of the old school. After the explaining was over, he called everyone to prayer out on the veranda. René was excused, claiming he was feeling faint. Probably blood loss, Anna told him.

Bannerman stood in the dark beside Bloom, his head bowed low, listening to the station manager whisper his plea to God in his native tongue and feeling the enormous grief that had settled upon this tiny community of Swiss citizens so far away from their homeland and in such an isolated part of the world. Then there were five. Less than a month ago, there had been eight, and all three had died accidentally.

Like hell they did!

Bannerman couldn't quite grasp why they were being killed off, but was more convinced than ever that their deaths had not been accidental. And René Simard was involved right up to his pretty brown eyeballs. His mind suddenly fired across the island with an abruptness that startled him: Shaleen, if only she was here. There was a calming manner about her, an impression that had hit him as sort of an aftereffect. She had a certain presence about her, as if everything would be okay as long as she was near.

This knowledge, that his need for her had finally surfaced, made him sweat. Charlie kept reminding himself that the girl was just nineteen years old. So why did she appear so damn mature, as if an older, wiser soul was harbored inside that magnificent body? How could she be so young and move like that? How could she be so goddamn gorgeous and still be his for the asking?

Marina was still sobbing, her blond head partly buried beneath her husband's thick red beard. Charlie had come to realize that the foresters were all one big family and that to Marina, losing Gerhard was like losing her own child.

It broke up slowly, with people drifting away reluctantly, one at a time. Bloom and Bannerman each muttered a few hopelessly inadequate words and wandered across the compound to Charlie's little Swiss chalet. He wanted a beer and knew Sam could use one.

Bloom plunked himself down on the steps leading up to the tiny veranda. It was almost three in the morning, but neither man felt like sleeping. "Some nasty stuff we're into, Lieutenant. Sure hit Marina hard."

Bannerman nodded, sinking his weight into the lone chair on his veranda. He handed Bloom a Foster's. "They're all her kids. Guess I didn't pick up on that till tonight. Jesus …."

Ten minutes later they watched Anna hobble her way across the compound. In the moonlight she looked kind of pathetic, and when she drew close, they saw her eyes were red and moist. Charlie stood up to give her the chair, but she chose instead to lean against a post, with her injured foot on the step beside Sam.

She fixed her sad eyes on Bannerman. "You blame René, don't you?"

The policeman rolled his head around, appearing to consider her question. "Maybe," he said finally.

"You're wrong, Charlie. René risked his life by going down that crevasse. Rinday told me he even begged him not to do it. How can you be so cruel?"

This time he didn't bother to reply. Bannerman could see she was all strung out and not too rational at the moment. He yawned and stood up. "I'm beat. A few more days like this and I'll be ready for a pine box myself. In any case, looks like we all get to sleep in tomorrow."

Anna wondered at his inconsistency. "I thought you would be anxious to inspect the scene of the crime, since you obviously believe that's what it is."

Charlie shrugged. "While you were talking to Simard at the clinic, Dr. Terroux told me it looks like the forecast just changed. There's a storm moving in. Rinday won't fly in a storm."

"Damnation!" Anna said.

Bloom cursed under his breath. He had been looking forward to getting inside Tsingy.

Bannerman paused at the door. "As for this latest so-called accident, don't worry. We'll find out the truth sooner or later. And don't call me in the morning."

After Bannerman went in and closed the door, Sam reached out to place his hand gently on Anna's injured ankle. Once Charlie switched on the inside lights, he saw that she was looking down at him. "How does it feel?" he asked.

She began to smile, because his hand had started to move slowly up the calf of her leg. "How does it feel to you?"

He ran his fingers a little higher, raising the hem of her gray woolen skirt. Then he realized they were in full view of the compound and squeezed her behind the knee before withdrawing his hand. "Just like I imagined it would: perfect."

She said nothing and stood there quietly, with one side of her face almost in complete darkness. When Sam got to his feet, he was just inches away from her and could feel his heart racing. Despite the layer of grief that had fallen upon their little encampment, he felt a near-desperate yearning for this incredibly beautiful woman.

She reached up to his eyes, forcing them closed, then allowed her thumb and forefinger to rest on his eyelids. "Marina told me about the pencil and paper. It's about your eyes, isn't it?"

He took hold of her hand. "How did you know?"

"Partly a guess. Will you show me?"

"Maybe. Answer a technical question first. The bomb blast, and the shock that went with it — do you think it's possible that it could have affected me psychologically?"

Her face turned serious. "How do you mean?"

He grinned at her reaction. "I'm not going loony or anything like that. This mental problem, left over from my days as a guest of the Vietcong, is never far beneath the surface, especially in a country like Madagascar where many of the natives resemble the VC. Well … since yesterday I've tried every way I know of to psych myself out, like bringing to mind some of the sadistic cruelty I saw over there. And nothing. I just couldn't care less. In twenty years it has never been possible for me to calmly recall the past, but now it seems that I can. So what's the verdict, Doctor? Is it real? Is it illusionary? Is it temporary? What the hell is going on inside my head?"

Anna came down a bit. She could feel some of Bloom's exuberance and welcomed it. "You know such questions are well beyond the scope of a general practitioner. I have only my medical school experience and a few well-known cases to draw upon. The truth of the matter is that the human mind is only slightly less a mystery than it was forty years ago. We only know for certain that anything is possible. If you have a strong sensation that your affliction has left you, then I suspect it has."

Bloom nodded. "Good. I'm prepared to take it at face value, anyway. Come on, then, we'll sneak down to my bedroom."

"Now?" she asked.

He took her hand and helped her down the steps. "Why not? Klaus and Marina are on the other side of the house. We won't disturb them."

Anna placed her arm around Sam's waist for support. "Very well. Lead on, Dr. Bloom."

Once inside his room, Sam switched on the lights and led Anna to a seat on the edge of his bed. After a few seconds of hesitation, he sat beside her and reached under his pillow to remove the two diagrams he had worked on during the afternoon. "Never thought I'd be able to do this, but it doesn't seem to matter now."

Anna took them with a questioning look and studied them for a few minutes in silence. In time the full impact of the special torture Sam Bloom had been subjected to in Vietnam hit her full force. She threw the papers on the floor as if she had just found a poisonous spider in her hands.

"How were you able to survive at all?" she whispered.

"At least I kept my eyes. I can still see. Some of my buddies weren't so lucky. They'd lose one eyeball that way, or two, and you could always see three or four guys groping around the yard with just holes. The little shitheads were always telling us, each one of us flyboys, that we were next. Some guys … it just blew their minds, you know, all the waiting. They cracked. Jesus, I can't believe I'm finally talking about this."

Anna took his left hand in both of hers. "I am a physician, a good one I like to think, but sometimes I despair of mankind. I truly do despair. I see atrocity after atrocity and find myself questioning where we are going, where we expect to go. And nothing changes. Throughout all of human history, nothing changes. If anything, we are becoming worse. Our capacity to kill and maim and torture is only growing more sophisticated, and our marvelous communications network lets us view it all in the privacy of our homes. Do you know my greatest fear? That we will become immune to it. That this endless parade of horror and violence will become a way of life for everyone. God help me, but sometimes I'm damned if I can see us ending up any other way."

Sam could feel her reaching out. She was no big brave woman tonight, just a lonely, confused little girl. He slipped his hand away and placed it around her shoulder, drawing her closer. "I know Charlie told you about Zurich. With the storm moving in, tomorrow is shot. So if we can book a flight out, we're on our way. Anna, I want you to come with us."

She stiffened, uncertain just what he was saying to her. She played for time. "What about the golden orchid you told me was so important? And why is it so urgent for you to go to Zurich? It's to do with this drug thing, isn't it?"

Bloom tightened his grip on his prize. "Charlie's been ordered to go, and it's more or less my responsibility to go along with him. But I've been thinking—Zurich is your home, you know your way around. You know the people. Why not a trade, a pact between us—you help us, we'll help you."

She frowned, and he could imagine the indecision that was running through her mind. He was tempted to tell her the real reason: That he was in love with her and could not possibly leave her in the care of a man Charlie was certain was a murderer. "You told us in Tana that you had considerable flexibility in your job. Look, I'll take care of the costs. You won't have to worry about a thing. Come with us—we need you, Anna."

Her eyes fell upon the drawings at her feet. Along with his other talents, Dr. Samuel Bloom was an accomplished artist. The first sketch showed a three-dimensional rendering of an odd contraption hanging from the ceiling of a small room. He had taken great care to get the scale correct. It was a type of pendulum, suspended within a crude framework of thin bamboo strips. On one end of the pendulum there was a sharpened bamboo point. The top extended through the roof into a rotary-shaped wind-catcher. As the speed of the wind increased, so did the distance the pendulum moved back and forth. It was a meaningless device until one studied the second drawing. This one too was in fine detail: A man tied upright to a pillar, his head held in place by straps of webbing, tears gushing from his eyes as he watched the bamboo point draw closer and closer. In the foreground, against a wall, the instrument panel of a small but sophisticated aircraft was displayed on a screen.

Bloom saw that her attention was taken. "I heard later that Mai Lok was only for pilots. Perhaps it was, because there were never more than thirty of us, and their torture programs seemed to be centered around the eyes. They'd play that bastardized film over and over, a dozen times some days, and feed you all sorts of psychological drivel while they were doing it. Then every evening when the wind started up, they'd play just the soundtrack as that goddamned bamboo pendulum swung closer and closer. In the darkness you could only feel the wind and hear the ropes creaking. It was a special hell created for pilots, always waiting on that big gust, the one that would drive it into your brain. I was one of the lucky ones."

Anna shuddered. "I can hardly conceive of anything so cruel. No wonder you carried it around with you all these years."

"It's caused a lot of grief in my life," he said with only mild bitterness. "And in the lives of others, including my ex-wife. When she couldn't take it anymore, my crawling around the floor like a wounded animal, throwing things around and crying out for God to put an end to my miserable existence, she pulled out. I never blamed her. I'm grateful she stayed around as long as she did."

"And now you're all alone?"

He nodded. "All alone."

She stuck her leg straight out to study her swollen ankle. She had felt something close to hostility tonight, not from Marina, but from the others. Nothing would ever be said, she knew, because the Swiss were too polite. But it was there, and no one would be sorry to see her leave. René was the problem. He had come all the way from Palermo to help her, and if she accepted Sam Bloom's offer, René would probably be furious.

"The offer has a certain appeal, I admit, especially since it will take several days for my ankle to return to normal. But don't you see, I can't, not now. René — "

"The hell with René! He's your cousin, not your husband. He's the big international policeman. He can stay here and sort it out while we're up in Zurich. You won't be a damn bit of good to him like this."

Anna was intrigued by his obvious jealousy of her cousin. But the uncertainty lingered still. "Those wide scars up and down your back, what caused them?"

Bloom released his hold. He knew Charlie was right about her and the Frenchman. He was overcome with a feeling of frustration and deep embarrassment. This was as close as he had come to baring his soul to any woman since the war.

"Barbed wire, had little wooden handles on each end. They'd rip it across your back, see how deep they could go. That was the first time—the first time I was shot down, I mean. I've always believed they hated us more than the others, probably something to do with all that napalm we were dropping on them."

"The first time … did you escape?"

"Three of us. A lucky break. Later I led a Special Forces team back and we managed to get seventeen of the guys out. It was after the second time I went down that they took me to Mai Lok."

"And were you kept there until the war was over?"

His response was slow in coming, because she had touched upon a deep secret he had kept buried all these years. "On the morning of my thirty-eighth day we were all out in the compound when this guy called me over, a Marine chopper pilot, name of Jones, Herbert Hoover Jones, black guy. Told me he had just a few days left; his wounds had turned gangrenous; the stink was so bad I had to hold my nose talking to him. He set it up for me, distracted the guards with a fake breakout. I got away clean. Heard the shots two minutes out. It was what he wanted, he said, to go out doing something useful. Looking back at it now, maybe the only reason he picked me was because I still had both eyes."

Anna glanced at the sketches again. "It all sounds so completely inhuman—so utterly, utterly inhuman."

"The Orientals, they got a special knack for it. Sanctity of life as we know it didn't exist in their society." He added dryly, "I doubt if it's changed that much."

Anna felt herself falling under his spell. For this man to have survived so much and still be capable of carrying on a normal life was a miracle in itself. She could feel her indecision slipping away. She knew Tsingy held an array of mysteries that had to be resolved before she could carry on with her own life. But now, having been forced out of commission for several days ….

There was still one tiny puzzle she wanted to solve. "Your accent is quite unlike anything I have heard before, much more lyrical than I encounter every day in Geneva. Where did you learn it?"

215

This caused Bloom to smile. She was not the first European to ask that question. "My mother's family was Louisiana French, their language a peculiar introverted mixture that had survived in the south for over three hundred years. She died during my birth, but I spent eleven wonderful summers in their big old house just outside of New Orleans. The accent stuck, I guess."

Well, there it was, a man who had completely captivated her. Despite her recent loss and the turmoil surrounding Lind's death, Anna suspected that she was very close to falling in love with Dr. Samuel Bloom. "You said you would help me if I went with you to Zurich. What do you mean?"

"When we complete our business there, we'll come back and comb every inch of that reserve. If necessary I'll hire a team of experts — commandos, hired killers, whatever it takes. I promise you, we *will* find out what's going on."

"A team of commandos? Where would even a world-renowned botanist get the financial backing for such an undertaking?"

Sam placed his arm around her shoulder again, pulling her close. Too bad, René old boy, this one belongs to me. She's mine. She could be firm, and tough when she needed to be; but for all that, Anna Grenier was definitely the most purely feminine creature he had ever known.

"I'm almost ashamed to tell you that I have more money than I know what to do with. Believe me when I tell you this: We — you and me and Charlie, if he wants to come along — will set up an operation that will blow this thing to out of the water. You have my word on it."

Chapter Fourteen

Bannerman had been in Zurich for less than twelve hours when he came down with a cold. A change of climate, according to the hotel doctor, who presented him with an array of medicines to take and told him to go to bed. They were now in Bloom's room at the Hotel Excelsior waiting for their police liaison, an Inspector Lemieux, to arrive. Due to the sensitivity of the subject they were to discuss, Lemieux had told Charlie he preferred not to have them come down to headquarters.

The time was two-thirty in the afternoon, exactly three weeks before Christmas, and two days before the *Lucinda V* was due to dock in Djibouti—the first opportunity ZIAN would have to unload their cargo, according to the ship's manifest. But Charlie wondered what was to prevent the captain from pulling in anywhere he wanted along the African coast and caching the suspect containers.

Even though the three of them had arrived late the previous evening, Anna had decided to take an early train to Geneva, as she wished to explain personally to the WHO assistant director her reason for returning so soon to Switzerland without ever having reached her destination in the Sudan.

As for René Simard, once Anna informed him that she would be returning to Zurich with the Americans, the Frenchman tried his best to make her change her mind, bringing the full extent of his considerable charm to bear. Then, seeing her determination, he went about his investigative role in apparent good faith. But the man from Interpol was to uncover nothing of significance, as Charlie had predicted.

When Anna and her American escorts were met at the Tana airport by Curtis Johnson, he confirmed that Simard had been seen in Toamasina at the time of the bombing. The news shocked Anna, for now she realized that her cousin must have been part of this whole dreadful affair, right from the moment of his sudden appearance in her Geneva office. It was a bitter pill for her to swallow, and the ramifications brought her close to tears. The CIA operative told them that the Frenchman had covered his tracks well, having booked his flight from Antananarivo to Toamasina under a Moroccan alias.

Bloom suggested that such information be turned over to the Malagasy authorities so they could pick up Simard for questioning. If the man was a killer, and it now appeared almost certain that he was, far better for him to be held for questioning in Madagascar than to be free to follow them around Europe waiting for the opportune moment to rig another car bomb. Since the intended victims had diplomatic passports, Johnson was reluctant, as he feared the embassy might have to field some awkward questions. Only after Bloom talked it over with his friend, the ambassador, were the details telephoned anonymously to the police. Bloom's call to Johnson that morning revealed that Simard had been taken prisoner at the Morondava airport as he was about to board a regular flight to Tana. He had been scheduled to depart the island that afternoon, and his final destination was Zurich.

Inspector Lemieux arrived with a scowl on his face. He was a tall, slender man close to retirement age, with a sprinkling of white hair, thick eyebrows, and a bushy moustache that had not been trimmed for months. He had received a call from Anna Grenier around midnight, giving him the details of her experiences on the island of Madagascar. It was from Anna that he learned the city police had been asked by the NYPD commissioner to assign a liaison to the American detective.

In view of the fact that he was the senior investigating officer into two murders that appeared to be related to Anna Grenier in some oblique fashion, he had pressured Superintendent Milland into allowing him to serve as liaison officer. Four years ago it had been a toss-up between him and Milland as to who would be chosen to head the Zurich City Police Department. Milland, the more politically sensitized of the two, had won out. But that did nothing to alter the close relationship that had developed between the two men over the previous three decades.

Lemieux knew it was only this friendship that had convinced Milland to allow him to act as official liaison. His boss had already assigned another, perhaps the most prolific bungler in the whole force, to the job. That was when Lemieux first caught a whiff of something that smelled suspiciously like a cover-up. He knew Milland and Dietrich Brower were old friends, but Lemieux had been just as astonished as his superintendent by the allegations against ZIAN. He was most curious to learn what the Americans had to say.

After the pleasantries were over and he had recommended his favorite cold remedy to Charlie, the Swiss detective got down to business. Three days earlier, while the police in Geneva were questioning the driver of the lorry that ran down Wilhem Strouss, they managed to trap the man in a lie. Just yesterday morning he had finally confessed. Unfortunately, the party who hired him had done so by verbal instructions over the telephone, so the driver never once laid eyes upon him. As for Dr. Lyon, the other physician who had been in that examination room, whoever was responsible for throwing him off that train was still at large.

Charlie had made an earlier decision to play it by ear and check out the level of cooperation he could expect before deciding how much he should reveal. It didn't take long to see that Lemieux could likely be trusted. The fact that he was also Anna's lifelong friend convinced the detective to give the man most, but not all, of what he knew.

Since he was sneezing constantly and forced to blow his nose every few minutes, it took him the better part of an hour to get it all out. Bloom sat quietly throughout the whole account, marveling at Bannerman's capacity to recall detail.

Once he was done asking questions, the inspector sat in silence for a full minute. He finally rose, pushing up with long bony fingers on the knees of his navy blue trousers, and walked across the spacious room to watch a light fluttering of snowflakes touch down upon the dark, still surface of Lake Zurich and then disappear. His head moved from side to side in a motion that was barely perceptible.

Then Lemieux made a strange noise, not unlike a whale clearing its blowhole. "I suppose Anna has already informed you that you are treading upon sacred ground. If you had arrived with an indictment of President Aubert himself, it would be only slightly more astonishing than an indictment of ZIAN. Herr Brower himself is almost an institution in Zurich." He blew out with his cheeks again. "Perhaps I was too hasty in requesting this assignment. Such introverted affairs, I have found, are quite capable of terminating one's career."

He was speaking with his back to the two Americans. Sam gave Charlie a quick glance, rolling his eyes before speaking. "But perhaps, Herr Inspector, you do not have so many years to go before retirement."

Lemieux turned around, his face cocked in an unexpected grin. "Not a bad accent, Herr Doctor, for an American. Your grandfather, I am given to understand, emigrated from Austria just before the turn of the century. Blumenauer then, was it not?"

Sam nodded. He noticed the deep crinkles around the man's eyes and realized that Lemieux was a man easily given to laughter. He returned to English. "You found it necessary to check us out, I see."

"Not at all. Your dossiers were on the superintendent's desk when I arrived this morning. He was the one who had you checked out."

Charlie removed the handkerchief from his nose. "Nothing unusual there. If the situation was reversed, we'd do the same."

Bloom stood up, suddenly restless. "You know, fellows, this isn't my line of work, but it seems the answer to most of your questions lies aboard that ship. If her captain decides to ditch that cargo, or worse still—from Charlie's point of view, that is—if the cargo's clean, where does that leave us? I would suggest nowhere."

"Maybe," Bannerman agreed. "Unless we can roust this Brower character, which is why we're here. I figure there's a good chance this whole operation is being controlled by someone in Zurich, and if so, Brower's our number one candidate."

Lemieux leaned back against the window ledge. Behind him the sky appeared to be growing brighter. The Quai Bridge, the first to span the Limmat River at the end of the lake, was now clearly in view. "You had better be told now, right at the start, that it is completely out of the question to obtain a search warrant to look inside the old opera house. Superintendent Milland has specifically ruled out any direct contact with Herr Brower, his board of directors, and his employees. He was quite firm about this. And I assure you, only the most irrefutable proof will make him change his mind."

"Wonderful," Charlie said through a sneeze. "I take it we're up against the old boy network. Who's looking out for Brower's ass? Is it Milland, or does it go higher?"

"Ah, Lieutenant, I suspect it is natural enough for you to view such matters from an American perspective. Let me explain how the system works in Switzerland. Here, I am pleased to inform you, a citizen of proven moral character and high standing in the community has earned, as it were, certain rights and privileges that are not easily revoked. In the case of ZIAN and its chairman, we have additional knowledge that makes your investigation all the more delicate. Before passing on such information, I want assurances from both of you that it will not leave this room, at least not without my permission. Agreed?"

Sam nodded. Bannerman grunted.

The inspector returned to his seat. He removed a dark cigarillo from the inside pocket of his dark blue suit and gave Bloom a questioning glance.

Sam said sorry, but nobody smoked in his bedroom — not the president, not the pope, nobody.

"It is a foul habit, Dr. Bloom, I couldn't agree more." He grinned as he replaced the offending object. "One day I must give it up. So, on to Interpol. I have no idea of your connections with their organization; but perhaps, in the case of narcotics at least, you may have noticed that Interpol is more predisposed to monitoring such operations on the continent than in North America. Part of the reason for this, I suspect, is the withdrawal of financial support by your government. Oh, they still help out from time to

221

time, but let me put it this way: I don't think their heart is in it, if you know what I mean.

"We, on the other hand, have a great deal to do with Interpol. Europe may be a land made up of many countries, but all in all, those of us in the west are just a small family. I've known this young man you mentioned, René Simard, since he was a child, when he used to spend his summers with Anna's parents. I also happen to know he is one of Interpol's bright and upcoming young stars. He played a key role in the combined undercover operation that just brought down half of the mafiosi in Sicily. A major feat, I can assure you, when you consider just how paranoid the Italians are when it comes to the Mafia."

He swept back each side of his great moustache with a flourish. "Why am I telling you this? Because of the relationship ZIAN has developed over the years with Interpol. You will know by now that their people—biologists, naturalists, whatever you wish to call them—have access to many remote areas of the world. This has proven to be of great benefit to Interpol and to the European community at large. In the case of Indonesia, Thailand, Kampuchea, and so on, information filtered back to Interpol from ZIAN field personnel has resulted in the seizure of more shipments of heroin than you could imagine."

"Why?" Charlie asked. "What's in it for them?"

"What indeed? A natural enough question, one which still raises its head from time to time, even here, in Europe's last bastion of conservatism. I, personally, would never think of confronting Herr Brower with such a question. He is by nature a modest man and would probably deny his involvement. But my information comes directly from St. Cloud and is correct. Perhaps, and this is leading into an area I do not particularly wish to enter, but perhaps the man is attempting to make up for the sins of his past. And I will say no more about that. In any case, he presumably answers to his board of directors, a group of highly respected and now-retired Swiss citizens, so it may be that such direction is handed down from above, as it were."

Bannerman could feel a big fat headache coming on. "Do you think we could cut the BS? Brower's a Kraut. His board of directors are Krauts. All ex-Nazis, who probably crossed the border around the end of the war with a piss-pot full of money, enough to buy each one of them new identities and set themselves up in a profitable business venture. They started up this ZIAN affair with Brower in charge, recognizing even then the vast potential of an international organization that could walk into most any country in the world under one umbrella or the other — protection of species or harvesting of species. And you're telling me as far as the Swiss police are concerned, ZIAN's record is clean because they're not crapping in their own backyard. That's just marvelous! Problem is, I got damned good reason to believe the bastards are crapping in my backyard, and I don't like it. So what I guess I'm saying, Herr Inspector, if this is the level of cooperation we can expect — you draping your precious Swiss flag over a bunch of Nazis just because they appear to be fine upstanding citizens and help out Interpol now and then, which used to and probably still does have its own share of Nazis — but that's another story — then thanks a whole lot, and there's the door."

Bloom could easily see through his partner's little charade. He wanted to shame the guy into cooperating, no matter what instructions he had to the contrary.

Lemieux didn't appear annoyed at all. In fact, Bloom thought he saw the ghost of a smile play across his weathered features. "Strong words, Herr Lieutenant. But where is the proof?"

Charlie shrugged. "Not much of that floating around at the moment, which is why we were hoping for a little local input. I think ZIAN is up to its ears in shit. I think they've been in the racket for a long, long time. Nothing to back that up either, except the few bits and pieces I got to date which point to a definite pattern."

"I'm interested," said the Swiss police inspector. "Tell me about your pattern."

"What's the point? You think this Brower's such a prize, on top of which you got your instructions."

"You jump too readily to conclusions, Lieutenant. I have repeated, for your sake, the *official* position both of us must take in this matter. Now that I have done so, perhaps we can get on with it."

Sam found himself grinning. It was Bannerman who was being suckered all along.

Charlie sniffed a few times before continuing. "I believe it's an integral part of their operation, this arrangement they got with Interpol. ZIAN is competition-oriented, doing everything it can to keep the other guys in line. They keep an eye on the Orientals, the Colombians, the Jamaicans, the Turks, the Italians, and so on, passing on what they learn to Interpol. Their staff makes certain the information reaches the right ears and the competition's shipments get nabbed, which gives ZIAN a bigger cut of the market. It's just good business practice."

Lemieux screwed his face into a scowl before shaking his head. "I cannot believe that Herr Brower is personally involved in any aspect of the narcotics trade. You are speaking of a kindly old gentleman somewhere in his mid-eighties who is worshiped by his staff—a most unlikely drug lord."

Bannerman didn't like what he was hearing: Simard a hero and Brower the original Mister Nice. Nevertheless, he could hear the footsteps of his old enemy, doubt, creeping up the stairs, trying to get in bed with all the other crap he had stored in there. He turned his watery eyes upon his Swiss counterpart. "You think you're a little close maybe, a little biased?"

The Swiss raised one bushy eyebrow. "But of course. It is a natural reaction for me, is it not? After all, protection of the innocent is more important than prosecution of the guilty."

Lemieux stayed for another twenty minutes. Using one excuse or another, he shot down each plan of action Bannerman presented. In the end he told the two Americans that he would make certain surreptitious inquiries on his own. He invited them to take in the sights and to relax after their arduous week in Madagascar. He would get back to them soon.

The inspector was emphatic about guns. The Americans had turned their weapons in just prior to their Tana departure and now felt a little naked without them. But there was no question of their being allowed to carry handguns in Zurich. If they feared for their lives, Lemieux told them, he would assign a policeman to keep watch on them.

Charlie was thoroughly pissed off by the time the guy left and darkened the air with a few choice oaths. It was the first time Bloom had heard him cut loose.

"I wouldn't write him off yet, Lieutenant. The man plays them close to the chest. I'd say he knows, or suspects, a lot more than he's letting on."

Charlie sneezed three times before he could respond. "Jeez — I come all the way to Switzerland to die of a freaking cold. So what the hell are we supposed to do, go Christmas shopping while we wait?"

Bloom chuckled at his partner's predicament. "You'd better jump into bed before that hotel doctor returns to check you out. Go on back to your room, call Shaleen, and ask her to cheer you up."

That idea brightened up the policeman somewhat. He'd called her twice before leaving, each time feeling the velvet noose draw a little tighter. He told her they would be returning to the island soon, as their business there was far from finished. He just needed a week or so in Zurich to check out a few loose ends. When he returned, they would sit down and have a serious talk.

Twice Hans attempted to enter the director's office, and twice he was told to get out. As this was highly irregular behavior for the usually stoic Herr Brower, his secretary was concerned.

The director, on the other hand, was distressed by his secretary's conduct. Who else besides him and the controllers knew about the serious threats brought on by the interference of this Grenier woman and the two Americans? The men in the old house up behind the hospital had been hired many years ago by Brower himself and rarely had contact with other company officials. To them, Herr Brower *was* ZIAN.

A board of directors meeting had been called for that very evening, and Chairman Brower was expected to provide answers to a number of difficult questions. Instinct told him it had to be his secretary, either letting it be known on purpose or letting slip some questionable piece of information in his grandfather's presence that had been picked up by General Backmeyer's well-tuned antenna and relayed to the other board members.

He was expected to give an account of his actions. It had been many years since Oberst Von Rudel was called to task, and it sat heavily upon his shoulders. It seemed almost a betrayal of his tenacity and dedication in building up one of the most profitable privately-owned organizations on the continent. The generals were old men now, as he was; and each man, or each family estate, in the case of those who had passed on, had grown accustomed to accepting their division of the enormous wealth that continued to flow from the great well of ZIAN. Up until now they had been content to leave the multifaceted day-to-day running of the Zurich International Association of Naturalists entirely in the hands of the exemplary field officer they had lured away from the Reichmarschall forty-four years earlier.

The former Gestapo colonel knew they had been searching for a suitable replacement since his first heart seizure in eighty-one. But that replacement had yet to surface. It was unlikely to be Hans Backmeyer, as the man was much too young and sadly lacking in organizational ability. Plus, there was something else about him that disturbed the director, as if his attention were frequently elsewhere. Once Herr Brower had followed through with his rationalization, he buzzed for Hans to enter.

"You know about the meeting this evening?"

"Yes, Herr Director."

"I have not been told how many are coming, but prepare eight places in any case. General Strobber is in America at the moment, so it appears he will not be attending. You will be there, of course."

"Naturally, Herr Director. Ah, there is further news on the Americans. Inspector Lemieux was just seen leaving the Excelsior. Our man learned that he spent a full two hours with Dr. Bloom and his companion. You will recall, Herr Director, that Lemieux was the official placed in charge of investigating both the disappearance of Dr. Lyon and the Wilhem Strouss accident."

The old man said forcibly, "Which has now been reclassified as murder! That imbecilic truck driver. So much for Simard's brilliant handling of the loose ends. He sits in a Madagascar prison awaiting arraignment, while these two wretched Americans have the effrontery to show up here, in *my* city." The director's gravelly voice rose a few notes. "Do you not realize that everything that man touched has gone wrong! That was my first mistake, Hans: assuming this amateur was capable of carrying out a proper assignment."

He threw up his hands in frustration. "It was stupid of me, I admit, to place so much trust in a Frenchman, any Frenchman. They are all a pack of sniveling dolts!"

His secretary made no comment and waited patiently for ZIAN's patriarch to continue. He noticed one frail hand gripping his vial of heart pills.

"Lemieux is a bloodhound. What has gotten into Milland, appointing that man as liaison? Am I being set up? Is ZIAN being set up? Each turn of events, it seems, is for the worse. Perhaps the board of directors has reason to be concerned, with close to ninety million francs tied up in the Tsingy operation and now the specter of defeat looming over us like Banquo's ghost."

The director had been fighting a cold for weeks. He rotated his big leather chair to view the Christmas decorations along the Bahnhof through his snow-flecked window, then sniffed several times as he mulled over the mess he seemed to have gotten himself into. *Double, double, toil and trouble; Fire burn, and cauldron bubble.* He scratched around the area where his stump entered the Teflon prosthesis. Up till now it had always come down to the same two questions: What did the Americans know? What did the Grenier woman know? But another, more urgent question had just surfaced: What had they told Lemieux?

Fifteen minutes after Lemieux's departure, Sam took a taxi to Bahnhofstrasse. They had left New York prepared for hot weather, so both men were in need of heavier clothing. Once over the Quai Bridge, he asked to be dropped off at the intersection of Talacker and the Bahnhof. Clad in the only sweater he'd brought along for the trip, he soon realized that the store he had in mind was three blocks away from where he remembered it. He shivered as he walked rapidly down Talacker, thinking it was a lot colder than it first appeared.

It also crossed his mind that if ZIAN really was behind the attempts on their lives in Madagascar, then the same forces might still be at work here in Zurich. Keeping this possibility in mind, Sam needled his way through the crowds of Friday evening shoppers, arriving finally at the big Bovet-Kleidung department store, the one with the elephant, he recalled. He wasn't looking for anything stylish, just something practical to see them through their presumably brief stay.

Christmas, in all its rich European glory, was everywhere. Once his purchases were made, he walked outside to be greeted by thick snowflakes. He had already pulled on his new overshoes and donned his navy blue mackinaw inside the store. Secured against the weather, he set off for the Bahnhof in comfort. Each store played its selection of music through a loud speaker, and the shoppers seemed carefree, their laughter and the children's high-pitched squeals blending well with the old carols sung in German. He stopped at a window where a small crowd had gathered. Over their heads he could see the subject of their attention: Dozens of animated wooden figures, including Saint Nicholas in a fur-trimmed robe, his helpers in pointed caps and grotesque face masks, and a few other church figures related to local traditions, he supposed, going about their business of preparing to distribute bags of gifts to little children. The life-size figures were exquisitely carved and seemed to move without wire or any visible means of support.

Evidence that Zurich had one of the highest per capita incomes in Europe lay in the bags and packages toted by everyone in sight. It was a festive atmosphere, with beaming smiles and happy greetings when old friends met, like Christmas was tomorrow, not three weeks away. There were no beggars here, he realized, nor was there the slightest indication of poverty to be seen.

Before he knew it, he was standing in front of the old opera house, the home of ZIAN. He had somehow became caught up in the maze of intersecting streets and ended up on Fusslistrasse without knowing it. Bloom stopped, having recognized the building almost by accident. It was in a small business section lacking much of the decorative glitter of the shopping district. Less than a hundred paces ahead, he could see the colorful storefront windows on the Bahnhof.

He walked by the place slowly, head turned, recalling the suffering and death over the last eight days, and wondering .... It was a typical Baroque structure of cinder gray color, four stories high and capped by the heavy mansard roof that characterized many of Zurich's older buildings. Several upstairs lighted windows showed figures moving about. Despite so many indications to the contrary, he still found it difficult to believe that the gracious old gentleman he had last met five years ago was behind all the killing. By the time he reached the Bahnhof, Bloom had made up his mind. Fifteen minutes went by before he was able to hail a taxi. He gave the driver the two shopping bags containing Charlie's jacket and overshoes and told the young man where to go, sealing the bargain with a twenty-franc note. In Switzerland, he knew, honesty was taken for granted.

Walking up the steps, he did feel a mild sense of foreboding, as if he had no right to be there. Sam had reasoned that since no official inquiries were to be made, there was nothing to prevent him, as a longtime member of the association, from making a social call on the director. He thought it unlikely the man would be there at six-thirty on a Friday evening, but unless it was the cleaning staff, someone was in there.

The large foyer was empty. Poking his head through the auditorium doors, he saw the lights were off. He took the stairs leading from the right side of the foyer, noticing the various bills previewing upcoming speakers. These were interspersed with more radical posters from Greenpeace and other environmental groups. At the top of the curved staircase, now the fourth floor level, he came to a long hallway that paralleled the street. Bloom slowly made his way down the corridor, his rubber soles on the carpeted runner dead silent.

He thought he remembered Brower's office as being at this end of the building, but that brief visit had been a long time ago. He began to read the door plaques, listening as he went. He had almost reached the end of the hall when he heard a voice raised in anger. The sound of Simard's name stopped him cold. He listened, hearing the distinctive resonance of the director's voice leveling a blast of incompetence against a man called Lapierre.

At that moment a stout, gray-haired woman stepped out of the door beside him. She gave him a start, as he did to her, since she had almost walked into him.

After recovering, she asked briskly, "Who are you looking for?"

Bloom gave her one of his best smiles. "Forgive me if I startled you. I was here once, several years ago. I thought I remembered Herr Brower's office at this end of the hall."

"That is correct. But who are you, and what is your business with the director?"

"Ah, my name is Bloom, Sam Bloom. I gave a lecture here in nineteen eighty-two. You are Frau Foch, are you not?" He could scarcely forget that name, considering how the Swiss pronounced Foch.

She smiled, remembering. "Of course, Dr. Bloom. My memory is not what it used to be. Is the director expecting you?"

"Not at all. I was shopping on Talacker and just making my way to the Bahnhof via Fussli without knowing it. All of a sudden, there was the old opera house. I saw the lights on and thought I'd see if Herr Brower was working late."

She frowned. "He is. A full board meeting has been called for this evening. The directors should be arriving soon. I would be surprised if they all make it, though."

"Why is that?" Sam asked in all innocence.

"Well, this time of year, and being called so quickly. They are old men, you know, most of them even older than Herr Brower. Usually, to get them all together at once is quite a task."

"Something urgent, I suppose."

She sighed. "Yes, I expect so."

"Well, I hope they won't keep you too late."

"Me?" she asked abruptly. "Only members of the board attend such meetings. And Hans, of course, Herr Brower's secretary, who happens to be out at the moment. Dr. Bloom, I would prefer not to interrupt the director while he is preparing for an important meeting."

"You're right, of course. Perhaps you could mention that I stopped by and tell him I'll be in town for a few days, at the Excelsior. I just returned from a short trip to Madagascar. Fascinating place, but serious problems with the number of native species they stand to lose in the very near future."

He quickly realized that his words were like blows to her body. Frau Foch placed a hand over her heart. "Oh, Dr. Bloom, it is such a sad, sad case, Madagascar. We know, because one of our field parties is just now completing a two-year harvesting project. Perhaps you ran into them?"

"No. Too bad, we could have compared notes."

"But you see, Dr. Bloom, unless their government changes course very quickly, that island could have the distinction of destroying more unique species than any other country in the entire history of the human race."

He nodded, thinking she was probably right. He bid Frau Foch good evening and took the winding staircase down to the auditorium, one story above street level. The same sharp chemical odor he had noticed on the way in still lingered. He wondered what it could be, since it seemed familiar in a distant sort of way. If the auditorium was on the second floor, what, he wondered, would be taking place below, at street level?

He was tempted to take a look around but knew if he was caught in the act, the cat would be out of the bag for sure. Better he should retain his credibility and try for another meeting with Brower. He descended the snow-covered steps thinking that Charlie was going to be upset by his jumping the gun, as it were, but at the same time satisfied that his brief chat with Frau Foch had proved worthwhile.

Bannerman called him a damned fool. Sam protested. This was not the wilds of Madagascar, he told the angry policeman as he opened the bag to remove Charlie's winter overshoes and mackinaw. Back in his room, he'd just found a phone message from Herr Brower asking Dr. Bloom to call him late in the morning. "Hell, if we're supposed to keep up this innocent scientist façade, isn't it natural for me to go visit the old man?"

Bannerman blew his nose, sniffed a few times and said, "Maybe you're right, but I can't have you wandering off on your own and making contact with the enemy without letting me know up front. For all we know, your stopping in like that might have stirred up a hornet's nest. So from now on you'd better keep me posted if you intend to do any more snooping around."

Bloom was considering telling Lieutenant Charlie Bannerman to go get stuffed, until it occurred to him that it was really his safety Charlie was concerned about.

Bannerman eased himself up until he was leaning back against the headboard. "This Frau Foch—how do you spell that?"

Sam told him.

"What a handle to carry around. Imagine checking into a New York hotel and saying 'My name is Missus Foch'."

"The Swiss don't seem to have difficulty with it. Matter of fact, in Holland they got a beer by that name. Waitresses just love to come up to American tourists and ask if they care for a foch."

Charlie shook his head. "I'll be go to hell. Okay, you went upstairs and heard someone giving this Lapierre guy a blast. Simard's name was mentioned. You believe it was Brower doing the talking. You hear anyone answer him?"

"Hardly. And his voice was raised for just those few seconds before—"

"Frau Foch. Yeah, I know. Just wondering how could you be so sure it was the old man's voice? Didn't you say it was five years since you were in Zurich?"

"It's distinctive, sort of nasal and gravelly-like. I'm certain it was him." He walked over and pulled out a can of Lowenbrau from Charlie's minibar. "Adds a little more meat to the bones of your grand scenario, doesn't it?"

"That big meeting this evening, what I wouldn't give to be a fly on that wall."

Sam grinned. "One big, fat mother of a fly—who couldn't understand a word of German."

Bannerman ignored the reference to his weight. "Suppose we told Lemieux about the board meeting. How do you think he'd react?"

Bloom didn't have the answer to that, as he had found it difficult to judge the man. On the one hand Lemieux had made it clear he was not going to disobey orders; but if he was a true cop, Sam told Charlie, he'd want to get at the truth, no matter what.

The detective sneezed twice while reaching for a card on his night table. "Here, give him a call. Ask if he knows anyone by the name of Lapierre."

Bloom took the card and wiped in on his sleeve. "But nothing about this evening's meeting?"

"No way. Then he'd know you were snooping around. I get the feeling this thing is real touchy, and if we step too far out of line, we're likely to find ourselves turfed out of town."

"My exact impression," Sam replied. He dialed the number and waited until Lemieux came on the line. Bloom asked if he knew anyone by the name of Lapierre.

"Poof! Lapierre is as common in Switzerland as Smith is in America. But not so many in Zurich. You are speaking about Zurich?"

"Well, I don't rightly know. Let's say in relation to Simard. Would that narrow the field somewhat?"

"In the context of René Simard," the man replied formally, "you would be speaking of Henri Lapierre, head of European Affairs at Interpol."

"Simard's boss?"

"Exactly. And now, Dr. Bloom, suppose you tell me in what context you heard Henri Lapierre's name mentioned. I don't suppose you happened to pick it up during your visit to the old opera house?"

Sam glanced at his companion, wondering how he should respond. But if he was followed and the tail had seen him go in, denial would be pointless. "Is it considered good manners in Zurich to have visitors followed?"

"I would say so," came the dry reply. "If there were two attempts on their lives during the previous week."

Bloom noticed the Swiss detective did not seem unduly disturbed by his having gone there in direct contravention of instructions to the contrary.

This observation was quickly confirmed when Lemieux continued. "As a member of their organization, you paid a social call. Perfectly understandable. And perhaps Herr Brower was unable to see you due to a board meeting this evening. What else did you learn during your little chat with Frau Foch?"

Cupping his hand over the receiver, Sam said, "Lapierre is Simard's boss. Lemieux already knows about the board meeting and my talking to the ZIAN woman. They had me followed. I think you'd better take over from here, Lieutenant."

Bannerman stumbled out of bed and snatched the receiver away, glaring at his partner. Bloom shrugged his shoulders in innocent denial. How was he supposed to know the police were following him around?

After bringing Lemieux up to date, Charlie waited for the blast he was sure would come. Instead, to his surprise, he heard, "Well done, Lieutenant. I had hoped you were able to recognize my posturing of our official position for what it was. And now, according to the telephone message, Herr Brower would like Dr. Bloom to call him. Interesting, is it not?"

Charlie still didn't completely trust the Swiss cop, so he held back. "Maybe. Why do you think he wants to talk to Sam?"

"If you wish me to speculate, I would say that Dr. Bloom's involvement in all this puzzles him. It even puzzles me a little. If your friend is willing, I believe he should return the call and accept an invitation to visit, if one is extended. With caution, naturally, and keeping in mind that I made no such recommendation. In fact, Lieutenant, this conversation never took place. And neither you nor Dr. Bloom is to go anywhere near the old opera house tonight."

"Sheesh, you gotta be kidding. I'm not going anywhere. But if you or one of your men could see fit to—"

"Out of the question, Lieutenant. That *would* cost me my job."

Bannerman saw Sam trying to get his attention. "Hold on a minute, Inspector."

"Ask him about that chemical smell, sort of sharp and sweet."

After hearing the question, Lemieux said, "It arises from the taxidermy studio below the auditorium, some kind of acetate they use. They have a cold storage center, plus a large studio with eight full-time taxidermists and a number of students in the south half of the building, where it faces Fussli. The remainder of the ground floor is used for general storage."

Charlie was going to say that it sounded like the perfect cover for a cocaine operation, but that was obvious. At this point, he figured, Lemieux was way ahead of him.

Bannerman passed the receiver back to Sam and after hanging up, began to voice his opinion about the taxidermy studio. A knock on the door interrupted him. It was Dr. Grenier.

"I thought I would find you here. Not causing the patient any undue stress, I trust?"

Charlie scampered back under the covers while Sam took her hand, but he really wanted to take all of her. He asked about her ankle, noticing her faint limp. The woman became more gorgeous every time he saw her. There was no doubt now: He was hopelessly in love with Anna Grenier.

He helped remove her luxuriant lynx coat and shook off the wet snow while she went into Charlie's bathroom to freshen up.

Bloom muttered under his breath, "If she gets any more delectable, I swear to God I'm going to eat her, clothes and all."

"Know what you mean," Charlie replied. In her own way, Anna Grenier was every bit as beautiful as his Shaleen. *His Shaleen!* Oh, Christ, I've gone and said it. He'd called her earlier and told her what was going on. Something was happening between him and the young woman from Somalia, he knew. He didn't understand what it was or how it could be, but it was real.

Anna came out of the washroom and caught the look on his face. She smiled a knowing smile of considerable warmth and beauty. "I know what you need to make you forget all about your cold, Lieutenant."

"Hey now," Sam cried, misunderstanding Anna's seductive tone.

She took his arm. "You may relax, Dr. Bloom. Charlie knows whereof I speak, even if you do not." She led him to the settee beside the window. "Tell me all about your meeting with Andre Lemieux."

"How did you know about that?" Bannerman asked.

"Because he told me last night, when I called, that he would make certain he was appointed your liaison officer. Andre is a very determined man and a very good policeman, according to my mother, who knows everything."

"Devious SOB," Charlie said. "Didn't even say he spoke to you. So he already knew most of what I was telling him."

"I expect he wanted to hear it from a professional. Have you heard anything new on René?"

Charlie decided to let Bloom answer that one. Sam nodded. "They picked him up at the Morondava airport. Sounds like he was all set to follow us. His tickets showed Zurich as his final destination."

Anna didn't reply immediately. Sam was still holding her hand and could feel the shudder run through her. "He told me he was returning to Paris," she said, almost in a whisper.

"So he lied again. You should be used to it by now."

Sam expected her to let fly at Bannerman, but she just nodded meekly. "You're quite right, Lieutenant. You would think by now I would know better. I don't consider myself a naive person, it's just that René and I were once so close."

"Too close," Bloom said gently. "You couldn't see him for what he is—a professional assassin, and God knows what else." To change the subject, he told her about his visit to the old opera house.

But Bannerman decided to pursue it, to knock this bullshit about family relationships out of her head once and for all. "Are you aware of the implications of Brower giving Simard's boss hell?"

Anna nodded again. "He was angry because René was not able to carry out his assignment."

"You got it, sweetheart."

Sam flashed a hard look at Charlie, warning him to back off. Then he said, "Which begs the question of whether the whole Interpol outfit is rotten, or if this is some minor operation they have going on the side to make a little spending money."

It was much the same question Ulansky had asked in the commissioner's office, and Charlie still didn't have an answer.

Something occurred to Bloom. "You know, talking about Simard, I'm getting a bit confused at this point. Frau Foch told me their team in Madagascar was just winding up a two-year harvesting operation—harvesting, meaning the specimens that were loaded in those crates we saw in Toamasina. Which tells me their operation is legitimate. So where did that final load come from—the same team or a different one, located somewhere else on the island? According to Lamont, the original shipment was transported by train. Then, in the middle of the night, the balance arrives by truck."

"From Tsingy, probably," Bannerman replied.

"Most likely. I wonder, the two names I overheard, Victor and Karl … I don't know …. Charlie, if this Frau Foch is crooked, so is the pope. Why don't I call her up right now and ask if those guys were part of the ZIAN team? If they were, then we can take it that the whole outfit is crooked. If she doesn't recognize the names, could we not then assume that ZIAN has an entirely separate operation going on down there, something the government doesn't even know about? What do you think?"

Anna cut in. "But my mother knows Frau Foch very well. She has been to my house on several occasions, and I know her well enough to call her up and say that I ran into these two men who said they were from ZIAN. If Sam contacted her again so soon, would she not grow suspicious?"

Bloom studied the Swiss physician with a bemused expression. "Maybe. It's up to Charlie."

Bannerman sniffed a few times as he rolled his head around. No matter who approached the old gal, the result would be the same: She would tell her boss, which would confirm Brower's suspicion that they knew something about his secret operation on the island. The pressure would be on, as he would feel trapped. But would he have the captain of the *Lucinda V* dump such a valuable cargo? Depending on just how valuable it was, maybe not. The detective wondered again if tonight's special board meeting might not be for the express purpose of making that very decision. Then again, Charlie figured, they had come to Zurich to apply a little pressure. What better way to do it than to let on that they knew about his goons?

He gave Anna the nod. "But don't say any more than you have to."

She squeezed Sam's hand before letting go. Despite Gerhard's death and the bad news about her cousin, Bloom got the distinct impression that Anna Grenier was getting a kind of perverse enjoyment from all the intrigue surrounding her. Watching her now, he fervently hoped it didn't turn nasty again before it was all over. But even as the thought occurred to him, there was no longer any doubt that the three of them had poked their noses into a massive narcotics smuggling ring.

It would be stupid to believe they would go unpunished.

CHAPTER FIFTEEN

As it turned out, six members of the board were able to attend. Herr Brower had figured five at the most. Two were in wheelchairs that were pushed into the boardroom by their chauffeurs, who then abandoned them for the pleasures of the *kaffeehaus* across the street. Old, old men, he thought, looking around the table. All those years, almost half a century, and they were still striving to grow wealthier, to amass more money, more power. But, he asked himself again, aside from the pleasures of one's own family, what other worthwhile goals were there?

The whole enterprise should have been turned over to younger men twenty years ago, he thought as they completed the final toast to fallen comrades. And indeed, that had always been their intention—a family business, where one generation after another would carry on the ZIAN tradition, or the NAZI tradition, as General Bront still claimed. With some the dream died hard. But just one had come. Sons, daughters, grandsons, and granddaughters had been interviewed, but only Hans Backmeyer, now seated slightly behind the chairman, had passed the test. Only he had been willing to submit to the oath of loyalty and proclaim absolute obedience.

After the war they were deluged with hundreds of senior party members desperately seeking employment, men whose prior deeds led them to believe they must be on one execution list or another. They filtered into Zurich throughout the late forties, many still in shock that they were no longer in power. Nearly all were unsuitable, men of raw arrogance, even then, whose only quality was blind obedience. A few, like Victor, General Meisner's adjutant, had been absorbed into the organization. These men, eleven all told, soon proved themselves capable and trustworthy.

As this was only the second board meeting of the year, Herr Brower began with an overview of the various activities ZIAN was involved in, starting with legitimate undertakings and then moving on to the important parts: An update on the Mafia arrests and how this was sure to enhance their business; the latest intelligence on Asian drug movements; the current status on their long-time Turkish opium supply; and so on. He informed them that cocaine was number one in North American sales again. Then he presented an overview on their current difficulties, the reason General Backmeyer had called the meeting.

After hearing the chairman's evaluation of the present status concerning the shipment and the American involvement, General Bront opened the floor with, "I say get rid of the damn stuff, right now!"

"Dump it in the ocean," echoed General Hauppman. "We cannot afford to gamble with our reputations at this late stage."

Oberst Von Rudel was appalled by these opening remarks. "Think carefully, *mein herr*s. Ninety million francs has been invested in this enterprise. And we stand to lose more, much more, as I have already explained to you. My plan, to have every drug addict in America tremble in fear at the very sight of cocaine, will work. Our initial experiment has proven this beyond a shadow of a doubt. Since the altered drug cannot be detected among the pure cocaine, once this special blend is mixed in with the vast supply we have stored away in the US, we shall have enough to keep the North American market saturated for years. As far as the future use of cocaine is concerned, paranoia will reign. I guarantee this will be the case."

Hardening his voice, the former Gestapo official said, "Make no mistake: The amount of blended essence we now have on board the *Lucinda V* gives us the capability to wipe all significant sales of cocaine from the face of the North American continent and to destroy the Colombian cartel in its entirety!"

Herr Brower took a deep breath, calmed down, then went on to point out that knowledge of the secret of the golden orchid was entirely meaningless if access to its precious nectar was denied.

And the opportunity to return to Tsingy, at least in the foresee-able future, would be extremely remote. There were good reasons for this. First of all, he reminded them, the illicit Tsingy operation had been carried out within the shadow of its legal counterpart. The government of Madagascar had granted ZIAN permission to harvest certain common birds, animals, and insects. It did not monitor the movements of ZIAN personnel, which allowed the workers at Tsingy relative freedom to move around the island when they were in need of supplies, or when it came time to move a doctored shipment of cocaine to Toamasina. Such movements were tightly coordinated by the controllers on Moussonstrasse to ensure that the teams did not run into one another. Now that the two-year legitimate undertaking had expired and would not be renewed because of the Malagasy government's new environ-mental awareness program, the logistics of conducting a covert operation in a forbidden reserve on a remote island had become much too formidable.

An equally serious problem was manpower. Few men found living underground and in complete isolation for extended peri-ods of time appealing, and those who agreed to do so were forced to live with hundreds of thousands of bats. Gathering and sort-ing mounds of foul-smelling droppings week after week, month after month, called for the sort of dedication that could only be achieved by great resolve and with substantial funding. The last security chief had lasted just six months — half the time of his predecessor. With the help of Interpol, they had been fortunate enough to locate a West German mercenary, Karl Schuster, who had been living in relative poverty in Algeria. He had accepted the offer with gratitude.

Now they had to contend with the Americans and a nosy Swiss physician. Was this New York homicide detective likely to return to Madagascar to continue with his aborted investi-gation of the reserve? With Anna Grenier's constant prodding, would the local police finally grow suspicious and attempt to tie the recent increase in lightning victims to Tsingy? Since Simard was being held as a suspected terrorist, were they not likely to conclude that this latest death inside the reserve was murder? If the authorities were to conduct a thorough, professional search of the reserve, sooner or later they were bound to discover, like the deceased natives who preceded them, one of the entrances to the caverns.

While they were still discussing the Tsingy problem, General Backmeyer leaned over and whispered to Herr Brower. "And what of *our* little reserve, Dietrich? Is it safe?"

The director smiled. "This is Switzerland. The authorities would not dare to search a building without applying for a search warrant. Even if that were ever to happen, *mein general*, I would receive plenty of notice."

"And the Americans, do you not feel that they should be silenced, before it is too late?"

"I would recommend against the use of violence here in Zurich. The risk factor is much too high. Naturally, their movements are being closely monitored."

" — grand plan, and a brilliant one. If you had been commanding the Reich, Herr Oberst, we would surely have been victorious." This from General Leitz, the philosopher in the group. "But now, alas, we must face reality and assume that your plan has been uncovered. By what means is of little consequence. The truth of the matter is that when our ship docks in Djibouti on Sunday morning, there may well be a warm reception awaiting them."

After a few moments of one-on-one discussions around the boardroom table, the still-deep voice of General Steiner cut through the chatter. "I presume the treated narcotic is being transported in the same manner as previous shipments?" By this Steiner was referring to a method of injecting several grains of the deadly essence between two crystals of common silica gel, used to absorb moisture from the air and ensure the various specimens were kept dry.

Herr Brower nodded.

"But you obviously feel this device is no longer sufficient to avoid detection?"

"One month ago I would have told you that it would have been impossible to detect our little subterfuge. I no longer have that confidence."

"Very well," Steiner said. "Then why not transfer those fifty crates to another vessel at sea? Is this not a possibility?"

"An excellent suggestion, General Steiner," said Bront, "except that the East African coast is riddled with scoundrels, on land and at sea. One would need to employ the highest degree of caution. Is it even possible to locate another trustworthy vessel in the Indian Ocean before Sunday?"

"Indeed, indeed," wheezed General Schimmel from his wheelchair. "But is it not correct that the poor old tub has established a reputation for breaking down on a regular basis? If a trustworthy captain could be found, even in the Mediterranean, Demetrios could wait around a few extra days without arousing suspicion, at least from the harbor authorities. Whatever these Americans busybodies will make out of it, well …."

They were not true comrades anymore, like they had been in the old days, Herr Brower thought. Over the years he had watched them grow apart, each man developing his own life in isolation of the others, as if by close association they might reveal their dark secrets from the past. Some were even neighbors, with their estates lying close together beside the lake. But their families had little in common, except wealth. None had intermarried, as they had initially hoped. And now, all that remained of the original fifteen high-ranking deserters was a handful of shriveled old men. But rich old men, rich beyond their wildest dreams, thanks to the vision and administrative genius of one of them.

An innocent prank, tragically played upon one of the regular ZIAN workers during their first week in Madagascar, had uncovered this marvelous bonanza in Tsingy. Once the cause of death was determined, it did not take Herr Brower long to realize its enormous potential. He began buying up all the cocaine he could get his hands on, much of it obtained by trading from their vast supply of heroin two to one — two kilos of heroin for one of cocaine. The Americans, or the French, or the Italians, went away happy, while ZIAN continued to amass well over three thousand kilos of cocaine. This treasure was stored away in various warehouses in New York, Los Angeles, Detroit, and so on, under the watchful eyes of five well-paid employees. There it awaited the arrival of the Tsingy compound, which would be then be blended with the pure cocaine until the whole three thousand kilos achieved the same fatal potential. The amounts that had been previously transported from Buenos Aires via the *Lucinda V* were relatively insignificant, a few kilos per trip. But those shipments had served their purpose well.

At the end of a relatively vigorous debate, it was agreed to put out a call for another Greek-manned ship that would be allowed a maximum of five more days to rendezvous with the *Lucinda V*. Herr Brower was to first contact Captain Demetrios and seek his advice. From experience they had learned that the Greeks were usually dependable in such matters, provided the price was right. Pay a Greek well, and he will go the distance for you every time. If such a vessel could not be located, along with all the appurtenant assurances that went with it, then the fifty crates were to be destroyed and the residue sunk to the bottom of the ocean. The director would then get rid of the American cocaine and recoup what he could from its sale on the open market.

And with that, Herr Brower's master plan, the crowning glory of which would have seen the subjugation of his sworn enemies, the Colombian cartel, would come to a futile end.

It was this thought, the possibility of failure, that occupied his mind as they continued to discuss the fate of the seven men who formed the Tsingy operation. The takedown operation was nearing completion, and Victor had radioed in for instructions. This was Victor's last job. He had told them as much, and would now finally retire to his native Salzburg. Erich had been on permanent staff for four years. He was an unpleasant individual, despised by all who worked with him. But he was also a brilliant chemist and now drawing close to one million francs annually. He would remain as part of the organization. Karl had received good marks from Victor and would also be kept on. It was unanimously agreed that the other four were to be left behind in Tsingy and their bodies dumped into one of the many deep crevasses in the reserve.

Anna wondered if her impression was correct, that Sam Bloom had suddenly turned nervous. He hesitated in his speech, looked away in the midst of his sentences, and altogether seemed to be on edge. What now, she wondered through the slight mist that had gathered inside her head after three glasses of '78 Krug.

The main course, an exquisite chateaubriand, had been served and was eaten with considerable relish by both of them. Bloom passed on dessert, but Anna felt just wicked enough to order a chocolate torte soaked in brandy. She touched his hand. "Sam, what is it?"

A decisive man by nature, Bloom was suddenly overcome with indecision. He had purchased a gift after his visit to the old opera house, a token of his gratitude for the loving care she had bestowed upon him. But the article he had chosen was not your everyday trinket. He had it in his jacket pocket and continued to finger the small package throughout dinner. What if she refused he wondered, almost in a panic. He was painfully aware that Anna had just lost her husband, so Bloom knew he was rushing things. Would he scare her off? Should he forget it, at least until they got to know one another better?

Even his smile looked nervous, he knew, angry at himself for his inability to rise above such adolescent behavior. Then he figured, the hell with it; he might as well find out now as later. He removed the box, gift-wrapped in a silky blue foil. Raising his eyes to hers, he made the offering, concentrating on his composure and making certain the words came out right.

"This is for the world's most beautiful healer, who came into my life and made me well again."

Anna's lovely gray eyes opened wide as she caught the intensity in his words. She started to say it was silly of him, that it was he who had come into her life, that it was he who had probably saved hers. To her surprise she found that she was quite speechless. She accepted the little package in silence, leaned back in her chair and stared down at it.

A full minute went by, a year for Bloom, before she opened it. He bit his lip in anxiety, his mind racing ahead to the next stage.

Anna's gasp turned the heads of those seated beside them. "Oh my," she whispered. "I never thought ... I .... Oh, Sam, I never dreamed ...."

Slowly, she raised the necklace with one hand, the diamonds and sapphires catching the candlelight. More gasps came from the adjoining tables.

Once Bloom saw them in her hand and had the opportunity to compare the color to her eyes, he knew he had made the right choice. There were five sapphires, the bottom one a ten-carat pendant. The next two on either side were five carats, and the two above that two carats. Each stone was embedded in an angular cluster of diamonds, the angle of each bed varying significantly from the other but complementing each other in a way that spoke of a master's touch. In all, there were seventy-eight diamonds; those surrounding the pendant were one carat in size, and those around the smaller sapphires, a quarter carat.

"The stones are rare, they tell me," he said casually, trying to lighten up the moment. "This particular cloud sapphire comes from a small river in northern Ecuador, the only known source in the world. The jeweler is a Brazilian chap named Sabino. Ever hear of him?"

"Of course," she replied, her voice husky, but still at a whisper. "Sam, they are exquisite, truly exquisite. Is it gold?"

Her question regarding the thick but finely interwoven chain came as no surprise, never being able to tell platinum from white gold himself. He told her it was platinum. Then she finally looked up, attempting to smile but not quite succeeding. "I don't know what to say. It's all too much. I—"

He cut her off fast, before she told him she couldn't accept his gift. "It was the color that did it. Don't you see, Anna? They're in the exact same color tones as your eyes."

He rose from the table, aware of the sudden silence in the Excelsior dining room. Without asking, he took the necklace and draped it around her neck, then stood back. She had worn a blue suit ensemble, a sort of cornflower blue, over a white silken blouse open at the neck. Again without asking, he slipped the jacket off so as not to distract from the sapphires. When he stood back, spontaneous applause broke out.

"Magnificent," said an older lady at the next table. Her husband, white-haired and rosy-cheeked, added, "Accept and enjoy, my dear. It is obvious the designer had you in mind when he conceived the idea."

Muted comments abounded, in praise of both Anna and the sapphire necklace. Bloom resumed his seat, grinning at the look on her face. "He's right. Your name was written all over it. Kind of drew me, like a magnet. I really had no choice."

Fingering the stones, she said softly, "I would not even attempt to guess the cost."

"Don't," Sam said, cringing a little himself when he recalled the price tag. "Besides, it's only money. So, do you like it?"

"I love it," she replied fervently. "I will always love it. Always."

Thank God for that, he thought. The chocolate torte arrived then, and the beaming waiter added his compliments to all the others. But Anna had lost her appetite. She was unable to keep her fingers off the stones and anxious to get to a mirror.

"Go on," Bloom said. "Go take a look."

She needed no second invitation and was off in a flash. While she was out of the room, the elderly gentleman from the next table leaned over. "Please forgive our curiosity, but this lady is your wife?"

Sam smiled as he turned in his chair. "No. But I'm working on it."

The man laughed. "Then you have made an excellent beginning." He reached over to touch Sam's arm. "Perhaps these eyes have grown a little dim with the years, but if you are successful, I think you will have the most beautiful bride in Zurich."

"No argument there," he answered. But would she consent to be his bride? That was the question. Having just lost one husband, he doubted if she would be receptive to taking on another just yet. But Sam was prepared to wait as long as necessary.

She had kissed him upon her return from viewing her prize, but once Bloom closed the door to his room, Anna placed both hands on his face and drew his lips to hers. It was a gentle touching at first, a mild caress, but it soon became more. Sam was aware of his heart pounding when they finally broke.

That night at the Swiss forestry station, they had kissed, but no more. With Gerhard's death still fresh on their minds, it did not seem proper to continue. But Bloom had wanted her. God, how he had wanted her. "You know, I was wondering if the parts I can't see are as nice as the parts I can see."

She giggled a little. "Other than being two kilos overweight, a butterfly birthmark on my rump, three moles on my tummy, a skating scar above my knee, there should not be any unpleasant surprises."

"Where are your sensitive spots?"

She backed away slightly, slipping off her jacket, then moved in again. "Besides the obvious, my neck, the inside of my wrists, but especially the base of my spine. There is a special little place there where it all comes together, my everything. Touch it, and all resistance breaks down."

He slipped the blouse free from her skirt and allowed his fingers to reach under the band. Pressing softly, he began a small circular movement, increasing the pressure until she moaned against his shoulder. "Oh God, you have no idea how good that feels."

"You do realize, Dr. Grenier, what it is you just told me?"

She looked up into his eyes. "How to seduce me, I hope."

Bannerman felt in tip-top condition the next morning, a living testimony to the effectiveness of Swiss medicine. He decided to let Bloom eat breakfast alone — if he was alone — and ordered his sent up. After a long relaxing shower, wherein he gave himself free rein to fantasize about the pleasures he might look forward to with Shaleen, he figured he had better call the commissioner, even if it was four in the morning in New York.

"Suppose I should have expected this ZIAN group to have a lot of clout," the PC declared after a long yawn. He was not upset that Charlie had called him. "Big money usually does. You think Lemieux did anything about the board meeting last night?"

"You mean listened in? No way. He's prepared to help, but only up to a point."

"Up to the point where his job is on the line, no doubt. What's your next move?"

"Depends on Lemieux. But I might have a little something he can use in the Strouss murder investigation. Then maybe I can squeeze a bit more out of him. How about the ship, Commissioner, any joy with the CIA?"

"You had it figured. Dates and times are downtown, but your little tub was caught on the west side of the island about one hundred twenty miles off course."

"North?"

"North—meaning a rendezvous, to drop off a payload."

"Um-um. Get it all fixed up in the Tsingy lab, then ship the stuff overland just in time to catch the *Lucinda V* before she pulls out."

"That's not all. The satellite has four-hour windows, meaning it views the same terrain every four hours. They calculated that your little old tub averaged twenty-three knots between sightings."

"Souped-up engines. The kind they use to haul drugs."

"You got it. But I'll tell you what bothers me about that, Charlie. Why not fly it in directly? I mean why ship it through all these ports of call and run the risk of being caught each time?"

"I put that one to Lemieux. First of all, he said, the Swiss run their airports like their banks, real heavy security, while nobody in these African ports gives a shit. Even Venice, he says, is looser than a sixty-year-old hooker, baksheesh being the order of the day."

"But it still has to cross the border into Switzerland."

"All their stuff enters the country by train, always has. And on the trains, he says, you could smuggle an elephant across the border if you wanted." Hearing the commissioner's snort, he added, "Yeah, I know, weird. But that's the way it is, he said."

"I hope the guy knows what he's talking about. Just a minute—here it is. I took this list home in case you called; it names the companies that are shareholders in the Shuller Foundation, which owns the *Lucinda V*. They weren't easy to ferret out. Let me know if your Swiss inspector objects to running down the names. Maybe I can light a fire under his boss."

Charlie took down the names, fourteen in all, six of which were estate companies. Then he told the PC about Bloom ordering a large scale map of Tsingy. "First thing he did yesterday morning. Got on the phone to some outfit he knows in Nairobi, told them to get it flown today, price being no object. He was talking about orthophoto mapping, something they could do up real quick. Said he's damned if he's going into any killing ground without knowing the terrain."

"That's his military background. However, there is no way this office can become involved in any kind of a paramilitary operation. You go in by the back door, Lieutenant, you're on your own. Know what I'm saying?"

Bannerman knew. The PC could hardly place himself in a position of complicity with the kind of operation Bloom had in mind. "You might find it interesting to know that Sam is carrying the cost himself. Insisted on it. He and the Grenier woman, I'd say they got something going on between them. Said he owes her this one."

The commissioner chuckled. "Those hot climates tend to loosen people up. I'd advise you to be careful, Lieutenant, or some sweet young thing might just come along and blow a hole in your bachelor status."

Bannerman bit down on his tongue, tempted, but said nothing. They talked about the progress of the special task force, the rash of crack houses going under the torch, the usual pre-Christmas lunatic killing binge. After hanging up, he tried to get Lemieux on the line, but the inspector was out.

When breakfast arrived he was ready for it, having eaten hardly anything since getting off the plane. It had occurred to him that maybe he should try to lose a little weight, especially if he was thinking about walking down the aisle. But the tempting aroma of poached eggs on steak effectively killed any thought of diet. Lemieux called as he was cleaning his plate with the last heel of rye bread.

"Yeah, I feel great. Whatever the guy gave me did its job. What about last night, you work up the nerve to do a little eavesdropping?"

"As I told you, we rarely consider violating a citizen's rights for mere expediency."

Charlie wondered how far he'd get in a murder investigation back home with that kind of attitude. "Well, here's your thought for the day: Why don't you find out where they're holding Simard, call him up and have a little chat? You should be able to bullshit your way past the local cops. Tell him you were shocked to learn of his incarceration. Maybe ask him if there's anything you can do to help him out."

"What exactly is that supposed to accomplish?"

"Arrange to get your truck driver in Geneva on the other line. You said he received verbal instructions only. Let him listen in, maybe you'll get a little surprise."

Bannerman heard that whale sound again, Lemieux blowing out his cheeks. "Isn't that a bit far-fetched, Lieutenant? Simard has a known history as a well-respected field agent with Interpol."

"Hey, I don't care if you do it or not. Where I come from, we don't pay a lot of attention to a guy's occupation if we got reason to believe he's a killer."

Then he gave the Swiss cop the list of shareholders and said it would be nice if he could check them out, but Lemieux already knew the estate companies. They belonged to the heirs of the deceased directors of the Zurich International Association of Naturalists.

After receiving that piece of news, Charlie stretched out on his bed. The time had come to have another look at the over-all picture, see where it was heading. Anna had been told by Frau Foch that ZIAN had no employees named Karl and Victor in Madagascar. The old gal even wondered aloud why Anna would think so, which more or less confirmed Bannerman's good-team/bad-team concept. So ZIAN, a central European consortium, had nosed its way into the traditional South American-run coke trade. That was a definite. As movers only? Maybe, but not likely. The way it was coming across to him, ZIAN seemed to be calling all the shots, probably right down to the wholesale level. Yet Professor Carswell claimed the samples he analyzed had been blended in three separate locations, meaning this killer shit wasn't turned into crack in any one place—maybe not in Madagascar, maybe not in Zurich, maybe not even by ZIAN.

He had to remind himself again that as big and juicy as the whole scenario appeared, drugs were still a secondary consideration. He was the investigating officer in a series of cowardly murders where the victims had been killed off by a deadly substance supposedly extracted from an orchid unique to Madagascar. This substance was then combined with cocaine through the use of some kind of advanced chemical process to make the final product undetectable on the street. Only Carswell, with his giant twin computers and the most advanced biology program in existence, had been able to get a handle on it.

After running through everything he had learned to date, Bannerman acknowledged that he had most of the flat pieces now, the outside edges of the puzzle. Now he had to work on the guts of the problem. It continued to bother him that these heart-related deaths had been in evidence for a couple of weeks at the most. And according to the commissioner, there was no indication of a similar problem in any of the other major centers. Allowing his imagination full reign, he wondered if it could have been some kind of trial run, a small test of the product's ability in the marketplace. With the test over, and successful, was the main shipment now on its way, perhaps intended to flood the entire North American market and destroy the public's confidence in cocaine altogether? No, that made no sense. There was something else too, a shadowy form that lingered just beyond the limits of his psyche, near enough and big enough to cause him concern.

He consoled himself with the knowledge that sooner or later all mysteries fell victim to the orderly mind. And when it came to order and method, he owned one of the best minds in the business. He admitted this with only a twinge of pride. There were those who claimed Charlie Bannerman could have made it to the top—One Police Plaza—if he had cleaned up his act and learned to kowtow to his superiors.

But that was history. Now, for the first time in his career, he realized he was up against something ominous, like a big tornado was headed his way and there was nothing he could do to stop it. He was suddenly anxious for Sam to meet this enigmatic

Herr Brower, to see if he could glean a few more pieces of the puzzle. Charlie would have loved to go himself, but Brower already knew his reason for being in town. Maybe Bloom, as a bona fide scientist and a member of ZIAN, might still have a little credibility.

Maybe.

CHAPTER SIXTEEN

Victor did not like the problem that was brewing. Members of the auxiliary staff — their own men — were to be left behind, and Karl had refused the job outright. He had even refused to participate in the slaughter. His refusal created difficulties, because the unpleasant task now fell upon Victor's shoulders. While the former Nazi *oberstleutnant* had no compunction about following such orders — after all, an order was an order — he knew that the intended victims, all fugitives from the law themselves, might be alert to deception. For a man of Victor's age, it would take clever planning to bring off a multiple execution without risking his own life.

There was, of course, Erich. This was his third major assignment with ZIAN's only full-time chemist, and Victor had observed his cool disregard for life on more than one occasion. When the younger man arrived in Victor's office shortly before noon, he went directly to the bottle of sherry and poured himself a drink.

"Well," he said, sporting that half smile and half sneer he usually wore, "the last of my paraphernalia has been crushed into little pieces and dumped into the well. So much for the great orchid enterprise."

The well was not a real well, but the deepest hole they knew of inside the cavern, a fissure which ran so deep that objects fell with no sound at all, unless they bounced off the sides on the way down. This, thought the old soldier, was where the bodies of the men he had lived with for the last two years would have to go.

"We have one final logistical problem, Erich. Can you guess what it is?"

Erich was a true Teutonic blond, the kind of man the Führer would have seen run the world if the war had gone his way. He looked down over the rim of his glass at the old man. "Something serious. And something that requires my help. Unpleasant, I expect."

Having been with ZIAN for several years, Erich was familiar with the fate of casual labor once the termination point in any major drug operation had been reached. It had recently occurred to him that just two of the seven men, three at the most, would survive Tsingy. With his own tenure secure, Erich did not need to concern himself with minor logistical matters.

"I heard the broadcast this morning about Simard being pulled in by the local gendarmes. Can you imagine how exasperated he feels, this big-time Interpol agent ending up in some sordid Malagasy prison for the rest of his life?"

Victor scoffed at this. "What do they have on him — traveling under a false identity? Everything else is circumstantial. They will never be able to tie him to the bomb in Toama, nor to that forester's fall into the crevasse. Do not forget that Interpol continues to exert an inordinate amount of influence upon French police everywhere, even here on the island. I'll wager he'll be out within days."

Erich shrugged. "You may be right at that. A little closer to home, what about Karl? Is he in or out?"

"In. Herr Brower is satisfied with his performance and his talents can be put to use elsewhere."

"But he has refused to do it?"

"Indeed. In a way I can't blame him. They have naturally grown close during these last few months."

The sneer increased. "Let's not cover his deficiencies in grandeur. The man is a coward. I really have no idea what Herr Brower sees in him. So I take it you wish me to resolve your logistical problem."

"I was wondering, Erich, if you have ever taken human life directly, face-to-face I mean, so close that you can smell your victim's fear and feel his hatred; and then have the satisfaction of knowing that your action has reduced the number of parasites in this world."

Erich helped himself to another sherry. "Your philosophical drivel is wasted on me, Victor. When do you want it done?"

The old man tilted his papery-skinned face to the overhead fluorescent tubes, which gave his already pale features a deathly sheen. During the war Victor had developed an allergic reaction to the sun's infrared rays, something no doctor had been able to find a cure for.

If Erich hadn't been so completely obnoxious, he thought, he might have grown to like this young man from Stuttgart. "Do you know how they are progressing with the solar panels?"

There were four sets of six solar panels — two sets in the main complex, one in the middle of the five-kilometer tunnel to the vehicular entrance at the north edge of the reserve, and another at the entrance itself. It was a long, laborious process to dismantle the six-by-six meter square panels, which had each been affixed to a hydraulic tilting device to allow for full sun exposure. The panels could be pulled back inside the vertical ridge of the sheltering pinnacle when necessary, as in the case of nearby aircraft. From these panels came the energy to power the 130 deep cycle solar batteries used to generate light and electricity. Victor, who had achieved his doctorate in mechanical engineering before the war broke out, had designed the complex system himself and took immense pride in its operation. Though he knew there was no other choice, it still upset him to see it all destroyed.

"It seems to be taking them a day and a half per set. With no interruptions, by noon tomorrow they should be ready to begin on the overhead ones. Never fear, I'll make certain all the hard labor is completed." Erich swirled the rich amber liquid around in his glass for a moment, studying it. Then he held the glass at arm's length, appearing to take aim at Victor's head. "Since the terms of my employment do not stipulate such matters, Herr Doctor, I assume there will be a suitable reward in store."

"Of course, my boy. You can depend on it." Victor rolled his chair back from the desk, stretching his legs. He had been reasonably certain Erich would do the job. "You have a three-month vacation waiting after we get out of here. A warm climate, or do you still yearn for the Fatherland?"

Erich quit his pacing and took a seat finally. "I've been thinking about South Africa, which for some obscure reason holds a particular appeal for me. I intended to go the last time, but ended up spending the whole six weeks with some horny bitch in Paris. It was just too damn comfortable to leave. This time around, after spending two of the dullest years of my life in this stinking hole, I crave some excitement, something more on the adventurous side."

Knowing his dislike for blacks, the old man questioned his choice of vacation spots. But Erich explained that the problem with the natives was part of the appeal.

Henri, a heavyset man of average height in his late forties, tapped on the door with the claw hammer he was carrying and walked in. "That same aircraft has returned. It seems to be flying parallel lines about one kilometer apart, north to south, south to north. Karl's shut us down until the bloody thing goes away. Do you want us to start pulling the living quarters apart?"

Victor glanced across his desk at the chemist. "Aerial photography. Government, do you suppose?"

Erich shrugged. "There have been rumors of their intentions to upgrade the mapping on the western section of the island ever since we arrived. Perhaps they finally came up with the money."

"I expect that must be the case. By all means, Henri, start pulling apart the recreation center and perhaps the frame around the kitchen. Leave the sleeping quarters for the time being. And leave the antennas and gasoline generator to the very end. I trust someone is making sure the batteries are fully charged."

"My job," Henri answered, twirling the hammer in his hand. "We could go for a week on what we have now."

"Good. Well, use your own judgment; anything you know we won't need, dump. And make certain my last case of Harveys doesn't disappear down that hole."

Henri grinned as he closed the door. "Not much chance of that."

"Pleasant sort," said Victor, watching the chemist closely. "Perfect attitude for this kind of an operation. Still think you can do it?"

Erich reached for the sherry bottle again. "You need not worry, old man. To me, he is no different than one of those filthy bats I step on every day."

Herr Brower did not wait for Sam to return his call. Instead, he called again around midmorning. Was Dr. Bloom going downtown to see the parade? If he was, why not drop in, as he was anxious to hear his impressions about Madagascar.

Sam knew nothing of any parade but said yes, he had intended to watch it. He would be certain to drop around and pay his respects. He called Bannerman's room to inform him of the invitation, but Charlie was out. Through his window he could see it was a brilliant sunny day, the lake sparkling and the snow-covered mountains surrounding it a picture of gleaming grandeur. When Anna came out of the shower, he told her about Brower's call and then mentioned that Charlie had gone out.

She had tied the towel high around her breasts, the bottom barely reaching her thighs. She padded across the room and placed both hands on the windowsill. "Have you ever seen a nicer Christmas day?"

Bloom instinctively glanced at his watch calendar: December fifth. "What are you talking about?"

She turned around. "Christmas. In Switzerland it is today that Samichlaus comes to the children."

Seeing his shocked look, she added, "You didn't know?"

"No, I didn't ...." No wonder everyone was in such a festive mood last night. "But what about the twenty-fifth?"

"Yes, that is the religious festival." She stared at him oddly for a moment, then twirled her hair around, catching him with a fine spray. "As for Charlie, I think that perhaps a man who has spent his entire life within the confines of a giant metropolis must be awed by such a spectacle. He is probably drinking in all our Swiss beauty."

"Probably not," Sam told her in a soft voice. "That's what I'm doing."

Anna took the sapphire necklace off the dresser and fastened it around her neck. But when she moved the towel down around her waist, the jewels diminished to mere baubles in the midst of her own magnificent ornaments.

Sam shook his head. "Dear God," he whispered, hypnotized by the sight of her. The curves of her body were so soft and perfect. She bent over him. "Care to inspect your purchase, Dr. Bloom?"

He wasn't certain if she was coming on to him again or just fooling around, but he wasn't taking any chances. He kissed each dark nipple twice and eased her away as he rose from the chair. "Gotta go find Charlie. See you downstairs at eleven."

From the door he glanced back, seeing her wide grin. She said, "I was only joking, honest."

He found Charlie on a wooden bench near the edge of the lake, just across the road from their hotel. He was staring off into space when Bloom sat down beside him. "You know this is Christmas Day?"

"Found out this morning," the policeman replied. "Weird, isn't it? A guy spends his whole life in one country and never really thinks about anyone else, like they might do things different from us."

"True enough," Bloom agreed. That same thought had often occurred to him over the years. Sweeping his vision across the gleaming alabaster peaks beyond the lake, he said, "Pretty darn nice, don't you think?"

Bannerman nodded vaguely. "Yeah, but it lacks something."

First Sam thought he was referring to the scenery, but then noticed that his eyes weren't focused on anything in particular. "Brower just called. Apologized for missing me last night. Said he'd be in for an hour or so this afternoon, if I happen to be downtown to watch the parade."

"Anxious, wouldn't you say? Christmas day and all. You'd better let Lemieux know before you go in. What's your opinion, think they're still as desperate as they were in Madagascar? Or is everything just dandy since their ship got away clean."

"Lemieux thinks Brower is just curious."

"He's probably right. Be pretty dumb to start pissing in their own backyard."

Sam recalled the explosion in Toamasina and shook his head. "According to Lemieux, these guys own this town, meaning they can do what they want. Tell you, I'd feel safer if I had a gun."

"Yeah. You know, Sam, I figure the commissioner made a mistake moving us up here without having a chance to look around that weird limestone reserve. We went down there for the specific purpose of tracking down your super flower and never even got to see one. Maybe the orchid's not there. You ever think of that?"

Bloom shivered. He had been fooled by the bright sunlight and left his mackinaw inside. He glanced at his watch: 10:50. "Shit, I don't know, Charlie. Anna thinks she may have spotted one from the chopper. I'm going in. Come on, I'll buy you a coffee and maybe one of those exotic Swiss desserts for your Christmas present."

The detective pulled himself up. "Sure, what's another thousand calories?" When they began walking back to the hotel, he said, "See that character to the left, on the corner? Been there since I came out. You figure he's counting seagulls?"

Bloom glanced toward the corner of Seehofstrasse and spotted a man in a heavy camel hair coat with a black fedora pulled down over his eyes. "Police?"

"Maybe. But if that's the case, who's the guy in the lobby?"

"Huh?"

They were just crossing Uto Quai, a major thoroughfare running along the lake, threading their way between clusters of cars whizzing by over a thin layer of packed snow. "The one standing in the window. Betcha dinner tonight he's back on to us when we go in."

"You're on." Sam couldn't lose that one, since they were going to Anna's place for dinner.

The guy had disappeared from the window by the time the Americans began stamping loose snow off their overshoes. Once inside the warmth of the hotel lobby they saw him again, back on, intently studying the dining room menu posted on the wall.

"See what I mean? Tail number two."

"Maybe they're both police?"

"It's not impossible — one for each of us if we split up. Probably got another one hanging around for your girlfriend."

As they were about to enter the dining room, Charlie turned to Sam. "Talking about girlfriends, I'd be curious to know how much you paid for that little token."

Bloom allowed the cop to go in first. "Forget it, Lieutenant, it'd just give you heartburn."

"I bet. And talking about money, that offer you made on the island still good?"

"Come on, Charlie, how many Randolph Scott movies you seen? You ever know him to break his word? Marry that gal, you're a rich man. Temptation getting a bit much for you?"

Bannerman couldn't help working up a small grin. "She's a lot of woman, that one. Probably lay me to rest permanently after the first week."

"But what a way to go, Charlie, what a way to go!"

Anna joined them a few minutes later, her face lit up like a beacon. She kissed Bloom on the cheek, touched Charlie on the hand, wishing him a Merry Christmas, and lowered her gorgeous frame into the chair between the two of them.

"You're looking bright and cheery this morning, Madame Doctor."

Her eyes sparkled at Bannerman. "Oh? I can't imagine why."

"Something to do with the birds and the bees, probably."

Despite her flippancy, Anna found herself blushing. She quickly changed the subject, telling them that she had just spoken to her mother about dinner. "She does not want you to eat so much today. She wants you to arrive ravenous. And Marina phoned her to leave me a message that René is in jail. I told mother that I already knew. She was shocked by the news, as you can imagine, and asked me to find out if René's mother knows yet. I had to tell her I was shocked too."

Charlie was trying to get a good look at the guy out in the lobby. He decided to warn Anna, just in case. "But don't turn around and stare," he added.

Her features clouded over. "Do you really believe we are in danger, here in Zurich?"

"Maybe he's a cop, maybe not. There's another one outside the hotel. Problem is, the last two guys who were keeping an eye on us had machine pistols, with silencers, which they were carrying for the express purpose of making little holes in our bodies. I'm satisfied they were hired by someone in the ZIAN organization. And here we are, smack in the heart of ZIAN country."

She angled her head to look at Sam. "It's not over yet, is it?"

Bloom placed his arm around her shoulder. "No, it isn't. But don't worry, Charlie will look after us."

She smiled up into Sam's eyes. "Do you know, up until you two dropped into my life, I've had practically no direct contact with Americans."

Sam gave her a hug. "Lucky you."

"Yes," she said dreamily. "Lucky me."

Bannerman laid down his fork and dug a little wax out of his ear. All this lovey-dovey stuff made him feel like he was intruding. Then he caught a glimpse of the man in the lobby, the watcher. He was pretty sure this guy was no cop.

It was just after two when Bloom reached the steps of the old opera house. He paused, turning once to check on his colleague standing in front of a store window out on the Bahnhof.

Charlie had wanted to get a look at the place. Before leaving the hotel, he called up Lemieux to tell him of Sam's pending visit. He also let the inspector know about the two watchers, describing both men in detail. As he'd already figured, only the outside one was a cop. Lemieux said he already had a man on Bloom and would check out the mystery tail. Then he broke the news about Simard.

"The call was arranged from Geneva. They gave our killer driver no hint why they wanted him to take up the phone. But his reaction was apparently something to behold. Afterward he said yes, the owner of this voice was the one who paid him to arrange the accident. The accent, he said, as well as the tone, made it a near certainty. So it appears that I am very much in your debt, Lieutenant."

"Good. Ten to one he did your Dr. Lyon too. When do we get the guns?"

The line was silent while the Swiss cop considered the ramifications. "Do you use throwaways in New York?"

After some hesitation, Charlie said, "Some guys carry them."

"When one is used in this part of the world, it is usually from an Eastern Bloc country. How about a pair of Czech semi-automatics?"

"I'm not real particular, as long as they work. You going to try and extradite Simard?"

"I have already set the process in motion. A formal charge is being drawn up and will be forwarded to the Madagascar consul in Bern. But such proceedings sometimes take months, as you know."

"By then he'll be out, guaranteed, unless they come up with something real heavy. Even a bribe, laid in the right hands, might see him sprung."

Lemieux disagreed, saying that Madagascar was not a typical African country and that the system of government they have in place, although socialist in nature, seemed to lean toward honesty. He had even heard good things about their police force, which in any case was run mainly by ex-Sûreté types.

Charlie wondered vaguely if that wouldn't make them more susceptible to pressure from Interpol. He considered asking Lemieux to plant a wire on Bloom, but then figured it wasn't worth the risk since Brower was sure to be careful about what he said.

The director was all smiles when Hans showed the American into his office. "The very best of the season to you, Dr. Bloom. I never thought a time would come when I would be forced to work on Christmas day; but alas, my never-ending battle with logistics takes little heed of the season. Did you see the parade?" He was saying this as he walked across the carpeted floor. Sam noticed the slight limp, remembering then that the man wore a prosthesis.

"A Merry Christmas to you, Herr Brower, it has been a long time." The director's solid handshake belied his frail condition. "Yes, I caught part of the parade. A crime, surely, that you had to leave your family, even for an hour. At least it is a beautiful day to be out and about."

"Indeed. It was so kind of you to drop in last evening. If only Frau Foch had told me."

"Think nothing of it. I merely happened to be in the area doing some Christmas shopping."

Sam let himself down into the deep leather chair he had been offered and watched Herr Brower slip into his, which, Sam noticed, was several inches higher than the one he was in.

"There is little doubt that you have come to the right city. Zurich, in its Christmas finery, is unmatched anywhere in the world, wouldn't you agree?"

"Well, I can't disagree."

"I heard you were in town and naturally assumed that you had come directly from Washington. But Frau Foch tells me that you have been down in Madagascar. This is true?"

"Yes, but just for a week or so."

"Research, I assume?"

"Started out that way. Then we ran into a couple of problems."

"We? Were you on some kind of expedition?"

"No, no. Just me and an old friend, Charlie Bannerman. Charlie's been working on his doctorate for years, finally made it this fall. Our trip to the island was sort of a celebration of a successful end to his struggles."

"I see," said Herr Brower, his small dark eyes anxious. "And what kind of problems did you encounter? The natives, perhaps?"

"Hardly natives, Herr Director. But the culprits could have been locals, I suppose, who either didn't care for Americans or mistook us for another party entirely. Someone planted an explosive device in our rental car that killed a teenage boy."

The director's face turned serious. "Did this take place in Toamasina, on the east coast?"

Bloom feigned surprise. "You heard about it?"

"I received a radio message from the captain of the *Lucinda V*, which was in port at the time. He had just begun to load the results of our final six months' work aboard his vessel when a bomb went off not far from the dock, he said. He assumed it was some kind of terrorist activity. This anti-government sect, the Kung Fu I believe they call themselves, violently object to the Soviet presence in Madagascar. And I understand that nowhere on the island is this presence more visible than in Toamasina. But I had no idea, no idea at all, that American citizens were involved."

Sam didn't quite grasp the relationship. "Why did you say the captain called you?"

"Because he was surrounded by Soviet vessels. He feared they might become the next target, thereby placing his vessel at risk. Truly, I thought the man was overreacting. I told him if he was that concerned, he should load up and get out of there."

"She must have been your ship, then, if you were giving the orders."

Herr Brower smiled. "It is leased to ZIAN from time to time. Were you aware that we have a harvesting team on the island?"

"Not until Frau Foch told me."

"Ah, then you have not read your annual report. There was an excellent review prepared by Dr. Hargraves."

Bloom shrugged, grinning a little. "If you saw the number of reports that cross my desk ...."

"Of course, of course. You mentioned problems. Was there something beyond this terrorist bomb attack?"

"Something much more serious, I'm afraid." Bloom had stated this in solemn tone and watched for Brower's reaction.

"More serious than a bomb? But what could this be?"

"I fell in love."

"Really?" the director replied, lightening up when he saw Sam's smile. "Yes, I see where that could be a serious matter indeed."

"Not only that, but she happens to be a native of Zurich."

"Ah, I begin to understand the reason behind your visit."

"We're off to her home for Christmas dinner tonight, where I get to meet the folks and all that."

Herr Brower appeared to consider this for a moment. Then his face broke into a warm smile. "I do believe that I sense a story here, and I insist you tell me, to humor an old man who has all but forgotten that people still fall in love. But first, let us celebrate your new relationship with a fine Napoleon brandy."

As he summoned his secretary over the intercom, Sam thought — that's your second mistake, chum. First the *Lucinda V*, then mentioning my *new* relationship with Anna.

Even so, it was still near impossible for Bloom to accept the fact that this kindly figure was behind all the killing.

Two blocks north of the old opera house, a dark green Volvo turned slowly into a narrow alleyway just off Uraniastrasse. Earlier, a cab had dropped the two Americans at Anna's house for all the world to see, including their watchers. They met her mother, who was simply an older, shorter, heavier, but still attractive, version of her daughter. Five minutes later, after effusive apologies and a few words of explanation, they were on their way back downtown in Mrs. Vandenburg's car, having made their exit through a rear door.

Earlier, back at the hotel, Bloom had been completing the knot in his tie when the idea struck him. "I told Brower we were going to Anna's house for dinner."

Charlie glanced up from playing with his fancy nine millimeter Makarov. "So?"

"Don't you see? Christmas night, us accounted for. We'll never get a better chance."

Bannerman had been looking forward to a turkey dinner all day, but couldn't argue with Bloom's logic. Both men knew it was essential to take a look around ZIAN headquarters.

The snow had picked up over the last few hours, as had the wind off Lake Zurich. Slowly but surely, it seemed, a storm was in the making. As they had hoped, the streets were near deserted. But the upper levels of most of the four-to-five-story greystone buildings were residential apartments alive with Christmas merrymaking. Charlie wanted to try the north end of the building first, which fronted a lane running between Sihlstrasse and the

Bahnhof. Lemieux had told them this section was used for general storage.

After abandoning the Volvo, they made their way out to Sihl where they turned south into the full force of the wind. Five minutes later the two huddled figures departed Sihl by turning left into the relative calm shelter of the alleyway behind the old opera house. Under the cover of throngs of people gathered downtown that morning for the annual Christmas parade, Bannerman had carried out a thorough reconnaissance. At the front of the building, facing Fussli, he determined that the only entry point was the main door on the second level. But at the rear, where they were now heading, there were two doors at street level, both of heavy metal construction. If the doors were barred from the inside, they would have no choice but to try the main entrance or the few windows within reach. Since the front entry was in plain view of any number of commercial buildings, that option would have to be left until the early hours of the morning.

As the alleyway was shrouded in near darkness and the buildings butted up against one another, it took Charlie a few minutes to be certain he had the right place. Each door was enclosed by a tiny decorative fence of wrought iron with a gate, prompting Bannerman to comment on the pointlessness of placing such things in a back alley. They saw no footprints in the fresh snow, nor any indication of light from inside the building.

Once inside the gate and up against the northeast door, the cop dug out his lock picks, which resembled a set of flip-out Allen wrenches.

"Bet this door is two, three hundred years old," Sam whispered as Charlie dropped to one knee to direct the beam of his flashlight into the lock.

"Big goddamn hole," he said. "Must be one big mother of a key. These spindly little suckers will probably break, but …."

Bloom switched on his light, as Charlie had put his own back in the pocket of his mackinaw.

"Don't need light for this kind of work," Bannerman muttered. He was down on both knees now, digging around inside the lock, his left ear close beside it.

Sam scanned the area, searching the darkness with nervous anticipation. For him tonight was a test, his first real test since being caught in the bomb blast. If he could survive the stress of breaking and entering without coming apart at the seams, perhaps the headaches would be gone forever.

"Son of a bitch—she's open!"

"Well done, Lieutenant."

Charlie pushed gently at first, then harder. After hitting it with his shoulder, he backed off. "Barred from the inside. Bastard!"

"It seemed too easy. Well, have a go at the next one, see if you can't beat your record."

The next lock was from a more modern era and considerably smaller, but still required several minutes of patient tinkering on Bannerman's part before he was successful. Again he gave a gentle push, this time feeling the door give slightly. Both men became aware of powerful chemical odors rushing by them.

"Okay sweetheart," he whispered as Bloom pulled out his Makarov. "Let's see what kind of security you got."

He unwound a two-foot length of thin, neoprene-coated wire and pushed the door open just far enough to insert the wire, running it slowly and gently around the three sides. "Nothing there."

The sound of singing washed over them when someone in an adjoining building opened a window. It was open just for a moment, then silence fell again.

"Phase two," said the cop. "This is the tricky part. If they got the thing beamed or a pressure plate installed, we're not going to make it. You got any pull upstairs, now's the time to get a message through."

"You're the churchgoer, not me," Sam replied.

When the door was open four inches, Bannerman exchanged the wire for his gun and pulled out his light again, shining it around the open seam. "Looks clear." At ten inches he pushed his arm through, casting the beam across piles of stacked tables. "There's a staircase, so watch it."

Once the door was fully open, Charlie shone the light around some more and took one step, then another. No alarm went off.

Following the cop's example, Bloom kicked the snow off his overshoes before entering and removed them while Charlie shut the door. The stairs dropped about twenty feet to a floor made of granite blocks. At the bottom he used his light to scan the contents of the large open space, which appeared to run the full width of the opera house. Ahead and to their right, dozens of folding wooden tables had been stacked close to the top of the thirty-foot-high ceiling, making it impossible to tell if there was a wall beyond them. Aside from all the tables, the room was vacant.

"No heat," Bannerman commented as he walked across the floor to inspect the other staircase leading to the first door they tried. Sam headed right, making his way along the wall until he came to the far corner of the room. There, hidden from sight by the tables, he found the dividing wall with a heavy oak door about five feet in width.

"Door over here."

"Seems to be the only one around," Bannerman said after shining his light over it. He dropped the pistol into his mackinaw pocket and began the same procedure he had used on the outside doors. While he was on his knees, Sam could hear the cop's stomach rumbling.

"Sounds like the food larder's getting down," Bloom observed.

Charlie grunted. In a few minutes he had the door open.

"Where did you learn to pick locks?"

"Police academy. Back in those days it was considered part of the job. Not anymore. Christ Almighty, what a stink! What is it, formaldehyde?"

"I'd say, mixed in with a whole range of acetates and whatever else these guys use."

Their narrow cones of light swept across a mixture of amphibians and reptiles in their various states of undress draped over wire hooks dangling from the ceiling. Electric heaters kept the room around sixty degrees.

"Just look at this shit—a goddamn reptile morgue," said Bannerman. "I don't mind telling you, this is not my idea of how to spend Christmas."

"Nor anyone else's, which is why we're here."

Standing in the midst of all the vats, steel-top tables, wooden boxes, and hanging reptiles, Bloom suddenly found himself wondering why *he* was there. Now that he had Anna — at least he hoped he had Anna — the danger of what they were doing came sharply into focus. He unzipped the front of his mackinaw as he felt his throat go dry.

The New York detective switched on the overhead lights and began to dig into the crates. Sam choked back his sudden rush of anxiety and took the other side of the room. He peered into the boxes, trying his best to identify the contents before poking his hand in. His side had the turtles, lizards, frogs, and a few large fruit bats. Each creature had been gutted, dried, and coated inside and out with a fine white resin powder. From his continued sharp curses, Sam figured Charlie had found the snakes.

The box inspection complete, they examined everything else in the room, starting with the chemicals, liquid and granular. Having found nothing there, they went on to check out the various detergent products, bits and pieces of fur, feathers, treated flesh, rows of plastic reptile eyes, the different implements used by the taxidermists to prepare their specimens, and the two tables used to mount butterflies, moths, and other large insects. One, a stick beetle, Bloom recognized as being a species unique to Madagascar. Finally, Bannerman climbed up a stepladder to have a closer look at the drying reptile shells hanging above them.

There were two more doors in the room. The one on the left had a large folding handle. "This is probably the cold storage. Okay if I pull it open?"

"Go ahead," the cop replied as he moved the ladder along to the next row. "Check around the door before going in."

The door had no lock. Bloom flicked the light switch. The storage room was about twenty by twenty feet square with a ceiling of normal height, but some forty to fifty degrees colder than the main studio. Inside he found several dozen more crates stacked neatly, one upon the other.

Sam's pulse jumped when he saw the familiar ZIAN stamp and quickly realized these crates looked to be the same as the ones he had seen in the warehouse in Toamasina. Then he noticed all the lids had been removed. He peered into the first box and saw that it contained a single specimen, a mandarin duck, he guessed. Its head, wings, and body had been cut open and the insides scooped out. It too was covered with a fine white powder.

Bannerman joined him, and several minutes went by before they were confident that the other crates also contained birds or small mammals.

Having replaced the last wooden box back on top of the pile, Charlie blew several times on his fingers. "I took a sample of that white powder, but I know it's too fine for cocaine." He glanced at his watch—9:17. "Man, you're looking at one hungry mother. Come on, let's try the next door."

That one led them into the south portion of the building, a smaller section with stacks of metal chairs and wooden containers partly filled with musty old costumes and a few stage props that probably hadn't been used since the last opera was performed. They spent ten minutes digging around in the dust until they were satisfied there was nothing of significance hidden away. A thorough search failed to reveal another door.

"Damn funny thing. You'd think they'd have some way to get down here from upstairs."

Bloom splashed his light across the ceiling, wondering the same thing. "In the old days, when the operas were playing, there was probably a trapdoor in the stage."

"Maybe, but unless they keep their drug shit upstairs, and I doubt that like hell, this place is clean."

Reluctantly, Sam had to agree with him. They went back into the studio, studying the ceiling one more time before returning to the main storage room.

"This is where the trapdoor should be, if there is one, because I figure we're under the stage right now."

Bannerman nodded, carefully searching the ceiling with his light. But there wasn't a crack bigger than a hairline to be seen in the dull yellow mortar. "Too bad, I'd hoped to get upstairs, maybe get a look at some of your buddy's papers. Anyway, that's it, ball game's over, and we lost."

Bloom nodded his agreement, but decided to voice the obvious. "Who's to say they don't have another building? For all we know they could have several."

"It never even crossed my mind to ask Lemieux about that. I'll call him from Anna's place." Charlie had reached the small landing at the top of the staircase, and was bending over to pull on his rubber boots when he began to mutter away to himself. He glanced down at Bloom, a few steps below him. "I think my gurgling gut's affected my brain."

He walked back down the stairs, pushing Sam ahead of him. "Come on, Professor, I'll need your help for this one."

Five minutes later, having picked the studio lock a second time, they were back inside the cold storage room. Charlie switched on the light. "See what I mean?"

"No, I don't," Sam replied, wondering what his partner was up to now.

"The ceiling, for Christ's sake. It's what, nine or ten feet high? Everywhere else it's about thirty feet high. So what do you suppose they got tucked away up there?"

Bloom wasn't overly impressed. He had noticed the lower ceiling earlier and assumed it had been done simply to cut down on the amount of space they needed to keep cool. Studying the ceiling, it looked like a single piece of white fiberglass.

"Bottle of Napoleon brandy, the expensive kind, says there's nothing up there."

"You're on!" the cop answered, an unusual note of excitement discernible in his voice as he left the locker. In seconds he was back with the stepladder and a broom. Sam stood back and watched him use the broom handle to poke at the ceiling.

After covering only part of the ceiling, Charlie said, "You hear that double thump? Every time I strike it, there's a double thump."

Sam had heard it, but didn't realize the significance until the cop mentioned it. "A false ceiling?"

Bannerman climbed the ladder to examine the section of ceiling where it met the dividing wall with the studio. Then he went back into the studio, taking the stepladder with him. Puzzled, Bloom followed him out. Charlie switched on the overhead studio lights and then placed the ladder against the other side of the wall.

"You left me behind there a bit, Lieutenant. What's going on?"

But Bannerman had gone silent, moving his ladder twice more before letting out a whoop. He climbed back down the ladder, grinning from ear to ear. "Up you go, Professor."

Sam found a block of wood, painted the same color as the room, sticking out where the cop had left it, an inch or so from the wall and tight against the ceiling. Charlie pulled over a stool to search the other end.

"Bingo! Here she is. Okay, remove your block and be careful not to leave any marks on it."

Sam did so and slid it into his coat pocket. The block of wood had occupied a space about four by five inches, large enough for an average hand to fit inside.

"Now, see that handle? Get a grip on it, okay? I've got the other one here. Now, start pulling … easy, easy …."

By now Sam realized that the steel handle was attached to the fiberglass ceiling in the next room.

"That's far enough," Charlie said after the heavy panel had slid forward about five feet. "Now let's see what kind of goodies are waiting for us."

Bloom climbed down the few steps, shaking his head. He was now very definitely impressed. Bannerman took the ladder and placed it under the trapdoor that had appeared in the center of the far side of the locker room. He took his time, going through the same careful procedure as before until the trapdoor had been pushed all the way back.

Charlie's head disappeared, then Charlie himself. After several minutes of moving about, he called down, "You'd better poke your head up here."

Sam did, resting his arms on the reinforced opening in the ceiling. Bannerman's light scanned the rows of neatly stacked wooden boxes for his companion to see. Then he held up a clear vinyl bag of white powder. "Maybe this is half a kilo. Each box holds thirty bags. There's four hundred boxes, near as I can tell, and all full."

"Six thousand kilos. That's over two hundred thousand ounces. Street value, what, for the pure stuff?"

"For eighty percent pure, wholesale, maybe ten grand."

"We're looking at two billion dollars' worth of cocaine."

Bannerman was squat down, his face close to Bloom's. "No, we're not."

Sam could see Charlie's face, the faraway look in his eye. "You want to tell me why?"

"Because this stuff is not cocaine, that's why."

"Then what the hell is it?"

"It's heroin. Frigging shitface heroin! And the missing piece to this freaking puzzle. And if I was any dumber, I'd be shoveling shit against the wind for a living."

A fierce wind was blowing from the southwest when they lowered Gerhard into his grave. The kid had been twenty-five years old, Charlie was told by Klaus Scheuchzer after the church service. He was two years out of university, and the island had been his first assignment. Someone had given the cop a heavy woolen hat to wear, which he'd pulled down over his ears. He was surprised to see the manager of the Madagascar Forestry Training Center show up at the funeral. He would later learn that Klaus had been recalled by the Swiss government to explain the loss of three of the seven foresters assigned to him.

Gerhard Schlossein had been born and raised in the small village of Winterhausen, some forty kilometers northwest of Zurich, where he was now being laid to rest. Anna had come for them just before nine in her mother's Volvo. Bloom sat in the front, leaving Charlie the spacious rear seat. The cop used the half hour's drive through the snow-covered countryside to review the steps he and Sam had taken that morning. He had already decided the night before to keep Anna in the dark about their find, at least for the time being; not because she couldn't be trusted, but because such knowledge could endanger her life even more. And, although Charlie's decision had come as a shock to Bloom, neither was he willing to share their discovery with Inspector Lemieux. Not yet. Once the reasons were made clear, Sam agreed that his companion was doing the right thing. Commissioner Hennessey's concurrence had proved more difficult, but in the end he too had relented in the face of Bannerman's unassailable logic.

Last night had been an incredible stroke of luck, even down to the full-scale storm that came along, blowing enough snow down that alleyway to cover all signs of their little visit. The flat wooden boxes had been stored away in that loft for some time, as they were covered with a layer of dust. Waiting, he knew, for the day when the value of heroin would take off like a rocket, if and when Herr Brower's ingenious scheme came to fruition. How could he be so certain it was heroin, Bloom had wanted to know, since both were a bitter white powder?

But Charlie knew. He could see the brownish cast, rub the starchy texture into his fingers. Cocaine was usually snow white, with a distinctive crystalline feel to it. It was the perfect cover – a built-in lab that used acetates to mount animals, the same kind of acetates used to break down the principal alkaloid of opium, morphine, into its diacetyl derivative, heroin. Boil morphine in acetic anhydride, a substance close to household vinegar, and you get heroin. Bannerman had no doubt that the whole process was carried out in ZIAN's taxidermy studio and had been for a good many years. Meaning they had a well-established supply line running directly into Turkey and probably the Far East.

The clincher had come that morning, when Lemieux called to say the man they had found waiting in his car outside of Anna's place the night before was from Interpol. He had refused all attempts at cross-examination and had to be released. The knot between the two organizations was growing tighter all the time. In essence, only one question remained as far as Interpol's involvement was concerned: Who was running the show, Interpol or ZIAN?

At least two hundred people were huddled together on the sloping hillside, overshadowed by giant peaks that made their presence known only during momentary breaks in the cloud cover. Had they come out of love, or respect, or was it merely tradition? Charlie Bannerman didn't know enough about the Swiss to understand why they stood now in silent defiance of the blowing snow and biting cold. Nearly everyone who had crowded inside the little church had come, from babes in arms to the oldest members of the community. The turnout affected Bannerman more than he would have liked, forcing him to acknowledge his own humanity in a manner that made him feel strangely restless, as if he should begin living his life in a more meaningful way. Before long, he realized, they'd be doing the same thing to him. And how many people would bother to show up to see his carcass lowered into the ground? A dozen, two dozen at the most.

He knew he was still a long way from grasping the whole picture. Could there be another equally large cache of cocaine hidden away somewhere in the city? Somehow Bannerman didn't think so. In any case, once Lemieux discovered the heroin, he would naturally want to check out everything belonging to ZIAN. Short of extracting a full confession from Brower or one of his henchmen, Bannerman was now convinced that the other half of the puzzle could only be solved by returning to Madagascar.

There was a reception in the town hall. They apologized, pleading an urgent matter to be attended to in Zurich. Even though both men had been on the telephone since before seven that morning, placing calls to New York, Madagascar, and Nairobi, a number of important calls still needed to be made and logistical matters sorted out before their flight departed at eight that evening.

They knew why. Now they had to find out how.

CHAPTER SEVENTEEN

It was Sam Bloom's show now. After all, what did a big city cop know about military operations? Bloom had his record going for him—two successful raids into the heart of enemy territory and would be running this one the same way, he'd told Bannerman. They had arrived in Nairobi at eight that morning, picked up the hastily-prepared orthophoto maps of Tsingy Reserve, purchased new tickets, as their destination out of Zurich had been Brazzaville, then flew on to Dar es Salaam and finally into the coastal city of Nacala in Mozambique, where a big helicopter awaited them. Bloom had tracked it down in Lusaka, Zambia, just off assignment to a British oil firm. The machine had been flown out to the coast while they were making their way down from Zurich.

Their Boeing-Vertol Sea Knight, a castoff from the US Navy, had crossed the Madagascar coastline ten minutes earlier. With the 270-mile stretch of ocean between mainland Africa and the island now behind them, the passengers began to relax a little. The French mercenaries continued playing cards. They had begun as soon as the helicopter lifted off from Nacala. These were Lamont's men, four guys he knew from the old days, he'd told Bloom on the phone; not young, he said, but true professionals.

Anna had been alternately reading and napping until they reached the island. Now she was engaged in animated conversation with the pilot and owner of the helicopter, a white South African named Lear, and his Canadian navigator, Downing. Bannerman had dozed off. As it was still another three hundred miles to the spot Sam had selected to rendezvous with Lamont, the idea being to avoid any villages along the way, he figured it wouldn't be a bad idea for him to get a little shut-eye as well.

But for Bloom, sleep was proving to be elusive. Everything had moved so rapidly over the last few days, the whole mad scramble through Madagascar and Zurich, that it now seemed to take on panoramic proportions with scenes and events flashing across his mind in strobe light manner. He had no idea what was waiting for them inside the enormous limestone maze. Maybe nothing. Maybe the white face Anna spotted had been a lemur after all. Rinday said it was. A man living in this climate would be tanned, wouldn't he? Gerhard's fall could have been accidental. And all those deaths by lightning, could they not also have been a series of unfortunate accidents, even that of Anna's husband?

It was twilight when Anna placed her hand on his arm. Bloom could tell by the sound of the rotors that they were in descent. He glanced out the window to see a campfire just ahead with the dim outline of a tent beside it. There was no vehicle in sight, so Sam figured Lamont had been successful in getting Rinday to drop him off.

He yawned, turning to Anna. Sam had tried to talk her into staying behind in Nacala, but she wouldn't hear of it. The fact that she was also a physician presented a strong argument in her favor.

The Sea Knight touched down, rear wheels first. "Phase one complete," Charlie said. "We made it."

"Surprise!" shouted Lamont as he helped Downing lower the steps.

"Holy shit!" Bannerman whispered. Standing a few feet behind the Frenchman and holding her billowing hair in place with both hands, was Shaleen.

Downing went down the steps first, then held out his hand for Anna. By the time Sam and Charlie made it down, the Canadian had moved her away from the dipping blades and already introduced himself and the Swiss physician to Lamont and his sister-in-law. The rather shy greeting that took place between Shaleen and Charlie was drowned out by the noise of the dying turbines and the boisterous embraces between Giles Lamont and his old military buddies.

"You rotten old bastard," said Marc, the leader of the four. "Look at that goddamn gut!"

"Too much easy living, eh, Giles?" said another, who went by the name of Hazz. The other two, Mitts and Rossal, were a bit more reserved and apparently did not know Lamont all that well.

The Frenchman's enthusiasm had not run out by the time he got around to Bannerman, giving him a great bear hug with a firm kiss on both cheeks. "Guess what? A little gift from your Uncle Sam just arrived."

"That's great," Charlie replied, marveling at Commissioner Hennessey's ability to lay his hands on a hundred grand in just a few days.

Then Lamont stood back, his arm around Bannerman's shoulders. "Hey, you soldier boys, you see this magnificent piece of female machinery?"

He was indicating Shaleen, standing to Charlie's left. "My sister-in-law. And she belongs to my friend here. So if you get drunk tonight and start looking around with lustful eyes, remember this one is spoken for."

"So is the other one," Bloom added hastily, in case someone should get any ideas about Anna.

"That was quite unnecessary," she whispered, giving his arm a good pinch.

They were men in their late forties and early fifties, men who had participated in enough suffering and death to become immune to it. Bloom had noticed their raw stares in the chopper. "Maybe it was, but I prefer to head off any problems before they arise."

One tent had already been pitched. With nightfall imminent, the next half hour was used to set up the two nylon tents they had picked up in Mozambique. It was decided that the women would take the smaller tent while Lamont and his friends were assigned the larger one, leaving the Americans to bunk in with the helicopter crew.

They had settled in at a point twenty miles north of the northerly extremity of the reserve, well beyond the visibility and audio range of anyone who might be inside. They were also perched at

279

the heavily treed edge of a long escarpment, where the plateau began to drop away into the westerly lowlands. A large troop of ring-tailed lemurs that had been frightened off by the screech of the turbines began to return, dropping low in the branches of tall tamarind trees to check out their visitors.

For obvious reasons no one had come dressed in military attire. Anna, in her light khaki jacket and bush trousers, looked more military than any of them.

"Sam, the girl is beautiful, absolutely beautiful," Anna said when she finally had the opportunity to speak to him alone.

"I know, and it worries me." His first impression had been that of a cheetah, long and lithe and built for speed. He couldn't help but wonder if she wasn't more than Charlie could handle. "Lamont told him about her being raised a Christian, not able to bear children, and so on. Still, a woman like that ...."

"Don't worry, by morning I will know what there is to know. But somehow, she seems so ... honest and forthright."

"Check her out, but cautiously. I believe we owe that to Charlie."

Shaleen was also the cook, having prepared a meal of honeyed chicken with rice and yams over the open fire. They were sitting around the folding aluminum tables on their little canvas seats drinking tea when Sam mentioned to Anna that their party numbered eleven, a lucky number. Did Anna believe in luck? he asked.

She raised her head and stared at the dark outline of the Sea Knight before replying. "I believe that most people are capable of making their own luck. Some are not. I have seen examples where bad fortune drove men to suicide."

"Their karma was adversely affected," Bloom said casually.

They were seated at the end of one of the three tables. Anna turned the full power of her remarkable gray eyes upon him, uncertain if his remark was intended to be frivolous. She concluded that it was not and continued eating. But after a few seconds she laid down her plastic fork. Sam's remark had distracted her, making her aware of their surroundings, where the air was warm and sweet with the scent of wildflowers. The sky was clear, its canopy of diamonds just emerging. The lemurs were still there, moving about and settling in for the night. She thought it a very romantic setting indeed.

But before she could voice her thoughts, the bats arrived, hundreds of them, having been drawn to the growing insect population gathered around the gasoline lanterns.

"Dear God, just look at them." They seemed to hold no fear of the humans, diving within inches to catch a fat moth.

"You're not afraid of bats, I hope."

Anna shook her head, smiling as she recalled some of her early experiences in West Africa. "Once I became convinced that they were not going to land in my hair after all, I didn't mind."

"Sure is a pile of them," Sam observed thoughtfully. He hadn't told Anna about the black wings that had shown up on Carswell's computer screen. But the sight of so many bats brought that particular puzzle into focus again, as he wondered what kind of deviant attraction an orchid would need to encourage pollination by bats. The amount of nectar generally contained by most orchids was insignificant for a creature the size of a bat. There had been stories, of course, but nothing substantiated. If it were a bat, he reasoned, there had to be a special environmental quirk that caused the mechanism inside the flower to seek out aggressive pollinators. Dwelling on the possibility of such an important discovery almost overrode the more urgent task at hand.

"I'd better get on with it, I suppose." He noticed then that Anna had been studying him, perhaps wondering what was going through his mind.

She touched the back of his hand with her fingertips. "You know, Sam, I never thought you meant it when you said you would come back here with these men."

"Hey, you didn't think I would lie, did you?"

"No, I just assumed you were joking." She paused before adding, "Have you thought about what might happen to us? When this is all over, I mean?"

"I have," he replied firmly. "I've given it a lot of thought. How about you?"

"Yes, naturally. It is so much clearer to me now."

"Good," Sam said. He had yet to tell her that he loved her, nor had she used words to that effect. Better to put all this behind them first, he knew, and take it from there. "Time to assemble the troops."

With Anna's help he laid the three tables end to end and placed lanterns in the middle and at each end. Then he unrolled the bundles of maps. Six large sheets, each about four feet by four feet, had been required to cover the entire Tsingy reserve. All six were laid out and held in place by empty cups.

"Gather around, fellows, and let's see how we're going to tackle this thing."

They drifted in, the pilot first, then Bannerman with the exotic Shaleen close behind him, Downing, the navigator; and finally, Lamont and his former colleagues.

"I've oriented the maps to the north, and since I'm looking north, the reserve is behind me. In case you don't know, what we have here is called orthophoto mapping, a quick method of using the imagery of the aerial photographs to create the map. If we had more time available, I would have had contours added. Instead, we'll have to settle for spot elevations on top of the spires, which will allow us to pick out the higher ones for navigational purposes."

"Scale?" Marc asked.

"One inch equals two hundred feet. One in twenty-four hundred metric."

"Large," muttered Lamont.

"Very large," Bloom agreed. "I wanted the exact configuration of every razorback to show up loud and clear. Anyone who can read a map shouldn't get lost now, which was the whole point of the exercise."

The men were bent over the tables studying the map sheets. "I don't see anything resembling a trail or an access route," said Mitts, blowing his cigar smoke across the tables.

"How are we supposed to find our way around?" Rossal asked.

"No one here has actually been inside, but I can tell you that in certain places there is barely enough room to place one foot. In the true sense of the word, there is no trail."

"Then what the hell is there?" demanded Rossal, the oldest of the four.

"A route, marked with fluorescent paint, up to the point where one of the Swiss foresters fell down into a crevasse. Presumably it extends beyond that, perhaps deep into the heart of the reserve, to where we have reason to believe some kind of experimental undertaking is in progress."

"Which means we move in single file," said Mitts.

"How many men are we likely to encounter?" Marc wanted to know.

"Unknown," Sam replied, "which is why we need surprise on our side. My plan, and I want your input into this, is to break camp and be on our way well before dawn, circle far and wide of the reserve and the local villages, then come in low and set down a few kilometers to the east. I asked the mapping firm to pick up an orange DayGlo patch at the entrance and plot it. See," he said, pointing to a small red square on one of the map sheets. "Charlie, me and Giles will trek into the entrance with the four of you, and once we're inside and know it's safe, Lear can bring his machine up. Until I say otherwise, Anna and Shaleen are to remain with the helicopter."

"It was my husband who lost his life inside that terrible place," Anna pointed out. "So I feel I have the right to be there."

"Excuse me, doctor lady," said Marc. "I think you should wait until we clear the zone."

Bloom caught the look on Anna's face, that firm set to her mouth he had come to know. "Sorry, Anna, it's out of the question for you or Shaleen to come along." He saw her winding up for a rebuttal and put up his hand to stop her. "Soon as Marc declares the area safe, I promise someone will return and guide you in."

Lamont removed his pipe. "Will your radios carry far enough inside all that rock?"

He had directed this question at Marc, who nodded. "The specs call for twenty kilometers in broken terrain, up to eighty line of sight."

Good radios had been one of the criteria Sam had given Marc over the telephone. "Which brings us down to the details of achieving effective penetration. It is entirely possible that whoever is in there could decide to let us to walk through without giving away their position."

Despite her assuredness that bats didn't bother her, Anna had placed both hands on top of her head, like a prisoner. This stance caused her full breasts to stretch the material of her rose-colored T-shirt to its limit, a fact that was not missed by any of the men. The Canadian navigator, Downing, could not take his eyes off her.

"Yet there must be something obvious to be seen," she said. "Otherwise, why have so many bodies shown up during these last two years?"

"I'd be inclined to take that one step further," Bannerman said. "If we assume Gerhard's death also falls into that category, the logical conclusion is that he spotted something which warranted his execution. Since Simard damn well knew all suspicion would fall on his shoulders, there must have been an urgent need for him to murder that young Swiss."

Bloom didn't want to get into that now, since the question of who did what to whom was academic at this stage. "Everyone who goes in is armed, even the women once they arrive. Marc, you guys are going to take the point, so I'm open for suggestions."

Marc appeared to be the youngest of the four, a handsome man who, except for his pencil moustache, could have been a taller, older version of Simard. He shook his head. "I think this one is going to be a new experience for all of us. It's sure as hell as close to play-it-by-ear as I want to get. Without map coverage I wouldn't touch this thing. Even with it we're running almost blind. There could be an ambush waiting behind every one of those razorbacks. But, such are the joys of the trade."

Marc went on to explain exactly how they were to conduct themselves, how each person was to respond instantly to orders, even Sam, until the area was declared free of danger. Listening to him, Bloom knew Lamont had come through for them again.

Sam was satisfied he had done his best. He could have asked for more men, and would have if they had been going into more open terrain. Lamont was a bonus. He had not expected the Frenchman to insist on coming along, but gladly welcomed his participation. There was a kind of aura around Lamont that imparted a strong sensation that all was going to turn out well. Bloom was beginning to understand the attraction such a man would hold for the beautiful Somali woman who had become his wife. Just as he was beginning to understand the attraction someone like Bannerman might hold for her sister. He didn't understand it completely, but knew it had to do with the distorted Western emphasis on superficiality. Shaleen, at least four inches taller than Charlie, stood beside him with one hand resting on his shoulder. It was obvious to anyone in the group that the young woman had staked her claim. Good for you, Charlie, he thought. Glancing at Anna, he said to himself — *and good for me.*

The party drifted away from the tables after Marc's recommendation to hit the sack early. They were to start pulling up stakes at four. Since all had traveled far that day, there was no resistance. Bannerman suddenly found himself alone with Shaleen near the lip of a huge granite boulder. Far below was dark jungle, then the coast, some eighty miles away, and beyond it the Mozambique Channel they had crossed just a few hours ago. Shaleen had linked her arm into his.

"Do you know what I sense, Charlie?"

"Not really."

"I sense that you are afraid of me."

He thought about it for a minute. "Afraid, in mortal fear of my life? No. Afraid of who you are and what you represent? Yes."

"I understand. I am a colored woman from a foreign country and I represent an intrusion into the life of a confirmed bachelor."

Bannerman took her hand, shaking his head. "Forget about the colored part. The color of a person's skin means nothing to me. Besides, the average New Yorker's darker than you are."

"Giles told you of my inability to bear children. Is this a difficult matter for you?"

The policeman turned, again astonished at the degree of maturity in so young a woman. "It's not difficult at all. Tell you the truth, I'm not real fond of the little rug rats."

She laughed, an instinctive reaction. "What a terrible thing to call a baby."

Bannerman took a deep breath, sensing that the time had come to crap or get off the pot. "Shaleen, I'm having a whole lot of trouble wondering why someone like you, who has her whole life ahead of her, would want to get mixed up with me. Giles gave me some reasons, as he sees them, but I want to hear it from your lips."

The woman folded her legs gracefully, like a gazelle. She indicated Charlie should sit on the rock beside her. "I was born in Berbera, on the north coast, which used to be known as British Somaliland, while my mother was visiting with her brother, a shipping merchant ...."

"A tempest in a teapot, Dietrich. Even Inspector Lemieux is annoyed at them for wasting his time over the holidays."

Two of his great-grandchildren had followed Herr Brower into his study and plunked their little bottoms down on the carpet to watch him speaking on the telephone. It was past their bedtimes, but rules were always bent during the holidays.

"Naturally, I am pleased to hear that the Americans were unable to find anything to enhance their preposterous suggestion that ZIAN is involved in illegal activities, especially drugs. But I must confess to a certain morbid curiosity about how such a ridiculous accusation could have surfaced in the first place."

Milland chuckled, saying, "There is an expression they use, something about throwing a lot of stuff against the wall to see what sticks. I would be willing to wager that this is an example of that kind of mentality at work. I can only hope, my dear Dietrich, that this American foolishness hasn't spoiled your Christmas."

"It has not, my friend, and I hope someday to be able to repay your concern with something other than words."

After the superintendent hung up, Herr Brower reached down to pick up one of the boys. He was eleven months old and had been given his name, Dietrich. The child hauled himself up and began to bounce up and down on Herr Brower's knees. Milland hadn't mentioned Simard, but the word was already out that he had been charged with the murder of Wilhem Strouss.

The Frenchman had been a bungler and a fool. He toyed with the idea of silencing him while the man still could be found. Neither had Milland mentioned the other Interpol agent who had been caught following the Americans. That one had been ordered out of the country. More bungling, he thought again. It was difficult enough to administer a complex organization like ZIAN, even with good help.

The head of European Affairs at St. Cloud, Henri Lapierre, would probably fall as a result of Simard's charge, but Interpol would go on, supported by the same ill-placed confidence, just as it has for the last fifty years. Their spokesman would make the same excuse used by every police agency in the world: Some were bound to fall victim to the seduction of personal wealth. There would be another minor scandal, and Lapierre, a millionaire many times over, would retire to some warm climate in style. And Hitler's heritage, the great enterprise taken over by the Gestapo and personally honed for surreptitious activities by Colonel Otto Steinhausel even before the war, would remain unbroken.

Their mother, a fair-haired Swede, stood in the doorway, smiling at her children's constant desire to follow her husband's grandfather everywhere. "Let me take them now, Gramps."

"A few more minutes, Lieta, just a few more minutes."

She left, shaking her head. The *Lucinda V* was due to arrive at its first port of call within the hour, some eighteen hours past its originally scheduled time. Let them search away now, he thought. The special cargo had been transferred to the *Valfredo*, another ancient freighter that had been plying the Arabian Sea since the thirties. It had just dropped its final consignment of cargo at Karachi and was due to go into dry dock in Port Said. For a huge sum of money it would now undergo maintenance at Venice.

And all is well, thought Herr Brower as he placed little Dietrich down beside his older brother, though he was still puzzled by Dr. Bloom's apparent involvement in the whole matter. Bloom was a renowned and dedicated botanist. His friend, Bannerman, who was also a policeman, had recently received his own doctorate. They had taken a field trip to Madagascar in celebration of the event. Bloom had fallen in love with Anna Grenier, a beautiful woman indeed, and had accompanied her to her mother's home for the holidays. New York Police Commissioner Hennessey had attempted to make use of Bannerman's trip to conduct an investigation into the activities of ZIAN—an investigation that had failed miserably. And now, it seemed, both men had decided to join Dr. Grenier as she resumed her regular work in Brazzaville, as the Congo capital was the destination for all three one-way tickets.

Their mother was back, gathering up her precious ones and planting her own kiss upon grandfather's brow. And Hermann Von Rudel was alone again with his thoughts, and his memories.

For Victor, the end was near. Life, first inside the Reich and later within the comforting arms of ZIAN, had been good to him. There would be a quarter moon tonight, he thought as he stepped through one of the three automatic doorways they had constructed in the limestone. He would probably not see it because of his restricted view of the sky. He flopped open his canvas camp chair, breathing in the pure, warm night air as he did so. Like the bats that provided their reason for being there, Victor usually came out only at night. His sensitivity to sunlight had been the result of an exploding phosphorous grenade during the Soviet invasion of Berlin.

His last assignment was over and had been successful. It had provided the means for ZIAN to reap more wealth than the gross national product of most countries. They were currently working on disassembling the last solar panel that was located no more than one hundred meters from where he sat, the sound of their voices and the impatient clang of hammers trickling around the spires. The panel would then be broken into pieces and follow the others down the well. There remained just the sleeping pallets, the emergency gasoline generator, the radio and its various antennae, and a few kitchen things to get rid of.

And the men, of course.

Erich's plan was simplicity itself. Victor would announce that they were to throw their weapons down the well, since guns were forbidden by law in Madagascar and they could conceivably be stopped by the authorities during their run to the fishing trawler waiting for them out on the coast. The men were conditioned to taking orders and would do as they were told. He expected no difficulties.

When their huge helicopter lifted off forty minutes after reveille, there was a sense of anticipation among the group, a peculiar attitude that seemed too frivolous for the potential dangers that awaited them. The mercenaries bounced one-liners off each other as rapidly as a tennis ball crosses the court. It didn't take Bloom long to realize this was just their way of covering up their own nervousness. *One or more of us might die today*, they were saying underneath all the bravado and silly remarks, *but we won't let that worry us.*

Twenty-three minutes later the Sea Knight came down in a dark swirl of dust. Marc and Hazz jumped out first, not waiting for the steps to be lowered all the way. Mitts and Rossal stayed inside the machine to hand down the armaments: A Bofors AT4 rocket launcher with a case of rockets, a dozen H & K assault rifles with two boxes of ammunition, three heavy cardboard containers loaded with ropes, flashlights, medical kits, flak vests, flares, and so on. Two folded nylon stretchers were the last items to come out.

Within minutes of touchdown the seven heavily-armed men were on their way, and soon vanished inside the murky predawn light. They were headed into one of the most hostile pieces of terrain on the face of the Earth.

Their arrival had been timed to have the rising sun at their backs and in the eyes of anyone who might be waiting for them near the perimeter. Struggling to keep up, Bannerman tried to watch where he was walking, remembering Anna's twisting her ankle in a hole. Like the others, he was wearing thick-soled paratrooper boots.

As they drew closer to Tsingy, dawn came and the skyline began to take on a magnificent surrealism. For a moment it seemed to be suspended in time and space, like the towers of a grand futuristic metropolis. Then the sun broke suddenly from the east, its first rays stretching across the plains, turning the soil a blood red and the dark jagged teeth of Tsingy a fiery crimson.

"Spooky-looking place," Charlie commented.

"The devil's teeth," Sam said, taking in the awesome sight. "That's what the natives call them." It was a tortured landscape, as if some kind of harsh punishment had once been inflicted upon it.

The seven men were now casting long, tapering shadows before them. The fluorescent orange square Gerhard had sprayed on the entrance spire caught their eye with half the distance still to go. Upon reaching the perimeter of the limestone sentinels, Marc stopped and told them to take a break. It had been previously agreed that the five professionals would enter the reserve first. Marc would notify the Americans when they had the area secured.

Bloom and Bannerman sat down on their packs and began to discuss the current state of affairs concerning the *Lucinda V* and its special cargo. The ship had been due to dock in Djibouti last evening, and Commissioner Hennessey had formally requested the US State Department to pressure the local government into conducting a search of the vessel with a United States agent in attendance. The PC was concerned that once ZIAN officials learned the two Americans were back in Madagascar, they were sure to scuttle the shipment.

The first radio call came at 06:55. "Point Leader calling Eagle. Come in."

Sam glanced at Bannerman as his pulse started to climb. The game had begun. "This is Eagle. Go, Point Leader."

"We appear to be at a dead end here. No crevasse wide enough to fall into. No sign of life either. Suggest you come ahead."

"Roger, Point Leader. Will do."

"I'll be damned," Sam said as leaped to his feet. "What do you make of that?"

"Nothing, until we get in and take a look around. Too bad Rinday isn't here, since he was the one who went in with Simard."

Bloom had originally thought of contacting the Malagasy pilot, but concluded that he had no right to ask the man to become involved in a mini-invasion of his homeland. They donned their flak vests and helped each other adjust their packs. Marc had assigned the ropes, stretchers, and medical kits to the Americans.

Sam took the lead as they began to make their way through the limestone gauntlet.

Both men were soon astonished at how easily the honed ridges cut through their heavy leather gloves.

"Christ Almighty! A guy could shave with these bloody things."

"For sure," Sam said. "You hear them ringing when your foot skims over one? Like a little Chinese gong."

It was an excruciatingly slow journey. Rinday had warned them that the terrain included extremely narrow gaps, and they found themselves having to hold onto the limestone and balance on one foot while searching for a spot to place the other. At least the route was clearly marked, with one bright splash of orange always visible from the next one.

The floor of the tsingy was anything but bare, harboring an amazing number of trees and shrubs, even bamboo, which came as a surprise to Sam. He had assumed the reserve would be mostly dry, its ample supply of rainwater having seeped away through cracks in the limestone. Yet it teemed with life. Multicolored birds and butterflies were everywhere to be seen. Large golden hawks studied them from lofty perches. Lizards of all sizes darted ahead of them. Miniature fluorescent green chameleons backed away in fright as gloved hands groped around the ridges. In places they walked through colorful profusions of wild flowers, including several kinds of orchids, each more or less familiar to Bloom.

And then, just fifteen minutes into the reserve, there it was: the golden orchid, almost exactly as the computer had created it. Both men studied it for a minute, saying little. Bloom picked one and stuck his nose into it before they moved on.

The radio sounded again, calling Red Knight for a reception check. Lear came in ten by ten. Another half hour went by before Hazz appeared about twenty paces ahead of them. He had called out before coming into view to make sure the Americans didn't take a potshot at him.

"You guys never gonna win no steeplechase," he cracked, watching Charlie get ready to jump a small fissure in the rock. "Only a hundred fifty meters to the end of the line."

The end of the line was just that—the last splash of orange. They found Marc squatting down on his haunches, studying his folded map. "I've plotted the route we took, but it doesn't seem to mean much."

Lamont had his pipe going. He shrugged his shoulders. "We scanned every rock within one hundred meters for sure. No more marks."

Bloom nodded, squatting himself. He didn't dare sit on the surface for fear of losing a chunk of his ass. "This is bullshit, fellows. Rinday told us that Gerhard fell down a crevasse—and that crevasse has to be at the end of the line."

"Maybe not," said Bannerman, drawing all eyes to himself. He inclined his head toward the last orange splash, saying to Marc, "Come back here, I'll show you something."

He ran his hand over the color, a diagonal slash running from lower left to upper right. Turning to the taller Frenchman, he said, "Tell me how you think this was put on."

Marc stretched out his own hand, studying it for a few seconds. "From the bottom. He took the can and sprayed across and up."

"How can you tell?"

"Because the tail of the spray is obviously at the upper end."

Charlie broke out a small grin. A New York cop, light years out of his element, could still teach these boys a thing or two. "Walk back two, three hundred yards, you're gonna find my handkerchief hanging on a piece of rock. Go back to the next mark and you'll find every one from there on back was put on the other way, starting at the top right and running to lower left. I'd suggest you nose around there a bit; you might find something."

"La, la, la!" Lamont said. "Do I have a smart almost brother-in-law or what?"

Bloom couldn't help but smile. "I guess that's why you're here, Lieutenant."

Like before, the mercenaries went ahead to check out the area. Sam squat down again and asked Charlie what he made out of this unexpected turn of events.

Bannerman shrugged, rolling his head around ever so slightly. He dropped his gear and leaned back against the limestone, unconcerned about its treacherous ridges. Bloom watched him, noticing the intensity, the narrowing of the eyes.

"You got it, haven't you?"

The detective smiled. "Maybe."

"Come in, Eagle." This time the voice came through in a whisper.

"This is Eagle. Go."

"We've located the diversion, very cleverly done. You better come on back here with us. Maintain silence, and keep your eyes and ears peeled. Rossal will be waiting on the trail. He'll wave when he spots you."

"Roger on that. We're returning now."

They moved faster this time, the excitement building. Rossal came into view, waving both arms. When the Americans closed in, he said in a low voice, "We heard some muffled noises up ahead. Something we can't get a fix on. And we found a couple of holes drilled in the rock. Weren't no woodpecker did it, that's for sure."

Once the point of diversion was reached, Rossal turned left, indicating silence with his finger. He moved his Heckler and Koch 5.56 automatic across his front, adopting the ready position. Sam unslung his own weapon, carrying it in his right hand. They went along like this for five minutes or so until they were suddenly back onto Gerhard's diagonal splashes, from upper right to lower left. Charlie silently pointed this out to Bloom. Marc was waiting for them.

The four closed in a tight huddle. "We got some life up ahead. Lamont and Hazz are checking it out. Mitts is off to my right. Rossal, you get out to the left, around a couple of those razorbacks, and stay there till I signal you. Make sure your radio's switched to LIGHT."

After Rossal disappeared, Marc tapped Charlie on the arm. "You were right. They scraped the paint off the next half dozen spots and then laid out a false trail, the one we took, which leads nowhere. But they couldn't get it all off. You go right up to the rock, the next logical place, and traces are still there."

Bannerman nodded. "Someone's gone through a whole lot of trouble to cover up the real trail. Meaning it's gotta lead to something they don't want anyone to see."

"No shit," Marc commented. "But what about the crevasse?"

Charlie shook his head. "I figure now that's just a place they dumped the body. Probably not related to anything special."

Marc pointed over their heads. "Maybe these holes mean something. They look burned around the edges. Must have some kind of use."

The holes were back a few meters, about eight feet above the ground. Sam reached up, rubbing the tips of his fingers on the powdery black residue surrounding them. He tasted it.

"Carbon," he said, spitting it out.

Charlie had backed away a little to study the narrow gap. He saw the darkened patch of grooved limestone at Bloom's feet and recalled the details of Lind Grenier's autopsy as related by Anna during that first night in Antananarivo.

He nodded, jamming his lips together. He eased around his partner and bent over to pick up a rounded, glassy-looking rock. "You know what this is?"

Bloom knew. "A fulgurite—meaning lightning's struck somewhere near here."

Bannerman jerked his head from side to side. "Uh-uh, not near here. Right here—exactly where you're standing."

Marc, having no knowledge about the background of their investigation, asked the policeman to explain.

"Over the last couple of years there's been an unusually high number of lightning victims showing up in an area about five to ten miles east of the reserve. We've had reason to believe some of them were killed inside and their bodies carted out and dumped on the open plains to shift suspicion away from Tsingy."

Charlie said no more and watched as Bloom stood between the drill-holes, pointing his arms toward each one. "What, a heavy steel bar fixed into the rock, with a long metal rod reaching above the razorbacks to attract the lightning?"

The detective nodded. "Something like that. It explains why Grenier had exit burns on his hands. They had him strung up like a goddamned chicken, waiting for the next bolt of lightning to fry the poor bastard."

"A simple and effective method to make death look natural," Sam said, his face grim. "Anna will have to be told about this. But what about Gerhard? We know he came this far, because his last mark is right here. Do you think he was able to recognize ZIAN's version of the electric chair?"

"Yeah, he figured it out, which left Simard no choice. He probably pulled his gun, marched the kid off to that hole, then dumped him. Except the way I see it, Simard must have had help, since as far as we know the guy had never been inside Tsingy."

"Was he carrying a radio that day?"

"Uh-uh. I know what you're getting at. No, I'd say that whoever hangs out in this place somehow knew they were there, maybe heard them talking."

Lamont's wide frame came around the base of one of the spires, followed by Hazz. "We found it. A doorway cut into the limestone — very professional."

"Never would have found it," Hazz admitted, "except for all the racket they're making down there."

"What kind of racket?"

Lamont pulled off his straw Panama and wiped the inside band with a handkerchief. "Hard to say. Throwing things around, maybe."

"Or breaking something up," Hazz added. "We looked around for a lever or handle of some kind. Nothing. Must be electronic."

Their leader pressed the LIGHT button on his Motorola four times, the return signal for Mitts and Rossal. Within minutes all seven men were standing near the place where Lind Grenier had come face-to-face with his Maker less than one month earlier.

Marc quickly laid out the plan they were to follow and then moved in for the attack.

CHAPTER EIGHTEEN

The last items to be thrown down the well were the solar batteries and the entire radio system. These pieces followed in the wake of the bed frames and the kitchen table and chairs, which had to be knocked apart with a hammer, creating a great racket that echoed back and forth through the tunnels and up into the hollow spires.

They were vulnerable now, Victor knew, their security system dismantled, the last directional antenna pulled out of its niche directly above the office. He was not concerned. So what if another one of these honey-gathering wogs heard the noise and began snooping around? In minutes they would be off, silently riding their battery-powered tunnel buggies up to the north entrance where their lorry awaited them. His men were now in the process of carrying out a final search of the area, scouring it to make certain no trace of their clandestine activity remained behind. Someday, Victor felt, ZIAN might well wish to resurrect Tsingy. But he wouldn't be around to see it. At his age, he thought while walking back to the well, life expectancy could be counted in months.

With the overhead lighting having been stripped away along with everything else, Victor directed his powerful beam ahead to avoid squishing bats. As always in the mornings, the areas below the roosting domes were strewn with bat carcasses. Most nights a few dozen would fall, but occasionally they died by the hundreds, a mystery that had no apparent answer.

Erich joined him from a side tunnel, where the sleeping quarters had been. An automatic carbine was slung over his shoulder.

This looked wrong, Victor realized with a mild surge of panic, since the chemist never carried a weapon.

Karl was waiting beside the well when the two arrived, his face grim in the moving light reflected off the stark cavern walls.

"I trust you understand that I have no choice in the matter," Victor told him in a low voice. "None whatsoever."

The big German nodded. "When the boys arrive, I'll be off to the buggies. I just ask that you do it quickly and thoroughly."

Victor breathed a sigh of relief. He had thought Karl might pose a problem.

Just then the sound of automatic gunfire rattled through the cavern, startling Victor and Erich. They turned to run back.

Karl's harsh laugh stopped them. "Did you think they would leave without sending a good-bye message to their stinking little friends?"

The men had grown to hate the bats as few creatures in this world had ever been hated. Five or six times a night for nearly two years, they had scraped and cleaned their reeking feces off the plastic sheets laid out below the roosting spots high above in the hollow spires. Then there was the matter of sorting through the whole stinking mess so Erich could begin the purification process.

Victor nodded in agreement. "I can understand their feelings. Tell them to collect their casings and come in here. Now."

When Karl departed to round up his colleagues for the last time, the ZIAN chemist used the fingers of his left hand to wipe the sweat from his forehead. "I thought—"

Victor smiled. "That they had decided to turn the tables on us? You need not worry. Intelligence was not the prime criterion for this job."

The sound of echoing gunfire, followed almost immediately by the swoosh of thousands of bats escaping from the tops of nearby pinnacles, brought the seven men to a standstill.

"Jesus Maria!" exclaimed Rossal. "They're playing my favorite tune."

Hazz rolled his eyes. "At least we know they're armed."

Marc cautioned for silence. He watched the bats for a few seconds, then turned his attention back the doorway Lamont had found. For several minutes they had searched unsuccessfully for some means to open it up. He sensed now that they were running out of time.

"Decision time, chief," prompted Rossal.

Marc looked at Bloom. "Even if we find another entrance, it will probably have the same kind of opening mechanism. We're going to have to use the RL and blast our way through the door, otherwise we could be hanging around out here all day."

"Agreed. Sounds like they're having a battle of their own in there. Might be just enough confusion to give us a little lead time."

"It might. Okay, get rid of your packs. Mitts, load up and put one midway up the left seam when I give the word. Hazz, have another rocket ready in case. Then dump the launcher and grab your HK. We'll go in fast, two and two on opposite sides, like usual. Giles will take the rear. One of us goes down, you move up. They're in some kind of underground tunnel or cavern, which could be blacker than Toby's ass. So break out the lights. And turn your radios off—I don't want an outside call to give away our positions. Problem is—these guys could have more holes than a goddamn ferret. Sam, you and Charlie hang back at the entrance and cover our tails. Bastards might sneak in behind us and we would never know until it's too late. So keep a sharp watch."

"Fun time for us soldier boys," said Lamont, slapping Rossal on the shoulder.

"You betcha, Mama-san."

"We hear and obey, Bwana."

They backed away from the door about thirty paces. Mitts loaded a rocket into the tube of the AT4, armed it, then glanced at Marc.

Karl had rounded up the four men and left without comment. "Well gentlemen, do you think we have everything?" Victor asked.

"Cleaner than your grandmother's tush," Freddie Gratin declared.

Victor smiled. It helped to maintain one's sanity by behaving like adolescents. "So, the end to a successful enterprise," he said. "So successful, in fact, that Herr Brower has decided to award each of you a fat bonus: fifty thousand Swiss francs."

One of the men let out a whoop. Another exclaimed, "Bloody good move!" With somewhat less enthusiasm, a third added, "Yeah, I'd say two years of scraping up bat turds rates a little extra."

"Don't forget helping to fry a couple of dozen blackies," said the fourth man. "Plus a few whiteys."

Victor nodded. "True enough, true enough. Unfortunate matters indeed. But that is all behind us now, and it is time to bid farewell to the tunnels of Tsingy Reserve."

He turned to leave, then removed his handgun from his belt, walked over to the well and dropped it in. "Since we no longer have anything to protect, there is no need for weapons. Once we reach the north end, we will simply be another ZIAN team riding down to the coast. If the authorities were to stop us, we would not want them to find any guns."

Erich laughed as he unslung his automatic carbine. "The last thing I need now is a stint in a Malagasy prison."

They all agreed wholeheartedly.

The rocket blast created a jagged opening about four feet in diameter. The five Frenchmen leaped over the piles of limestone rubble even before it had settled. Once inside they were greeted by darkness, a god-awful stink, and several thousand confused bats.

In seconds the swirling black hole had gobbled them up. "Brave men," Charlie observed, backing away from the hordes of escaping bats. "Either that or crazy."

"It's their job. Big money, travel to exotic lands, high adventure. The downside is they tend not to live too long."

A troop of white-faced lemurs had suddenly materialized in the high branches of a nearby baobab tree to see what all the noise was about. A colony of weaver birds in a bottle tree halted their activities to keep watch on the bats.

Inside, Karl had correctly identified the source of the deep rumble and blast of warm air sweeping around him. He ran back through the narrow tunnel into the main cavern in time to meet the others arriving from the well.

"What happened?" Victor wanted to know.

"They took out the east portal. Probably government forces. We better get up there before they get into the tunnel."

Karl directed his light toward the east entrance, picking up the dust that had been pushed ahead of the blast. "Whoever it is came in this morning and they came in fast, meaning they knew exactly where the door was. *The bastards knew!* And they must have known when our antennas were being pulled."

"Nonsense!" Victor replied. "No one had any idea how long it would take to dismantle the solar panels. A whole day was lost because of that aircraft taking photographs. Otherwise we would have left yesterday morning."

Karl relented. "You're right. So what are your orders?"

First an engineer and then an administrative officer during the war, Victor had spent little time on the battlefield. "Whoever launched this attack obviously knows who we are and what we have been doing. If we are captured, no matter who it is, we are certain to end up in a Malagasy prison, perhaps for the rest of our lives."

"Unless they kill us first," Erich snapped.

Victor nodded impatiently. "It would hardly matter then, would it? We stand to lose not only our freedom, but access to the substantial wealth each of us earned over the past two years."

"Fair enough," Karl said. He did not voice his concern that since the assault force knew where to find this entrance, they might also know where the other two were located. The attack on the east portal could even be a ruse to get them to run toward the north exit. It was better to face the music now, he knew.

"All right, lads, douse your lights. This is our home ground, so we have the advantage. Reimer, you take the south tunnel and work your way around to the east portal. Perhaps if there are not so many, we can catch them in a trap. You three will come with me to greet our visitors, whoever they are."

Five seconds after the men had vanished into the darkness, Erich whispered, "Time to leave, I'd say."

"My thoughts exactly," Victor declared.

Erich said, "We'll have to take both buggies."

Victor agreed, though with considerable reluctance. They couldn't gamble on leaving one behind, as the attacking force would surely seize upon the opportunity to chase after them.

There were two large tunnel buggies, each powered with eight solar batteries. With just one man aboard, even along the rocky shore of an underground stream that ran through the main cavern, the small machines could do in excess of forty kilometers per hour.

Minutes later, both machines were underway.

The French mercenaries found a slippery limestone surface waiting for them at the bottom of the steps. They soon learned, to their disgust, that it was littered with the carcasses of dead bats. They advanced cautiously, without lights, staying as low as possible, knowing that somewhere ahead automatic weapons might be waiting to cut them down. Daylight from the opening behind them quickly grew dim and then faded away to nothing. Darkness was now complete, bringing with it a strong feeling of disorientation. In the clammy coolness the men began to sweat in anticipation. The odor was powerful enough to sting their eyes, while the swoosh of thousands of wings and frantic echo location chirps made it difficult to hear what activity was taking place ahead.

"This is a real bitch!" Lamont whispered.

"Shhhh," Marc ordered. He knew they had passed at least two openings in the tunnel wall, and this worried him.

Despite the milling bats, Karl suddenly became aware of a human presence ahead of him. He was strongly tempted to call out, to ask who they were. For a moment he felt a sense of panic, his decision-making mechanism rendered inoperative. Perhaps he should have stayed inside the main cavern and waited. Victor's workers were not trained soldiers and could not be depended upon to conduct themselves properly under fire. But at least they are alive, he thought wryly. The invasion of their sanctuary had saved their lives.

A burst of automatic gunfire to his left put an end to the German's indecision. One of the unknown enemy was hit, his cry of pain familiar, his thud to the ground real. He heard a voice call out in French, "Jesus, they got Rossal!"

Marc flattened himself tight to the floor. He pulled a flare out of his belt and jerked the tab off with his teeth. Tossing it ahead of him, he shouted, "Daylight! Open up!"

There were no more words, only a ferocious blaze of gunfire. Even as the bullets struck him, Karl knew his wounds were not serious. It was hard to tell within the reverberating echoes, but he figured at least four weapons. Still, because the tunnel was so narrow, this allowed no more than a few to open fire at the same time. They spoke French, which confirmed his belief that they were government troops, meaning that the assault force could be a large one. He dove inside the lavatory doorway before the flare blossomed into full daylight, recalling that he had once reached into this room to get a towel for the condemned Swiss forester.

Grenier!

Was it possible, he wondered in desperation? Victor had been assured they had all gone to Zurich. Herr Brower had even met with one of the Americans personally. Karl wondered at the time why no investigation had followed the last execution, when the last Swiss forester had been dumped into that crevasse. They had worked all through the following morning to lay a false trail to divert the men he was certain would return in short order. But no one had come.

Was Simard so good an actor, or were they just now returning?

Marc and his men knew that night blindness could be caused by a flare and made certain to keep one eye jammed shut until it burned itself out. But one eye was enough for them to make out three forms ahead of them in the prone position: two very still, one just starting to rise. He and Hazz saw the movement at the same time and opened fire together. The rising one collapsed.

To make certain the others would never move again, Marc emptied his magazine into both men. He sprung the empty magazine, jammed in another and jerked the action back. The flare was dying now, and he scanned the route ahead to imprint it on his mind. He noticed at least three more openings, each capable of harboring an unpleasant surprise.

Karl saw Henri attempt to get up, then watched his body dance from the sudden influx of lead. He was reasonably sure by now that these silent men were not government troops. But who were they? That was the question. In any case, it was time for him to leave. He was certain Victor and Erich were already on their way, but that would still leave one buggy. Reimer was now on his own.

The German chief of security took the kitchen exit out of the lavatory, only vaguely aware of the burning sensation in his left shoulder and the hot blood flowing down the inside of his right leg. From the absolute darkness of the room that had served as their dining area, he entered the small cavern housing the deep well where all their paraphernalia had been dumped. Here he switched on his light and ran the rest of the way out to the underground stream where the buggies were kept.

But there was no buggy to be seen. Karl Schuster stood near the edge of the water, allowing his anger to give way to despair. It came as a shock to realize that he had been betrayed by Victor.

Erich, yes. Betrayal would come naturally to him. But Victor …?

The four French mercenaries advanced slowly. Rossal had been hit in the neck, the bullet severing an artery; not good. Marc left him in the Americans' charge and pressed on. In this kind of operation, he knew, hesitation invites disaster.

"Red Knight, Red Knight, come in, Lear."

Bloom frowned, wondering if his set was faulty. He refused to believe that the radios were incapable of carrying the few kilometers to the helicopter. He was about to tell Charlie to try his set when Lear's voice came in loud and clear. "This is Red Knight. Go ahead."

"Jesus! Where the hell were you? We have a casualty, condition critical. We'll need the winch, and make sure Dr. Grenier is aboard."

When his request was greeted with silence, Sam jammed his thumb on the SEND button. "Lear, what the hell is wrong with you? We got problems here. Get that goddamn machine in the air right now. I'll give you the coordinates when you're airborne."

"Sorry about that, just checking something out. Look, the winch was banged up in Swaziland, and we've been on the move ever since. It won't operate."

Bloom glanced at Bannerman. "Well, isn't that just ducky!" To the pilot he said, "That's marvelous, Lear. We got a guy here bleeding like a stuck pig. He could bleed to death because your effing winch is broke down. You should have damn well told me that last night."

The South African's voice took on a hard edge. "Look, chum, it's entirely out of my hands, okay?"

"No, it isn't okay. Put Anna on."

While waiting for Anna, Sam watched Charlie's vain attempt to keep the bullet hole closed without strangling the patient. The problem with this kind of wound was that pressure had to be applied constantly, but keeping the pressure on too long could lead to a shortage of oxygen to the brain. Each time Bannerman released his thumb, Rossal's blood gushed out in great spurts.

"I don't see her right now. She went out with Downing to look for fulgurites."

Fulgurites. *Christ!* Only then did Bloom become aware of a man standing at the edge of his vision. When he swung his head in surprise, the man raised his gun to fire.

Lamont thought the place was deserted. Marc didn't agree. Cautiously, they continued to scour the limits of each section of hollowed-out limestone wherever an opening took them. By the time they neared the underground river, the bats had settled down and the men could hear rushing water. Up to now they had been using their lights sparingly, as the sharp beams made a perfect target.

When Marc heard the water, he stopped, switched off his flashlight, and listened. Up ahead a loud splash made him raise his rifle.

"What the hell was that?" Mitts said.

"A crocodile," a deep voice out of the darkness replied in French. "In Madagascar it is not unusual for crocodiles to spend the majority of their lives in these underground streams. Perhaps that is what keeps them alive."

Marc told his men to spread out, then stretched out his arm to the left as far as he could before switching on his light. It took him a few seconds to locate the dark form, because the man appeared to be sitting at the edge of the stream with his back to them. When his beam picked up no one else, Marc swung the light back. "You are to stand up, monsieur, slowly, and turn around. If you have a weapon, do not think of using it."

His comment was met with laughter. "Professionals. Mercenaries, I'd bet, just like me. I'll be damned." He stood up then, a tall, broad-shouldered man, and turned to face them. His hands were empty. "I'm Karl Schuster. Algeria. Any of you heard of me?"

Marc moved closer. He knew Schuster, having met him on a few occasions. The face looked familiar. "Okay, so you're Schuster. How come you got stuck with these losers?"

"You mean those poor lads you just mowed down? They were not even trained. Rank amateurs."

Lamont moved up to look the German over. He noticed the blood seeping from his shoulder. "A guy runs with amateurs, you know, the risk factor goes out of sight. So why is Karl Schuster sitting here all alone?"

"Not by choice, I assure you. It happens that I was betrayed by my employer." He chuckled away to himself. "But betrayal is a double-edged sword, as those two will learn before long."

Sam stared at the man, saw the panic and indecision in his eyes, and shouted in German, "Don't shoot! We are doctors."

Perhaps it was his native language that stopped him, or maybe it was Bloom's deception. Either way, it gave Sam enough time to pull his rifle out from under his pack and open fire. His aim was way off, but he succeeded in making the stranger dart back into the limestone without firing a shot. Bloom took off after him immediately, as he knew the guy could reappear at any time, in any location. He shouted to Bannerman to pull Rossal back inside the cavern.

When Lamont heard the distant shots, he jammed his gun into Karl's ribs. "Move, you guys! I'll handle this one."

Schuster said, "That must be Reimer. I didn't think he would have the nerve to show his nose. Give me a light, and I'll lead you directly to the east portal."

"Okay," Marc said, reaching over to give the German his flashlight. "Get moving, and no tricks."

Karl moved swiftly, with the French mercenaries tight behind him. Marc reached for his radio, but Bannerman was already calling in. "Some fellow with a gun showed up and Sam opened fire. I'm pulling Rossal back inside the tunnel. Bloom's gone after the guy."

Marc called back that they were on their way. Karl stepped over the bodies of the ZIAN men, his former companions, and a hundred meters later, limped up the steps. Bannerman was trying unsuccessfully to pull Rossal through the opening while maintaining pressure on the artery. Schuster squeezed around both men without comment.

"Reimer!" he shouted. "Reimer, this is Karl. It's all over. You hear me? It's all over. No more shooting. Come on in, now!"

Reimer had just finished climbing to an elevated niche in the limestone, one of several observation platforms they had carved out in the early days. By moving his body just slightly, he commanded a four-way view. Sooner or later, he knew, the man following him would show. Reimer was angry at himself for hesitating and then falling for such a dumb trick. He listened carefully for the sound of the tsingy, the ringing trill given off by a razorback as a boot skimmed over it. He would make certain this time.

Sam heard the shouting, stopped, and listened. He heard Karl calling to Reimer and knew Karl was the big German at the warehouse in Toama. So Charlie had been right all along. And it was all over. Bloom did his best to tone down his adrenaline before making his way back.

Reimer trusted Karl and knew it was no trick. Reluctantly, he climbed down and headed toward the open area fronting the east portal.

Both men arrived within seconds of one another. Marc had just administered a shot of morphine to Rossal and was anxious to get moving. The Frenchman was on a stretcher, now conscious, and had just been told he would have to be carried. It was urgent to get Rossal to the helicopter as quickly as possible, but it would be difficult climbing over the tsingy and maintaining pressure on the artery. Marc knew the life of his comrade depended on how fast they made it out. He gave the orders. Reimer took one end of the stretcher while Mitts took the other. Marc applied pressure with his thumb, while Hazz pulled up the rear.

Bannerman bid them good luck. He looked down at his hands, then at his clothes. They were covered in Rossal's blood. He wouldn't lay any money on the French mercenary making it.

Karl had remained behind with Lamont and the Americans to explain the activities of ZIAN, but first they had to bind up his wounds, as he too had lost a fair amount of blood.

Sam was on the radio to Lear. "… and if Anna can patch Rossal up long enough to take him safely back to the mainland, then that's the way we'll play it. If not, take your rig down to the clinic in Analabe, a hundred or so miles to the south. Drop Rossal, and then get back up here. This exercise seems to have fizzled out, but we can't be certain, not yet. Give me a call when Dr. Grenier completes her examination. Keep me posted if there's any change of plans."

"I would like to know what status this raid has," the German said, after Lear acknowledged Bloom's instructions. He was attempting to remove his shirt and winced painfully from the effort. "What will happen to Reimer and me if we talk — or if we refuse to talk?"

Bloom helped Karl get rid of his shirt. He glanced at Charlie, who nodded. Sam gave the German the proper assurances, then turned the questioning over to the New York detective.

Convinced that he and Reimer would not be handed over to the authorities and be given a ride across the channel to Nacala, Karl opened up. A half hour went by, followed by a tour of the cavern and its various tunnels. Victor and the chemist, Erich, were on their way to the coast, he told Charlie. They would use the company trawler, which was moored in the protective custody of a well-paid Malagasy, to return to the mainland. The boat was an eighteen-meter, three-thousand-horsepower vessel capable of fifty-five knots per hour. And yes, it was the same one they used to meet the *Lucinda V.*

While Bannerman was being given the tour, Sam and Lamont dragged the bodies of the three ZIAN employees down to the well, as Karl called it. This was where Victor had intended the men to go in the first place, the German told them.

Sam did not wish to linger any longer than necessary, but had one particular curiosity that he wanted to address. When Charlie was through, Sam asked Schuster to take him to a spot where the golden orchids grew in abundance. Once there, he took several photographs, picked three of the exotic flowers, complete with stem, and packed them in the case he had brought along for that specific purpose. His suspicion that the golden flower did not hold the complete answer had been confirmed earlier, when he spotted the first orchid. It had taken him another twenty minutes to find the other half of the puzzle. He also picked three of those and carefully sealed them in beside the orchids before returning with Karl to the tunnel entrance.

Bannerman was satisfied. As far as Madagascar was concerned, he had all he needed and more. There was still the matter of locating ZIAN's American contacts, to learn exactly how the stuff was being moved from Zurich to New York. But he had also learned of the ingenious method used to disguise the treated cocaine while it was enroute to Zurich, and there was no reason to suppose they would not use the same method to ship it to the States.

The four men had just started to head back when Lear called in. "This is Red Knight. Come in, Eagle."

"Go ahead, Lear."

"Good news. Dr. Grenier was able to stop the bleeding and fix a neck splint. She feels surgery can wait at least twenty-four hours."

"Great. We'll see you in an hour or so." Schuster's leg was giving him trouble, so the return trip would be slow going, Sam knew. The bullet had completely penetrated his right lower thigh, missing the bone by millimeters, but tearing out a healthy chunk of muscle.

Fifteen minutes later they stopped again. The German's face was white with pain. He had been offered a shot of morphine but refused it. Something was bothering Sam. Why, he wondered, had Anna not communicated with him at all? He knew she was anxious to learn what had transpired. It would've been more natural for her to call in with a dozen questions. Instead, there was only silence.

Bannerman caught his companion's look and guessed at what was going through his mind. "I found it a bit hard to take, her wandering around looking for rocks with an attack underway. She's the type who would have her ear glued to the radio."

Lamont nodded. He did not know the Swiss woman that well, but was inclined to accept their word. "So why not call her now?"

Bloom did, and within a minute Anna came on. "I just wanted to get an update on Rossal's condition. The guy lost a lot of blood, several liters, I'd say. How is he making out?"

"Rossal is doing well enough, under the circumstances. Is there anything else you wish to know?"

Sam glanced at Charlie, feeling a little embarrassed. "No, that's it. Thanks."

"Jesus!" Bannerman exclaimed. "That sounded pretty cold for the Anna Grenier I know." He turned to the German. "I hope you don't have any little tricks up your sleeve, Adolph. You'll be the first to go."

Karl appeared to think it over. He consulted his watch and finally shook his head. "Victor and Erich could have driven their vehicle around the reserve by now. But why would they? Erich is a coward, and Victor is an old man. They have no idea who you are or where you came from. They assumed, like I first did, that government troops were behind the attack."

"There is no one else?" Lamont wanted to know.

"Absolutely no one! If there were, I would tell you."

Bloom was inclined to take the German at his word. "You believe him, Charlie?"

The policeman nodded. They must be imagining things. "Yeah, I do."

Lamont pulled himself up, grinning as he did so. "Who knows, maybe she's not over yet."

The Sea Knight was there when they reached the reserve entrance around three in the afternoon. The sun was high, the sky clear, and although there was a mild breeze blowing, the only visible piece of shade to be seen anywhere across the entire stretch of dry dusty plain was cast by the helicopter, at least five hundred paces away.

"Asshole pilots," Lamont muttered.

Bannerman agreed wholeheartedly. He pulled off his leather gloves, examining the multiple cuts on his hands. He didn't need this extra distance tacked onto the end of the goddamn obstacle course they had just emerged from. The front of the big helicopter was about five feet off the ground, with lots of nice dark shade underneath. So why, Charlie wondered, were the men standing around in the blazing sun?

They were nearing the halfway mark to the Sea Knight when one of the group broke free and came to meet them. It was Reimer.

Bloom stopped when he recognized who it was. "Something's up, sure as shit."

There was a hint of a smile on his face when Reimer stopped in front of them. Bannerman noticed he was unarmed. He asked if they had enjoyed their little hike.

"What is it, Emil?" Schuster wanted to know.

"Small change in plans." He began to walk back, the others following along beside him. "A wild card, so to speak, has entered the fray. Chap by the name of Simard. You have already made his acquaintance, I understand."

Lamont cursed. He had been right after all. But he was not pleased about it.

"Where is he?" Bloom wanted to know.

"Sitting inside your helicopter with a nasty little Mac-11 resting on your girlfriend's neck."

Sam was stunned by the news. Renè Simard was the last person in the world he expected to show up. Anna's terse reply made sense now.

"I have a message," Reimer said. "But first I should warn you that the man appears … how should I put it … not quite rational."

He stopped, looking Sam in the eye. "Believe me when I tell you that he is not to be trifled with. He has killed already today and will not hesitate to kill again."

Lamont lost control and grabbed the German by the throat with one hand. "If this is a trick, Lamont will spread your rotten Nazi carcass all over this *putain désert*! Who did he kill?"

Reimer pulled the man's hand away and rubbed his throat before answering. "How do I know his name? Maybe he was the navigator, I don't know."

Suddenly, it was a nightmare to Bloom. Anna was now the captive of a man who might well be a psychopathic killer. When she had not responded to his first call on Rossal, everything inside him screamed that something was wrong, but it was somehow beyond reason to acknowledge it. The enemy had been subdued. Two had escaped, but they had fled in the opposite direction. There was no enemy left to deal with.

Bannerman was becoming impatient, since he understood not a single word of German. Bloom gave him a quick rundown. Then he turned back to Reimer. "The message?"

"You are to surrender your weapons to me. The two Americans will approach the helicopter doorway. The Frenchmen are to go free." He looked at Lamont. "His jeep is behind the machine. Your men can take it to the nearest town."

"And Rossal?"

"Oh, Rossal." The German's face turned somber. "I am afraid the pilot was forced to lie about his condition. He's lost a lot of blood. I heard the doctor tell Simard that unless he has an immediate transfusion he will die within hours."

Bloom saw the look of exasperation on Bannerman's face, but there was no time to translate everything. "Just for the record, what happens if we don't do as he says?"

"First the mercenaries will go, one by one. Then the lovely Swiss doctor, whom he refers to as his cousin, by the way." Reimer glanced at his watch. "The first one has barely four minutes to live. I suggest we move along."

But Sam didn't move. He gave Charlie an update and asked his opinion. The cop wiped a sweaty hand across his brow. He was worried sick over Shaleen. "You said he's got a gun on Anna, but—"

Lamont's prod in the ribs shut him up. The German had not mentioned Shaleen, for one of two reasons: She was either dead, or she wasn't around.

After a brief discussion, the three men handed over their guns to Reimer. He gave the rifles and pistols to Karl, who took the weapons while silently shaking his head, as if to tell them it was not his idea.

The ZIAN men went on ahead, while Sam came to a halt about thirty paces from the helicopter. The wind had died away; complete and utter silence now lay over the land.

The expression on Marc's face accurately portrayed the anger and frustration he felt. Rossal was apparently inside the chopper, while Downing's body was nowhere to be seen. Lear was in his seat, his face set in stone.

After watching the two Germans board the helicopter, Lamont placed his hand on Bloom's arm. "If you and Charlie go aboard, *mon ami*, you are dead men."

"I already figured that out. You have a better idea?"

"Regretfully, I do not."

Bloom said, "I wouldn't bet on the sincerity of his offer to let you guys go free, but just the same, I'd like you to do me a favor."

"Of course. You have only to name it."

"Tell Simard Charlie and me are not coming in until Anna is in the clear. The deal is she goes with you, Marc, and the others. When they're out of sight, we come aboard."

Lamont was not impressed. "Why should he go for such a deal? Does he not hold all the cards?"

Sweat was running down Bloom's face. It wasn't from the heat, he knew, but from the knowledge that his time had just about run out. He watched the two Germans walk down the steps and move off a few meters to talk among themselves. He also saw they were unarmed and wondered how Simard had managed to pull that off, since they were supposed to be on the same side.

They were not quite within audio range of the three French mercenaries, but Sam still lowered his voice. "Listen, fellows, as I see it, we're playing for one life, maybe two. We haven't heard a word about Shaleen, so maybe she's escaped. Giles, when you're inside, take a look around. If she's nowhere in sight, we have to assume she's in the clear. Simard has two guys on his side, and I'm not all that certain about Schuster; he could go either way. Counting Lear, Simard has seven stacked against him, which means he has to move very carefully indeed. He's sharp enough to figure out that the German contingent just might not go along with seeing the French contingent shot down in cold blood, so he stripped away all their weapons. But just in case they might decide to rush him anyway, he assures everyone that only Charlie and me are his enemies and that no one else has anything to worry about.

"Now, maybe I can reverse that psychology. If he flatly refuses to let Anna go, and the men from either side think he is going to kill her, he risks the possibility of an uprising. He knows Marc's men are professionals, and they probably know by now that Rossal is running out of time, so they're antsy. And he knows they know a whole bunch of tricks he never heard of. But no matter how you cut it, Anna is toast unless we get her out. You have any trouble with that, Charlie?"

Bannerman shrugged. At thirty yards, Simard could cut them down at his leisure if he wanted to. And there sure wasn't anywhere to run. "I'll play it your way."

"This I do not like," Lamont said slowly. "But I will do it."

When Lamont drew near Marc, the French mercenary shook his head. "He was holding an Ingram machine pistol on the Swiss woman. There was nothing we could do."

Lamont placed his hand on Marc's shoulder. "I know, *mon ami*, but what of —?"

Marc shook his head to Lamont's unfinished question. He had neither seen nor heard from Shaleen.

The chopper had landed east-west, with its cockpit facing Tsingy. The three men were close to the door on the north side, presumably so that Simard could keep an eye on them through one of the four porthole windows. When Lamont vanished inside its dark interior, Bloom took a covert glance around. He was puzzled by Shaleen's apparent vanishing act.

Giles Lamont came down the steps with a long face. The rising star of Interpol, as Inspector Lemieux had referred to him, had another message to be delivered, and Lamont was his reluctant messenger.

"Monsieur Simard invites his countrymen who have been hired by the Americans to get moving; now, while he feels in a generous mood. The keys are in his jeep and you are welcome to it. It will be somewhat crowded with Dr. Grenier and the stretcher, but he has every confidence that good French ingenuity will sort everything out. The Americans are to lie face down out here in front of the doorway, looking away from the helicopter."

They obeyed the instructions with minimum discussion, except that Bloom had no intention of lying down or facing away. He told Bannerman that if he was going to be shot, he wanted to look into the eyes of the guy who was doing it. Charlie went along with him. Schuster and Reimer were called inside to lower the stretcher into the waiting hands of Rossal's comrades. Next came Lear, who walked silently over to stand beside the Americans. When Anna came out, she was unable to stifle the involuntary cry that escaped her lips. Simard was behind her now, a dark shadow in the doorway.

Marc was the last to leave and had to be ordered to get moving by Simard. He stretched out his hand in a final farewell salute. Only Lamont had not moved, and it was not until the jeep started up and began to pull away that Simard realized he had chosen to remain behind.

Still, the man from Interpol did not seem disturbed by Lamont's refusal to leave. From the doorway he watched his burly countryman walk over to join Lear and the Americans. "So, mon ami, you wish to throw in your cards with these men? As you wish. It is your decision."

Karl Schuster and Reimer moved into the Sea Knight's inviting shade and sat on the ground. To the east, a line of clouds had developed, getting ready to move across the plain. Simard moved out of the darkened doorway, smiling and elegant, the deadly Ingram machine pistol held loosely in his right hand. He sat on the steps and waited.

Chapter Nineteen

It happened in slow motion, scene by scene: Simard standing up, stretching, stepping down to the ground, walking toward the front of the helicopter, and turning; a blaze of rapid fire; Karl's shock at another betrayal; Bloom's rush, aborted by the Ingram's muzzle pointed at his face.

"Have you not considered, Dr. Bloom, that you may have been chosen to live? Perhaps Herr Brower wishes to have another chat with you and your pudgy assistant, Dr. Bannerman."

Sam instinctively knew this to be a lie, as Simard was a proficient liar. Hold out the chance of life, a man was sure to grasp at it.

"I suppose you were surprised to see me, thinking I was wrapped up nice and snug inside that rathole in Tana."

Bloom glanced over at the still-twitching bodies of Schuster and Reimer and sucked in a deep breath to steady himself. Then he asked their killer how he managed to escape.

"Escape? Really, Dr. Bloom. I believe you know who my employer is. Their influence extends even to this godforsaken part of the world. The Malagasy authorities admitted to making a serious mistake. They have even apologized."

"I see." In studying the Frenchman, Sam realized that René Simard was above all a superb actor. He was also a homicidal maniac. "How did you know where to find us? Or was it just coincidence?"

"Hardly coincidence. You forget that I am in the business of finding out such things. Three telephone calls: Zurich, Brazzaville, Nairobi. One does not need to fly into Nacala in order to reach Brazzaville. So, with three fresh tickets routed through Mozambique, where else would you be going?"

Bloom nodded. Where else indeed?

"So," said Simard, a self-assured smile fixed upon his handsome face. He had carefully edged over to the ramp again. "Phase two complete. Now, if our South African pilot and Monsieur Lamont would be kind enough to load the bodies aboard, we shall be on our way."

Bloom gripped the pilot's arm, holding him back. "Maybe it's time to stop cooperating with a mad dog killer. We're dead meat, all of us, even Lear once you reach your destination. You killed Gerhard, didn't you? And Willi?"

The smile thinned. "That stupid ox! It was his own doing. In any case, Karl had a hand in that one. As for Strouss, yes, I can claim credit there, as your fat friend has already figured out."

Sam knew what he should do next, but hesitated, because the results could be fatal. Desperate now, he decided to play for more time. "But you must have a soft spot somewhere; after all, you let Anna go. Or was it that you were afraid those mercenaries might move a little too fast for you?"

The man from Interpol gave him an odd look. "Attempting to provoke me at this stage seems rather futile. And are you so certain that my lovely cousin will live? She too has a price on her head, you know."

Simard reached behind the door with his left hand to retrieve a small metal box.

Bloom recognized it immediately. And then realized there were to be no prisoners. None!

Because this asshole had wired a bomb to the jeep!

Sam saw the dust tail from the jeep and watched his enemy smile as he opened the box and flicked a switch. All he had to do now was push the button.

Sam knew they had run out of time. He was about to speak the words that would result in the certain death of Giles Lamont, but was saved the trouble.

Simard's smile widened to a grin. "Ah, Dr. Bloom, I do believe you have been holding out on us. You are the only one who recognized my special package, and yet you are supposed to be a botanist, a man of peace. Could it be that my little gift in Toamasina is somehow imprinted on your mind?"

Bloom prepared himself for the leap, because when Lamont grasped the full impact of Simard's question, he would react.

He did — with a sudden roar.

Sam dove low and was in the air when the rush of bullets zipped by his head. Then there was silence. He had landed arm's length from Simard, whose knees were buckling underneath him. Confused, Sam reached out to grab the man around the legs and pull him to the ground. Lamont was already there, ready to tear him apart.

Bannerman knelt and seized hold of their would-be murderer to roll him over. The little crimson hole in Simard's forehead stunned all three of them.

The man from Interpol was stone dead.

Sam stood up, shaken from his desperate leap. He held onto Lamont for support as he looked over at Lear, about to thank him, but could tell from his expression that the pilot was just as astonished as he was. Bloom scanned the horizon, but within the stark terrain fronting him saw nothing but rocks and gravel.

Then Bannerman stood up and began to walk quickly away. Lamont muttered something under his breath and started after him. Lear turned to Sam in surprise. "What in the bloody hell is going on?"

Then they saw it: a rock. Just an ordinary rock in every aspect, except that it moved. Charlie was almost there. Bloom glanced down at the dead man at his feet, then went off to follow the others.

By the time he arrived, Shaleen was just getting to her feet with Charlie's help. She was the color of the earth, a coppery red. She was also completely naked. Bannerman stripped his shirt off and wrapped it around her. Bloom could only stare in utter amazement.

"Stealth," Charlie told him, his face breaking into a great wide grin.

"How's that?" Sam asked. He could not take his eyes off the woman. He did not see her nakedness, but rather the near-miraculous deed she had just performed. Then he noticed the gun at her feet and little rivulets of blood seeping from so many cuts along her arms and legs.

"Stealth," Charlie repeated, with obvious pride. "They take it in school in Somalia. Where you learn to creep up on your enemy and kill him before he knows you are there. Shaleen achieved perfect marks."

"Unreal!" was all Sam could get out. Lamont wrapped both arms around his sister-in-law and spoke something into her ear. Bloom thought for a minute that the Frenchman might get emotional. When he withdrew, Shaleen was finally able to smile, though she still had not spoken a word. Her face was a disaster, and it was apparent that she felt awkward with the four men crowded around her. It was also obvious to Bloom that she had been under considerable strain, as it had taken her God knows how long to maneuver into position.

Lear had run back to his machine for a blanket. He returned now and gently draped it around her. As he was doing so, he kissed her softly on the cheek. "My dear young lady, what you have done here today will remain with me forever. I promise you that my grandchildren will learn the meaning of courage and endurance from this story. Thank you for my life and for all our lives."

The young heroine took hold of Charlie's arm and started back toward the helicopter, but then stopped and whispered, "My clothing."

When Sam asked where she had left her outfit, she cleared her throat and told him in a scratchy voice that they were at least two hundred paces further north.

Bloom bent down to pick up her Heckler and Koch assault rifle, taking in the odd-shaped rotary diopter aperture sight. She had it set on one hundred meters, and he imagined her anxiously praying that the gun had been accurately sighted in. He looked back toward the chopper, trying to visualize the picture she must have had from flat on the ground. He saw now that she might have fired earlier, except for the condemned men lined up in front of the machine effectively blocking her field of fire. Sam shook his head in disbelief. She had done it with one shot from well over a hundred yards, as Lamont was charging and Bloom was flying through the air. She had been too far away to know what was going on, which told him she had fired without notice. Even a second's delay, he now realized, might have been fatal for the four men.

After dashing ahead to retrieve Shaleen's clothes, he remembered Rossal and Simard's little metal box. This prompted him to run back to the helicopter and scramble up the steps before the others boarded. Once inside, he gently took the electronic detonator in both hands and sat on one of the canvas seats to open the cover. The flashing red light told him it was all set to go. Sam read the instructions carefully, which happened to be in English, then laid his thumb on the master switch to the left of the detonator button. The instructions were clear: TO UNARM, TURN THE MASTER SWITCH TO OFF.

But Anna was riding in that jeep. What if he was wrong? What if Simard had wired the device in reverse? By now they would be several kilometers away, but just how far could such a radio beam reach out?

He wiped the sweat from his brow and saw that Lamont and the pilot were watching him intently. If he waited, would the vibration trip the mechanism when they became airborne? But if they waited until the jeep was much farther away, it might be too late for Rossal. Lamont's gentle reminder settled the matter.

Sam closed his eyes and turned the switch. There was no explosion in the distance, but the silence was inconclusive. He knew the jeep might already be too far away for the sound to carry back to them. "All right," he said, standing. "Let's get going."

They caught up to the jeep a few miles out of Manera, a small village east of Tsingy. Anna had felt it was best to get to a radio and have a helicopter come in for Rossal, as he would never last through the long ride back to Analabe. When the Sea Knight showed up on the horizon, Marc was forced to consider evasive action. He knew it was inconsistent for the Interpol agent to allow witnesses to Downing's murder. But the exuberant signaling from the open hatch was a happy sight. Somehow, Simard's prisoners had managed to get the upper hand.

As soon as the steps were lowered, they hoisted Rossal's stretcher up and into the aircraft. Next came Anna, taken up bodily by Sam. She clung to him until the three Frenchmen were aboard and Lear ordered them to be seated for takeoff. Still, she did not release her hold. Anna Grenier had been convinced that she had lost the man she loved, and only by working hard at keeping Rossal alive had she been able to hold back the despair that threatened to engulf her.

Once they were airborne again, Sam released Anna's grip and beckoned to Marc. "Come here, I'll show you something interesting."

The French mercenary was at the rear of the aircraft viewing the four bodies: Schuster, Downing, Reimer, and their killer — René Simard. He shook his head and came forward at Bloom's request.

Sam slid the metal box from under his seat. "You recognize this?"

Marc's eyes widened as he took his seat across from the American. "Jesus Maria! Where did you find that?"

Bloom opened the box and flicked the master switch. Seconds later a flashing red light came on. "Take a look back over your shoulder."

Marc turned around, jerking instinctively when the jeep vanished inside a ball of fire.

It was a powerful bomb, the kind that did not leave survivors. The others crossed over to stand around the four windows on the starboard side. They watched in silence until the jeep was just a column of black smoke in the distance.

"Simard had it armed and was set to push the button, when this young lady planted a slug smack between his eyes from about one hundred meters. She saved our lives, and yours."

Her clothing back in place and her face somewhat cleaner than it had been, Shaleen quickly became the center of attention. But it was Lamont who claimed the right to tell her story. It turns out that Shaleen had merely been wandering about looking for fulgurites. When the jeep came speeding up and stopped behind the helicopter, she was in plain view of the driver if he had bothered to glance in a northerly direction. But when she heard Anna call out René's name in a loud voice, this told her something was wrong and she immediately dropped to the ground. Then she heard a short blast from an automatic weapon, which prompted her to scramble even further away from the helicopter until she came to a small depression in the flat landscape. Here she removed her clothing and rolled around in the reddish earth until her body was the same color. Then she began her slow crawl back to a position where she was satisfied that she could get an accurate shot away if the opportunity presented itself. Which, of course, is exactly what took place.

"What made you decide to take a rifle with you?" Marc asked.

Shaleen gave a tiny shrug. "Considering why we were there in the first place, it seemed like a wise thing to do."

Grinning, Lamont said to Bannerman, "You see now what I mean?"

Charlie got the message loud and clear, but said nothing. He had been rendered speechless by this young woman's heroic action.

Marc jammed his lips together and glanced away. He had been right about Simard. He was also grateful that Rossal had a firm policy of sighting in new guns before going into action. Then he looked over at Shaleen with a wide smile. "What can I say? Thank you, I think, is not enough—you deserve the ultimate reward. I will marry you."

"The hell!" Mitts said. "You're too bloody ancient. I'll marry her."

But Hazz was already on his knees before the Somali girl. She was smiling, but holding tight to Charlie's hand. "These two reprobates are way over the hill. Take me, fair maiden, and I will guarantee your absolute happiness."

For a moment Bannerman felt a bit self-conscious. But he also knew the time had come to make his commitment. "The lady is taken, fellows. She's going to marry me."

Rossal was given a sixty-forty chance. Anna wanted to stay, but with two physicians in attendance there seemed little point. The police, who had appeared along with the rest of the residents of Analabe, were far from satisfied. The Americans were forced to produce their embassy cards in order to obtain permission to leave.

Two hours before sunset, the big helicopter pulled up into a heavily overcast sky and headed north. Bloom took Downing's seat and spread out the French aeronautical chart.

With a good fuel supply aboard, the South African cranked up his twin turbines to eighty percent revs. He knew they would have to move fast in order to catch up with Victor and Erich before dark. Even then, luck would play a considerable role in locating a small boat in the middle of the ocean. With the size of the engines in their fishing trawler, the two senior ZIAN employees could easily make the coast of mainland Africa before dawn and then disappear.

Despite their earlier triumph, the presence of four cadavers in the rear of the aircraft did not make for light conversation. The pilot in particular had been devastated by the loss of his Canadian navigator and longtime friend. Anna had moved slowly from her earlier exuberance at finding that Sam was alive, to a deep remorse over the actions of her cousin, and then to her earlier indiscretion when he had first appeared in Geneva. Having almost slept with René was a bitter pill for her to swallow. She said a prayer asking Lind's forgiveness.

Lear flew directly over Tsingy this time, about three thousand feet above the limestone forest. He took this route to avoid a lightning storm that was moving in from the east. Anna was seated to Sam's left and slightly behind. She placed her hand on his shoulder and squeezed hard when Tsingy came into sight. Everyone aboard glanced out their porthole window, thinking their own thoughts. Bannerman wondered how it all got started. As he watched the deadly flashes arc across the sky, Bloom thought of Lind Grenier and wondered how many others had been forced to wait in abject terror for the brilliant yellow bolt that would snuff out their lives.

They had only Karl's rough guess of how far up the coast from Morondava the trawler had been moored, having travelled it just once. But Sam figured that since the two Germans had no knowledge that they were being following by a seagoing helicopter, they would likely make their way up the coast to Cape St. André and from there cross the channel at its narrowest point, just as the Sea Knight had done the previous afternoon.

Maybe they would take that route. Maybe they wouldn't. When the Sea Knight reached open sea, this thought continued to torment Sam until his eyes were red from scanning the horizon.

The ID was made at dusk, with some ten minutes of light remaining. A plan of action had already been discussed. According to Karl, the two men were carrying nothing on them to indicate they were involved in narcotics. It would be pointless, even dangerous, to bring in the Malagasy government; and it was even more unlikely that the government of Mozambique would accept the word of one group over another. They pulled ahead of the trawler as Lear let down the rear hatch, providing a firing platform for Marc.

Only Bloom was able to positively identify one of the men, Victor, from having seen him inside the warehouse in Toama. He used Marc's field glasses to scan the two anxious faces below, to make certain. The pale, wrinkled face staring up at them was Victor. Anna also took a look and recognized the face she had seen staring up her in Tsingy.

Sam stepped back, summoning Marc to the rear. He placed one hand on the Frenchman's shoulder and called to Bannerman, "You got a problem with this, Charlie?"

Bannerman glanced at Shaleen, trying to determine what her feelings might be, but her eyes told him nothing. He never held a soft spot for drug runners, nor did he believe in indiscriminate killing. He would have liked to talk to the men, especially the chemist, to learn more about the deadly toxin. But he also believed in justice. He gave the nod.

"You, Anna?"

She was less decisive, but had earlier talked it over with Sam Bloom. She knew this old man, Victor, had ordered Lind's death, and Sam had convinced her that if these men were allowed to escape, they would never have to answer for it.

She gave her approval.

"Giles?"

"It is your decision, *mon ami*. Do what you think is right."

"Good." He let go of Marc's shoulder. "It's all yours."

The Frenchman knelt down on one knee, steadying the launcher. Mitts laid out five rockets and placed the first in the tube. He moved back ten feet and unfolded the big aluminum deflector used to contain the rocket's powerful back-blast.

They were to sink the boat, destroying all traces of it. Marc aimed directly at the two Germans in the bow to make their deaths as swift as possible.

By the time the two men from ZIAN figured out why the giant helicopter was hovering just ahead of them, it was too late to begin an evasive maneuver.

Hazz slapped Marc's shoulder. The rocket was on target.

The burial at sea took place forty minutes later, well away from the coast of Madagascar. Leaving Mozambique with arms aboard was one thing; being caught bringing weapons into the country was something else. The logical solution was to make use of the guns, rockets, and ammo to weigh down the bodies. Using his landing lights to pick up the chop on the ocean, Lear dropped down to about fifty feet. At his request, Bloom reluctantly took over the controls while the pilot said a few words before each of the four were dropped. Two hours later their dark journey ended in the twinkling lights of the Mozambique port of Nacala.

Commissioner Hennessey took the call at 3:10 in the afternoon, New York time. He interrupted just twice, and at the end congratulated Bannerman on a job well done. Then he broke the news about the *Lucinda V*. "She was clean. Stacks of specimen crates, like you said, but nothing in them that didn't belong."

"How many?" Bannerman asked.

"How many what?"

"Crates. How many?"

Hennessey searched around for the file and pulled out the message the CIA had forwarded to him. "One hundred and twenty-three."

"Is that a fact? Well now, looks like somebody's misplaced fifty crates."

"Explain."

"I got a copy of the shipping manifest right here in my hot little hand, and it reads one hundred seventy-three. And you know what else? The seven is written North American style, meaning it's not crossed, like they do everywhere else. Betcha if you got hold of that original manifest, you'd see that the seven's been changed to a two."

"Okay," said the PC somewhat impatiently. "Suppose you're right. Will that help us locate the other crates?"

"No, it just means they were set up to disappear in the first place if the going got rough. We closed in, and bingo, the seven's got a tail on it."

"So how do we go about finding the missing ones?"

"Call up your buddies — sorry, your acquaintances — down at Langley, get them to go through the ship routine again. Have them trace the movements of the *Lucinda V* since it left Madagascar. And then check out what other ships came close to it. Maybe you'll get lucky. Maybe the satellite will catch them in the act. If not, you're going to have to run down all the suspect ships, anything that was spotted within a certain range. That's the only way, Commissioner."

"What makes you so damn certain they wouldn't dump it?"

Bannerman didn't respond right away; he had to think it over. "More of a hunch than anything else. Karl Schuster claimed this last batch was the only large shipment that ever left the island. He also assumed that somewhere along the way it was intended to be mixed in with pure cocaine, which means they probably got a big supply somewhere waiting on this killer stuff. My guess is they won't dump it."

After hanging up with the commissioner, Charlie figured he had time for one more quick call. He had received clearance from the PC to break the news to the Swiss police. Shaleen was in the shower, and he didn't know what was going to happen when she came out. He tracked Lemieux down at his home.

326

"I left a message for you at the hotel. You can go pick it up now, and thanks for the loan of the guns. I'll be in touch when we get back to New York. And you can forget about Simard."

"Why? Does the Malagasy government intend to squash the extradition order?"

"A bit more serious than that. Monsieur Simard has disappeared — permanently."

"I see." There was a short pause. "What is in the message, Lieutenant?"

Shaleen came out of the bathroom then, a pink towel wrapped around her sleek frame. "Big trouble, Inspector. Real big trouble."

She plugged in her hair dryer and sat on the bed beside him, pulling one long, beautifully tapered leg up under her. The towel didn't cover much. Bloom had rounded up the cook in their swanky hotel, who promised to have a celebration dinner ready to go in about an hour.

"Will you help me out?" she asked innocently.

"Sure." He took the blower, got up on his knees and began to direct the warm air at her hair. Charles Bannerman, fifty-one years old, confirmed bachelor, was about to have his status changed.

And was damned grateful for the opportunity to start his life all over again.

Andre Lemieux took Rämistrasse down to the lake, turning left just before the Quai Bridge. The afternoon's rain had turned to a driving sleet in the late evening and would in all probability turn back again into freezing rain before morning. He thought about the American's call. Big trouble, the man said. Yet he had left so abruptly, without even saying he was leaving; which Lemieux had found annoying, not to mention downright rude.

The Excelsior was a popular hotel with the middle income bracket and boasted an excellent dining room. With the Christmas season well underway, there was a great deal of dining out. The lobby was filled with the last of the late night diners, all very much in a festive mood. He showed his identification to the desk clerk and was given the package. Then he took a seat in the noisy lounge and tore it open. He removed the envelope and read the contents twice, feeling a slight constriction in his throat. After ordering a Cointreau and downing it, Lemieux told the desk clerk that he wanted to use a private telephone.

Superintendent Milland answered personally.

"My apologies, Horst, but I must see you in your office as soon as you can get there."

"Is this necessary?"

"My friend, it is imperative that you do so. And plan on staying around, perhaps for the whole night."

It was nearly midnight when Herr Brower was awakened by the sound of a police klaxon nearby. To hear it so close in this neighborhood was unusual. Then he became aware of flashing blue lights reflected in his bedroom window. The door chime came next. He strapped on his prosthesis, his fingers groping about in the dark. By the time he arrived at the foot of the main staircase, the others had already gathered. In silence they turned around to stare at the old man as he crossed the entry hall, giving way a few at a time until Horst Milland was revealed, standing at the head of a contingent of uniformed policemen.

The superintendent said it was a sad thing for him to have to do, especially at Christmas, but he really had no choice. Herr Brower said he understood and asked how he had found out. The American detective, he was told, had telephoned from Mozambique earlier in the evening.

It was not a long drive to the headquarters. They sat together in the back of the superintendent's Volvo, Milland on the right, each man silent. Finally Herr Brower reached down to rub his knee.

"This damn Teflon thing, if it isn't fitted perfectly, it cuts a ridge into my leg. Do you mind if I remove it and put it on properly?"

Milland was feeling terribly embarrassed, for several reasons. "By all means, Dietrich."

The little .25 Beretta semi-automatic fitted his hand perfectly, and Herr Brower was amazed at how comforting it felt. Now he was once again in control of his own destiny. "I believe you should know that ZIAN has worked long and arduously at keeping drugs out of Western Europe. We have used our entire resources to this end. And we have been successful to an extent that you would find difficult to believe. Everything that has been carried out of a criminal nature—"

"Please, Herr Brower, I would urge you to say no more until you speak to your lawyer."

"Lawyers, a lot of good they are. Did you know that the Führer once classified the legal fraternity on the same level as the Jews?" He allowed himself a small chuckle before going on.

"What I wish to state to you categorically is the fact that I, and I alone, was party to the movement of narcotics." He stuck out his chin defiantly. "It was done for reasons you may not understand, but it was done by me alone. The directors of ZIAN are entirely innocent of such actions. I want you to protect them as best you can."

Milland muttered that he would. They had passed the Quai Bridge by now; just a few blocks to go until they reached police headquarters. In the driving wet snow, Herr Brower was unable to make out the twin towers of the Grossmunster church, nor the elegant needle-like steeple of the Fraumunster, dating back to the days of Charlemagne. He had lived for more than forty years in this jewel of Europe, and life had been good to him. Now it was time to say good-bye.

The gun was in his left hand. He felt for the safety catch and pushed it down. When he raised his arm as if to scratch his head, he realized that he must be careful with the trajectory. "Horst, do you mind, I am feeling somewhat faint."

Oberst Hermann Von Rudel dipped his head low, thinking of the Rhineland where he had been born and raised and how green it was in summer. The single shot was just one more embarrassment for the head of Zurich's police force.

All of a sudden Bannerman was caught up in a serious case of déjà vu: the pre-Christmas rush all over again. Three days had gone by since the bodies had been dumped in the middle of the Mozambique Channel. Sam and Anna had accompanied the policeman and his beautiful fiancée back to New York. Bloom had booked rooms for the three of them at the Marriott near LaGuardia Airport, which was close enough to Manhattan for the women to be able to take a cab downtown to shop for Shaleen's wedding apparel. Much to Bannerman's surprise, his sisters, once they recovered from the initial shock, had been delighted. Charlie and Shaleen were to be married right here in Manhattan on the twenty-first day of December, with Sam and Anna standing up for them. Giles and Loyola Lamont would be arriving tomorrow evening.

The commissioner was not pleased with Charlie's decision to take early retirement. Using some of the new money the president had earmarked to fight drug abuse, Hennessey had just finished setting up a new narcotics investigation unit with access to the latest in computer technology and authority to conduct out-of-state research. Since the Drug Enforcement Agency had recently fallen under the wing of the FBI, it was routinely shunned by many police departments. Bannerman, now a captain, had been selected to run the new unit.

A second ship, the *Valfredo*, had been spotted less than a quarter mile away from the *Lucinda V*, almost certainly the vessel now carrying the killer cocaine. Having learned from Karl Schuster how Erich had sandwiched the treated substance between silica gel crystals, the Greek authorities knew exactly what to look for when the vessel docked in Athens sometime tomorrow.

As for ZIAN itself, the board of directors was in apparent shock over the news that their chairman had been mixed up in the drug trade. According to Lemieux, there were mixed feelings in Zurich about Herr Brower, with many believing he had been framed and others believing he had been murdered. And Interpol's credibility, already badly eroded, sunk a little lower. That, and the forced retirement of a single man. So much for the great international police force.

The city was in a cold snap at the moment, with biting winds and drifting snow. The guard who watched over the Schermerhorn entrance off Amsterdam waved Bannerman's Chevrolet in. Carswell was wearing the same gray turtleneck sweater he had on when the cop first met him. Charlie could tell from their smug expressions that they had it figured out.

Bloom had spent much of the last two days barred inside Columbia's computer center with Carswell. The answer to what exact ingredients constituted the killer cocaine had proven to be nearly impossible to determine and would never have been resolved without Bloom's personal inspection of Tsingy reserve.

This was Charlie's first visit to the university since their return, so there was some small talk about the trip, most of which had been censured by the commissioner. Coffee in hand, the detective leaned back and waited for the explanation.

The golden orchid was on the screen. Carswell turned off the lights. "Our first mistake, or mis-assumption, if you will, was in thinking that the computer was showing us two separate and unrelated forms, a bat and an orchid. We now know that Dan is showing us parts of three separate, intrinsic life-forms. Sam confirmed this when he saw the first real orchid, with its slender green stem. The one on the screen has a twisted brown stem, dramatically different from the real stem. If the program was able to give a close representation of the actual flower, why not its stem?"

Bloom took over. "I suspected something was wrong when I first looked at this, since the stem is not the usual monocot type belonging to the subtribe *Angraecinae*. With these bat wings hovering about, I didn't pay a lot of attention to it at the time. Along came Anna, who had seen a photograph of the real orchid and mentioned its stem. That's when I began to think the answer had to be more than just a matter of finding an orchid that was being pollinated by bats."

He took a narrow-capped, long-stemmed mushroom off a table and handed it to Charlie. "I was also having difficulty with the apparent proposition that a single chromosome was capable of producing a catalytic killer. If the flower's nectar or pollen is so deadly, then it would hardly be capable of reproducing. Another element was needed, something natural, I reasoned, and something again native to Madagascar. While Karl was taking me on a little tour of the orchid clusters, I looked around for another source of food I figured the bats might feed upon. That's when I spotted this long, spiral-stemmed cousin of a common parasol mushroom; which, along with the orchid, is an unlisted species. The stem, as you can see, is very close to the computer image. As it turns out, the mushroom is capable of producing a moderate-strength toxin."

Carswell jumped in again. "This leads to the inevitable conclusion that the resultant by-product is a molecular combination of both species. Which leaves us with the bat. It's common for certain flowers to release their pollen only at night, at the same time giving off a powerful odor, similar to rotting meat or fermentation, to attract major pollinators. What usually distinguishes such flowers are their outsized nectar pods, since bats, after all, are considerably larger than, say, a bee."

Charlie twirled the stem in his fingers, trying to keep it all straight in his head. Bloom took over. "So what we have here is a proven example of a common African Little Brown Bat pollinating an orchid. A breakthrough, in fact, and the subject of a paper Dr. Carswell and I shall do together. The difficulty that presented itself next is that this orchid has little to offer in the way of nectar, nor does it give off the kind of odor that usually attracts bats. Another mystery, at least on the surface. But we have since learned that our golden orchid is a very unique species indeed. It is the first known example of an orchid offering a narcotic as a reward to the pollinator. You remember all those dead bats inside the cavern?"

Bannerman nodded. He wasn't likely to forget them.

Sam leaned back against the computer table. "The orchid didn't kill them, it simply made them feel high. Nor did the mushroom, much to our surprise. At that point we came back to Dan on bended knee and asked him to sort it out. I fed in everything Karl told us about the collection and sorting process, the various steps he had seen the chemist carry out. The answer lay in these fluttering bat wings. Sure, by now we knew that molecules from the plant and the fungus had combined inside the bat's intestinal tract, and it seemed obvious that this was the key. Still, by using samples blended in every conceivable way, we were unable to duplicate the process by which the combined elements turn deadly."

Appreciative, but growing impatient, Bannerman asked, "So what the hell did it?"

"The bat itself turned out to be the modifier," Carswell told him. "They were also committing suicide. Once the hydrochloric acids and enzymes found in the digestive tract, used to break down their food supply, combined with the narcotic from the orchid and the dormant but unstable toxin from the fungus, the chemical process that resulted was explosive. Only because they defecate every twenty minutes or so were the majority able to survive. But a good percentage, depending on how many fed on both the nectar *and* the fungus during the same night, would die soon afterward — perhaps within minutes of this powerful amphametic toxin leaking through the stomach wall and entering the bloodstream."

Bloom nodded. "This explains Karl's mentioning that some mornings there were a couple of dozen, and other mornings there were hundreds of the little buggers scattered all over the cavern floor."

"The point is, Lieutenant," Carswell went on, "Dan didn't indicate a bat simply because it was feeding on nectar. The wings appeared on the screen because they represented the third element in the process. The creature had left its own DNA signature on the chromosomes belonging to the pollen contaminants that found their way inside its stomach. Indeed, the orchid's pollen played a vital role in the identification process. But only by passing through and reacting with certain of the various acids found inside the creature's intestinal tract does the toxin become deadly. I sincerely doubt if even the ZIAN chemist was aware of this interaction. And then, of course, its coincidental DNA structure allows it to be blended with cocaine via a simple heating process, hence your killer crack. But it could just as easily be blended with any other narcotic."

Bannerman rolled his head around. "How in the name of Christ could something like this have developed?"

Carswell fingered his stringy blond beard. "Not known, but in all likelihood it was accidental, like so many other discoveries."

Sam agreed. "There are a number of things we may never know. For instance, what special environmental restriction forced the golden orchid to develop a narcotic in the first place? There are usually clearly defined reasons for such odd behavior. And why bats? I would guess simply because there are so many of them in an environment that is ninety percent sterile limestone rock. The golden orchid was forced to compete with every other flowering species in Tsingy for its share of the action. And it did this successfully. It has also shown us that the drive for preservation of species — good old-fashioned sex — is still the most powerful force in nature."

Bannerman smiled. There was a lot of truth in that.

THE EXORDIUM
(DUE FOR RELEASE IN 2013)

If you enjoyed Bloom and Bannerman's very first adventure, hold onto your hats when Sam and his colleagues are taken hostage by a mysterious Arab terrorist. Once Charlie learns that his friend's life is at risk, he joins forces with CIA operative Nick Manzoni as they set out under extremely dangerous conditions to rescue the captured botanists. But nothing had prepared them for what Sahallah has in store for those who would subvert his ingenious plan of world domination.

Check out *The Exordium* at http://www.rodpower.com/?cat=8

Rodney Christian Power grew up in Grand Falls, Newfoundland, joined the Canadian Corps of Engineers at an early age and entered the military survey school in Ottawa. Upon returning to civilian life, he became a Professional Land Surveyor and planner, establishing his consulting practice in Vernon, British Columbia. Rod's overseas experiences as an international consultant often took him to isolated parts of the world and into dangerous circumstances. The seeds for *The Case of the Golden Orchid* resulted from one such trip. His first novel, *Shadow of Light*, was published in November, 2011.

For more information you can visit www.rodpower.com

Made in the USA
Charleston, SC
22 February 2013